Tangled Roots

Tangled Roots

Mary Williams

Copyright © 1990 by Mary Williams

First published in Great Britain in 1990 by
Judy Piatkus (Publishers) Ltd of
5 Windmill Street, London W1

British Library Cataloguing in Publication Data

Williams, Mary
    Tangled roots.
    I. Title
    823.914[F]

ISBN 0-7499-0027-X

Phototypeset in 11/12pt Compugraphic Times by
Action Typesetting Limited, Gloucester
Printed and bound in Great Britain by
Butler & Tanner Ltd, Frome and London

Introduction

Letter from Julia Gort to Chetwyn Shane

                                        Trencathra
                                          St Taloc
                                          Cornwall

My dear Nephew

    As you will see from the above address, I am now installed for a period at Trencathra with my son-in-law and grandchildren, who are attempting to turn their home into an individual kind of guest house for 'people with a cultural trend of mind'. On paper, the suggestion seems somewhat absurd, I know, and I am not attempting to prophesy the outcome. I came here to give them a little financial ballast for the beginning, and am contenting myself in a top sitting room, where I can be as quiet as I like and watch the guests disporting themselves in the garden below.

    I do not know how long I shall be able to stand it – already I am picturing autumn on the Embankment, with the dark little balls of the plane trees bobbing against the yellow sky; and I'm thinking of your new show at the Garrick, after your years away. It's seldom I have missed a first night of yours. However, when one reaches my age – and I am eighty-five this month – a little generous philanthropy is good for one's arteries, heart, and self-esteem. It is pleasant, and excusable I think, to be able to relax warmly in the knowledge that one can still be of use – if only financially. And the family need all the help they can get. Publishing, as you know, is at a low ebb, and Nicholas' books are no longer popular. He is a dear, bless him! but vague, like many writers, and does not adjust himself to the age. However, his name still counts for something — if only to draw inquisitive lion-hunting females to Trencathra. Not that they see much of him. He has esconced himself, like the doormouse in Alice's teapot, at the lodge which has been equipped for him quite comfortably.

He comes to the house only for the midday meal and occasional dinners, and picnics for the rest, which, with Susie-Jane's help suits him quite well, I think. It must be some years since you saw Susie-Jane. She's eighteen now, and was in the Land Army for a year at the end of the war. She's quite delightful — a tall, clear-eyed Rosalind kind of young creature. One wonders what she will become. Fifty years ago there would have been no doubt about it — my father would have bullied her into playing Goneril and Ophelia with equal capacity. But she has no desire for the stage, which is perhaps as well.

Merlynne seems restless. She has her husband here — Hugo Lane — who's recuperating following his demobilisation. But he still limps, and there's something about him which worries me; a tiredness, a hurt and frustration which is not, I think, physical so much as spiritual. It's very hard to explain what I feel about Hugo. Maybe I am just a sentimental old woman imagining things.

Richard is attempting to bring the land into some sort of order, and is doing very well. He's certainly the reliable one of the family, and it's hard to believe that Nicholas could have had such a son. Catherine is as beautiful as ever, and more remote. I know, poor girl, that she has missed her husband terribly. But after six years — he was killed, if you remember, in 1940 — one would expect her somehow to be now more adjusted — escapism should not be indulged in for too long. Still, she is very decorative, and despite her aloofness, perhaps because of it — seems to manage the home very well. The whole scheme, I believe, was her idea, and apparently there was no argument about it. The family were willing to make any effort necessary to keep Trencathra — they couldn't possibly have done so as things were, what with heavy taxation, bad investments, the high cost of living and all the hundred and one other penalties of this post-war world.

I can forgive their sentiment, too. I can do more – I can understand it. Trencathra is unique in its way, standing as it does, on its own headland overlooking St Taloc. And after all it has belonged to the Nankervisses now for several generations, and I suppose this does – forgivably – breed an inherent mediaeval possessiveness. It is something I cannot personally feel, but I can appreciate it. Like you, Chetwyn, I'm a roamer at heart, born of vagabond stock; and despite your success – and you have lived through the war, thank God, to go still much further – the fact remains that your great-great-grandparents were strolling players giving *Lear* and *Hamlet* in village barns, and that an ancestor of ours was a juggler at a fair.

I'm not ashamed; I'm proud! It's the adventurous strain, and it goes on. Even now – and I am an old woman, or I shouldn't have time to reminisce so much – the smell of sawdust and greasepaint comes back to me with a pang, and I remember a host of things I ought by now to be forgetting. Something stirs in my old blood which is very invigorating and refreshing; gratitude, a kind of glow: that friendship, alomost love, Chetwyn, which is the only right relationship of artist to a kindly audience. Of course, the technique is different nowadays – to play less to the heart, and more to the mind and eye. But, if I have any advice to give, it is – never lose your love for your audience. Never forget that actors belong primarily to the world, dear boy. If you do, you will lose something. The intellect means progress. But great things are given from the heart.

You must forgive this retrospection, a habit, I'm afraid which is growing on me. But luckily I still have Marianne with me, and Marianne understands – she recognises the sign for a little subtle flattery, and never fails to respond. A great deal is talked of psychology these days; but psychologists are born, not made, and Marianne is a 'natural'. I have only to turn my head in a certain manner, smooth my hair in the mirror, sigh, perhaps, in a particular way, and she will say, 'It is one of your young days, madam – what about wearing the plum-coloured taffeta?'

And I answer, 'Yes, Marianne, perhaps I will. Do me good.' Symbol of vanity — the plum-coloured taffeta.

Once again, dear boy, forgive my wandering. I've told you all the news, I think, and when you have a spare moment you must come down for a few days. It would please the family, and you'll be a welcome guest. The other visitors — there are three of them at the moment — are all unique in their way and a little odd. But one must be tolerant. There's Miss Spring, poor dear, who wears sandals and draperies, and belongs to some strange religion which impels her to walk bare-footed in the dew in the mornings, wearing a bathrobe. She chants and performs Yogi exercises outside the Lodge, which amuses Richard immensely. He says she's repressed and has designs on Nicholas. He, generally so detached, is profoundly annoyed, and I shouldn't be surprised if she was submerged one day by the contents of the water jug.

Then there is the 'artistic' young man with romantic eyes and long hair who paints pictures which neither himself or anyone else understands. He's looking for a studio, I believe, in St Taloc, but I've noticed that he looks at Merlynne a good deal as well. On the whole, therefore, it is perhaps all to the good that we have, to balance things up, a typical North Country businessman, the inventor of a face cream and hair oil, I believe, with jovial blunt speech and very twinkling blue eyes. I've not yet discovered what possible interest he can have in the culture of Trencathra but no doubt I shall, before I go. I have an inkling that the little man, despite all his bluffness, has a sneaking sentimental urge to unfold his life story to someone with a sympathetic ear. And I flatter myself that I can hopefully offer that.

So you see, it's really all quite amusing. As I have already said, the only worry is Hugo. He bothers me; and I'm fond of him. He's really nice, but it's obvious something more than a physical wound worries him. It appears to me as though he's looking for something Merlynne can't give. But I may be wrong. I hope so. Perhaps when his health bucks up things will be different.

Well — the gong is about to go for dinner, so I must

close, dear boy. Write to me when you have time, and good luck with the show.

    Your affectionate Aunt,

    Julia Gort.

Chapter One

On a certain evening in 1946 as Susie-Jane dressed for dinner, she was conscious of an anticipatory sense of excitement which was all bound up in the guests, the knowledge that the family was together again on a new project, that Hugo was back, and that it was fun after a period of muddy boots and backache to be facing herself in the mirror wearing a new green dress which suited her. The dress had a high neck, short bunchy sleeves, a tight bodice, and a full skirt reaching her toes. It was the first sophisticated long dress she'd ever possessed, and it accentuated the curving lines of her young figure, and radiant quality of her glowing golden skin flushed to a deep rose on the high cheekbones.

Susie-Jane was happy. Her greenish eyes, faintly tilted, danced through the mirror with the same electrical vitality that sprang with every touch of the comb from her dark curling hair, and in the lively impish quality twitching the corners of her full lips. She could not exactly have defined her happiness, but was aware that it had a good deal to do with her own perfect health and spirits, and something, also, with meeting Hugo on the rocks after tea. At the thought of him, her face sobered a little. Hugo had been *thinking* down there, all alone. Descending the cliff path she'd watched him for some minutes before he was aware of her; and he had not looked happy. There was something about his posture — the way he'd stood, contemplative, leaning on his stick, looking out to sea, that expressed a curious loneliness.

Yes, that was it — lonely. Hugo had been lonely. Susie-Jane could not bear loneliness in others, and Hugo's hurt her. For a moment she'd paused, wondering whether or not to break in upon his mood. Then she'd dislodged a stone with her foot which rattled on the rocks, making him turn sharply. He'd smiled at her, and she'd gone to him, scrambling like a boy in her slacks and sweater over the wet rocks lately washed by the tide.

'Hullo, Susie-Jane,' he'd said, and there'd been no mistaking the welcoming warmth in his voice.

'Didn't it hurt your leg?' she had enquired, 'coming down here?'

'The leg's got to be disciplined,' he'd replied, 'or I shall be a very useless fellow.'

'Useless! The very idea. And you've only been out of hospital a fortnight.'

'Still – the quicker I'm normal the better. It can't be very helpful to Merlynne seeing me drag around like this.'

'It's for Merlynne to help you!' Susie-Jane had started in quick instinctive judgement of her sister. 'After all –' more charitably ' – it's all she really wants to do, I'm sure.'

'I know, my child. But it's not quite all – with Merlynne. And why should it be? She's got a tough enough job as it is – all of you have – with the visitors and so little help in the house.'

'Oh, I don't know, there's Ann – and the boy as well. Besides, we don't mind as it's for Trencathra.'

'How you love the place, don't you?' he'd said, watching her.

'Of course. I don't think I could live anywhere else, ever. Unless I cared for someone very much. But maybe I'm exaggerating. I don't know – I suppose no-one can really predict the future –' She'd broken off, unable adequately to explain her feelings about the house, in case Hugo thought her childish, over-emotional. Most people, anyway, regarded Trencathra as an odd-looking old place with its queer little jutting towers and medieval windows. And indeed it was. But this, to Susie-Jane, was one of its attractions. There was an air of enchantment about it which had reminded her always, ever since she had been old enough to look at picture books, of the castles in fairy tales; and she'd invested it, in consequence, with a host of her own legendary imaginings, which had compensated in some measure for the gap in her life caused by her mother's death when she was a year old. Its ancient atmosphere had soothed her during her childish ailments and unhappiness; and when she'd lain seriously ill with pneumonia her first conscious impression following the long delirium had been the rhythmical sound of the sea breaking on the rocks beyond her window, lulling her with the peace of a cool hand on her forehead to a weak, placid contentment.

Rumour had it that the house – which had been built originally by some eccentric hermit who had founded his own religious order there – was haunted. But if there were ghosts, they were friendly ghosts to Susie-Jane Nankerviss. She loved the wide picture gallery with the smaller corridors leading from it, the shadows which lurked in the doorways, and the twisting narrow staircase up to the tower room, which until her father's retreat to the Lodge, had been his study. Now this was Susie-Jane's particular sanctum, as Nicholas would allow none of the guests to use it.

For many years, half the rooms had been shut, since help was difficult, and the Nankervisses being squires of the district had obligations to meet which took an undue toll of their diminishing and over-taxed income. Nicholas had never been a businessman, and before the war had allowed the land to grow wild. During the war years, under the wing of the Agricultural Ministry, it had been cultivated with some sort of efficiency; and Richard, the eldest son, had now returned from the army, determined to make its husbandry his career. It was not easy land, being so near to the sea, and somewhat stony. But Richard had an inherent capacity for understanding the rotation of crops, and planned the following year to have another twenty acres under the plough.

At first Susie-Jane, following war experiences with the W.L.A., had wished to help him. But Richard hadn't wanted this, and Susie-Jane had been secretly relieved because it would be nice, anyway, to become a real girl again, to be able to wear dresses when she chose, and keep her loving, possessive eye on Trencathra. It was a little intimidating, of course, seeing strangers wandering down the long corridors and across the lawn and garden; but Susie-Jane was a friendly person; their appreciation pleased her. And the house couldn't mind, not really, she told herself childishly. The scheme was only a temporary measure after all. Next year, when Richard was making the land pay and the guests had brought in enough to tide them over the difficult period, there might be no necessity to have any more. Nicholas, too, was convinced that his current book would be a 'seller'. But then, her father always thought this.

'The trouble is — ' Susie-Jane told herself, fixing a clip into her curls ' — he *preaches* too much. He thinks he can reform the world by saying what he thinks. But he doesn't *amuse* people, and people won't listen unless they're at least a *bit* amused.'

Susie-Jane herself had an infinite capacity for seeing the bright side of most situations in life, and was what Richard called the 'sanguine one' of the family. She had 'temperament', but it was unsullied as yet by shaken faith or a cheapened viewpoint of men and women. She believed that what was to come must eventually be for the best. Only one thing in her life had shocked her violently, and that was the death of her youngest brother Julian, who had been killed flying in 1942. However, her youth and inherent optimism had stood her in good stead; Julian wasn't really dead, she'd told herself many times. Something of him remained. People like Julian, with laughter and happiness and goodness in them, didn't die. They couldn't. And there were times even now when, alone in the tower room, or in the shadows of the gathering dusk about the house, she felt him quite near to her — so real a presence that it seemed her secrets were his, and those of the house also. They three in communion. She never spoke of this to anyone. It was the kind of thing you couldn't mention, even to your own family. But on the rocks that evening, she'd almost started to — to Hugo.

He was different somehow; she felt he'd have understood. The fact it was which had given Susie-Jane that sudden rich sense of happiness — the realisation flooding her of a secret bond between two people that would remain so, unsullied by mundane practical realities.

In such a mood she put the finishing touches to her new

leaf-green ensemble on that far-off evening, feeling that something new and very precious was beginning. Her eyes were dancing and her mouth smiling as she fastened her brooch and prepared to go downstairs.

It was good to be alive; good to live in a world with people like Richard and Hugo in it. But Hugo was lonely. She would help him and be his friend. Whatever happened he must get well again.

'Thank God for onions!' said Merlynne, whose turn it was to cook the dinner. With onions you could make the dullest thing interesting, and though the guests had come to Trencathra chiefly, perhaps, for atmosphere and interest, yet their tummies counted also. You could not feed a hungry person on conversation, however intelligent it was. And really, Merlynne's thoughts ran, it isn't as if they get much of that, with Nicholas shutting himself away, Grandmother writing letters all the time, and Richard concerned with compost. Then Hugo – so reserved now. He doesn't seem to want to talk, or to do anything else for that matter.

She opened the oven door to inspect the savoury pie, and hot fumes rose against her forehead. 'Ann,' she called to the girl who was helping her, 'get the plates ready, will you? It's nearly seven, and I must do a quick change.'

She hurried up the back stairs to her own room, and found Hugo looking out of the window, smoking. He was still wearing his daytime tweeds. They suited him; anything suited Hugo's careless good looks, with deep-set blue eyes, and rather stern profile. But Merlynne, hot and tired, was quickly irritated. He should have changed. Something drove her, irrationally, to the stimulus of a scene, although it was the last thing she really wanted at the end of the day, especially with Hugo, with whom she knew she should be patient.

In spite of herself, the words rose sharply to her lips. 'You haven't changed. Aren't you going to?'

'Need I?' he enquired, turning. 'Is it necessary?'

She shrugged her shoulders, with a quick impetuous gesture. 'Necessary? Oh, Hugo! What do you think?'

'Oh, very well.'

Because she was tired, and depressed by a feeling of futility, tears threatened her violet eyes, although they didn't fall. She knew she appeared unfeeling and cold to Hugo, but she did not *feel* cold. That was the trouble — since his demobilisation things had never become relaxed between them. It was as if, all the time, they were hammering at a mutual wall of misunderstanding, so different from the quick giddy month of their courtship, when filled by a sense of danger and separation, a mutual flood of passion had held them close, unimpeded by the trivialities of convention. They had met at Plymouth where she'd been stationed as a WREN, and he was with his regiment prior to embarkation. It had been natural they should fall in love; both were young, attractive and unattached; and Merlynne, with her tawny soft hair and mobile mouth in the pale heart-shaped face, had attracted him by her subtle promise, the look of dew on her, of a glowing future which might, for him and countless others, never come to flower. Caught in the fever of uncertainty and longing to live before it was too late, they had speedily married, and as quickly he had gone abroad. She had not seen him again until her visit to the hospital ward three years later, where, wounded and changed, he'd waited for her in an invalid chair overlooking the garden.

In the first few moments she'd sensed the difference — spiritual as well as physical — in her husband. It was not so much his looks that shocked her, but the expression in his eyes, and a certain hurt, defeated twist of his lips. The minute had been charged with a perilous expectancy, and as perilous a betrayal; she knew, watching him, that he was alien to her. She had come to meet the man she had loved and married so blindly. But he was not there. This was someone she did not know — had never known — this stranger demanding in his integrity and defeat something she could not give. Merlynne had none of Susie-Jane's intrinsic faith or capacity for giving. Her moods were more wayward, her will weaker. And she was spoiled. She was honest enough to know this, and to admit it. But it did not help the issue; because one couldn't so easily break the habit of years — years which for Merlynne had been filled with the excitement and the attention of many men. She had grown used to attention, grasping it as the drug and food that had seen her through. If Hugo was going to fail her, where would she be?

But of course he won't fail me, she'd told herself insistently since. He's wounded and not well. It's up to *me* to see I don't fail *him*. In the end it will be better — when he's normal again. It will come right. It must.

So far there had been no sign of it. Hugo was different — his kisses less passionate, his eyes strangely inscrutable when he looked at her, as though he were searching her soul. And Merlynne had no wish for soul-searching. She hadn't married him for that. She'd married him because she loved him and the pressure of his lips was heaven to her; and because the feel of his arms straining her to him was all that had mattered in that crazy world of war of which she'd been a part.

But now ...

'Don't bother, if you don't want to,' she said wearily, referring to the argument about his clothes. 'I suppose it doesn't matter.'

And she thought. If only he would come over and hold me and make me forget. If only he would be *my* Hugo, even for a minute.

She heard him saying behind her, 'Those things aren't really important, are they, Merlynne? Don't let's jar each other.'

She felt his hands on her shoulder turning her round to face him. The contact gave her pleasure. She was a passionate woman. But she didn't want to look at him because she knew it would be there still — that small questioning frown.

She shivered slightly, closing her eyes, as his cheek touched hers briefly.

'Darling, we must be happy. Be patient, Merlynne. It will be all right — it's just a question of adjustment.'

She leaned against him, a trifle more sensuously; but he still held her gently, quietly, as though she had been a child. She tore herself away, striving to hide the unwarranted rush of anguish she felt. It was dreadful, this feeling of having nothing when once she had had everything.

'We must hurry,' she said in an icy level voice. 'I've the gong to ring in five minutes, and I've not even washed.'

'I'm sorry,' he said with cold abruptness. 'I know I'm a failure. I apologise.'

She laughed on a high note, taking her blue dress from the wardrobe.

'Oh, Hugo, don't be ridiculous.'

And he thought, what are you made of, I wonder? What's happened to change the girl I married into this moody, impatient woman?

He watched her wash quickly and pull the dress over her head, noted the silky toss of her hair as she combed it and shook it from her face. The outline of her cheek was smooth as a child's under the light – pale and shell-like, moving him to swift emotion.

'Oh, Merlynne,' he said, 'we mustn't bicker.'

'I'm not bickering,' she answered, the tug of tears at her throat. 'But don't you *see*, Hugo, it's no good – if – if you can't love me any more.'

'I do love you,' he protested. 'But good heavens, Merlynne, can't you understand that I'm tired? Have I got to go on, day after day, proving it – is that how you want it to be?'

'Certainly not,' she said, despising both herself and him for their mutual humiliation. 'What a beastly thing to say.'

'Again,' he said bitterly. 'I seem to have put my foot in it.'

'Yes,' she agreed tartly. 'But what does it matter? I'm getting used to it.'

'Oh, Merlynne, Merlynne.'

She winced, and suddenly looked younger, more vulnerable. 'Pretty ghastly, isn't it, Hugo? That we should have come to this?'

She drew lipstick across her mouth, while the tears fought themselves once more to the surface of her eyes.

'It will be all right,' he said doggedly. 'It must be all right.'

She tried to believe him; but as he stood there, resistance suddenly went from her, and she longed for nothing so much as to be a child again, long before the war or Hugo had happened to her. In those brief moments her life seemed to race through her brain in a succession of pictures. If the war hadn't come everything would have been different. She wouldn't have known or missed him, and she'd have continued with the career she'd set her heart on. Uncle Chetwyn would have helped her, she had the looks and temperament for an actress. It was in the blood – something vivid and deeply emotional which must have its outlet or turn violently upon itself in a welter of unhappy frustration. It was not that she couldn't be happy. She'd been acutely happy as a child; she hadn't wanted parties or games or to be amused like many children did. She'd been perfectly content at Trencathra so long as there was some prospect ahead of fulfilling herself, of giving fullness and meaning to her life. She had been innocent then, yet curiously alive in her senses and imagination; her resources had been within herself and Trecathra. It seemed only yesterday that she'd played Ariel to Julian in the wild part of the garden called the Nut Grove.

That had been her happiness – feeling her nerves and body respond to an emotion which fulfilled, rather than demanded from her – losing herself in something far more vast than the child Merlynne. Her failure now was that she could no longer express herself, because Hugo witheld contact from her. It wasn't altogether her fault, surely? It was true she was not as patient as she might be; but couldn't he understand – even have an inkling of how desperately she needed to be needed? She, Merlynne, was his wife. She, too, had known war and its after effects. It made you either weaker or stronger. She was not one of the strongest. She wanted support and help through this reactionary period – warmth and an anchor – peace for her tired nerves. Trencathra meant much to her, but alone it was not enough; not sufficient for her to devote herself exclusively to a few guests, even when it meant saving the loved home.

Later, of course, she told herself repeatedly, some change must come. It was bound to, because nothing stood still. When he was better Hugo would take up his post again as lecturer on International Affairs at Linchester College. This was her hope. She would be with him there, and things would surely be better between them.

But try as she would – and she had tried hard during the past month – she could never clearly now visualise the future. Deep within her, as days went by, she had less faith in their mutual course, felt less certain of the outcome, and consequently endured guilty feelings, because he was ill and needed help and sympathy. This fact alone only served to depress her further.

As she went downstairs she tried to shake the mood from her, but it was no use. She felt old, far older than her twenty-eight years.

'I'm not really alive,' she thought. 'Why can't something happen to make me *live*?'

Nicholas chose to appear at dinner that evening, taking the special place that was his on these occasions, at the end of the long refectory table, next to Susie-Jane and his mother-in-law, Dame Julia.

From her position at the other end, Miss Spring, one of Trencathra's first guests, thought with a stab of excitement how distinguished was the gathering – how intellectual Mr Nankerviss looked with his remote, thoughtful eyes set deep beneath the brows and high domed forehead. True, he always appeared a little untidy, but great men frequently did, she decided charitably, living on a higher plane than most people in the everyday world. One day, when he knew her better, she hoped he would unfold some of his ideas to her. Despite his cleverness she was not sure that he was really happy. He spoke so seldom, and though she took any slight chances of stimulating his attention, he had refused, so far, to enter into any serious discussion with her. Such a pity. For she was sure that fundamentally they had much in common. She, too, had studied Eastern philosophies and religions on which subject he was an authority, and in her own small way she might, she felt, be able to add further light to his lustre. Not that she was in any way conceited. At heart, Miss Spring was a humble person. It was just – she told herself reassuringly – that *she* had discovered the truth of Karma, and that whatever happened in life to her must in some way be the fruit of self-experience. It was obvious that Mr Nankerviss had as yet not savoured this truth.

As for the old lady – Dame Julia – she was someone quite alien to Miss Spring's world: unpredictable, and despite her age theatrical with a touch of adventure about her, sitting there in her plum-coloured taffeta and crystals, with the lively, almost reckless, gleam in her fine old eyes, her mouth curved whimsically above her small pointed chin, the gestures of her hands extravagant and Frenchified below the fine lace at her wrists. She was the live wire of the party, sustaining the conversation with touches of irony and wit directed at Nicholas, or at the pale young man, Laurence Dale, on her right, who, charming as he might be to some, did not charm her.

She appeared kinder to Mr Murgatroyd, an ordinary, commonplace little Yorkshireman, drawing him out with subtle touches of flattery which were, Miss Spring felt, quite misplaced. For obviously there was little that Mr Murgatroyd could contribute to the gathering beyond bursts of crude, well-intentioned humour which somehow broke into the finer vibrations of the party with disastrous results.

On the whole Miss Spring was not quite certain of her opinion concerning Dame Julia. A fine old lady and a remarkable character, but one had a feeling that she was being amused all the time at matters not originally meant to be amusing. And her tongue had a very icy edge to it. After all, modern painting might not appeal to her, but there was no reason to condemn it with quite the acerbity she showed to the young artist.

'If people are such fools as to be taken in, young man,' she said, 'take 'em in, and it serves them right. But don't expect me to see beauty or spiritual significance in a dirty smudge on a piece of paper.'

Miss Spring had thought, at first, that the young man was going to show annoyance, but instead he'd smiled with singular charm and remarked equably, 'I don't expect you to, Dame Julia. When I invite you to my studio I'll be sure I have something coherent to show you.'

'Good. Now we know where we are.'

Miss Spring had been unable to resist putting in her own little word any longer.

'But isn't it true —' she urged in defence of the young man '— that modern expression demands a modern tuning-in, so to speak. And that something which is a perfect jumble to us — like much of the modern music — may mean a great deal to some people?'

There was a grunt of annoyance from the end of the table where Nicholas sat.

'Rubbish!' he said with finality. 'The function of art — of any art — if it has any function, should be to be understood by the world. If it fails in that, it fails altogether.'

With mixed feelings, flattered that the great man should have been stimulated to conversation by her remark, yet anxious to establish herself in his esteem, Miss Spring hastened to add, 'Oh, yes. Of course. Naturally. But —'

'In any case,' Nicholas said, looking up at her, 'I never like talking art over my dinner.'

Oh dear! thought Susie-Jane. He's irritated now. He's going to be rude.

'Will you have some more gravy, Miss Spring? she said, offering the tureen in an effort to detract the poor lady's attention from her father's slight.

'Oh, yes, thank you — I —'

Miss Spring looked confused, and a little flushed and Susie-Jane felt swiftly sorry for her. But she could quite understand why Nicholas was irritated. He had always despised odd and self-consciously arty people, and in her green kimono-looking gown with her pseudo-golden hair piled high and a ribbon threaded through it, there was something affected and almost macabre about Miss Spring. Yet beneath it all, Susie-Jane felt, she was a really nice, old-fashioned little person, with a heart full of sentiment and kindness. What a pity she didn't dress and behave more normally. But then perhaps she was lonely — like Hugo — and just wanted to impress people. If so, it was very sad.

Loneliness had never touched Susie-Jane herself, because from being a tiny thing she had learned what it was to have inner resources, and that 'alone times', if rightly lived, could be the least lonely of all. But Miss Spring was different. When, for instance, she went for a walk on the cliff, with her cape flying, it appeared always as though she were having a race with herself and her own loneliness. She didn't see what Susie-Jane saw, she was never still enough really to feel the silences about her, or to absorb the lovely things that were happening all round — she had her mind filled with a number of highly evolved theories and ideas which seemed to pursue her wherever she went, so that she was never properly herself but instead some pattern of another Miss Spring who convinced her she was happy. But she wasn't. Not really.

As she helped herself to a second portion of vegetables, the thought flashed through Susie-Jane's mind that of all the people in the room, perhaps only her grandmother and herself could be termed happy at that moment. Richard was absent; and Hugo silently pre-occupied. Merlynne seemed restless and on edge, and Catherine with the aloof, vague little smile about her lips appeared removed materially from them altogether, although she was by far the loveliest in her simple mauve medievally-cut gown with its full sleeves fitting tightly at the wrists, a low, square neck and tight bodice. All the same attention wandered from her after a moment or two to concentrate on Merlynne who was less good-looking but more compelling with her silky page boy hair, violet eyes and tempestuous mouth. Merlynne, like her name, had something restless about her, restless and unsatisfied and ever-changing.

As if she's searching for something she never finds, Susie-Jane thought, with instinctive shrewd insight. And it's all wrong — having Hugo. She ought to be happy, having him back again. I would be, if I were married to him.

The mere idea caused a deepening of the colour in her cheeks, which accentuated her arresting, ardent look.

Watching her, Dame Julia was struck anew by her air of pride and awakening maturity.

She's beautiful, she thought. None of the others can compare with her in character or breeding. How my father would have revelled in her now. And yet she's not all Shane. There's a look of Nicholas about the forehead and high-bridged nose. A mixture — my Susie-Jane.

Susie-Jane was completely unaware of her grandmother's scrutiny having forced her attention from Hugo to the young man, Laurence Dale, who had commenced a conversation with Merlynne. They were talking of modern theatrical production, and for a few moments enthusiasm lit Merlynne's eyes, changing her completely from a certain rebellious indifference to a creature of light and shade and unexpected charm. Like that, how attractive she was. No wonder Hugo had fallen in love with her, Susie-Jane thought, no wonder he had married her. But there was something subtly dangerous about her, holding the beckoning elusive quality peculiar to the Shanes; and she had it to a large degree. What she wanted, she would take — somehow. Perhaps Laurence realised this, too. For he was watching her closely. And his eyes, under their long lashes, had something in them which Susie-Jane had not observed before — interest, yes. But it was deeper than that. And Merlynne was aware of it. Raising her eyes for a second from her plate, she faced Hugo across the table, and her expression said, There, you see. You mustn't value me lightly. See what I can do.

All of a sudden Susie-Jane wanted the meal to end. It was silly to feel like that, but something suffocating had crept into the atmosphere — something which shouldn't have been there — some secret sensation which, if left to itself, might flourish and destroy part of the fabric of Trencathra.

I don't like him, Susie-Jane said to herself, attacking her baked potato with vigour. I'm sure Gran's right. There's something pseudo about him. But it was not really Laurence she mistrusted — it was the look in Merlynne's eyes, the way she'd glanced at Hugo. There had been no tenderness in it, kindliness or real affection. Perhaps she didn't love him, then. Perhaps that was it. The suggestion kindled many conflicting emotions in Susie-Jane's warm heart, but by far the strongest was a sense of pity and compassion for Hugo. He had suffered enough. It would be unbearable, somehow, for him to have to suffer further.

Chapter Two

After the meal the guests either went for a walk or sat in the lounge. Merlynne helped Ann clear the table and wash up, while Catherine saw that the eiderdowns in bedrooms were turned down, and all the other hundred and one little things which are indicative of a well-run household. Yet the house was far from being perfectly run, Catherine knew. Cobwebs had gathered again in the picture gallery, some rooms were not cleaned as thoroughly as they should be, and dust had accumulated behind much of the furniture. The stairs needed polishing, but they had neither the time nor necessary help to do it, and Richard did not help matters, coming in late frequently with dried mud on his clothes, and boots far from clean. He had promised Catherine time after time that he would remember to change them in the kitchen, or at the back door. But his good intentions weren't always carried out, and it was not fair to be on at him all the time, poor boy.

If there was anyone, now, for whom Catherine, as eldest of Nicholas' children, had any deep love, it was for Richard who came next to her in years and was completely dissimilar in looks and temperament from the rest of the family. He was a true Nankerviss, resembling his paternal grandfather in a way Nicholas never did. Nicholas, vague and intellectual, took after his own mother, the daughter of a country doctor, from Somersetshire, whereas Richard had the imperious features, dark curly hair and swarthy colouring of generations of Cornish forbears. He was neither artistic nor scholastic in any way. His interest lay in the land and sea, and reverted to the strain which had bred yeomen Nankervisses. He liked the smell and touch of the earth; the sight of a straight furrow with the gulls swooping above the brown soil gave him an excitement, a sense of fulfilment which none of the others, except perhaps Susie-Jane, could remotely appreciate. He was thirty now, and before the war had been training as a surveyor. But the war had shown him where he stood. Returning, after years of strain and hardship abroad — he had been both at Dunkirk and Alemein — he had known that he'd returned for good. This was his place, and this his land, difficult as it might be. Let other men plan the world, order society and make of it the best they could. His roots were here, where he might tackle a job of work far from industrialism and the stress of modern times — something to tax both his mind, and will, and magnificent physique — the business of bringing Trencathra land under the plough, of utilising the estate to the very best advantage.

This evening he came in late, having helped with the milking and other jobs about the sheds. It was almost dark, and the air was pungent with the heavy damp smell of decaying chestnut and oak leaves. He drew its richness into his lungs with a thrill of satisfaction, realising that he was hungry.

Along the drive he met a figure in a loose grey wrap coming moth-like towards him. Catherine. She stopped for a second when she saw him, and told him Ann was keeping his dinner for him.

'OK,' he said. 'And I'm hungry, by God! Don't get cold,' he added, giving her an affectionate pat on the shoulder, 'in that loose thing.'

'I shan't,' she said. 'Don't worry.'

He did not enquire where she was going. He knew, and there was that sympathy between them which forbade any comment, although it sometimes worried him that his sister should still, after six years, make her nightly sojourn to the clump of beech trees where, in the old days before her marriage, she and her husband had said goodnight. Once, recently, quite unawares, he had stumbled upon her, and had stood in the shadows shocked and silent while she lifted her arms to the empty air, raised her chin as though to invisible company and whispered, 'Goodnight, my love. My dear, dear, love.'

Richard abhorred unnecessary sentimentality. But there had been something tragic and pitiful about that lonely interlude. He'd tip-toed away, betrayed only by the cracking twigs. Catherine knew he'd seen and heard. But because it was Richard she'd not minded; rather it had drawn them closer together.

He walked on now, thoughtful, a little abstracted, wishing she could forget a little. Catherine was thirty-two, too young and too beautiful to live for ever with ghosts. One could, he felt, be a little too constant.

In the kitchen he found Ann already preparing the potatoes for the next day.

'Still working,' he said.

She looked up. She had a very white skin, and very clear grey eyes set wide in her head below level brows framed by smooth sable-dark hair.

'It's got to be done,' she remarked, with a shrug. 'I'll get you your dinner. The table's still laid for you.'

Quite suddenly he had no desire to go into the large, lonely dining room. He wanted to be by the friendly fire in the lamplight of the kitchen, with this quiet girl moving about him in the routine of her domestic tasks.

'I'll have it here,' he said, drawing a chair to the table.

'Here, Mr Nankerviss?'

He grinned at her boyishly, revealing a set of very white teeth. 'Do you mind?'

'No,' she said. 'Of course not.'

But it seemed a little out of order to her, and she wondered what Miss Catherine would say. After all, he was the young master, and they might think she was running after him. She would not like that. Although she was the daughter of humble people – her father had a small impoverished moorland farmstead near Cripple's Rest – she, Ann Chenoweth, was proud, and would run after no man. Besides, everyone knew that he was keen on that wild Miss Deborah of Stark End Hall, although for all her money and looks she wasn't half good enough for him, running after the fellows as she did. In the village they thought that young Mr Nankerviss would marry her. But Ann hoped not. There was bad blood in Deborah Cavin, despite her charm and breeding and beauty.

Without realising it she was frowning as she laid the cutlery on the table and took the dinner from the oven.

'I believe you're annoyed with me for descending upon you,' said Richard. 'Is that it? Or are you tired? I guess you are. Do you ever sit down like normal people and read a paper?'

'No,' she said. 'Not much. There isn't time. When Miss Catherine gets a cook it'll be easier.'

'Is the boy much help?'

Ann dimpled in a way which gave her a sudden country charm.

'As long as you don't expect to get any commonsense out of him. If he's kept in order, he is. Poor Robin! He can't help his wits.'

'It's hard on you, though.'

'My dear life, I'm used to it,' Ann retorted with a sudden quick impatience. 'We're a large family at home, Mr Nankerviss, eight children, and seven younger than me. We don't expect to be idle.'

'Most young women do.'

'Maybe I'm different then.'

Yes, he thought, watching her with new interest. Maybe you are.

She had nice arms, he observed, slender but firm and round, with capable quiet movements that put one at rest. Ann Chenoweth would one day make some man happy, lucky devil.

He sighed, comparing her quickly with Deborah Cavin. The comparison was to Deborah's disadvantage, but it brought to him, nevertheless, a heaviness of heart, a hunger for her which was against all his judgement. He could not rid himself of the picture of her as he had last seen her, riding with Barry Stokes across the moor, slender and spirited in her grey riding suit, her red gold hair bright in the sun, eyes brilliant in her radiant face. He could not forget — despite her brief, polite greeting — how anxious she had seemed to be off again with Stokes, the impatient, half-apologetic note in her voice, and obvious relief when he himself went on. Yet only two evenings previously he had held her in his arms, felt strained against him all the sweet wilfulness of her body. For months now, it had been like this — the sight of her was torment to him, for he knew she was teasing him, yet he couldn't relinquish the friendship. Sometimes he was angry with her, they would quarrel, and he'd determine never to see her again. But later, always, he made excuses to himself for her, pleading youth and high spirits, arguing that she could not help her bad heritage. He knew it was bad. Her mother, daughter of mad old Lord Trevane, had run off with some man in the early years of her marriage to John Cavin. That she had been provocative, unstable, with a neurotic thirst for passionate amours had been a fact well known. It was distasteful to Richard that Deborah, her daughter, should be showing ominous signs of the same weaknesses.

But after all, he thought, time after time, she's young, attractive and wealthy, with nothing to hold her. And her father spoils her. It doesn't give her a chance.

It was true that John Cavin fussed unduly over his daughter. The adoration, in a sense, was but the outcome of his own frustrated love for his wife. Her leaving him had shocked and hurt him acutely, but beneath his bluff exterior, he'd not been surprised. His wealth, as founder and chief shareholder of the Cavin Cafés and Restaurants Ltd, was self-made; there was nothing very dashing or attractive about him, and he had always been conscious that his wife was the daughter of Lord Trevane, who except for John's money would probably never have looked at him twice. And so he'd determined that Deborah at least, should have nothing with which to reproach him.

But this — as Richard saw clearly — had been the very worst thing for her. Deborah needed discipline and an anchor above all things. He'd played often with the suggestion as to whether or not he might be able to provide that safe anchorage for her. And, as always, when contemplating the possibility frankly, he'd felt extremely doubtful. Try as he would, he could not fit her into the picture of Trencathra. Had he been a weaker man he might have allowed the strain to tell on him. But Richard was not made of such clay, and when indecision intermingled with his desire for her, he fought it away with purpose and commonsense, applying himself instead to the work waiting to be done about the place, to the job that was in hand. Always, sooner or later, the vision of her returned again, though he was determined that she should not disrupt his life.

In an instinctive way, Ann Chenoweth knew all this. And whereas she knew, also, that Richard Nankerviss could mean nothing to her, she resented the power this girl's wanton charms had over him. As she laid the potatoes on the table, she recognised that Richard's mind had turned to thoughts of Deborah, and was quickly irritated.

'There,' she said. 'Get on with it now, or it'll be cold, Mr Nankerviss, sir.'

Richard gave her a quick glance, his eyebrows raised. At that moment Merlynne came into the kitchen. Seeing Richard she looked surprised, and he knew that she disapproved.

'You here?' she said. 'I didn't know you were in.'

'Oh, yes,' he said easily. 'I'm enjoying my meal in peace.'

'Well, there's not much peace for most of us. A prospective guest has just rung up from Penzance asking if we can put her up for an indefinite period. She's a strict, fanatical vegetarian and she must come tonight. She's had a row at the place she'd booked at, and had us recommended to her. She's vague about money and seems prepared to pay anything. But it's going to be a dreadful rush, with no bed aired, and the blue room upset with Susie-Jane's trunks in it —'

'Steady on, steady on,' said Richard equably. 'If it's all that bother why not say no to her?'

'At first I was going to, but Catherine came in and thought we shouldn't miss the opportunity. All the same, it's a bit thick at this time of the night.'

'I'll get the hot bottles ready,' said Ann practically. 'I don't know about sheets. Robin never called for them this morning, and I used those in the linen cupboard.'

'Ask Miss Susie to run along for them, then,' said Merlynne. 'It won't take her long.'

Susie-Jane was quite ready for a walk. It was dark now, and the first dim starlight threw a dancing pale pattern of leaves to the ground, from trees meeting over her head. For a short way the lane continued in this way until it led into the open, revealing a wide tract of country under the arch of sky, against which a few humped trees from the hedges were silhouetted darkly. She walked quickly, half-dancing, her chin held high and her nostrils sniffing like some exuberant young animal's the strange damp smell of undergrowth and earth. There was a faint wind, and a very slight prediction of frost in the air. In the distance the light at the corner of the lane by the hotel winked like some great jewel. Life was suddenly inexplicably wonderful to Susie-Jane. Beauty that was timeless caught her with a stab of wonder, and she felt for a moment that she must rush along the road, that she must run and run into the dark luminosity of night until she was swallowed up by the great mystery of the Universe. Some of the excitement lingered in her eyes still when she reached the cottage. In the light from the lamp her face was radiant, her dark curls blown in the wind.

'Why, Miss Susie, you're out of breath,' Mrs Evans said, opening the door. 'Been running, have you?'

Susie-Jane nodded and smiled. 'A bit,' she said. 'It's so lovely out. I couldn't help it.'

'Don't you go and get pixie-led, now,' the woman chaffed her. Then she added, 'You'd better come inside and I'll give you a cup of tea. My boy Joe's just arrived from Fowey and the pot's all ready.'

'I'd love to,' Susie-Jane said, 'but I've got to get back. A new guest's coming, and we want the sheets.'

'Dear life! What a world it is. Somehow, Miss, I can't get over these goings on at Trencathra.' She fetched the parcel, and Susie-Jane, suddenly business-like, asked, 'How much is it?'

'The bill's inside,' said Mrs Evans. 'Don't bother now, next week will do.'

As Susie-Jane went back she found Sam Murgatroyd, the little Yorkshireman, leaning over the top gate at Trencathra. He stood there very quietly, watching the sky, and she wondered what his thoughts could be. He was smoking. Little sparks blew from his pipe into the dark air, and he was so still that she thought at first he'd not heard her. As she approached, however, he turned round.

'Eh, lass!' he said. 'It's a grand night.'

'Yes,' said Susie-Jane, pausing. 'Isn't it?'

'I've been watching those little stars shoot,' he continued, 'and was reminded of the tale told when I was a boy of a shooting star being a soul passing. Rum idea – very rum. But no stranger, when you think of it, than that all those up there should be suns.'

'Yes,' Susie-Jane said, 'it's queer.'

'It is that.'

'It's funny,' said Susie-Jane. 'I was thinking the same sort of thing when I went for the washing. And now I come back and find you doing it.'

'Yes. It comes to all of us sometimes, I suppose – even a tough old chap like me – not much education or anything of that sort, but it suddenly comes over you. Queer thing – you're back again where you were as a lad, wondering what the whole bag of tricks is about.'

'Yes, I think I know what you mean.'

'I'm not an imaginative chap, in the ordinary way,' Sam Murgatroyd went on, 'but there were times, in my youth, when I had my little thoughts. I remember walking back from the mines and trying to puzzle it all out. I was a young fellow then, only a bit of a lad, and it started all sorts of odd things in my brain – you know, about reforming the world, doing things to help, all that socialistic stuff. Hm! You mean to do everything, when you're a lad. Then, when the time comes, you look back, and beyond making a bit of money, perhaps, you find you've done nothing at all.'

'You've probably done more than you think,' Susie-Jane said. 'Probably it's the little things that count, Mr Murgatroyd. You know – like talking to people, and cheering them up – the little friendly, funny things.'

'Yes,' he said ruminatively, 'maybe.'

Susie-Jane would have liked to talk longer. It was not often such opportunities arose. In her heightened mood she felt a stab of warm sympathy for this little man who before had seemed to them all so commonplace and dull. It just showed that life was even more exciting that one imagined. People were strange and hidden. You thought they were just what they appeared to be on the surface. But they weren't. Underneath there were strange currents of emotion and hidden desires, of yearnings and frustrations which emphasised the great mystery of existence. Half an hour ago, if she'd thought of Sam at all, it would have been with kindly tolerance, as a rather common little man who tried to be funny at meal times. Now, suddenly, there was a bond between them — the magical bond which Susie-Jane, in her adolescence, had felt at certain times for all things — for the seething throngs of men and women in unknown far away cities, for the farmer and labourer returning at night from the hayfields, for the small birds soaring and dipping above the grey hedges in the autumn mornings, for the myriad of living, crawling, flying things of which the universe was composed. It was inconceivable to her that anyone could be dull, in such a world.

She didn't want to go into the house. She would rather the confidences had continued between them. But the light shone from the window of the blue room, and conscientiously, she remembered that Catherine and Merlynne were waiting for the sheets.

'I must go,' she said. 'But I've enjoyed talking to you.'

'Me?' said Sam. 'Bless your heart. I'm no company for a lass.'

'All the same,' said Susie-Jane, 'we'll talk again, won't we? I'd like to.'

In the house she found Catherine and Merlynne in argument over the prospective guest whose name it appeared was Miss Fothergill-Briggs.

'I think Richard was right,' Merlynne was saying, shaking a pillowcase, 'we shouldn't really have taken her. After all, it's going to be very difficult catering for her kind of vegetarian. No animal fats at all. Miss Spring is at least tolerant — up to a point she's willing to compromise. But this — it will mean two different menus all the time, and it's significant that she's already had a row at the other place.'

'We mustn't turn people down,' Catherine said with quiet stubbornness, 'especially when it's for a long period.'

'You know,' said Merlynne, 'if we get too commercial we shall get no fun out of it at all. What's the point of wearing ourselves to the bone for Trencathra if we have no time to enjoy it? Probably the whole thing's been a mistake, anyhow.'

'You're tired,' said Catherine, 'that's what's the matter. You've been cooking. Cheer up, Lynne, tomorrow's your "off-day".'

'I very much doubt it. Soon there'll be no "off-days" if we persist in taking any oddity who comes along.'

'She may not be an oddity,' Catherine said with gentle persistence, 'and if she is, ther may be an amusing side.'

'I'm afraid I haven't your faculty for always looking on the bright side,' Merlynne said wearily. Her head ached, and she knew that even when Miss Fothergill-Briggs had been properly ensconced in the blue room there would be no real rest for her. For there would be then the coolness and tension between herself and Hugo to face.

Catherine's eyes clouded. 'It isn't always easy but I want to make a success of something, that's all.'

'Oh, I know,' Merlynne said. 'I'm sorry. Susie – do those sheets seem aired? Or ought we to put them by the fire?'

'They seem all right,' Susie-Jane said. 'And anyhow there are the bottles, aren't there?'

At a quarter to ten a taxi drew up at Trencathra and out of it stepped Miss Fothergill-Briggs. In the darkness she presented a somewhat bulky spectacle, but it was not until she stood in the light of the hall that Catherine and Susie saw why. Besides being 'amply upholstered', as Richard described her later, she carried under one arm a Pekinese dog, and under the other a cat of Siamese origin.

'There!' she said, putting the dog down. 'At last!'

She spoke in a hearty voice, and was attired in masculine-looking tweeds, though her high piled hair under her small hat was frizzed elaborately into the semblance of an Alexandra fringe. 'Poor little things!' she went on. 'You've no idea how badly treated they've been. The unpleasant welcome we received at Lyndale! It was really unbelievable.'

'Are they yours?' asked Catherine, for want of something better to say.

'Of course,' replied the lady. 'Didn't I mention them?'

'No,' replied Catherine, 'you didn't. You see – we don't really take animals here.'

'Don't take animals!' began Miss Fothergill-Briggs. 'No, perhaps not in the usual way. But these two are quite exceptional. And believe me – I could not possibly leave them behind. They won't be any trouble,' she continued, giving Catherine no time to interrupt her, 'the dog is Tito, and the cat Tush. And they're perfectly clean and well-behaved – Tush has his own little toilet box which can be put in some convenient place. I shall take strict charge of that. And when he knows the vicinity he can use it outside.'

'But really – I don't think –' Catherine began helplessly.

'And they can sleep with me,' the lady went on indefatigably, 'I'm quite used to it.'

Catherine shook her head determinedly. 'I'm sorry,' she said. 'I can't allow animals in the bedrooms, Miss Briggs.'

'Fothergill-Briggs.'

'I'm sorry, Miss Fothergill-Briggs. If we once started it, everyone would expect to do the same, and we really can't allow it.'

'In that case, I'm afraid I shall not be able to stay.'

Catherine's lips tightened. 'Very well,' she said.

Miss Fothergill-Briggs was silent for a few moments, evidently considering the whole matter well. Then, after the pause, she resumed, 'Supposing I gave in to your rather – if I may say so – narrow-minded and prejudiced point of view? Where would the two little dears be able to sleep?'

'There's the stable,' said Catherine.

'The stable?' echoed the lady, throwing up her hands. 'The very idea! They've never slept out in their lives.'

'Really, it's all very difficult.'

'What about the lounge? Haven't you some corner in the lounge where I could put their cushions? As I've already explained, they're both perfectly clean!'

In the end, tired of argument, Catherine gave in, and when Miss Fothergill-Briggs' two cases had been carried upstairs and the good lady had removed her hat, Tito and Tush were deposited upon their respective cushions in the lounge.

Chapter Three

The next morning, aroused quite early by the dirgeful note of Miss Spring's chanting, Nicholas at the Lodge rose and prepared to do a little work before breakfast. It was not yet seven and the sun was just rising above the sea in a flood of crimson against which a few bare branches of the trees stood out like jagged black arms against the sky.

'Drat that woman!' he said to himself, seeing in the distance the figure in the bathrobe doing her perambulations in the dew. 'Talk about a guest house. This is more of a lunatic asylum.'

He found to his chagrin that he had left a book he wanted in the lounge. This caused him added annoyance because it meant that, to get it, he had to cross the garden and run the risk of being pounced on by Miss Spring. He peered through the window, wondering whether or not to risk it. Then the ludicrousness of the situation swept over him and he drew back, flung up his head, saying in a loud voice, 'The idea! A Nankerviss afraid to cross his own lawn.'

Despite Susie-Jane's constant reminders not to walk about in the wet grass in carpet slippers, Nicholas did not change them but went out as he was, with his thick dressing-gown over his suit. Seeing Miss Spring take the footpath into the shrubbery he made full use of the opportunity to avoid her, and managed to reach the side door of the house without running into her.

Miss Spring had left it open, and he entered quietly, anxious not to rouse the household though he could hear Ann moving about above.

He padded up the corridor, opened the door of the lounge and switched on the light. Instantly a terrific scream penetrated the room. Aghast, he looked round, and was amazed and shocked to see a woman − a large middle-aged woman in a négligé, with her hair in elaborate curl papers, half lying, half sitting on the couch, a dog in her arms and a cat on her stomach, such horror in her eyes that he involuntarily stepped backwards.

'Good God!' he exclaimed.

'Don't swear!' shrieked the lady. 'Get out − get out quickly, do you hear, or I'll call for help. Intruding at an hour like this, and when I've had little sleep in all conscience, having to come down half through the night to comfort my poor little dears!'

Nicholas did not need twice to be told to get out. He fled.

In the hall he met Ann, who hearing the outburst had hurried down, followed by Susie-Jane, to discover the cause of it.

'It's inconceivable,' said Nicholas. 'Inconceivable that a man of my age and reputation should have to meet with such treatment in his own house.'

'But, Daddy, what is it?' asked Susie-Jane. 'What's the matter?'

'There's a woman in there − ' Nicholas said, indicating the lounge − 'an immense hysterical woman surrounded by a zoo who would have murdered me if she could. It's outrageous. Outrageous! One can't walk in the garden for them, and they're even dotted about the furniture waiting to spring out everywhere. I tell you, Susie-Jane, this can't go on.'

'Of course not,' she soothed him, trying hard not to smile. 'I can't understand it. It must be Miss Fothergill-Briggs, although when we left her last night she was in the blue room.'

'That's just it!' said Nicholas. 'You never know where you are with them. I tell you, they're all mad, and the sooner my home ceases to be a guest house, the better.'

For the next few days Nicholas kept severely away from

the house, and Susie-Jane took all his meals to him at the lodge.

'It's upsetting me,' he said one day at tea time. 'All these goings on are affecting my work. It's lost its poise somehow. I find myself bringing a lot of odd characters into my stories which have a cheapening effect, to say the least of it, on the main theme.'

Susie-Jane was silent for a few moments. Then she said, 'Don't you be too sure about it, Daddy.'

Nicholas jerked his head up, regarding her quickly over the top of his glasses.

'What do you mean?' he said.

'Well,' Susie-Jane said deliberately, 'I think perhaps it's what you need.'

'Oh!' grunted Nicholas, slightly annoyed. 'You do, do you?'

'Yes,' said Susie-Jane, 'I do. Oh, Daddy, don't think I'm criticising you. Don't think I don't appreciate how good your writing is, and your style. Everyone knows that. But sometimes people don't always want only that – '

'What does it matter what people want?' Nicholas queried irritably. 'They're pandered to too much as it is, what with bad films and sensational novels.'

'Yes. But I'm not sure that's what they do want,' Susie-Jane said sagaciously. 'I don't think it is, really. I think they want to read all about themselves – you know, their funny little ways, and crudenesses, and oddnesses. They don't always just want to read about great people. That makes them feel out of it, and somehow small. They want to know all about human beings like themselves with failings and habits they recognise. And probably that's what you're doing now.'

Nicholas studied her intently.

'Quite a lot seems to go on in your head,' he said.

Susie-Jane smiled. 'No,' she said. 'I'm not clever at all. But I feel things, and often I'm right. And I think your books will be more living things through letting these people jump into them.'

Nicholas shrugged his shoulders. 'Well,' he said, 'we shall see. But I doubt it.'

After a silence he resumed: 'What's the matter with Merlynne these days?'

Susie-Jane drew her brows together. 'I don't know,' she said. 'I don't think there's anything really, but — '

'Well?'

'I think it's Hugo,' Susie-Jane confessed, with a little tightening of her chest.

'Hugo? But what's he been up to?'

'Oh, nothing,' said Susie-Jane warmly. 'It isn't that. Hugo's wonderful, and so patient with her, but of course he's not really well yet, and somehow that seems to jar Lynne.'

'I see. But she should make allowances.'

'Yes.' Susie-Jane's mouth hardened. 'That's what I say. But of course — ' she continued trying to be fair ' — there is a lot to be done, and I don't think Merlynne really likes housework. Anyhow, it may be better soon. We've got a help coming — an Austrian refugee, at the end of the month — Catherine engaged her yesterday.'

'Hm,' said Nicholas despondently. 'A foreigner.'

'Well, you don't object to that, do you?'

'Not if she's a normal one,' Nicholas replied. 'But don't expect me to welcome any more cranks to this place.'

'I don't think Catherine would have engaged her if she hadn't been suitable,' Susie-Jane said.

'My dear child, Catherine's the worst judge of character I've met with yet,' Nicholas answered with a twinkle. 'Everyone, to Catherine, has some sort of halo, however muddy.'

'She can stick up to people, though,' Susie-Jane said. 'You should have heard her the other night when Miss Fothergill-Briggs arrived and wanted those animals in the room with her!'

'All the same, I expect the old termagant has got her way in the end.'

Susie-Jane dimpled. 'Yes, she has. We thought it was the lesser of two evils.'

Nicholas threw up his hands. 'There! What did I say? Not content with cranks, we have also to take wild animals into the family ménage.'

'Oh, they're not so wild,' Susie-Jane said. 'They're really

quite nice little things. And Miss Fothergill-Briggs isn't so bad as she sounds, despite her roaring voice. She belongs to lots of humane societies. She's already trying to get Mr Murgatroyd to invest money into her animal league.'

'Is she now? Kind of her! But I thought she had plenty herself.'

'I'm sure she has. I'm sure she's quite rich. But she's always extending into something or other. At least – it sounds like it.'

'Well, so long as she leaves me alone.'

'Oh, she's sorry about you. She wants to apologise.'

'She needn't,' Nicholas said. 'The further she keeps away from me, the better.'

Secretly, Susie-Jane enjoyed the numerous little complications now revolving round Trencathra, disturbed only by Merlynne and by Hugo, who as days went by seemed to withdraw more into himself, appearing to avoid even Susie-Jane herself.

One afternoon she happened to meet him again by chance, down by the cove. He was seated by himself on the rocks, below the dark cliffs which in the late pale sunlight glinted black, dark red and a pale yellowish green. At this time of the year, autumn, it was strange to find another human being on the beach. Susie-Jane went there frequently because the loneliness appealed to her and she enjoyed watching the birds on the edge of the sea – gulls, cormorants, sandpipers and puffins. That afternoon the beach shone wet, lately washed by the tide. The air was warm for the time of year, holding the salt tang of brine and weed, carried from dark clumps lying black and shining along the ridge of sand, where thin drifts of foam still lay, and myriads of small pale shells.

Hugo was staring out to sea, his leg thrust out in front of him, one hand on his stick tracing unconscious patterns in the sand at his feet.

When he saw Susie-Jane he stood up and went to meet her.

'This seems to be a favourite haunt of ours, doesn't it?' he said.

'Hugo,' she said impassively, 'what's the matter?'

'The matter?' he said, feigning surprise. 'My dear child, what do you mean?'

'I'm not a child,' she replied. 'And you know what I mean. It's so obvious, Hugo. Everyone notices it. You're not happy, you and Merlynne.'

'Do they, by jove!' he said, with his jaw thrust forward. 'Just what are they saying?'

'Nothing much,' she said. 'It's just pretty clear, that's all.'

'I suppose it is,' he said grimly. 'But you mustn't blame Merlynne, understand? It's not her fault.'

'A bit of it is,' Susie-Jane insisted stubbornly.

'Fifty-fifty, then,' he agreed. 'Let's leave it at that. What does it matter, anyway?'

'It *does* matter, if you're both miserable.'

'Who said we were miserable?'

'I know you are.'

'Well, this sort of thing happens sometimes. It happens from a number of causes – of which you probably know nothing – and it's just tough luck, that's all. Somehow it has to be lived with.'

Susie-Jane was silent for a minute or two, wondering how to say what she had to without butting in or appearing to be impertinent.

'I expect you'll be angry with me, Hugo,' she said at length, 'but do you love Merlynne?'

He stared straight ahead of him, not looking at her. 'Of course.'

'Very much?'

'Oh, Susie-Jane, what questions!'

'I know. It's awful of me. But I feel somehow I've a right to ask. After all, I'm a kind of sister, aren't I? And I can't bear you to be unhappy, Hugo. Really.'

He looked at her, a wry little smile about his lips. 'You mustn't be so sensitive,' he said, 'or you'll never get through life successfully. Have you never realised how very few people, comparatively, *are* happy? After all, perhaps we shouldn't expect it. We're lucky enough, some of us, to have a precious glimpse of it, and then we coolly expect it to go on all the time, whereas it can't. Surely you realise that?'

'No, I don't think I do,' Susie-Jane said. 'I think happiness is supposed to go on. If it doesn't there's failure somehow, in us, or in the kind of happiness.'

'Very well,' he said, 'We're failures, Merlynne and I.'

'If you love each other,' Susie-Jane told him, 'you shouldn't be.'

'But my child, life − or love, for that matter − isn't so simple. There can be a hundred and one complicating factors in a relationship between two people, just as there are many kinds of love.'

'I wasn't speaking about ways of loving,' Susie-Jane persisted, 'not little separate bits − if you love in a certain way it's only a kind of half love. I was meaning something much bigger, Hugo.'

For a moment he looked really sad. 'But I'm afraid very few people find it.'

'I know,' she said slowly.

They were both silent after this, and Susie-Jane sat completely still, her hands in her lap, her chin raised, with the dark hair swept back in the breeze behind her ears. Watching her, he was struck anew by her innocent dignity, the pride revealed in the youthful static pose and fearless profile. Sitting there she seemed to symbolize for him the spirit of the place. Whereas other people like himself and Merlynne, he mused, could become jaded and spoiled, this girl surely never would.

After the pause they walked on.

'Susie-Jane,' he said gently, 'you expect a great deal, don't you?'

'No,' she said. 'I don't really think I do. At least, not to hold on to − except Trencathra. Perhaps I expect a lot from Trencathra.'

'Trencathra is only a symbol to you,' he told her. 'One day your love for it will be given to some person, and I only hope you won't be disappointed.'

'I don't think I shall be,' she said.

'But you can never tell.'

'I suppose you say that because of Merlynne?'

'Well,' he said, 'there was a time, you know, when neither

of us would have believed things could become as they are between us. People change.'

'Have you changed, Hugo?' she asked, looking at him.

He nodded. 'Yes, I'm afraid I have. But none of us should be afraid of changing; it's inevitable. It would be queer if we didn't. The difficulty's the adjustment.'

'How are you different, Hugo?' she asked simply. 'Do you mind my asking?'

'No,' he replied. 'I don't mind. But it's hard to put into a few words. I'm older, of course. And I think I'm sick of sensation. My senses are a little tired, too. I no longer want the things I did, with such gusto. And Merlynne doesn't understand. That's the devil of it. She's kept her exuberance and hold on life, and she naturally wants it satisfied. But at the moment I can't do that. It's the kind of situation that must be happening times without number at the present time. And there seems no answer except waiting.'

'Perhaps in the end it will work out all right.'

'I'm not sure,' he said slowly, more to himself than to her. 'It will work out somehow, of course. That's obvious. But how? I expect she thinks she's got a raw deal – and I can see her point. But – it's difficult.'

'I know, It must be.'

'I'm tired,' he said. 'That's the long and short of it. The war has tired me. People don't seem essential to me any more. Personal things irritate me; I want most of the time to get away from it all – to something beyond human desires. I suppose –' he added, turning to look at her '– this all sounds complicated and rather boring?'

Susie-Jane shook her head. 'No. Not a bit. Do go on.'

'Shall we rest a bit again then? Do you mind?'

'Of course not.'

They sat down on a flat slab of rock washed smooth by countless tides, and he went on: 'I don't know why I'm talking to you like this but you're – composed, somehow. You don't exact anything like most women. So many won't give their interest unless they get something in return. But you don't behave that way.'

'Go on,' she urged for want of something to say. She felt a little shy. It seemed strange Hugo shouldn't realise how much this meant to her, just sharing his confidences and friendship. That, after all, was uniquely hers; he'd as good as said so. He'd loved Merlynne as a woman, but she, Susie-Jane, was his friend. Nothing could take that away. She was suddenly irrationally glad that she possessed something of Hugo which was not Merlynne's, and couldn't help wondering how she'd have felt if Hugo had married her instead of her sister. The thought did not bear contemplating. The mere suggestion sent a flood of sweetness through the whole of her being which for a moment was acute pain. She wouldn't have let him be lonely; no. Never should he have suffered in spirit as Merlynne had allowed him to suffer. She forced herself to regain her composure, and stilled the tremor of her body.

'Go on, Hugo,' she repeated once more, in a small quiet voice.

'I was thinking — talking to you has brought it all back to me — of an experience I had at the beginning of the war, following my first leave ...'

'Yes,' she prompted.

'I went for a holiday to the mountains in Wales.' He was staring out to sea as though once more he was re-living the occasion. 'It was before I met Merlynne. I stayed at a small inn in a valley of the Black Mountains, and I spent the time walking. Everything then was at a high pitch of tension. You won't remember much of it but we hadn't got used to war. The fall of France had shocked us. Many of us, I suppose, wondered if it couldn't have been avoided. It was only the Jewish persecution and Czechoslovakia which at that time seemed to justify the violence and degradation of war. For war always brings its degradation. There may be a strange glory alongside, but the result, in the main, is degradation. I thought so then, I think so now.'

'On that holiday I tried to puzzle it all out. I knew I was going to do my best, along with all the other good fellows, to put matters right in the way society thought fit — it was my duty. The torment and torture of a whole race of innocent people demanded it. But up there, in the quietness, I tried to find a philosophy that would satisfy my inner conscience and the part human integrity demanded I should play. And

I couldn't do it. I faced it all quite squarely, went to the deepest heart of what I believed, and I knew that Christ, the Nazarene, was right. I knew that the Sermon on the Mount preached the highest doctrine of all. If the churches of the world had stood together and lived according to true Christianity there would have been no war. They would have led people out of the mire, and Nazism would have failed. There'd have been no persecutions and ultimately no revenge. But the church, in compromising, went along with the political powers-that-be, like most of us who accepted it was the inevitable course to do the wrong thing for the right end.'

'You mean you were a pacifist?'

'At heart, I suppose.'

'Oh, I see.'

He smiled gently and gave a sigh. 'You don't, you know. How could you? There was the other side. It seemed to me that our little nation was fighting for its soul, and that counted more to me at the time than the philosophy preached by a great idealist nearly two thousand years ago.'

'Well, that was natural. You worry too much,' said Susie-Jane.

'Maybe. But that day, up the mountain, the truth seemed so clear. Those hills are unique in their way, very lost and lonely, filled with shadows and quietness. I had climbed the highest ridge of all, and was walking along the top with peak after peak before me just tinged with pale sun through a thin mist. It was all very mysterious. I had seen no living soul all day – nothing beyond a few sheep on the hillsides. Then, it seemed to me that I heard singing – '

'Singing?'

'Not physically, you understand – nothing tangible. But with my heart and mind I heard it. And through the mist I imagined shapes moving, hooded shapes of indeterminate colour, but moving in a vast pilgrimage along the mountain and down to the valley. And I knew them to be the martyrs – the souls of the truth-seekers, Susie-Jane, still concerned with bringing their light to the world.'

There was a long silence, after which he remarked, 'It was a kind of vision. For a time I was uplifted. Then, of course, I went abroad. The war continued. I did my job, like everyone else, and the memory of the experience was naturally submerged temporarily in more practical affairs. And, of course, there was Merlynne. But lately – I've been remembering. I realise that you've all thought me sick and possibly neurotic. I'm probably both. But it's more than that. Merlynne spends her time trying to convince herself and me that we must get back to what we were before I was wounded, that I must somehow become the man I was when I first met her. But I never shall. That man was not the whole of me. Most of him has died, anyway.'

'But, Hugo, that sounds so sad.'

'No, it isn't sad at all,' he told her. 'It merely means that I know more about the direction I want to take and that my appetites count less. That, surely, is important.'

'You said "direction", Hugo. What *is* your direction?'

'You may think me a little cracked,' he said, 'but if I was free to choose, I think I should first of all spend a period alone – quite, quite alone – then afterwards go out in the world speaking and doing what I know to be true.'

'Preaching do you mean?'

'In a way,' he admitted.

'And what about Merlynne?'

'I said if I was free,' he reminded her. 'But, of course, I'm not.'

'Perhaps Merlynne feels all this,' Susie-Jane suggested. 'Perhaps that's what worries her. After all, if she loves you, and knows all the time that you've changed – that you don't – '

'I do love Merlynne,' he said, 'but it seems not enough – in the way she wants. That's my concern – to try, somehow, to *make* it enough, for both of us. Do you understand?'

'Yes,' said Susie-Jane, 'I think so.'

All of a sudden she saw Merlynne more clearly, and was deeply sorry for her. To Merlynne, who had loved the flesh and blood Hugo, this remote mystic must have come as a shock and a frustration. Even she herself, against her will, felt a pang. Susie-Jane, despite her youthful idealism, was woman enough to be concerned with Hugo the man, as well as with Hugo the dreamer and friend. And although she would have shrunk from intruding in any way into that part of his life which by rights belonged to Merlynne, Hugo, remote and self-sufficient, raised a barrier between the easy flow of their relationship which temporarily chilled her.

He must have sensed something of what she felt, for he said presently, 'Have I worried you, Susie-Jane?'

'No,' she said. 'Except that – '

'Well?'

'Couldn't you ever care, ever again, about any one individual?' she asked. 'Do you mean you think it's wrong to?'

'My dear child,' he said, 'I never said that. One can't speak for the future – life is never static. It goes on, and we go with it. I only told you what I did,' he added, 'because I felt you would understand. I didn't want to depress you. I haven't, have I?'

'Oh, no, Hugo,' she said, worried by the anxiety in his eyes, ashamed of her brief selfishness. 'Of course you haven't.'

'I've told no one else all this,' he resumed, 'only you.'

'Thank you.'

'It's for me to thank you,' he said. 'Most girls would have been bored or irritated. But I feel I can talk to you.'

'Oh, yes,' she said. 'You can – always.'

He gave her one of the swift, rare smiles which so changed him, making him instantly human and approachable once more.

'I shall remember that,' he said. 'And when I feel a mood coming on me I shall think – where's Susie-Jane? So you see what you've let yourself in for.'

She gave him her hand. There was no more to be said.

'Come along,' she said, 'we ought to be going.'

He stood up, and presently they commenced walking back along the pale sands in the direction of the path.

All was very quiet now. What breeze there had been had died down, and no sound disturbed the silence save the gentle lapping of the water below, and the sudden shrill squawking of the gulls as they approached over the stones. Susie-Jane was impressed anew by the immensity of everything, by the eternal, constant ebb and flow of the waves breaking on the beach, and by the great fading dome of the sky which had seen so many ages pass, so many millions of nights and days come and go since the beginning of creation. Before them the face of the cliffs rose, towering in passionate primeval colours to the summit. Clumps of dark shining ivy had made their tangled way over the stone, and a few dried roots of scabious and thrift had become implanted in the shelved layers of earth. The path took a zig-zagged course up the side, and Hugo frequently had to rest. Susie-Jane noted the lines of pain on his face, the involuntary stiffening of the jaw and mouth, and beads of perspiration on his upper lip; but she said nothing, knowing at that moment that he would have scorned her pity or compassion. Before their conversation which had revealed so intimately the inner secret Hugo, she would have been tempted to take his arm, to help him with all her strength up the incline. But recognising his innate independence, she refrained.

The light caught his profile, finely carved, with its well-balanced head and firm outline of nose and jaw. Seen thus, there was something about him which reminded her suddenly of Durer's 'Pilgrim' – something which took her from the present to eternal regions of the imagination wherein from time immemorial heroic deeds had been achieved in the mystical search for good. As they trudged on, she felt that she could follow him through the world, if he asked it of her, exacting nothing of her but her loyalty and devotion.

Then, as they reached the top and made their way across the short turf towards the house, Susie-Jane pulled herself together with a jerk. Hugo was Merlynne's husband. He loved her, and was determined to make her happy. She, Susie-Jane, must help him – she must do what she could, in any way possible, to make this course easier – however hard it became, however deeply she, too, felt for him.

That night she couldn't sleep. A strange sense of companionship mingled with sadness kept her awake, and a yearning which had changed her in those few hours from girl to woman. Sometimes the tears were wet on her lashes – because the world was so beautiful, and life was such an aching business, and because she knew now that suffering was a part of it, and that none could escape. From henceforward there was a secret which she must keep to herself — the secret of her love for Hugo.

Towards dawn, however, the house, as of old, lulled her to oblivion. Taking her into its shadows and quietness, soothing her heart and burning eyes. A piece of ivy tapped at the window; from the trees outside there was the sleepy chirrup and rustle of wings. The first pale streak of dawn presently lit the sky, and the fishing boats trailed dark against the sea, into the harbour. A new day had begun.

Susie-Jane slept.

Chapter Four

Miss Fothergill-Briggs had been a week at Trencathra when the Austrian help, Lotte Eberhert, arrived, and from that time she had an ally in food reform; for Lotte, if anything, was even more pronounced in her views than Miss Fothergill-Briggs, and between them they put up a united front in the cause of strict non-animal fat vegetarianism. Soon the house had arrayed itself into two groups – the Carnivori versus the Vegetarians. Miss Spring, with her Eastern tendencies, adhered to the former, and Hugo, the humanitarian, was inclined to, on the whole. Richard was frankly and good-humouredly sceptical, but as most of his meals were taken apart, the whole scheme affected him very little. Nicholas now refused to come to the house to eat, save for very rare occasions. He had an aversion to nut roasts and he considered the whole atmosphere 'cranky' in the extreme, as, also, did his mother-in-law, Dame Julia. She, however, was amused by this new state of affairs. Catherine became worried, because the regime seemed to put her in the wrong. She was a kind person and resented the moral slur laid upon her erst-while menus, asserting that she would be the last person in the world to cause undue suffering to any living creature. There were times when she regretted ever having engaged Lotte. But the fact remained that the Austrian girl was efficient in the extreme, and apart from the question of the food, the house was run considerably more easily than before. She took charge of the bedrooms, with Ann's help, and was mostly responsible for the vegetarian side of the cooking. In appearance she was a heavily built tall girl, with very dark hair drawn demurely back from a centre parting to a knot in the neck. She wore colourful clothes, gay little blouses and very bright and clean flowery aprons which Dame Julia found rather pleasing.

But Ann Chenoweth, in her quiet way, disapproved.

'She's turning the place upside-down, Mr Richard,' she said to him one day when he sat in the kitchen — a growing habit of his — eating his dinner. 'It's not like home anymore. I don't like it.'

'But you have an easier time, don't you?' he enquired.

She shrugged her shoulders. 'Oh, that! I'm not so sure of that, either. In any case, I'd rather work day and night than be ordered about — *and* see Miss Catherine ordered about too — by someone who doesn't know our ways. It isn't that I'm against foreigners — dear life, no. I've always been broadminded in that way. But there are limits. People shouldn't try to inflict their ideas on those who've got their own. This Eberhert girl, now — she talks a lot about a proper spirit and brotherhood and kindness and all that sort of thing. But it seems to me she's stirring up something quite the opposite. There's no peace about the place any more. Well, I ask you! Look at Miss Catherine and Miss Merlynne, the way it's taken them. They look guilty every time a piece of steak comes on to the table. It can't go on — mark my words, something will happen.'

It did.

A few days later Miss Fothergill-Briggs, supported by Lotte who always took her meals in the dining room with the rest, to Ann's annoyance and humiliation, decided that she could no longer eat with the Carnivori and retired instead to the lounge, where she and the Austrian girl had their lunch on a small card table in the window, the dog and the cat on the floor beside them. The next day the same thing occurred; only this time there was a second card table at which sat Miss Spring.

This was too much for Ann, who declared to Catherine that she simply refused to carry in any meals to the lounge. Why should she wait on a foreigner who, 'help' or not, was an employee like herself?

'But, Ann,' begged Catherine helplessly, 'what are we to

do? After all, it's not much trouble, and if they prefer it that way — '

Ann set her mouth stubbornly. 'No,' she said. 'I won't do it.'

Harrassed and tired, Catherine said quickly, 'if *I* ask you to do it, you *will* do it.'

'I'm afraid not,' said Ann. 'Someone's got to take a stand, and if no one else will, I must.'

'Ann, I won't have you talking to me like that. You're forgetting yourself.'

'Am I?' retorted Ann, with temper in her eyes, and two spots of flame burning the cream of her cheeks. 'Very well, then. If I'm to be put in the wrong, Miss Catherine, I must leave. I must give you a week's notice.'

She turned abruptly, going into the scullery, leaving Catherine to carry the meal into the lounge.

'You will have to do the waiting in here, Lotte,' she said to the Austrian girl, 'if you and Miss Fothergill-Briggs still intend to have your meals here. Ann refuses to. I've left the vegetables on the table.'

She went from the room, tired and dispirited, and later in the afternoon confided her troubles to Richard.

'It's so hard arranging things,' she told him, 'you've no idea how difficult it is trying to please everyone, Richard. And I'd been cooking all morning and was utterly tired out. I'm afraid I flared up at her — but after all, I can't allow even Ann to defy me completely. What am I to do? She's such a standby. If she leaves I just can't contemplate going on.'

Richard was thoughtful for a moment or two. Then he said to her quietly, putting his arm round her shoulder, 'There, old girl, don't worry. I'll speak to Ann. I'll make it all right if it's at all possible, and I think it is. She's a good girl — and at heart she's fond of the family, I'm sure of it. But, you know, between you and me — Miss Fothergill-Briggs was a mistake. And I'm not at all certain we ought to keep Lotte.'

'No,' agreed Catherine. 'Neither am I, really. Only she's such a good worker that I've been prepared to overlook other complications because of it. Help *is* difficult. There really is a lot to do. And, after all, if people have principles they're entitled to stick up for them. I don't blame her for that. No, it's just not too easy running a guest house. There's the rationing too. Miss Spring wants marmalade both for tea and breakfast, and as she won't take beans or toasted cheese insists that we buy her some on points. But the points won't run to it.' She broke off, drawing her hand across her brow wearily. 'That's only *one* thing,' she resumed. 'There are hundreds more. It really is trying, sometimes.'

'I know. Try not to worry, Cathie. I'll see what I can do about Ann, anyhow.'

Although he was sorry for Catherine in her predicament, he was secretly pleased to see her getting worked up about any practical matter. It was proof, he thought, that she was coming alive again, and had other interests now to disturb her beyond the ghost world of her married life.

That evening he found Ann in the kitchen garden picking sprouts for the following day. The sun had almost gone and in the half-dark she was pale, though when he drew near to her he observed her eyes looked red, as though she'd been weeping. The scent of herbs filled the air. Despite the sturdy grace of the young figure before him there was something hurt and reserved about her that touched his sympathy.

'Well, Ann,' he said, 'nice night, isn't it?'

'Very,' she said.

'You don't sound too cheerful,' he said, thinking it best to come to the point quickly.

'No, I'm not,' she said. 'But that doesn't matter.'

'Oh, yes, it does. At Trencathra people must be happy.'

'Well,' she said with a sudden stubborn lift of her chin, 'I shan't be long at Trencathra anyhow.'

'Ann,' he said slowly, looking at her hard, 'you're being a rather silly girl, you know.'

'No I'm not,' she asserted, with a faint quiver of her lips and a suspiciously quick intake of breath. 'Miss Catherine showed me today just where I stand in this house, and after that, I must tell you, I don't intend to stay.'

'But, Ann, Catherine was tired and upset, just as you were –'

'I wasn't at all tired,' she contradicted, 'I never get tired. I can work night and day for those I care for, and never get tired – so long as I'm treated properly. But I'm not going to be put in the wrong falsely just to please the high and mighty whim of a foreigner. Oh, I know I'm only a country girl, Mr Richard, but for some time now, I've resented certain things.'

'Have you indeed?'

'Yes, indeed I have,' she said. 'And not least of them having to run round after Miss Fothergill-Briggs' dog, and take second place to Lotte Eberhert. They're in league together, and they allow Tito to eat his dinners off the best satin cushion that was Mrs Nankerviss's. But that's only *one* thing. There are lots,' she concluded firmly, turning round again to proceed with picking the vegetables.

This show of temper and independence pleased Richard. She was really a fine girl, he thought, watching her, attractive – with her hair tumbled softly about one temple, cream skin glowing.

'Look here, Ann,' he said. 'I agree with you over most of what you've said. But you're going to forget this bit of trouble now and settle down again like a good sensible girl, aren't you? Because of course we can't get on without you.'

'Oh, yes, you can,' she said, still defiant. 'I'm sure you'll find that Lotte will run you all very successfully.'

He forced his mouth into grimness, though his eyes twinkled.

'Ann!' he exclaimed.

'Well?'

'She won't run *me*, I promise you. And I must have someone to see I get my dinner at nights when I'm late. You can't desert me now, can you?' Even in the dim light he noticed a deep flood of crimson staining the high curve of cheeks and forehead. For a second, seeing her so young and vulnerable, he was prompted to kiss her. He took a step forward but restrained himself, remembering Deborah.

His voice had changed slightly when he said, after a pause, 'Well, Ann?'

She looked up at him quickly, a smile like sudden sunshine flooding her face. 'All right,' she said. 'If you want it, I will.'

'Thank you,' he said, adding with slight embarrassment,

'it isn't only for domestic chores we want you. You're our friend. We like you. We're used to you. You must remember that, when things seem difficult. Will you?'

'I'll try,' she promised.

Presently she watched him stride up the path until he reached the gate leading to the shrubbery by the house. He walked with a swing, his figure lean and spare against the dying light. A glow filled Ann's heart, followed by a pang of loneliness. She knew it was only for him, Mr Richard, that she'd stay on, and she knew the situation from her point of view was impossible.

From the distance somewhere a fox barked. Over towards St Taloc the lights were beginning to sprinkle the fading sky. The air, intermingled with the scent of herbs, smelled deep and rich and autumnal, fanning her smooth face like a caress. But Ann noticed nothing of this. Another picture was in her mind which she would keep there always – the picture of Richard's figure, swinging away from her into the dusk.

One evening Dame Julia invited Sam Murgatroyd to have coffee in her room, following dinner.

'I like the little man,' she confided to Merlynne, with a playful tap of her finger. 'He's worth the whole bunch of your cranks and geniuses put together. And I don't like the way "that woman's" setting her cap at him.' By 'that women' she referred to Miss Fothergill-Briggs. 'If we allow her to she'll have half his fortune in the twinkling of an eye. I must have a talk to him.'

On the evening mentioned Sam was very careful to flatten his hair immaculately with his own 'Smootheen' cream, and to trim with his nail scissors his greying moustache. He was flattered and humbly impressed that the old lady had singled him out for attention. He couldn't fathom the reason for he was, after all, only a simple kind of fellow, despite the fortune he'd amassed through luck, kind friends, and a certain business acumen rather than any particular merit. As he adjusted his tie his thoughts turned to his wife, Tilda, who'd died only the preceding summer, and he wondered what she'd think of him now; for Tilda, as the years went by, had evinced an increasing contempt of his personal attributes, having him remember that she'd married him when he was only a poor chemist's assistant in Bradford, and that any social success he might have achieved had been due purely to her. Not, he thought wisely, that there ever had been much genuine success of this kind. He'd never deluded himself that anything but his money had counted in the eyes of the world, and was conscious always of the pit-boy he'd started as, rather than the business figure he'd become.

That was nearly sixty years ago, but a chance phrase or thought easily took him back again — as on that night when he talked with Susie-Jane at the gate — remembering with a stab of nostalgia the hardship, the secret ambitions which had fired him to better himself during his first youthful days. And he'd done that all right.

At seventeen he'd run away from an unsympathetic home and the uncongenial work underground, found employment in a small chemist's in Bradford, after which, step by step, he'd worked himself up, until in partnership with a young Jew of commercial instincts he'd launched 'Smootheen' upon the market.

The rest had been a phenomenal climb from obscurity to fame. But he knew that quite half the battle had been the advertisement campaign, the slogans and apt phrases which had originated in his partner's mind.

He'd married Tilda when he was twenty-five. She was an attractive little thing in those days, a little sharp-featured and sharp-voiced, perhaps, but bright and lively. Unhappily, though, in the years that followed, her brightness had evolved into something like shrewishness, and any affection she had in her revolved solely round their son and only child, Robert. Well, Robert had been killed in forty-three and Tilda had died following an operation three years' later; so here he was, adrift and alone at sixty-five, with no anchor save his duties on the council of Blackhampton, and a few business interests which were mere routine. He had a fortune behind him, with nothing or no one in the world personally to expend it on. Looking back, his life appeared to him very mediocre and intrinsically unimportant. If Robert had lived, at least a portion of him would have gone on. As it was, except for the rather sterile achievement of amassing money, he thought, he might as well not have lived.

His visit to Trencathra had resulted from the chance glimpse of an advertisement in a daily paper which had informed him of the cultural interests to be found at Trencathra, near St Taloc, Cornwall. Something about the wording of the paragraph had caught his interest, and on the spur of the moment he'd decided to go there. He knew the name of Nicholas Nankerviss, though he'd read none of his books, and the word 'culture' meant for him artists and the type of people he had never really mixed with at all. Why not take the opportunity? Why not, even at his age, savour something else other than the boring, stiff-shirted, dinners and social life connected with his business acquaintants and people whom he well knew were interested only in his brass? Besides, he'd been suffering recently from indigestion. A change would do him good. And so he'd come to Trencathra.

It had been with a sense of belated adventure that he'd arrived there, on an autumn evening just as daylight was fading above the yellowing hedges and narrow lanes and a faint film of mist hung above the sea.

The approach down the winding roads, and the freshening evening air tangy with the smell of brine and blackberries, had quickened his senses and given him a brief feeling of being a boy again. He had no idea what awaited him behind the gaunt wall of the strange, mediaeval-looking house, and was prepared for anything. Nervousness, for the first few days, had made him behave and speak boisterously at meal times when confronted by the family headed by the elegant old lady and actress of her time, Dame Julia. He'd decided he must show them he was not quite a ninny, and had endeavoured, when the opportunity arose, to amuse them all by the few jokes and funny stories he knew. But after the first week he realised that his efforts had fallen rather flat, and had settled down into more or less being an onlooker and spectator.

The only member of the household up to now with whom Sam had exchanged any real confidences at all was Susie-Jane who'd been so friendly to him on the night of her return with the washing. He'd liked her from the beginning, and time had cemented his regard for her. If he'd only had a lass like that for a daughter, he told himself, things would have been very different for him. And if it hadn't been for Tilda always imagining she was delicate, there might well have been another child. Come to think of it – after the first few years Tilda had never been especially friendly to him. She had nagged more than was necessary, and many times he'd rued the day he'd married. But when she'd gone, poor thing, he'd missed her. It was odd how much one depended on a woman, even the nagging kind.

Ah, he thought, putting the finishing touches to his toilet before going to meet Dame Julia, there's no mistake about it – we waste our lives bickering and bothering about little things that don't matter, and when we wake up it's too late to do anything about it. Poor Tilda! What would you think, old girl, if you saw me now, all toffed up to meet an actress?

He smiled at himself in a manner meant to be jocular and debonair, but the eyes that confronted him in the mirror were wistful – they were the eyes of Sam Murgatroyd the pit boy who had once dreamed his dreams of being a power for good in the world.

In her room, meanwhile, Dame Julia also was concerned with preparations. Marianne had helped her into her plum-coloured taffeta gown, and she wore the velvet ribbon with the diamond clasp at her neck. She displayed most of her rings on her fine old hands, and sprayed her handkerchief with the merest suggestion of lavender water.

The Dresden coffee service, with the genuine apostle spoons which had belonged to her daughter, was already laid on the walnut table by the fire, with a plate of shortbread beside it. And she had not forgotten the cigars. Men like Sam Murgatroyd, she knew, never smoked cigarettes; it was always a pipe or cigars.

He arrived shortly after eight, a little nervous and ill-at-ease but smiling, faintly excited, with a slight odour about him of brilliantine and soap which to Dame Julia was characteristic of the little man's homely, essential cleanliness of mind and body.

He displayed the qualities of a small boy, she thought,

on his first visit to Sunday School; carefully washed and groomed, and slightly awed, keenly anticipating the occasion.

'Sit down, Mr Murgatroyd,' she said, indicating the easy chair by the fireplace. 'Don.'t stand on ceremony. I'm glad to see you. It isn't often an old woman like me takes it into her head to receive visitors.'

'Indeed, ma'am,' said Sam. 'It's very kind of you.'

'Kind? Tut, tut!' she said, tapping her fingers on the table. 'Nonsense. I asked you for my own pleasure. And why shouldn't I? After all – I'm eighty-five, old enough to be your mother. And that's the best of old age – tongues can't wag any more.'

She crossed the room and sat in the chair opposite, her silk skirt billowing out around her, looking very like a painting of some ancient Duenna, with one slender ringed hand still upon the knob of her ivory stock. She rang the bell for Marianne, and resumed: 'Never believe that old age is a tragedy, Mr Murgatroyd. It can be – but it needn't, if one keeps one's sense of humour. A sense of humour is a blessed thing. I've always had it, thank God! But the present generation seems to be losing it. That's the fault of the wars, and all these dictatorships. Everything has become so dreadfully solemn. Even my grandchildren are solemn – although Susie-Jane's the right sort, bless her! But in my day, how we could laugh – kindly, without malice. How we could flirt and play with life – what an adventure it was. But now –' she broke off, turning her shrewd brilliant old eyes full upon him, and resumed after a pause – 'tell me, what do you think of all this?'

She waved her hand round the room airily, taking in at one gesture the cream walls, maroon hangings and antique mahogany furnishings which had belonged to generations of earlier Nankervisses.

'It's a grand, handsome room, ma'am,' Sam answered.

'Ah, I didn't mean that! I meant the whole thing – Trencathra – the guest house. What do you make of them all? My family and the guests?'

'Well, it's hard to say,' Sam replied. 'I've only been here a fortnight, and most of that time's been observation on my part. You see, ma'am, I'm not that much used to writers and artists and such like. Most of my life's been given to business and this is a kind of fling on my part.'

Marianne entered, carrying the coffee on a tray which she placed on the small table on the old lady's right hand side.

When she'd gone again, Dame Julia continued, 'A fling? But you must be worth a great deal of money. Do you mean you're not used to holidays?'

Sam shook his head. 'Oh, no. Not that at all. When Tilda – that's my wife – was alive, she got so that she always had to be round and about somewhere. But it wasn't this sort of thing at all. Bournemouth, Torquay, Biarritz, Monte Carlo, ma'am, that's the kind of place she wanted, expensive hotels all the time, tea-time music and massage – not that Tilda was fat – but that was her fancy, to take 'cures', and listen to bands all the time. Sometimes we wintered at Harrogate or Buxton. But, it's a rum thing; I never got to like it. My fancy was for other things.'

Dame Julia passed him the shortbread, and handed him a cup of coffee.

'What other things, Mr Murgatroyd?'

'Ah, that's what I never knew,' he said ruminatively. 'That's just what I never exactly knew.'

'What do you mean by that?' queried the old lady. 'Do you mean you never knew your own mind?'

'Maybe that was it,' he agreed simply. 'When I was a lad I used to plan things. I worked in a pit in Yorkshire then, and I meant to do a great deal for the world. It seems rum a chap like me talking like that, I suppose. But in those days it wasn't so much money I thought about, ma'am, as power. I wanted the power to help my pals, and the kind of folk I mixed with, to better things.'

'We're all socialists in our youth,' Dame Julia said with a little nod of her head. 'Go on, Mr Murgatroyd.'

'But somehow,' he said, 'time went by. And when I'd got on a bit, there was Tilda and then the lad. And then things seemed to have changed. As I've said, Tilda had different ideas about it all. And we went on and on – and here I am, both of them gone now, not knowing quite what to make of it all. You see, ma'am — however much you may differ from a woman, however much of a tyrant she is — when she goes, you miss her. There's no doubt about it. You miss her, like you miss an old pain that's nagged you for years, and life doesn't seem right any more. And that's the queer fact of it. Half our lives Tilda and me bickered away in misery. And yet, believe me, if I could have her back again tomorrow I would. Queer, that!'

'You're lonely,' Dame Julia said. 'That's your trouble, you're lonely. And it's dangerous for a man like you.'

'Dangerous, ma'am?' he enquired innocently, with brows raised in his small round face.

'Of course,' she said. 'You may once upon a time have been a working man, but that's nothing against you these days. Look at our politicians. Look at myself, for instance, who came of tramp and vagabond stock. No, one's beginnings are not all that important today. But the fact remains, you're a very rich man, and I shouldn't like you to make a mess of things now.'

'That's very kind of you.'

'Oh, no it's not. I like you. You're one of the few *real* people in this house at the moment. And I don't want to see you eaten up by cranks.'

'Eaten up by cranks?' he reiterated. 'What do you mean, ma'am?'

'My dear man!' Dame Julia said with a twinkle. 'I was not born yesterday. I mean, don't get entangled with that Fothergill-Briggs woman in any financial scheme until you've properly considered it.'

'Well, really,' he said, confused and a little doubtful, 'it's odd you should mention that —'

'Oh, not so very,' she interposed quickly. 'It's been perfectly obvious, I can assure you, and it has afforded me a certain amount of amusement too, watching her from my window, stalking you with her little tracts and pamphlets and schemes.'

He flushed. 'She seems a very kind sort of lady,' he said rather weakly.

'Kind? Fiddlesticks! When she's already caused trouble between the staff and my grandchildren? Oh, she may not have meant to. She may mean well enough. But, mark my words, the only people who can afford to be in any way cranks are middle-aged spinsters and romantic young men like Hugo. A man like you should keep away. You're not the type.'

'Oh, as to that,' he said, 'I know I'm an ordinary kind of chap. But you see how it is, ma'am, I've got no roots. And that's the long and the short of it. I may've spent too much time bothering to make my pile when I could've done other things as well. But there was always my boy. He'd've had the chance to make good use of it. Now he's gone it's all so final. There's nothing. Nothing any more.'

'Have another cup of coffee?' suggested Dame Julia after a short silence.

'Thanks. This is the best coffee I've had for years.'

'Marianne made it,' the old lady told him. 'She's French, and the French know what they're doing. Anything that needs taste or flavour about it – anything to do with the senses, whether it be scent, touch or flavour – trust the French, I say. We're amateurs in comparison.'

Flattered by the companionable 'we', Sam leaned back in a more leisurely manner while she poured him the second cup.

'There,' she said handing it to him. 'And what about another biscuit?'

He shook his head. 'I had a large dinner, thanks.'

'Your pipe, then. Or a cigar. Take a cigar,' she told him. 'I like to feel the men-folk comfortable about me.'

'Presently,' he agreed. 'Excuse my saying so,' he went on, 'but you're a very wonderful woman. It seems to me, Dame Julia, there's not much you don't know about human beings.'

'Hardly anything at all,' she agreed. 'It's been my life's work, you see. To play as many parts as I have in my day, you have to understand them. You have to know their secret yearnings and humiliations, their hopes and their fears, and to be able to touch the secret spring in the heart of the ordinary man and woman, so they think instantly, Ah, that's how *I* feel! That's how *I* suffered. That is *me*!' She laughed a little indulgently. 'Bless you! That's the job of an actress – to flatter, with human sympathy. To understand people, without illusion, but always if possible kindly. And when people are real it's not difficult to be kind, believe me. But the others – ah!' A little coughing sound of contempt came from her throat, 'I cannot put up with them.'

'No?' he echoed.

'No,' she averred. 'I don't like anything pseudo, Mr Murgatroyd.'

He frowned slightly, and appeared a little perplexed. 'That Miss Briggs,' he began hesitantly, 'I'm not sure she's – what you say, ma'am. Her ideas may be rum – they're not *my* kind of ideas at all. But she seems a kind sort of woman – even if it's a mistaken kind of kindness! Take the orphanage, for instance.'

'What orphanage?' asked Dame Julia so sharply that he involuntarily started.

Making a vague gesture with his hands, Sam shrugged his shoulders slightly. 'Just an idea, Dame Julia. Just an idea.' His tones were soothing, half-apologetic. Then he leaned forward and continued with more enthusiasm: 'It was like this, you see. Miss Briggs had a fancy for running an orphanage on international lines, different from what has been done before, a philanthropic kind of idea, but I admit it took my fancy, ma'am. I admit it. Well – that's natural enough if you consider that I've no-one of my own to follow on. Then the question of finance arose.'

'Ah!' said Dame Julia significantly.

'Naturally,' he resumed, 'it takes a great deal of money. And though Miss Briggs may be comfortably off, she's not all that rich. And so she put it to me, and the suggestion – well, took my fancy. And that's about all, so far.'

'Hm!' Dame Julia's brows met above the bridge of her fine old nose.

'That's all very well,' she said after a moment, 'that's all very well, Mr Murgatroyd, and I don't want you to think I'm an interfering old woman – although I am, of course, very interfering when I think it's necessary! But the point is what kind of an orphanage this is to be. International, you say. Yes, that sounds good. Very good. But what else? Food fadists, I suppose, and a lot of other taradiddle that ordinary folks don't believe in?'

She waited for his reply and, after a short pause, he agreed slowly: 'Yes, I believe so. But the vegetarian part, ma'am, at least that's progressive. Look at Bernard Shaw now, and after all, why should we kill animals if it's not necessary? Though I must admit *I* shouldn't like to go without my little bit of steak on occasions.'

'I'm not interested in propaganda,' Dame Julia said inconsistently, 'it may or may not be right. But I advise you to think things over well, my friend. Don't get mixed up in anything too cranky. I can see your point over the orphanage, bless you. But if you go in for anything like that, do for heaven's sake see that it's sound. You're not the age now to go in for hare-brained eccentric schemes. I don't say you should stay in a rut and never venture far from it, but wisdom and commonsense do count, you know.'

She leaned towards him. 'Look at me. I've had my fun, and achieved a bit in my own line. But I wouldn't have if I'd not had my head screwed on the right way. There was a time when I had my temptations – not your sort, but just as exciting.'

She leaned back again while a faint reminiscent sigh escaped her. 'Yes, it seems a long time ago now. And so it was; Vienna, sixty years ago. Have you ever been to Vienna, Mr Murgatroyd?'

'Once, ma'am,' he answered, 'but Tilda didn't care for it. She had stomach trouble, and blamed the water. We didn't stay long.'

'Ah, well, I had a season of Shakespeare there,' she told him, 'Henry, my husband, was in London at the time. We hadn't been married long and things had not been too easy between us just then. It was before the children came, and though I loved Henry ... well, you know what human nature is. Vienna was very romantic then. Mischa Friedman – that was his name, he was half-Hungarian – was in opera there. Ah, what a voice he had! And what looks. What a flatterer! And in my day, you must understand, I was not unattractive myself.'

She waited, with a lift of her brows, and he said, smiling, 'Aye, I can well believe that.'

'The long and short of it was, of course,' she went on, 'we fell in love. Not easily and comfortably, as I had been in love with Henry, but very violently.'

'Dear, dear,' he remarked, at a loss.

'I might well have run away with him,' she said with a faint touch of vanity. 'He wanted me to, he begged and threatened, and I must say it was all very charming and tragic and exciting while it lasted. And how I adored him. But,' she said significantly, 'he was a very extraordinary young man. And that, I think, held me back. For while these episodes give a zest and beauty and pain to life, they do not form an adequate background to it. And I realised this in time because, as I have said, I have my head screwed on in the right way. And do you know what I did?' she said, chuckling.

'No,' he answered.

'Well, of course you don't. I just ditched my season, wired my husband, caught the first boat home and told Henry I wanted to start a family. And so we did.'

'Ma'am!' he gasped.

'Yes,' she said, 'and everything was all right after that. But if I'd obeyed my wild and foolish fancy it would not have been. Now, do you see what I mean? I'm not inferring, of course, that you have any such fancy for eloping with the Fothergill-Briggs woman. But you keep your schemes earthbound. That's the advice of an old woman who knows a few things.'

'Aye. But I've always been on the earth, ma'am, until now,' he said. 'Too much. And a time comes when it doesn't altogether satisfy.'

'Sam!' She tapped his arm with her forefinger. 'I'm going to call you Sam. You don't mind, do you? The people who really do things − things that count − aren't the impractical dreamers. No, they're the people with a vision, but they build *up* from the earth, step by step. Remember that. And they build soundly. Dreamers are right. We must have our dreams, but there's no short cut to success. You should know that. It took you years of effort, didn't it? Of hard work and slogging, to get where you are now? Well – don't despise it. Don't despise being practical. Where would you be if you hadn't been that? In no position to consider any scheme for an orphanage or anything else. Don't forget it.'

'And don't go wasting yourself now. Too many people in the world are doing that at the moment. The war, I suppose, and a general namby-pamby moral weakness. There's a kind of pseudo quality creeping into everything – into art, music, literature, and living itself. And the man in the street, poor creature, is in serious danger of being gulled by it all, unless he wakes up. Take this young man here at Trencathra, this Laurence something-or-other. What do you make of him?'

'I don't know,' Sam confessed. 'A high-falutin' sort of young fellow he seems to me, and yet there's something likeable about him.'

'Yes,' Dame Julia agreed grimly. 'Charm. Well, charm's a pleasant quality to possess, if it's used right. But between you and me, I don't like the way our young friend is utilising his opportunities.'

'In what way, ma'am?'

'He plays up to people. Haven't you noticed? To Miss Spring and the Briggs woman. And yet all the time he's laughing up his sleeve. He may imagine he's got some sort of a message to give through his surrealistic horrors, but if so he's gulling himself. Then again, I don't like his attitude to my granddaughter, though perhaps I should not be sitting here saying all these things to you.'

'You mean Mrs Dale?' queried Sam.

She nodded. 'Yes, I do. Merlynne. Perhaps I shouldn't worry, but I'm not at all happy about her, Sam. She's restless. Restless.'

As if tired, the old lady fell back into her seat, a perplexed reminiscent look in her eyes. For a moment the fire left her and she looked what she was, a very old woman. Her face, in repose, had paled and looked more drawn. Yet the bones were good. And watching her Sam envisaged her, for a moment as she would appear when dead – cold, waxen, and immobile, with a static dignity upon her which mortality could not destroy.

Presently she sighed. 'Ah, well. It's what I said. The age.

No roots, no commonsense, and Merlynne's a child of it. Greedy for life, because she's lost her faith. But I'm anxious for her, and for that husband of hers.'

Sam was silent. He would have liked to put the old lady's fears at rest, but he felt that nothing he could conscientiously say would do so. Her reference to Merlynne and Laurence had not surprised him, rather it had endorsed his opinion of the matter, and he remembered, with a sensation of guilt, an evening only three days ago when he'd taken a stroll along the cliffs and almost stumbled upon the two young people who were standing by the rocks in the shadows. It had been dark except for the starlight, and he would possibly not have seen them at all if the man hadn't struck a match suddenly which had thrown their two profiles into relief.

Sam had involuntarily stepped back into the darkness of the stone wall, but something about the pose, an intimate quality in the way the young man had bent toward her to light her cigarette, had discomfited him. There had been nothing wrong in the gesture itself but their faces had been pale, tense, both of them with a passionate unhappiness which he'd not liked to see. He didn't wish to suspect anything. He'd turned and gone back as quietly as he could, telling himself he'd been imagining things, that everything had been a trick of light, no more. In any case, it was not his affair. But Dame Julia had revived his memory of the scene. And he knew that what he'd thought, she also believed.

'I shouldn't worry, Dame Julia,' he said presently. 'Young people have different ways nowadays. You can never tell what they're thinking. And the more you try the less they like it, and are apt to go off at a tangent.'

'That's sense,' Dame Julia said. 'I thought you had sense, Sam, underneath. And though I've been moralising a lot tonight – women of my age are apt to – you've helped me, maybe as much as I've tried to help you. That's what a good friendly talk does.'

Sam was flattered. He left her room that evening feeling twice the man he had been on entering. It was not only that French coffee of hers, which had been good, very good; or even the stiff whisky and soda which she had insisted, later, on his taking, though for a moment recalling Tilda's strict Non-Conformist tendencies, he'd hesitated. No, it was not only these things but rather that she, a woman of her reputation and experience, had thought fit to confide in him and treat him as a friend. Tilda had never done that. Tilda, despite her many good qualities, had somehow always contrived to make him feel a very poor fish.

And after all, he thought, as he went to bed, that sort of thing downs a man. But tonight I feel a king – a real king.

For once the sight in his mirror of his small rotund figure in the pink-striped dressing gown did not mildly depress him. For once he had an air about him as he patted his thinning hair and surveyed with pleasure the small bristling moustache which despite his sixty odd years was not yet quite grey.

Life over for him? Of course it was not! Tomorrow he'd think over what Dame Julia had said about the orphanage. Tomorrow he'd have a few practical things to say to Miss Fothergill-Briggs. Tomorrow was another day.

Chapter Five

September passed into October, and the guests were still at Trencathra; leaves were yellowing on the branches of the stunted trees now, and the lanes smelt damp with the mingled odours of blackberries, brine, and decaying vegetation. Miss Spring still rigorously performed her exercises in the garden each morning, but she had given up hope of any friendship with Nicholas Nankerviss who had at last achieved what he had set out to do, by being consistently rude to her.

Laurence Dale, on the other hand, had flattered her with an appearance of understanding which, whether genuine or not, eased her loneliness and added a little to her confidence in herself, frequently at a low ebb though she did not recognise this. Her heart warmed to the young man whose talents she began to suspect were considerably underestimated by the less appreciative and sensitive members of the household. Beneath her fly-away exterior Miss Spring was a sensitive soul. All her life she'd been starved of affection, having been orphaned as a child and brought up by two maiden aunts whom she'd assisted when she'd left school in a suburban art-and-crafts shop popularly known as a fancy goods store. Life for her had been a repressed affair relieved only by weekly visits to the Literary Circle, and later a certain religious 'sisterhood' where she'd absorbed an Eastern trend of thought, adopting the rather absurd little rituals which caused amused irritation at Trencathra.

Despite the forced sanguine brightness of her manner, Miss Spring knew she was being laughed at. But she accepted the fact with the nonchalant veneer of those who know themselves to be square pegs in round holes. She liked Trencathra, and found the household stimulating. Although five weeks had passed and she'd gained comparatively little ground in establishing herself intellectually, she was determined to go on trying, blaming a lack of vision on the residents' part rather than any peculiarities on her own. It would be ridiculous, now, she thought, to turn her back on the place – to leave Cornwall and go elsewhere. Cornwall, after all, had been her secret ambition always. She'd had one holiday there as a child and had retained ever since memories of narrow curling streets, small harbours and gaunt coast. And here she was – free to stay, if she so chose, for the rest of her life, with an assured income and no need to worry about the future.

Even now – and her aunts had both been dead for a year, dying within a month of each other – Miss Spring could hardly believe that so much money was at the back of her. Forty thousand pounds! Who would have thought that her two shabby aunts had accumulated so much behind the windows of the little fancy goods shop? Who would have imagined a year or two ago that she, Elizabeth Spring, the rather nondescript shop-assistant, would be able in so short a time to fling it all up and come to Trencathra? Would be free to dress as she chose – within reason, of course – eat what she wanted, do as she liked, and make her own friends. It was like a dream come true, almost; if the people at Trencathra would only like her as she was prepared to like them. Somehow they didn't, yet. Miss Spring always knew when people liked her; everyone knew that. It was obvious in the way one's remarks were taken, and the kind of smile one received. And all too often, to hide her hurt from herself, Miss Spring had been driven to the lofty, chilly retreat of her inner philosophy and superimposed Buddhistic calm, rather than allowing herself to be upset.

Still, it was pleasant to find someone who seemed pleased to listen, and who did not hurriedly make a retreat when she approached across the lawn or down the corridor in her cape and flying skirts. Miss Fothergill-Briggs had also been quite friendly in her own way, so long as she, Miss Spring, had been content to listen and never say anything. But she was a domineering woman, and tired Miss Spring. Besides, Laurence Dale was young, and really rather attractive. There was a bond of sympathy developing between them which was becoming very precious to her.

So when he caught her up one day, walking along the road to the bus stop for St Taloc, she was pleased and stimulated, flushing faintly under her sallow skin, darting bird-like glances at him from beneath her floppy hat and simulating the light girlish voice which Nicholas so disliked. She was wearing a green cape over a lemon-coloured dress, with a string of amber beads round her neck and a touch of Indian red at the wrists and at the throat. Cornelian earrings dangled from beneath her fuzz of yellow hair. Her mouth, strained into a smile, was tired at the corners, a rather pitiful, pathetic, mouth which belied the gaiety of her voice.

'Well!' she said. 'How nice. Are you going to St Taloc, Mr Dale?'

'Yes,' he said. 'I'm going to see a fellow about a studio.'

Miss Spring's eyes widened. 'Oh! Are you really? But how exciting. Do tell me.'

He gave that odd, half-veiled smile which she found so attractive, and said, 'Well, there's not much to say. I can get it, I think, a nice little place, too. But it's a question of pounds, shillings and pence.'

'Money?' said Miss Spring, with a little tug at her heart. 'Do you mean you can't afford it, Mr Dale?'

'I'm not at all sure that I can,' he admitted. 'You see — ' in a more confidential tone of voice ' — it's not easy for a chap like me, coming out of the army, with no capital and certain progressive ideas about painting which need a little push and publicity to make them accepted. Oh, I'm not broke,' he continued with a shrug of the shoulders. 'If the worst came to the worst I suppose I could do hack-work — pretty-pretty Christmas cards and calendars. But I'm damned if I will!' he added fiercely. 'Why should I? In any case, why worry you with all this? It doesn't matter.'

'Oh, but it does matter,' Miss Spring said eagerly, unaware of the quick glance suddenly turned on her from the long-lashed deeply set eyes. 'It matters very much. After all, one's work is one's life. And to prostitute one's message – that is a dreadful thing.'

'Yes,' he agreed. 'I thought you'd see it that way too.'

'My dear young man, we're intelligent people, you and I. How could we think otherwise on such a matter?'

'But I can assure you most people do,' he told her grimly. 'To use a new medium, or give a new message, is anathema to the general public. We are expected – we younger ones – to trip meekly along tied to the apron strings of our traditional elders, so that when the time comes and we ourselves are doddering into sentimental old age, we may be allowed to shine a little in the feeble ray of reflected glory. And that's it in a nut-shell.'

With his scarlet tie flying, his rather long hair blowing arrogantly away from his finely-cut Byronesque profile, Laurence did at that moment epitomise acutely all Miss Spring's preconceived notions of rebellious young poets and painters; and her heart warmed to him.

'Poor boy,' she said sincerely, 'I do sympathise with you, and I do agree. The only consolation is that it's their short-sightedness, and that they in the end are the losers.'

'Certainly,' he agreed, 'but it means in the meantime that it's my loss, too. I have to live. And if I can't live by painting I have to live in some other way. And if I do that, well, I shall frankly give up art. I couldn't stand the strain of doing two jobs. Besides, it means too much to me. I couldn't half do it.'

'I'm sure you couldn't,' she said warmly.

'If I had a little at the back of me,' he went on, not looking at her, 'I might manage. I might arrange an exhibition, and I could afford proper materials. Only, unfortunately, since I've already told you so much, I've already spent more than I should on this holiday, and at the moment everything looks a little dark for yours truly.' He turned upon her his slow charming smile. 'Never mind, Miss Spring. What am I boring you for? I ought to be kicked. What about having a coffee with me in St Taloc?'

'No,' she said firmly and recklessly, 'certainly not. *You* shall have a coffee with *me*.'

It was past eleven when they reached St Taloc, and the

autumn sun glistened quietly on the dark fishing boats in the small harbour. The tide was high, leaving only a thin pale rim of wet sand below the sea wall. There were not many visitors in the town now, and save for a few artists the cafes facing the quay were comparatively deserted. They found a table vacant in the window of the Blue Ship and Miss Spring felt a stab of excitement and romance as he guided her to it. It was not often that such things happened in her life. Indeed, she had never before had a rendezvous with an attractive young man, so obviously of the intelligentsia and anxious to please her.

He ordered coffee and cakes, and while they drank it he praised her gown and told her it was refreshing to find a woman who dared to dress individually. And all the time his eyes were smiling at her, so that Miss Spring was more than enchanted; she was quite entranced.

Not, she told herself, that there could ever be anything sentimental between them. He was only young, and obviously would be much sought after when he had made his way, whereas she had already passed her fiftieth birthday and could expect no serious attention from a man. Still – the fact remained, he liked her clothes, and that was something. It was nicer to be praised than not, and his friendly little attentions did somehow made her feel she counted more as a human being.

Later, when they had separated and she was making her way from the library to the bus, she reviewed the scene of their little talk together. It was a shame, she thought, that such a nice young man should have to face such difficulties. The government surely should do something about it. Always when such problems arose, Miss Spring, who really had no knowledge of politics at all, blamed the government. In her airy, vague way she considered that the world was badly run but that eventually, through the divine working of Karma, it must right itself. In the meantime, of course, as young Laurence pointed out to her, it was young men like himself who had to suffer. It really did not seem quite fair.

Although, she told herself philosophically as the bus jolted her along the high white road above the cliffs, spiritually there must be a reason for it. Some time, in some other life perhaps, he must have brought this on himself. Poor young man!

Then another idea occurred to her. But why, her mind went on, had all this come up today? Why should it have been thrust under her nose in this manner? What drove him to confiding in her so suddenly?

Electrically almost the answer — or rather a suggestion — hit her. She, perhaps, Elizabeth Spring, was connected in some intricate way with the spiritual working out of his destiny. It was her role to help him in it. The thought at once confused and exhilarated her. Because if this was so, there was no avoiding it, something would have to be done. The question was — what? As she travelled on, numerous ideas occurred to her, racing through her mind with the quick darting quality of the little birds rising and circling above the grey hedgerows.

As she walked along the narrow lane to the house in her fancy 'arty' clothes and absurd hat, something very young and childlike lighted her eyes.

'Why, Miss Spring,' said Sam Murgatroyd, meeting her at the gate, 'you're looking very girlish today. Quite a schoolgirl complexion that you have.'

Miss Spring smiled at him. 'It's the day, Mr Murgatroyd. Something about these autumn days goes to my head.' She quivered with self-indulgent laughter, then resumed, 'And I'm happy, you know. The world is really a very wonderful place.'

She hurried past him, taking flurried dancing little steps. And he thought, looking after her, poor thing. Poor little woman. Now what's she got into her head now? Something's brewing there.

He was right — something was brewing.

Chapter Six

Within a fortnight of Laurence's conversation with Miss Spring he was already ensconced in his studio in St Taloc. Miss Spring having considered the matter thoroughly for two days had eventually prevailed on him to accept from her a 'small cheque' in token of their friendship, and as a tribute to his art.

'Very well,' he had said, in conclusion, 'if you really insist – but remember it's a loan only. And when I've made my way I shall pay you back.'

'No, no,' she'd said, embarrassed yet pleased, 'certainly not. Loans are odious. You must not think of me as lending you money but as your patroness.'

It was very pleasant to be able to act in this generous manner, and the gesture gave her a heartening sense of power. She could afford now to be negligent even of Nicholas' opinion of her, which was perhaps as well, for if anything it was diminishing. Though he shut himself away as securely as possible from the house, Nicholas could not but help being aware of certain things that were going on. He had noticed, for instance, the intimate little conversations between Laurence and his benefactress at the far end of the lawn, and the sight had aroused in him a cynical contempt which he expressed one day to Merlynne when she returned from St Taloc with a book for him.

'How are things going over there?' he enquired, watching her and thinking how nice she looked in her green woollen frock, with her soft tawny hair falling straight to her shoulders. Generally she wore too much lipstick but today she looked young and natural, more like the child Merlynne who had fascinated him in the past with her renderings of Ariel and Miranda. She was pale though. And there was something vaguely lost and troubled about her which struck a swift chord of sympathy in him. Since they had grown up, Nicholas had not troubled unduly over his children, living very largely in his own remote world of philosophy and imagination. But when he cared to consider them his intuition was acute. And he knew Merlynne wasn't happy.

'Oh, all right,' she answered. 'Except for Lotte. She's had another row with Ann, and Catherine's told her she'd better go at the end of next month. It doesn't matter much. We're one guest less now, and the Fothergill-Briggs will probably be leaving some time in November, so I don't suppose we shall be full through the winter.'

'And that's a good thing,' Nicholas retorted. 'Get rid of them as quickly as possible, and let us have a little peace.'

'You're not very encouraging,' Merlynne remarked. 'After all, they've given us our bread-and-butter for the last few months.'

Nicholas made a sharp, clicking sound of irritation with his tongue against his teeth. 'We could have managed, with your grandmother's help,' he insisted. 'Besides, my book's about ready now, and it isn't as if we were all paupers. There are ways and means. By the way, I'm glad that long-haired gigolo's gone.'

Merlynne went a shade paler. 'Who do you mean? Laurence?'

He eyed her with a rare flash of shrewdness. 'Who else? Yes, I do, and if it hadn't been for that fool of a Spring woman we might have had him on our hands for ever more, until we kicked him out.'

'Daddy!' Merlynne exclaimed, quite shocked, for it was seldom he gave vent to such violent feelings.

'If you ask me,' he resumed, 'and you take this in, my child, that young man's been sponging on the poor creature. That's the kind of fellow our cultural guest house attracts.'

From the pallor of Merlynne's cheeks, two spots of flame burned their way, giving a heightened, hardened, dramatic quality to her face. Yet she strove to keep her voice casual.

'Oh, no,' she said, 'I don't believe he's like that.'

'You haven't used your eyes,' her father told her, 'for weeks now they've been having intimate little rendezvous and discussions in the shrubbery. I suppose the studio's the outcome.'

'No,' she said again. 'That's not true. I don't believe it.'

Nicholas regarded her closely. 'How do you know? I'm practically certain it is, but in any case what does it matter to you?'

'Of course not,' she said. 'It doesn't matter at all.' But her voice and demeanour belied her. There was a look of passionate misery on her face which alarmed her father. This was no mood, no casual whim of hers.

'Merlynne,' he said gently, 'what's the matter?'

'Nothing,' she said, pretending nonchalance, 'what could be?'

He sighed, 'If you won't confide in me, you won't. I wish you would.'

She was stubborn. 'There's nothing to confide.'

'Well, I hope not. But keep your head. I know you all think of me as a vague, queer old stick. But I'm fond of you all, I'm your father. I don't want to see you in a mess. Be good, Merlynne. For Hugo's sake.'

'Oh, Hugo!'

'And your own.'

'What's goodness, anyway?' she asked in a level, light voice. 'Everyone's always so certain about it for other people. That's what's so amusing.'

Her cynicism hurt him. 'Nobody can afford to set a general standard,' Nicholas remarked, 'but every human being can have standards for himself. That's what I mean. Don't let yourself down.'

'There'd be no sense in that, would there?'

'No, but sense doesn't always come into it.'

The result of this conversation, so unsatisfactory to Nicholas, was a second jaunt by Merlynne into St Taloc that same afternoon. It was almost five when she arrived, and the sun had already sunk behind the houses, leaving a streak of reflected gold across the sky which lit the roofs and tangled chimney pots with a pale radiance, rapidly fading.

The gulls were already gliding to their nesting places on the island, and the boats were dark on the horizon for their night's fishing. Odd lights glimmered from windows round the harbour, and a few people were seated in the cafes.

Merlynne walked quickly along the wharf, her fair hair blowing behind her, swept clear from her face, her chin up, her eyes reckless and miserable. Ever since her conversation with Nicholas she'd hardly known how to get through the day. For weeks now she had been unhappy and bewildered, denying even to herself the thing that was happening to her. For Hugo's sake, and for her own, she'd fought to keep in abeyance her developing passion for Laurence Dale. That it was requited she'd known for some time now, and the knowledge had brought upon her alternating moods of joy and despair. But for the most part it had been despair – the despair of knowing that though her body trembled at his approach, she must not give in; that though her whole being yearned for him, she must deny desire – pretend, make light of it all, when it was the one thing she'd ever wanted in that certain sexual way. That had been hard enough but this suspicion of him was worse. A 'gigolo' her father had called him. No phrase could be more contemptible. The inference that he'd played up to Miss Spring, a woman old enough to be his mother, for the sake of her money had been a knife-thrust she could not tolerate without response. She must see him and have it out with him – know the worst, whatever the cost to her own dignity and self-respect. As she walked along with her loose tweed coat blowing in the wind she recollected their last brief conversation before he left for St Taloc, when he'd asked her meaningfully to be sure and call in soon.

'You will, won't you?' he'd said. 'Promise me. I shall expect you.'

Mere words; but the atmosphere between them had been highly charged and tense, signifying a challenge she had no strength to resist.

'One day,' she'd answered with rapidly beating heart, knowing full well that it would not be long. 'Yes, I promise.'

'And I'll repay you that five pounds,' he'd said, for she, too, had loaned him money.

Money! Was that all, then, that he really thought about? Was that what it had all amounted to? The glances, the brief exciting contacts of touch, the meaning phrases and lowered voice? The sleepness nights and torments of desire which had possessed her when she'd remembered every word he'd spoken, imagined hopelessly the sensation of his arms about her, of her own starved body held tight against his own? Was that all it came down to in the end? Money?

She'd blamed herself many times for being faithless in thought to Hugo; many times had watched him with a feeling of blind angry impatience, as he lay beside her sleeping, impassive, not wanting her. There had been moments when she could have beaten against him with her fists, shrieking to him to love her, to save her from herself. Now it was too late. Even that had passed. If Hugo sought to take her now, she knew she could hate him. Indeed she sometimes did already, because he was so cold, and self-sufficient and remote and unseeing; because he had allowed her womanhood to betray itself – had married her and changed into someone she did not know.

If Hugo were normal, she told herself for the hundredth time, hurrying along, none of this would have happened. If Hugo, even once, when he'd come back, had shown that he really wanted her, Laurence might never have counted. But now she couldn't bear it. Couldn't see herself going on without putting all her cards on the table. Laurence Dale might be what her father had so ruthlessly implied – a sponger – but she wanted him.

The sky had darkened now, and a chill little wind crept from the sea, blowing down the narrow streets and twisting corners; whispering to her, it seemed, of the hollow aching quality of all the love in the world which had been lost or unrequited.

She found the studio at last, overlooking the rocks and Porthcarn beach. Its door was painted a bright blue with the words 'White Dolphin Studio' painted above it.

She clicked the latch up and climbed a few rickety wooden steps to another door which was half open. Inside she found Laurence arranging a few canvasses against the wall. The room was sparsely furnished, with a cooking stove at one end and a large divan at the other. A square table, three chairs, a curtained wardrobe, and a cupboard completed the furnishing. The light was good, but the room was not tidy; a few cobwebs were still slung from the ceiling, and the floor was a maze of paint tubes, saucepans, and odds and end of materials.

Laurence turned when he heard her, and a smile lit his eyes. He put his pipe down, and hurried towards her.

'Merlynne! I'm glad you've come.'

She took a step backwards, saying mechanically, 'I said I would.'

'What's the matter?' he asked, frowning. 'Anything wrong?'

Now she was here she wondered how to answer. She felt rather foolish. Walking along it had all seemed so simple. She would accost him, blurt out the truth, accuse him, do anything to have the doubt in her mind settled, even if it meant the worst. Now she realised she was on shaky ground. It wasn't as if there had been anything definite between them. Oh, no! He'd been too careful for that. Just subtle things — tricks of touch and glance, words and suggestions that had fanned her feelings to flame.

'Not really,' she said. 'No more than usual.'

He came towards her, unbuttoning the coat at her neck, removing it with fingers which sent a tremor through her. He laid it over a chair.

'You're not happy,' he said. 'Foolish you!'

'Why?'

'You know why,' he said significantly.

'Not completely,' she lied, 'I suppose everyone has moods.'

'A girl I knew once,' he said stuffing tobacco into his pipe, 'wasn't happy with her husband. He didn't satisfy her, and she'd not the courage to leave him. She made things bearable by pretending he was some other man when they lay together.'

Merlynne went very white. 'Why are you telling me this?'

His eyes — beautiful relentless eyes — narrowed as he stared down on her.

'I was making a suggestion,' he said.

'If the suggestion is what I think, then you must be — '

'A bit of a cad,' he interrupted. 'Too true.' He smiled imperturbably, yet she knew he desired her.

'I'm glad you admit it. But, of course, you had to after Miss Spring.'

For a second he was silent, then he laughed. 'Good Lord! That woman — well, what about her? Has she been telling you naughty stories?'

Merlynne's lips closed tightly over her teeth. 'No.'

'I suppose,' he said easily, 'you mean the money. Well — do you object?'

'I? How could I?'

'Exactly,' he replied. 'That's what I was thinking.'

'All the same, there *are* limits,' she continued. 'I'd looked on you as a friend. I thought — '

'You lie so badly, Merlynne,' he exclaimed. 'You know very well you don't care tuppence for my friendship.'

'Laurence!'

He came forward quietly, grasping her two shoulders. 'Well — do you? You know you don't. You never have. We both know. The truth is, darling, you're simply, starkly, crazily jealous. Jealous of a middle-aged little spinster who's been kind enough to help me a bit. Really, it's not very noble of you.'

The mockery of his voice and eyes humiliated and infuriated her.

'Let me go,' she said. 'I didn't come here to be treated like this.'

'Oh, but you did, you know,' he said, his breath warm against her ear. 'You knew very well what would happen.'

'Please let me go,' she repeated, struggling ineffectually against him. 'I shall hate you if you don't.'

'No, you won't — tiger-cat,' he said easily, his lips against her hair. 'This has been coming to you for a long time, Merlynne, ever since that first day, do you remember?'

'Don't,' she said. 'You mustn't. There's Hugo — ' She tried once more to push him away, but weakened and fell against him again, where he held her, trembling.

'Hugo doesn't count,' he said. 'Forget Hugo.'

'He's my husband. He must.'

'Not to you. And for Pete's sake stop acting the puritan. You came here today because you wanted one thing – me.'

'I –'

'Shh.' His mouth sought hers sensually. His voice was husky when he continued, 'And it's the same here. God, how I want you, Merlynne!'

'I –'

'Well, say it,' he urged. 'Say "I too want you, Laurence". Please, darling.'

She turned her head away, struggling with the truth, emotion thick in her throat.

'Need I? Don't make me. I want to be fair – I want to behave as well as I can. Don't make me feel worse than I do.'

He carried her to the divan and sat with her close, so his touch was thrillingly stimulating, waking all the hidden pulses of her body to life.

When she protested, he said, still holding her, 'Why the devil are you so nervous, Merlynne? There's no harm in this.'

'It's just that I – oh, you know why.'

He released her suddenly then, and stood up. 'Yes, Always Hugo. And yet – he gives you nothing that matters, and at heart you despise him.'

'No. I'm sorry for him.'

'Pity!' There was contempt in his voice.

'And I still care – in a way.'

'Bunkum. You're deluding yourself.'

'It's sometimes necessary,' she agreed.

He shrugged his shoulders. 'Maybe, if you happen to be one of the frightened conventional women content to lead a sterile life rather than take the little sweetness offered. But I can't see you as the eternal virgin somehow. The role doesn't suit you.'

'You're very blunt.' Her voice was bitter.

'Would you rather I went down on my knees to you, protesting undying fidelity and a great immortal love? I will, if you like, but it wouldn't be true. We need each other physically and that's it in a nutshell.'

'How cynical. And rather nasty. I don't believe there's a shred of tenderness in you.'

'Do you want tenderness?'

'I don't know what I want,' she admitted, moving further away. She pushed her hair from her forehead and he noticed her hands were still trembling. 'I really don't. I'm just — het-up, miserable.'

'You don't have to tell me. And it doesn't suit you.'

She crossed to the window. Before her, beyond the humped cottages, the grey stretch of sea merged now into the line of sky, eternal, unchanging, timeless. Her own desperate mood struggled for expression.

'It isn't,' she said, 'as if you and I were really suited, or thought alike, or had the same values at all.'

'You're wrong there,' he told her more seriously. 'On the contrary — we *do* think alike. And though you don't admit it, our values are the same. We're people of a type, Merlynne, requiring the same things. Oh, I know you've a lot of illusions — I know you blame me for taking money from Miss Spring. But that's only a conventional scruple. And you seem to have overlooked the fact that Miss Spring enjoyed bestowing it. It gave her no end of a thrill. In point of fact, I did her a kindness.'

Merlynne's mouth twisted itself into the semblance of a smile. But it was a smile of bitterness, and aged her. For a second he saw her as she might be when she was much older at forty.

'How you turn things to your own end,' she remarked.

'I should be a fool if I didn't.'

'You've been called her "gigolo", Merlynne said in a dry voice. 'Does that please you?'

'No,' he said. 'But it's unimportant. What matters is you and me.'

'I can't really see where *I* come in,' she said, 'under the circumstances.'

'Oh, don't fool yourself.'

His voice softened. He went over to her and took her in his arms again more gently now, though his lips on hers were urgent, explorative.

'Well,' he said after a moment, 'is that better – do you see now?'

She broke free desperately, blood and senses burning.

'I don't know. I shall have to think. I just don't *know*, Laurence.'

He straightened his tie with a show of indifference which was belied by his eyes and faint tremor of the hands.

'Okay,' he said, 'that's it then.'

'Don't be hurt,' she said swiftly, suddenly longing again for the moment she'd thrown away. 'Don't be angry with me. It's true,' she confessed desperately, 'I do need you. Of course I do – or I wouldn't have come here. But I suppose I am conventional in a way, and there is Hugo. These things count, Laurence. I can't just suddenly act as though they didn't exist.'

'All right,' he agreed coldly, 'have it your way. I understand. But remember this: no man appreciates being played with. I've had about as much as I can take.'

'Laurence!' She went up to him. 'I'm all bewildered. I must have a little time –'

'You've got it. But keep it short, darling, or else –'

'Kiss me!' she begged suddenly.

Quite quickly the tenseness seemed to drain from him. His mouth relaxed, his eyes softened. She was once more in his arms, throat arched backwards under the sweet violence of his caress. She could feel his heart pounding against her own, felt a weakness sweep over her from which, quickly and urgently, she dragged herself free.

'I must go,' she said. 'I *must*.'

'Go then,' he said. 'You'd better.'

He watched her walk to the door, where she stood for a second before lifting the latch.

'Come back soon,' he said softly. 'If you're wise, you will.'

She didn't answer, and just for a moment it seemed that she must turn, rush back to him and fling herself into his arms once more. Then there was a rush of air and the click of a latch. He heard her feet running quickly down the steps outside. Despite himself he was shaken. It was his creed to abhor sentiment, and think of women in the least idealistic sense possible. But there was something sweet about her. She had looked very young standing there at the door, so passionate and lost.

He sighed, and lit his pipe to soothe his torn nerves and frustrated sexual hunger. He wanted her, and she was in love with him. He had no scruples about Hugo who was obviously a neurotic having no use for a woman. But the fact remained that he could not afford for Merlynne to complicate his life. If she came to him it must be with her eyes open and on his terms. No pledges, no obligations, no regrets. He bit the stem of his pipe hard, puzzled, anxious, tormented by his desire and memory of her.

Then, abruptly, he turned once more to his pictures. Thanks to Miss Spring he would be able to hold a small show in the summer. Here, possibly, but preferably London. The thought stimulated him, erasing to some extent the emotion of the last half hour. Most of the paintings, he decided, should be abstract compositions. Meanwhile he would also settle down to doing a few seascapes and landscapes.

Really, he thought, it had been inconsiderate and absurd of Merlynne to resent the Spring woman's valuable help. That sort of interference he'd tolerate from no one. Besides, the pathetic creature had been heartened by playing the role of patroness, which alone was justification. She was an eccentric, and he'd no personal regard for her. She bored him completely. But he was mildly sorry for her, and if she wanted a little chivalry on occasion, he was prepared to give it. Also – he wanted her assistance. No woman in the world was going to be a cog in the wheel there.

Not even Merlynne, he told himself relentlessly.

All the same, he couldn't rid himself of the thought of her, and hours later her image was still with him – young, passionate, so appealing in her unhappiness, so feminine and subtle in her allure. But he knew she would return, and then they'd have this thing out; something flowed between them now which must either follow its course or be diverted relentlessly into other channels. Which would it be? Which? Ah, she was too sweet to lose! And after all – why should he? Innocent she might have been once, but she was innocent no longer; he'd known that by the feel and pressure of her, by her closed eyes and last urgent embrace. That had not been the gesture of a woman innocent in mind, else even then he might have hedged, and withdrawn. But now, he could not. He desired her, as she in her womanhood desired him. The end was already clear. It would have to be.

Chapter Seven

Letter from Julia Gort to Chetwyn Shane

Trencathra
St Taloc
Cornwall

My dear Nephew

    I am pleased to hear that 'The Lost Year' still goes well, and wish with all my heart that I could be transported for a few hours to Town. I had thought of coming up for a weekend, but at my age 'weekends' are hardly á la mode – and when I return I shall return, I think, for the season. At the moment I am held here by two things – a sense of duty to the family, and concern over Merlynne and Hugo who, I am afraid, are facing some kind of a crisis. This, of course, is strictly between ourselves – but at the moment I cannot see much good coming of the marriage, and although to some extent I blame Merlynne – she is a reckless, rather spoiled and demanding young woman – Hugo, also, has his eccentricities. I am fond of him, as you know, but at the moment he seems to live in a daydream and refuses to acknowledge what is going on beneath his own nose. Merlynne should not have married a dreamer. She should have married a man with his senses about him and the capacity to put her over his knee if she needed it. There are still some women about like that – and Merlynne is one of them. Beneath her lipstick and glamour, the gipsy streak is not far away. She is adventurous, and needs a lot from life. I am sorry for her. Whether I shall be able to be of help is a moot point, and I think doubtful. But for the time being, anyhow, I shall remain here, and only hope matters work out better than they appear to be doing at present. Quite three-quarters of the trouble is the war, obviously. It has done something to Hugo which may never properly adjust itself. And yet it is not purely nerves. He has tremendous control. Sometimes, I think, too much.

Ah, well! This is not like me, to be despondent.

The truth is, Chetwyn, I am aching for a little gaiety. Cornwall is dramatic and beautiful in itself, and I have made friends with a little Yorkshireman, Sam Murgatroyd, the 'Smootheen' man, from whom an eccentric mannish spinster is trying to diddle money – but something in me hungers for the lights and sound of traffic outside my window, for the sight of the curtain going up, and, yes, I must admit it, for my box at the theatre and the agreeable sensation of so many lorgnettes being raised, so many flattering glances and whispers in my direction. You see, I am a very vain old woman, Chetwyn – I cannot easily give up my love.

Could you not come down here for a few days? I should indeed like to see you – it would be one of the few civilized contacts I have had since being here. You might perhaps give me an extract from 'The Lost Year', or perhaps we might revive a little Shakespeare together. That would be nice. How I would appreciate one of the old all-Shane Shakespeare productions that we used to give in the old days! You never saw your grandfather in *Lear*, did you? A pity. His was the finest Lear I have seen. But, of course, acting was different then – more downright and spectacular, more dramatic. That, I think, is what we miss nowadays. I know it is what *I* miss; but that may be because I belong to the past. Life was simpler then. Good was good, and bad was bad. There were rich, there were poor, and there were morals. Superficially, anyway. Now one hardly knows where one is. Everything is so complex and jumbled up, and for all the talk of twentieth century freedom we don't seem to have got much. I often wonder what your poor cousin Adelaide would have thought now, had she been alive. Her suffragism doesn't seem to have done much good to we womenfolk – the only tangible result that I can see is a lessening respect from the opposite sex, and a confusion of thought and conduct which certainly doesn't make for contentment or success. I very much doubt that the woman of today has the power she had in my youth, when, through cleverness and charm — despite the male prerogative — she nevertheless contrived to rule her household like a queen.

Well, well! You'll be thinking me one of those interfering old bodies who always imagines the past is in advance of the present, and it may be that I am. But for the life of me, Chetwyn, I cannot see where we are heading. Not that this will affect me personally, except through the children — for Susie-Jane and for people like her one wishes something better than atomic bombs and the mass hysteria which seems to sweep the world on the least occasion. Slowly, insidiously, we're losing our personal identities, we are allowing ourselves to become puppets of the so-called democracy which in truth is no such thing, but something quite the reverse. And that is the only regret I have for being old.

If I were younger I might do something about it. That's where you are lucky. You're old enough to know something, and young enough to get it over. You still have your stage, Chetwyn, and the stage is comparatively free. It is one of the last weapons we have in the cause of individualism. That is why, in the early days, people like our vagabond ancestors followed it — because they were proud folk not afraid to taste and touch and feel life — because they had the courage to accept the world for what is was with its suffering and joy and hardships and sin and greatness. They took it, and they lived it. But nowadays people run away. Under the guise of some milk-and-water ideology they swarm together in a tabulated unification under the pretext that it is good for humanity. Rubbish, I say, and fiddle-de-dee! I don't like that kind of escapism. It's dangerous and of the stuff that goes to make dictatorships.

Even here one has glimpses of it. There's Miss Spring, with her fancy religion which is only a substitute for any real purpose in life. She's chosen it because it elevates her, in her own mind, to some sort of power, and there are thousands — millions — of people like her in the world, people wandering round in a woolly kind of way looking for something to follow, because they can't think logically on their own. Indeed, it seems to me that modern education rather than making people think more, has made them think less, and that's the reason they are willing to follow any sensational scheme that comes along.

Well, my dear, I expect by now I'm boring you. Don't let me depress you, Chetwyn, because – despite all this rigmarole – I'm far from being depressed myself. I still love life, I still wake up with a sense of pleasure to my morning cup of tea. I still like to help people, and cheer them up, and be admired. I like pretty things, and pleasant people, and reminiscing over old times. I feel a thrill of pride in my old bones when I realise that but for me and former Gorts this household would not exist as it does. Here they are – my family – with their numerous complications and strivings and disappointments, their little triumphs and defeats, their humanity, their differing characteristics. Unique, every one of them, and all revolving round me. Oh, how I run on!

I told you in my last letter, I believe, that I was not possessive. Neither am I in the 'have and hold' manner. But the fact remains that my blood runs in their veins, in Merlynne's, Susie-Jane's, lovely Catherine's and dear Richard's. I like to think that wherever any one of them goes, a little of myself goes also, and that where their roots are, something of me will still live. This is vanity, I know, and colossal conceit. But I have loved life, very eagerly, Chetwyn; and through these children of mine I shall never entirely 'not be'.

That is what, at the moment, is disturbing the little Yorkshireman – the fact that he is childless, with no one to carry on. He's in danger at the present time of founding an orphanage in conjunction with an eccentric spinster here who has a passion for cats and dogs and stalks him everywhere he goes, wearing mannish tweeds and very high hair, with a pile of pamphlets under her arm. Why he bothers with her, I don't know. But I have had several good talks with him lately, which I think are having some effect – for his idea now is not for the 'Fothergill-Briggs Orphanage', but for the 'Sam Murgatroyd Home' which I think sounds better.

This all appears as though I were rather interfering with

everyone's business, doesn't it? That's why you must come and see me, dear boy — take me out of myself. I don't want to become a mere fussy old busybody. Neither must I judge too harshly, even the Fothergill-Briggs. For, believe me, Chetwyn, everyone has a streak of sanity somewhere. Underneath I suppose we're not all that different from each other. Well, well! Time passes, and as usual I have written far more than was necessary or than I intended. Write to me, and tell me if there is a chance of your coming down here.

        For the present — au revoir.

        Your devoted Aunt,

            Julia Gort

Chapter Eight

One day in early November Hugo informed Merlynne that he intended to give a series of weekly lectures in St Taloc, in conjunction with a certain adult education society on the 'Trend of Modern Affairs'.

Merlynne who was tidying her hair before tea, was surprised, and pleased that Hugo should be finding something to occupy him.

'Oh, I'm glad,' she said quickly, turning round. Genuine pleasure lighted her face, and dispelled in a flash the look of strain which, during the past weeks, had hovered about her lips and eyes. 'You're feeling better then?' she asked.

He nodded, watching her. 'I shall soon be all right,' he said.

'Do you mean – really better?' she asked, hating herself for the stab of fear which swept over her, the fear of what his recovery might entail.

'I hope so.'

'Oh, good,' she said, trying to make her voice genuinely bright. 'That means that you – that we – shall soon be able to go to Lynchester. Do you mean that, Hugo?'

'Do you want to go?' he asked slowly.

'Of course,' she lied, 'if you do. Except that it's perhaps rather soon to leave Catherine and Susie-Jane. I mean the guests and everything.'

She had an uncomfortable feeling that he was watching her and summing her up, probing still into the recesses of her mind, as she combed her hair, striving in every way to appear casual and natural.

'Yes,' he agreed. 'I thought you'd think that. In any case, I'm not really ready yet. The chap in Penzance says my leg still needs treatment, though the wound is perfectly healed. He's got his own new kind of electrical device that may bring back full use to it.'

'Oh, Hugo! I am glad.'

'Perhaps everything's going to be OK in the end,' he suggested. 'I hope so, for your sake.'

'Oh, don't worry about me,' she said hurriedly, with a quick hurt feeling of guilt. 'I'm all right, Hugo. I – I've been more irritable than I ought to have been in the past. I'm sorry about that. I bothered too much about some things. But I'm different now.'

'Yes, you are somehow,' he agreed tentatively. 'What is it?'

She couldn't help a flush straining her from neck to brow, nor still the agitation of her nerves. Why, she thought, must Hugo question her at this point, when her deepening affair with Laurence was pressing her to make a final decision? It was ironic. For so long he had ceased apparently to have any interest in her. She fumbled in her mind for something to say, and, following an awkward pause, replied, 'I suppose I've more sense. Perhaps I've grown up. But – '

'It's more than that,' he stated. 'Still, I'm glad if you're happier. Whatever differences we may have, Merlynne, your happiness really comes first with me. You know that, don't you?'

'Oh, Hugo, not now, please!' she protested.

'Why not? It's important you should know. Maybe you haven't realised it in the past. And I can understand it. I haven't been a very satisfactory lover. But I've *loved* you, Merlynne. That's what women find it hard to realise when things like this arise – sex isn't the whole of love.'

'What things?' she asked through dry lips. 'What do you mean?'

'I was referring to my health,' he said. 'It's the first time I've felt able to talk to you about it. My – not impotence, exactly – but lack of passion. It's quite common, I believe, when men have been badly shocked. But later – perhaps – '

'Don't,' she said, 'please don't talk about it. It doesn't matter. I – '

She stopped, confused, not knowing how to continue. If Hugo tried to touch her now, she just couldn't bear it. Knowledge of his goodness, of his intrinsic unselfishness, only served to irritate and frustrate her, because she knew that according to his code and the code she'd been brought up to believe in, she was behaving badly. For a moment she tried to imagine herself in love again with him, switching her mind back quickly to the early days of her marriage – that brief bitter-sweet time. But in the face of this other, darker, wilder passion for Laurence, it was pale like a dream, having no substance or reality. She wondered now how she could ever have wanted Hugo so desperately; ever have suffered so during the past months over their frustrated union. Yet he was kind, he was good, and had all the attributes which, under other circumstances could have made her happy again – whereas Laurence, she knew, was quite selfish and without scruples. Yet it was *his* face now, with its mobile, impudent charm and slow smile, that swam before her eyes always – blotting out all other obligations and personalities – *his* voice, with its caressing mocking quality that haunted her, and must do so, she thought, for ever.

She pulled herself from the conflict of emotion to the present. 'Let's go on as we are, Hugo. Let's not go too deeply into it. There's no need. I understand more than you think, and I'm quite satisfied, really.' Oh, what treachery! What a lie.

He thought how beautiful she looked, standing there with her lips half parted, like a child's, and the warm, faint flush of confusion on her face, with the tentative, half searching little frown between her eyes. She said she understood, but did she? Ah, no. How could she? How could any woman appreciate the things that war could do to a man? The leg was a mere nothing. The leg was physical, it would recover, or not. The spirit was a different matter. He would have liked to be able to say to her frankly, more frankly even than he had spoken to Susie-Jane, 'Look here, Merlynne, just for a time, anyway – I'm tired of things of the flesh. I've had so much of it. Hurt flesh. Corrupt, bruised, maimed flesh. So many bodies – so many dead bodies! Don't you see, it revolts me? The body revolts me. My only desire is to get away from it. Sometimes I can't breathe for thinking of it. Even in my sleep sometimes, it's bodies, bodies, bodies! Maybe according to doctors I have a complex – maybe I'm a bit mad – but it's more than that. It's decency I want, and coolness and vision. Help me to follow my vision, Merlynne, and later I shall come back to you, because I love you, though you don't think I do.

But, of course, he could never speak thus to her. And so he remarked instead, 'It's nice of you to understand, though you can only get half way.'

He smiled at her, and the smile cut her to the heart, there was such trust in it. Impulsively she stepped forward and took his hands for a second, lightly, involuntarily, in friendship. He kissed her forehead, and the cool touch of his lips made her wince, ashamed. Then she released herself, and enquired, 'When do the lectures start?'

'Oh – in a month or so,' he told her.

'Where are they having them?'

'At the Fishermen's Hall.'

'In the daytime?'

'No. At night.'

'You won't have to overdo it, will you?' she said. 'And it will mean hanging about, unless you catch the nine bus – they've taken the ten o'clock off, and the last is at eleven.'

'Oh, well, if I miss the nine I shall have to call in at our artist friend's,' he said casually. 'Inspect young Dale's surrealist masterpieces.'

'Yes, you could always do that,' she said, trying to keep her voice steady. 'Not that he's got much to show.'

Almost immediately, realising her error, she caught her lip between her front teeth as he said quickly, 'Oh? Have you been there?'

She shrugged her shoulders. 'I've called once or twice. Miss Spring, you know, is a constant visitor.'

'Yes. I heard she'd taken him under her wing. Well, it will probably do her good. She hasn't many friends.'

Despite herself, Merlynne said, 'I don't see what they can

find to talk about. He's so cynical, and Miss Spring's such a sentimental little thing.'

Hugo said maddeningly, 'It's very hard for one person, ever, to judge the reaction of another to a completely different individual. Most of us only know one side of our friends or acquaintances – the side we're most interested in. To another person they may reveal an entirely dissimilar character.'

Jealous of his knowledge where Laurence was concerned she said quickly, 'I don't think he's so difficult to know. He may be cynical but he's quite honest. I don't think he'd pretend.'

'Don't you? But how do you know? Surely if he said what he *really* felt to Miss Spring, she'd not be so concerned with him?'

That was true. And although Merlynne had determined to put her doubts aside, indignation cut her again when she considered the innumerable times a week now that Miss Spring took the bus into St Taloc, presumably with the intention of calling upon Laurence. It was not that she felt in any sense a personal jealousy, but that her being recoiled from the game he was playing – the hypocrisy which must be involved in his friendship with the little spinster. At such times Merlynne hated herself for caring for him.

He's not worth it, she'd tell herself. He's really not worth it.

Then, as always, the indignation would die, leaving her lonely and longing for him, despising herself yet wanting him more. There was no way out that she could see. Soon the point would come when they could no longer go on as they were, having stolen inconclusive meetings which left them both spent and tired. A day would arrive when she could fight him no more, when Hugo would be forgotten and the issue clear. She would belong to him completely in the open, or in secret, as he wished. Either way would be difficult and put her in the wrong. But of the two the former would be preferable, though when she faced things squarely she was doubtful if Laurence wanted this; therein perhaps lay her greatest sorrow – that he could offer her so small a thing.

Chapter Nine

Lotte Eberhert left Trencathra at the beginning of November, and the following week Richard drove in his car to Cripples Rest to fetch Ann's younger sister, Olive, whom Catherine had engaged in place of Lotte.

The hedges, bordering the narrow lanes winding ribbon-like this way and that over the moor, were burnished brown and a flaming rich gold now, smelling pungently of berries, damp leaves and earth. The afternoon was very still, with a lowering yellowish sky which predicted rain, though none yet had fallen for some days. Over the high fields and jagged skyline of hills an indeterminate thin mist hovered. Smoke from outlying cottages and farmsteads lay low in the air, without movement, curling at last into the mist itself. It was the kind of day, Richard mused, driving along, for tea in a farm kitchen by a large fire, for the smell of chestnuts roasting, and an hour or two afterwards with a book in a comfortable chair. Not that he had leisure nowadays to read. For day by day the land exacted from him more of his energy and time. He didn't grudge this. He had already discovered that what one gave to the good earth was returned in some shape — if only the healthy tiredness and satisfaction bred from the knowledge that he'd been at grips with something real, that this business of growing things was at the heart of human existence, and that the toil and effort somehow made a man right with the world.

Though, as yet, the outlay had naturally been considerably in excess of the yield, Richard was satisfied with the way things were going. The potatoes had done well, and would have cleaned the ground for other crops the following year. He'd had several more acres ploughed up than he intended, and with the help of German prisoners and odd labour hoped to have it planted by the spring. He'd also had the fences repaired and the barn put right. Gradually, he thought with satisfaction, he was getting everything under control. Ultimately Trencathra land should pay as it had paid its way generations ago when the Nankervisses had first come there. True, he was up against the problems which all farmers had to face at the moment, of controlled prices, limited fertilisers, of transport and certain difficulty with labour. There were a number of controls and regulations which irked him, but beyond this, one fact predominated: that he was doing his job and meant to succeed.

He was grateful to his sisters for the ready way they'd rallied in the cause of Trencathra. But he did not intend, if he could help it, that the guest house business should continue; give him a year, two years' scope, he determined, and outside issues could be put aside. Trencathra should have its independence again, free of the numerous strangers whom circumstances had driven there. He was not possessive of it in the way that Susie-Jane was, but his roots went deeper — into the very soil itself. Susie felt for the house itself, loved it with a passionate feminine love. But he, Richard, wanted only to see it proud and self-contained in its own right; to have it cared for and at the heart of good things, a miniature land flowing with milk and honey in which he had earned a certain right to share.

These thoughts were in his mind as he drove up the steep moorland lane which led eventually to the main Penzance road. On one side of him were small cultivated fields bordered by stone walls from which a flock of crows and seagulls rose squawking as his car passed by. On the other, tracts of stonier land, tangled with bracken and furze, eventually stretched at a steepish incline towards the coast, surrounded by ruined tinmine shafts and cromlechs.

Cornwall. His own country. A stab of loving pride rushed through him as the age-old sense of place possessed him. He was only thirty, but here he knew he would live and die, marry, and breed his sons, if fate was kind to him. If fate was kind!

The suggestion led his mind immediately into another channel of thought, and he found himself wondering again, as he had wondered so frequently, about Deborah. He'd heard rumours, and believed them to be true, that she had been about again recently with Barry Stokes, and the knowledge perturbed him more than he'd admit, even to himself. He couldn't forbid her friendships, of course, he'd no right — yet. But he resented her evasiveness and light nonchalance about this particular one. It wasn't as though Stokes was a fit companion for any girl, least of all a highly-strung young woman like Deborah. In the first place he had a wife of his own, though he didn't live with her, more money and looks than was good for him, and a complete lack of conscience. The combination was dangerous, and Richard mistrusted the friendship. When he'd spoken of it to Deborah at their last meeting, she'd said airily, 'Him? Barry? Don't be so pie. He doesn't count, not with me. He's amusing to be with, and a good pal. I like him all right, that's all. Anyway I don't see him much now.'

Richard had to leave it at that. He'd hated to mistrust her, but something about her manner, her too casual air, had discomforted him.

'Supposing,' he had said, 'you were to marry me, Deborah, would you still want your "pals" as you call them?'

She'd smiled at him, and answered lightly, 'Probably I wouldn't. But you never know. Are you proposing, Richard?'

'No,' he'd replied. 'I won't risk it until you're in a more serious mood.'

She'd sighed then, whether from relief or disappointment had not been clear to him. But the interlude had depressed him. Despite her casual air, she was on edge, strung up. Her colour was too brilliant, and her eyes too bright, her laughter too frequent to be quite natural. There was no stability in her — no reliance. As a wife, she'd be a risky undertaking. The snag was no other woman had ever set him afire in just the ways she did, nor was ever likely to. He wanted her.

It was ironic. Yet there were times when she softened and was amenable, when she professed to care for him and promised to be reasonable and 'old-fashioned' and 'good for his sake'. He forgot, then, that other side of hers, preferring only to believe in the present. Her resolutions unfortunately, were temporary, and thus they went on, alternating between bickerings and reconciliations, between one mood and another, until it seemed there could be no satisfactory solution, and that the commonsense course would be to end the friendship. Somehow, though, he always gave in, and here he was on that very afternoon, thinking of her again, tormenting himself by the problem of her relationship with Stokes.

Almost as though there must have been some telepathic communion between them, he was suddenly aware of her in the flesh some little distance away on her roan mare, Sally. Though she had her back to the light, silhouetted against the sky, the slender, arrogant lines of her figure were unmistakable, and as she approached the lane at a canter, he stopped the car and waited for her. The glint of light was bright on her hair; she waved to him and presently drew alongside, jumping to the ground beside him. She looked excited, with a wild colour in her cheeks, her eyes starry beneath their fringe of dark lashes.

'Hullo, Richard. Hullo, darling.'

He'd meant to be aloof, dictatorial and censorious when he saw her; had intended that she should not this time have everything her own way. But when she ran up to him, slim and lovely like a tall child in her jodhpurs, raising her chin to be kissed, he weakened and took her in his arms.

'I was coming over to see you,' she said presently. 'Why haven't you been over to Stark End for so long? Even Daddy was asking.'

'Because, my sweet, I have a job of work to do,' he told her. There was a short pause before he added, 'Don't say you lacked company?'

She frowned. 'You mean Barry? Well, I told you. And I've decided, I'm not seeing him again,' she said decisively.

He was surprised. Always before she'd temporised and scoffed when the subject cropped up. But this time it really appeared as though something final had swayed the issue. Her mouth was set above her small firm chin. There were sparks of anger in her eyes.

'I'm glad to hear it,' he said.

Her mouth curved rather dangerously. 'You were right about him, Richard. He wasn't much good. I hate him.'

'Oh, I shouldn't do that,' he said easily, as though talking to a child. 'Why bother?'

'No. I suppose not.'

'Unless,' he added, 'you'd like me to beat him up, would you?'

She laughed shrilly, shaking back her curls. 'Oh, no. Why worry? He isn't worth it!'

'As long as you remember that.'

'I shall this time,' she said.

'Promise?'

'Yes. Yes, I do,' she reiterated with undue vehemence. He wondered what the fellow had done to upset her; that she'd been riled was obvious. The memory of him apparently still rankled. Even now it took her some minutes to recover; and when the conversation turned to other things a sense of strain remained.

They didn't stay long together that afternoon, but he arranged to go over to Stark End for dinner the following Saturday.

'Don't forget,' she chided him. 'You blame me for things, but you're not always so gallant yourself, you know, Richard. You could hardly call yourself a persistent lover — when you put an old field before me every time.'

'You wait,' he said. 'I'll show you, Deborah, my child.'

'I'm not your child.'

'What are you then — my love?' he enquired, teasing her, yet solemnly, half in earnest.

'I'll tell you on Saturday,' she said, jumping away from him to her horse.

'Very well. I shall hold you to it.'

Shortly afterwards she'd cantered away, and he was watching her as she broke at last into a gallop across the moor, turning to wave once before rounding the rocks of Torcrom.

For a minute or two he sat where she had left him, reflecting on her mood and what had been said. He lit his pipe, striving to recapture his earlier calm. But Deborah had spoiled this for him. It was ever so; instead of fulfilling and contributing to his joy in his work and land she disturbed him and tore him apart from it, taking him to matters which had little contact with the part he had chosen in life as master and owner of Trencathra.

Involuntarily a sigh escaped him, because his love and his life were not in unison. Then he squared his shoulders, and started the car. This was but another constructive job to tackle — the business, somehow, of bringing Deborah within the fabric of his existence as he had chosen to make it. He told himself that he could and would do it. But the outcome was not easy to visualise. Try as hard as he might, he could never picture her caged or conforming to any will other than her own. Even when she chose to give in to him, it was because at the time it pleased her to — not through any feminine concern or consideration of his wishes.

Driving along he felt his teeth closing hard over the stem of his pipe. He wanted her so passionately, but wished at that moment, with all his heart, that he could have cared for someone else less wayward and colourful — the kind of wife suitable to his position. Unfortunately these things couldn't be ordered. One loved or one didn't. A spark was lit, and the world became changed. However foolish it might be, the fact remained that if she'd have him, he'd marry her tomorrow and risk the outcome.

He reached Cripples Rest soon afterwards, and at the doorway of the small farm found Olive Chenoweth already waiting with her bag. She was a dark-eyed, russet-complexioned girl of sixteen, more impudent-looking than Ann, with her hair frizzed over her forehead and tilted pointed nose above a wide mouth.

Her mother, gentler in appearance, more like Ann in manner and features, came hurrying out with a second bag, followed by four younger children, one of whom was sucking a piece of bread and jam. Before the girl was properly ensconced within the car, Nathaniel Chenoweth, her father, appeared from the back of the house. He was as dark-skinned as Olive, but with a certain dignity about his features which held the hardbitten, rugged quality of the landscape itself. The farm appeared clean, but impoverished. Yet no one would have dared openly to pity Nathaniel Chenoweth. There was that about him which proclaimed an independence felt to the very marrow of his bones. It was this quality to which Richard felt so much akin, and which impelled in him always a sense of respect fully reciprocated by the other man.

'Well, there she be, Mr Nankerviss, sir,' he said, when the last bag had been put in the car. He turned to his daughter. 'You see you go to chapel of a Sunday, my girl – and don't 'ee go standing about the roads at night at all,' he added, almost as an admonition. 'If you have any time off you just catch the Penzance bus out here for an hour.'

'We'll look after her,' Richard promised him, 'and she'll have Ann with her.'

'See you do your duty,' the farmer resumed. 'Work well, and learn your manners right.'

'She'll do that f'sure,' his wife said, with a fond look at Olive. 'She'll be all right with Miss Catherine and Mr Richard. Besides – though she's my daughter, I must say it – she can work when she had a mind to, can't you, Olive? I shall miss her, I'm sure.'

Olive sat in the seat beside Richard looking a little shy, a little defensive and sulky, and wishing that her family would stop talking. She didn't think she would like Trencathra. She disliked domestic work – having a taste, unlike Anne, for a livelier kind of existence. However, she was glad to get away from home which would mean a change, at least, from the care of continual babies, and washing and stitching and scrubbing. And, who knows? She might get a better job from there. She might quite soon find herself in a city where there were lights and lots of people and pictures, and boys for a girl to choose from. Ann might be content with the country, but *she* wasn't. Anyhow, she was quite different from Ann; everyone said so. She had fuller breasts and a better figure. Bert Trevane, who worked in the grocer's at St Taloc, had told her that she had glamour, when she went to fetch the provisions the other day. That was something Ann hadn't got. That's why Ann had no ambition. But she, Olive Chenoweth, had other ideas. She meant to get on. One day, even, she might get into pictures. You never could tell. A producer might see her in the street, notice her face, and think, Ah, that's the type, and then her future would be made. These things happened. She knew all about it – had read it in the *Film Fan Gazette*, so it must be right.

These fancies were in her mind as Richard put the car into gear and presently swung out, down the narrow lane, towards Trencathra. As the car moved away the children and her parents waved to her from the gate. She put her hand out to them, and suddenly felt a qualm at leaving them; but it was soon dispersed, and she stole a look at Richard who was leaning back in his seat, driving easily, with one hand on the steering wheel.

Ann, she knew, thought Mr Richard handsome. She wasn't so sure about that. He didn't speak much, he was rather stern-looking, and his hair wasn't shiny like Bert's in the grocer's. She thought he might perhaps have made a joke or two on the way, said something to cheer her up, or that he liked her hat, which was a new one with a little green feather in it. But he made no attempt to please her in this way, and when at length they reached Trencathra, she was glad.

'There you are,' he said, opening the door and speaking to her as though she were a child. 'I hope you'll like being with us, Olive, I know we shall like having you – if you're anything like your sister, Ann.'

Olive tossed her head slightly, a look of faint annoyance on her impudent little face. Like Ann indeed! No, thank you. She had more about her than that. At that moment Ann herself came to the door, took Olive's arm and kissed her.

'Well,' she said, 'you are toffed up, and no mistake. How are the others, Olive? How's Mum?'

'Oh, all right,' Olive said, a little huffily. 'They're all right.'

Ann flung her a quick glance. 'Well – you come in now,' she said, 'and I'll show you your room.'

Olive followed her to the side door carrying one bag, while Richard brought the others. Catherine, with a tea towel in her hand, looking tired and hot, met them in the passage.

'I'm glad you've come, Olive,' she said. 'I'm so pleased to have Ann's sister here. And I hope you'll be very happy with us.'

Olive eyed her sullenly and defensively. She wished it

was not so much 'Ann, Ann' all the time. She would never stay if her sister was going to be thrown up at her in every sentence.

When she saw her bedroom, however, which was a small single one on the top floor, next to Ann's, her mood changed. It was a pretty bedroom with a sloping roof, white painted furniture and pink hangings. There was even a pink rug on the floor, and a bowl of anemones on her dressing table. She forgot, suddenly, her superimposed sophistication, her resentment, and the absurd little feather in her hat, running forward and saying in a childlike eager voice, 'Mine, is this mine? But it's handsome – handsome.'

Her eyes were sparkling, her cheeks aglow, as the bags were dumped on the floor. If everything was going to be like this, it would not be so bad after all. Fit for a film star it was – a real star's room. She giggled in her excitement, and sat on the bed, feeling its springs. It was only a very ordinary bed, a little uneven in parts, but Olive Chenoweth had never known one as good.

Catherine, in the doorway, smiled at her. She looked so young sitting there, so like a child on some Sunday School treat.

'Tidy your hair, Olive,' she said, 'and if you want a wash Ann will show you where to get the water. Then come downstairs and there'll be a cup of tea for you.'

'Will you have tea, too, Ann?' Olive asked, when Catherine had gone.

'Oh, just a cup,' Ann replied. 'Hurry up now, Olive. I'm ready for it.' But it was Richard she was thinking of, knowing that he'd be in the kitchen, taking tea himself; she looked forward these days to such little contacts – small interludes when they became for a brief moment friends rather than master and maid, and she could be of use to him, listening to what he had to say, giving him her advice over small matters within her province, seeing that his tea was brewed properly, and that there was enough hot water.

She wondered frequently how much he saw now of Deborah Cavin. Ann was not by nature a vindictive character, but there were times when she hated the thought of that other girl who had so much in her favour where Richard Nankerviss was concerned. She'd heard the gossip concerning Deborah and Barry Stokes, and had hoped and hoped that something would come of it. If Deborah had been a different kind of girl she might not have wished this so urgently. But, with shrewd insight and the peculiar intuition born of her Celtic ancestry, she knew that Deborah was bad for Richard, and wished her far away. Even now, though she accepted there could be no intimate bond between herself and the young master, the possibility of his marriage with another woman – especially Miss Cavin – roused very violent feelings in her indeed. The trouble was there was nothing she could do about it.

Such was her frustration and bitterness: that she must calmly wait and see the thing take place under her very nose, that thing which to her would mean her inevitable departure from Trencathra, since she could never bear to live in the same house with the wife of Richard Nankerviss.

Chapter Ten

The following Saturday was wet when Richard drove over to Stark End. The hedges and lanes were sodden with rain which fell in a steady deluge giving little promise of clearing that day. Rivulets of water coursed over the stones, and gusts of it were driven against the windscreen. The earth had merged into a landscape of indeterminate tones and greyness. Even the sea was grey, and the Mount but a shade darker, facing the Penzance Bay.

He reached Stark End shortly after seven, and the lights were shining cheerfully from the windows of the Hall as he drove up the drive. Stark End was not beautiful, but it was impressive with a stolid early Georgian grandeur which never failed to imbue in him a sensation of conservatism – of the middle-class luxury of a past epoch still clinging relentlessly to the present. Sir John Cavin, burly, a little pugnacious, noted for his good wines and hospitality, enhanced this; he had an air about him of bull-dog determination which seemed to suggest that for this he had striven and worked in the early years, to this end he had concentrated all the energy and initiative of which he was capable, and was not going to let it elude him now. He had been born poor, but he had no use for poverty or socialism. A man was worth just as much as he became and he was damned if he was going to give in to any democracy preaching equality. Equality? There was no such thing!

He greeted Richard with good-humoured patronage, slapping him on the back and calling him 'my boy' every time he spoke. He liked Richard, and if his little girl had a soft spot for him – which he knew she had – he was prepared to do what he could in furthering any possible marriage. The Nankervisses were poor, but on the other hand they had 'family', and this, to Sir John, who was an inveterate snob, meant a good deal. Besides, if it came to that, he could put the boy on his feet again, pay a good estate agent to take over Trencathra and make the place livable for Deborah. The family would have to leave, but something pleasant could be arranged for them; and, if Nicholas turned difficult, he would have a friendly little chat with him. After all, the fellow could not make much out of those highbrow books of his, there must be some way out which would please them all.

That was the best of money – it could talk. It had given him a position in society, and the reputation for being a good sport in racing circles and with the Hunt. It had given him his wife and daughter. If it hadn't been for his money he would never have had Andrea. Their time together had been brief, but by God it had been worth it! He knew that if his life was given to him over again, he would still marry Andrea Trevane. She and Deborah were the two people he had really cared for in his life, and he felt for his wife no grudge now, although at the time of her desertion he had felt like shooting himself. She was dead now, her body had been found some years ago, in rather doubtful circumstances, in the bedroom of a London hotel. He had been called to identify her, and the interview had sickened, hurt him. But when he saw her he had known no other woman could mean quite the same to him; she had still been beautiful, with the proud aloof little smile about her contemptuous lips, the gold hair, only threaded with grey, bright about her brow. Decadent she might have been – depraved and ill – but breeding and beauty had been hers to the end. Before this he had been conquered, dumb.

Deborah, in a sense, was her resurrection. She was a little darker than her mother, a little sturdier, and stronger willed. She had in her a strong streak of the Cavin realism, but she was lovely like her mother, with the breeding about her of a racehorse, a highly bred filly; she would kick and rear, and take her own course. But he, John Cavin her father, was determined, if possible, to see her in comfortable pastures.

If she wanted Richard he would see somehow that she had him, for this would mean her safety, her anchor against the wild tide of her heritage. He rather hoped the affair would not linger on too long, for he was not oblivious of her affair with Stokes, was conscious of it, perhaps, more acutely than Richard. He knew very well that the child had been infatuated for a time — it was obvious from her alternating moods of vagueness and irritation, from her excitement and those long hours at night when he'd heard her pacing about her room. He'd thought many a time of taking a horse whip to the fellow, but Stokes was in Parliament — what talk there would be; he mattered in the county, and had influence in a variety of ways. Also, Deborah was proud, she would never have forgiven his interference. So he'd let the matter go on unchecked, meanwhile doing all he could to divert her attention; wondering, like Richard, what the outcome would be. He'd no illusions over Stokes himself. In the first place, the fellow was married; in the second, he had a reputation for affairs, which always, ultimately, came to nothing. The interim had been unsatisfactory and upsetting, and he hoped now that it was ended. All this swayed him in Richard's favour. Do the girl good to settle down. She was quite ready for a husband of her own, and it would please him to have a grandchild or two to carry on.

That evening, therefore, Sir John was at his most affable, and Deborah charming, in a soft blue evening gown which gave her a more feminine, gentler look, altogether at variance with the recklessness which had beset her recently. She was particularly sweet to their guest, and at the conclusion of the meal at which was offered a bottle of Sir John's oldest and best champagne, Richard was feeling that all his doubts had been confounded. He had misjudged her, and owed her an apology.

This warmer, kinder, mood in him, resulted later in an outpouring of all he had felt for her during the last year. His defences were down; he told her that he loved her and wanted her to be his wife. Standing in the shadows where he'd left the car under the trees, he could not see her face, but her voice sounded young, a little frightened and tremulous, when she agreed.

'You'll love me always, won't you, Richard?' she queried with her face against his coat. 'You won't judge and condemn me, or ever be hard to me?'

'My darling, why ever should I?' he said, touched and puzzled. 'Why should I be hard to you, when I love you so much?'

'Some love is hard,' she said, 'and there is a queer streak in me, Richard. But you must keep me safe. Promise.'

'Of course I promise,' he told her, with his lips on her hair. 'That's what I'm marrying you for – to care for you and look after you. Oh, Deborah – Deborah!'

He broke off, confused by her sweetness, while she stretched up her arms to him, kissing his mouth of her own accord. The moon, breaking suddenly from behind a cloud, struck across her face, lighting its beauty to a strange pallor. The rain had stopped now, but little drops still fell from the trees, studding her hair with the brightness of jewels. Her eyes, suffused with a passion he'd not known she felt, were raised to his with a look in them he could not fathom – searching, but soft and yet demanding all in one. There was something he could neither comprehend nor fully understand about her, even now, which penetrated his happiness, leaving him faintly ill-at-ease.

'Are you happy?' he asked. 'The truth, Deborah.'

'Of course I am,' she answered. 'I love you, Richard.'

'That's all right, then. For both of us – always.'

He left soon afterwards. But the vision pursued him – the vision of her pale upturned face with the question in her eyes – the memory of her urgent impassioned appeal – 'You must keep me safe, Richard, promise?'

Safe? Of course he would. But why the need? From what? From whom? And why had she looked like that – so lost and uncertain? So wild and fey? Would he ever possess her, or be able completely to call her his own?

As ever, when removed from her presence, the old doubts began to return. He found himself going step by step over their conversation, worrying himself by endless unhappy explanations and possibilities.

It was after twelve when he got back. All the lights were out, save in Catherine's room, and the hall lamp which had been left burning for him. There was also a glow from the lodge where Nicholas was still, apparently, writing. Richard could see his shadow through the curtains. Letting himself in, he suddenly realised how apart from them all his father was. We're strangers, he thought. He hardly knows me now, or I him. It was true. Since adolescence they'd had little contact with each other, and as the years went by, Nicholas had drawn further and further into living the life of the mind rather than of the real flesh and blood world. Yet, when the children had been young, before their mother's death, he'd frequently played games with them, laughed with them, and taken them for walks of exploration along the cliffs. He'd had a keen sense of fun in those days, and been much closer to them all than he now was. Though they had missed their mother acutely — for the daughter of Dame Julia had been a bright, warm-hearted and lovely creature — none of them, Richard realised, had been fully able to realise what her death must have meant to her husband. Many men would have married again, carved some new life, formed new ties. Not so Nicholas who had preferred, obviously, to live for his books and his memories, rather than for some relationship which could only, to him, be second best.

These thoughts were in Richard's head as he went to bed, a retreat from the more tormenting memory of Deborah which, however, returned every time his mind relaxed. When at last he gave in, she was there to disturb his sleep, wayward and provocative, a figure of light and shade, and doubt and joy — at one moment pleading with him, at another in his arms. He saw her flying across the moor with Stokes, and again, gentle and subdued in her blue dress.

The next morning he woke with a headache, but with renewed determination to get on with his job. He said nothing at breakfast of his engagement, determined to tell Catherine later that evening, so she could use her own discretion in informing the family. He was aware, however, that Ann was watching him. He guessed that she suspected something and was vaguely discomfited. There was a disconcerting quality in the clear eyes of Ann Chenoweth, something faintly critical, which he didn't care to face. He was more abrupt with her than usual, and she was silent as though she'd expected it.

He knew she was unhappy over something, but, for once, had no energy or initiative to bother about it. Women were difficult. He could understand why some men preferred horses. They were easier to handle, and less upsetting. He would be glad to be in the open air for a time. He was tired of feminine moods.

Chapter Eleven

The sky was clear and the air holding a faint prediction of frost in it on the following morning when Dame Julia received a letter from her nephew, Chetwyn, saying he would come the next weekend from the Friday to the Monday, if they could put him up.

'It won't hurt Grierson to hold the fort for me for two nights,' he wrote, 'he's a good chap, and it will give him confidence. I feel in need of a breath of the country, and I always get a kick out of your company, dear aunt, so expect me some time Friday, unless I hear to the contrary.'

Dame Julia was sitting up in bed having her breakfast when the news reached her. She was wearing a frilly bedjacket, with something lacy on her head; beside her was the tray holding the small silver teaset with toast and butter and a glass dish of marmalade.

'Marianne,' she called. 'Marianne!'

Marianne, rouged, French, chic, sixtyish, and passionately devoted to her mistress, came hurrying through the door from her adjoining bedroom where she lived and ate her meals and cared for Dame Julia's clothes, and generally looked after her interests.

'Oui, Madame!' she said, for even now, after forty years, she still resorted to her native tongue in moments of excitement. 'What is it, Madame? Is anything the matter? Non? Ah!'

She sank with relief on to the chair at the bedside.

'Chetwyn is coming down — my nephew, Chetwyn Shane,' Dame Julia said, eyes bright, the colour deepening in her face. 'Ah, Marianne, there'll be something to talk about at last. It's made me feel quite young. Get my black silk out, Marianne, I'm going to get up. And the cornelian earrings and everything. But, no, fetch Miss Susie or Miss Catherine first,' she broke off, chuckling. 'This is the best thing that's happened since I came down here. I'm very fond of Chetwyn, you know, Marianne. A bit of the old life. Bless the boy. It does me good just to think of it. See what he says, he gets a kick out of my company. I like that. It flatters me. Run along, Marianne, fetch the girls.'

Marianne did as she was bid; a minute or two later Susie-Jane arrived, boyishly clad in navy slacks with a navy fisherman's jersey, which made her look very young.

'Catherine's cooking,' she said, 'so I came. What is it, Gran?'

'Your Uncle Chetwyn's coming down,' her grandmother told her, 'next Friday. I'm very excited about it, Susie-Jane. I want you to be sure to see that there's a nice room ready for him, with a soft bed and a good view.'

'But, Gran, all the best rooms are taken,' Susie-Jane said. 'Still, there's the yellow room on the third floor next to the one that was Lotte's. That's quite nice.'

'The yellow room!' gasped Dame Julia. 'That gloomy yellow ochre affair! Wasn't that supposed to be haunted or something by the ghost of some monk or other?'

'But you always said you never believed in such things,' Susie-Jane said, 'and I'm sure Uncle Chetwyn wouldn't mind. Besides, the poor ghost's never hurt anyone.'

'Of course not,' agreed the old lady. 'It's all fiddle-de-dee anyway. But why should poor Chetwyn have to put up with it, even if it *is* fiddle-de-dee? Half the things in the world are fiddle-de-dee, but they can be very disturbing to everyone else, for all that. Anyhow, my dear, what about the blue room?'

Susie-Jane looked nonplussed. 'But that's Miss Fothergill-Briggs' room.'

'Turn her out,' said Dame Julia flatly. 'You've got an excuse. The dog and the cat are scratching the door, and I heard that they are given food from the best cushions, so the sooner *they're* moved out the better.'

'I don't think Catherine would do it,' Susie-Jane said. 'After all, it's not very easy once people have been *in* a room.'

'You'd better send Catherine to me, my dear,' said Dame Julia imperturbably.

Susie-Jane considered her grandmother doubtfully for a moment or two, then seeing that she was in one of her more difficult moods, decided she had better humour her. Not that Dame Julia looked angry; but she wore the look of decision, of controlled excitement that betokened something was about to happen.

'All right,' she said, 'I'll see if she'll come.'

Catherine arrived shortly afterwards, with a cooking spoon in her hand.

'Gran, dear,' she said to the old lady, who was looking very pretty with her pink cheeks and sparkling eyes, 'you shouldn't get so excited early in the morning. You know it's not good for you.'

'But it's very good for me indeed,' Dame Julia contradicted her. 'Do I look sick? Do I look ill? Or worried? No, of course I don't. In fact,' she added with a swift smile of mischief and pleasure, 'I feel ready for anything. Now, my dear, as Susie-Jane may have told you, your Uncle Chetwyn wants to come down on Friday, and it appears that the yellow room is the only one available at the moment. I should like you, Catherine, to get that ready for Miss Briggs, and let Chetwyn have the blue room.'

'But I can't,' Catherine said, 'it's quite impossible.'

'Impossible! But why, my dear?'

'It wouldn't be fair,' pointed out her granddaughter. 'True, I didn't want her to have animals in there, but I gave in, and she's there. It would be inconsiderate to push her out now.'

'The yellow room is a most unpleasant room,' said Dame Julia, 'I don't like the idea of Chetwyn having it at all. I shall have to think.' And think she did.

Rubbish! she said to herself. I've had my way before, and I'll have it this time.

That same evening she prepared once more for a little rendezvous, and had Marianne arrange the coffee service on the silver tray, and cut small thin sandwiches of cress and marmite. She wore her plum-coloured silk dress, her best jewellery, with the little band of velvet ribbon at her throat. At eight-thirty there was a tap at the door, and after a moment or two Miss Fothergill-Briggs entered.

'Come in, my dear,' said Dame Julia affably, 'sit down, won't you, and make yourself comfortable.'

Miss Fothergill-Briggs perched herself on the edge of the armed Chippendale chair, her large legs in their flat-heeled shoes looming mannishly from beneath her dark tailored skirt. She wore a severe white silk blouse beneath the costume coat. Her hair was swept higher than usual, and two patches of bright colour burned her cheeks. She had, she explained, brought Tito with her. Tush had been left asleep.

'Good for the little dears to rest,' Dame Julia said maliciously. But her eyes were twinkling, and she was thinking, Why do these middle-aged virgins always sit on the edge of chairs? So uncomfortable. Really quite irritating.

'Relax, please,' she said. 'Lean back. Would you like a cushion?'

'No, thank you,' said Miss Fothergill-Briggs. 'I prefer sitting this way.'

'How extraordinary,' Dame Julia couldn't help remarking.

'I've probably lost the art of resting,' the lady told her. 'I'm always so busy, you see, and one does forget how, in the end.'

'Ah, but it's wrong!' Dame Julia said. 'Too much flibberty-gibbertying can make life a tiring business. No fun at all.'

Miss Fothergill-Briggs smiled condescendingly. 'But you could hardly call my work flibberty-gibbertying, Dame Julia. It has a purpose which exacts every ounce of my time and energy.'

'Yes. I know you're a very humane woman,' Dame Julia said, 'that's why I've asked you here tonight. I have something to talk to you about.'

'Indeed?' The brows crept up in a query under the Alexandra fringe. 'May I ask what?'

'First of all, I think, we'll have a cup of coffee to cheer us both up. What do you say?'

'Certainly,' agreed Miss Fothergill-Briggs. 'Mr

Murgatroyd – Samuel, you know – was telling me the other night how good your coffee was.'

Dame Julia smiled reminiscently.

'Yes, I think he was appreciative. A nice little man.'

She rang the bell, and presently Marianne arrived, with the coffee freshly made.

'Thank you, Marianne. And now,' when the Frenchwoman had closed the door behind her, 'do you take sugar and milk, Miss Fothergill-Briggs?'

'On certain occasions – just for a treat,' Miss Fothergill-Briggs admitted, 'although a time will come in the future, I'm sure, when we shall all be strictly non-cow.'

'Non-cow?' gasped Dame Julia, thinking to herself, Surely the woman's madder than I thought?

'Non-cow produce,' Miss Fothergill-Briggs explained. 'That is, a diet entirely free from any animal products whatsoever.'

'And what would you live on?'

'Nuts and nut creams. Oh, you'd be surprised, really, how very many alternatives there are to a meat diet.'

'I see. Well, in theory you may be right. Personally, in principle, I agree with vegetarianism. The trouble is – fitting in with other people. So often compromise is necessary. I'm not against you having your little whims, we all have 'em. They may be right or they may not. Same as mine. I've got my little whims, too.'

She chuckled, nodding her head, and resumed, 'But *not* nut creams. Now then, help yourself to sugar.'

Miss Fothergill-Briggs helped herself from the basin, stirred the cup, and put it to her lips. She drank in a self-conscious way, taking small dainty sips which went oddly with her mannish exterior. She strove hard to take command of the situation, but this was not easy; for against her will she found herself succumbing inch by inch to the strength and charm of the old lady's personality. Old as she might be Dame Julia could still exert a romantic influence when she tried. There was something essentially feminine, still, in the gleam of her eye, the slightly mischievous smile, and the slender curve of her wrists beneath the white frilling of the sleeves.

So, as the conversation proceeded, Miss Fothergill-Briggs

found herself listening with growing attention while Dame Julia took her along the path of reminiscence. It was not, of course, that she agreed with the old actress, whose ideas were frequently in opposition to her own, but that in the face of so much concentrated Shane charm her defences were down and she was victim to it, anxious only to please and be liked.

The conversation inevitably led to the matter of Chetwyn.

'Such a distinguished man, my dear!' Dame Julia said with a faint, retrospective sigh. 'A little like my father, but more sensitive, really terribly sensitive. But, of course, he's been overworking.'

'Dear, dear!' murmured Miss Fothergill-Briggs.

'Yes. And he'll only have a few days down here,' the old lady resumed. 'Not enough. Indeed, he'll be travelling half the time. That wouldn't matter if he had comfort when he got here. But poor Chetwyn! Those little minxes, my granddaughters, have only the yellow room to offer. What do you think of that?'

'Well – indeed!' Miss Fothergill-Briggs began. 'I hardly know. Isn't it a nice room, Dame Julia?'

'Oh, nice enough! Nice enough,' Dame Julia answered, 'to anyone who is not sensitive to yellow, of course. But Chetwyn had jaundice as a boy, and ever since it's affected him unpleasantly.'

'I'm sorry.'

'Yes. It will quite ruin the brief rest for him. I had hoped,' Dame Julia resumed, 'that Catherine, or Susie-Jane perhaps, might offer to change over, just for the two nights, you know. In my day I should have done so. But I'm very much afraid, Miss Fothergill-Briggs, that the young people of today have not quite so much sensitivity in these matters. What do you say?'

'Well,' said Miss Fothergill-Briggs, flattered to be thus consulted, 'perhaps not. No, I don't think they have.'

'Now if it had been *you*, my dear, if *you* had been asked to change rooms with my nephew, for a short time, I know very well what *your* answer would have been, because *you*, Miss Fothergill-Briggs, are a sensitive and humane woman.'

'Well, I do try to be,' the good lady admitted.

'Exactly. I knew I was right about you. Indeed, I seldom make a mistake where character is concerned.'

A flush of pleasure stained the sallow skin of Miss Fothergill-Briggs, driven by a tide of sympathy that caused her to say impulsively, 'Dear Dame Julia, if it is any help to you whatever I should be only too pleased to change rooms with Mr Shane for the weekend.'

Dame Julia looked up at her quickly, eyebrows raised, and queried, with one white hand gripping the arm of the chair, 'Really?'

'Certainly.'

'Miss Fothergill-Briggs, that is extremely kind of you. Extremely kind, if you mean it.'

'Of course I mean it.'

'Very well, then, and thank you, my dear. This will just be an example to the family, mark my words.'

The news of Miss Fothergill-Briggs' offer to renounce her room to Chetwyn was received by the family with amusement not unmixed with irony. They knew full well that Dame Julia was at the bottom of it, indeed, her tactics had been most blatant. However, although the change-over entailed a certain amount of extra work, the delight shown by the old lady over the proceedings made the effort worthwhile, and on Friday afternoon she was busy about the room itself, arranging flowers on the dressing-table, inspecting the coat hangers and etceteras in the wardrobe, flicking a little dust away, and nodding approval as she moved about, stopping to rest occasionally on her ivory stick.

It was past eight o'clock when Chetwyn arrived. Nicholas, who had been prevailed upon to come to the house to meet his cousin-in-law, came from the library to receive him. He liked Shane, and was pleased to have him there. Both, in a sense, belonged to a world which was passing, a world of culture and aesthetic values, to which they adhered even in the face of current materialism. It was something of a tonic to Nicholas to see the tall, elegant figure outlined against the light of the hall lamp, to feel the vitality in the slender hand, and hear Chetwyn saying in his well-modulated actor's voice, 'Glad to see you, old man. How many years?'

'Five at least,' Nicholas replied. 'More. It was in thirty-nine, wasn't it? At the Atheneum?'

'Good lord, yes. So it was. Before the war. How time flies.'

Catherine and Merlynne emerged from the hall and greeted their relation. A few minutes later Chetwyn was being taken upstairs. At the top, half in the shadows, Dame Julia stood watching the proceedings. As her nephew approached she moved forward tremulously and with excitement, saying a little breathlessly, 'My dear boy! My dear boy. Come here, my dear. Here I am. Why, Chetwyn, you don't look a day older.'

He took her hands eagerly, kissing her on either cheek where the soft flesh, faintly powdered and perfumed, glowed with excitement. Then, leaning on his arm, she escorted him to the bedroom.

'We've put you in the blue room,' she told him, 'because it's the nicest we have. And the roses – see them, Chetwyn? Susie-Jane picked them in the garden today. But *I* arranged them.'

'Dear aunt, you think of everything. You always did.'

'A room is never right without flowers,' she said. 'Even men need flowers, though they may not think so. And every woman, too. Ah, Chetwyn, what flowers I used to have. You don't see flowers like that now. The fault of the age. A pity. It's losing something – evening dress, lorgnettes, the grand manner – yes, the little subtleties of life! They are going, Chetwyn.'

'Our values are changing,' he agreed. 'It happened after the last war, standards toppled. Life became a see-saw business. But a few things have remained. You, my dear. I believe you're immortal.'

She wagged a finger at him, glancing at him roguishly from the corner of her eye.

'Flatterer.'

'Yes, she's incorrigible,' Catherine said. 'She does what she likes with us all.'

'Well – if I hadn't learned a *little* of how to get my own way in all this time I should be a fool stick of a woman indeed,' her grandmother told her. 'That's a woman's business – to get what she wants.' She paused for a moment, then resumed, 'Well, my dear, do you like the room?'

'I do. Very much.'

'There now. That's all right.'

Dame Julia flung a faint look of triumph at Catherine, resuming presently, 'I'm going to leave you now, Chetwyn, but later, after dinner we'll have a little talk. And tomorrow, perhaps, a little Shakespeare? Eh?'

He smiled at her. 'Why not?' he said. 'It will be a tonic to me. Shakespeare! And the lovely Shane.'

She shook her head, a certain brightness in her eyes. 'Oh, no, no. Lovely no longer, my dear boy. Old, Chetwyn. An old woman. But tomorrow, perhaps, I may forget it. That will be my little vanity, dear boy – a journey into the past. I shall look forward to it.'

For many hours after she had gone to bed that night, Dame Julia could not sleep. Scenes from the past crowded into her waking senses, so that even when the light was out, and she lay in the darkness listening to the constant murmur of the sea outside and soft drifting of the curtain in the wind, her mind became a vortex of colour and moving shapes, her old blood stimulated to warmth and a sense of youth again. Old times invaded her memory. Old scenes and situations. She was a girl again, in a peach-coloured crinoline with flowers in her hand, taking her bow following her first night of 'The Doll's House'. She was driving through the misty London gas-lit streets in her cab with Henry Gort, her husband, sitting by her side holding her hand. How good-looking he had been in his well-cut evening dress, with his stiff, waxed guardsman's moustache; how proud of him she had been; how proud they had been of each other; how excited and flattered she had felt by the stimulus and applause. Julia Shane! So soon to be the 'the lovely Shane', adored daughter of vagabond blood, of countless Shanes who had striven and swaggered and achieved success before the footlights. The charming Shanes. Adventurers all of them, yet with sense enough, withal, to mate wisely and with realism. Yes, beneath the adventurousness, always, she had had commonsense – something humourous and balanced derived from her Scottish mother.

She remembered Mischa, her early love. As she lay there

with the lids pressed tightly over her eyes, he broke once more upon her vision, as he had done those sixty years ago. Mischa, with the dark eyes and cleft chin, and mouth tender as a woman's yet relentless and whimsical as Pan's. She had thought of him persistently throughout the years. Memory of him had been revived at intervals, like the sweet ache of a tune becoming each time a little fainter. Success had crowded upon her in a steady rhythm until her epoch was reached, making the memory less compelling and easier to bear. But now, with her old body at rest and her mind alight, he returned to her for a second with the tormenting passion of youth. She wondered for that brief interim what, if she had gone with him, her life might have become. Sweet, for a time, but wild and lost surely. For she had loved him, not as she had loved Henry, with restraint and admiration and commonsense, but with abandon and despair, and if she had chosen to throw everything up for him, it would indeed have been everything. The Julia Shane the world remembered would never have been. There would have been no Dame Julia; no old woman lying now, in the autumn darkness of Trencathra. She would have been instead but an echo of Mischa, a shadow perhaps of a love too sweet to bear. For it could not, she felt, have endured as it was. The rose died. The scent lingered for a little, then faded at length into nothing; and where there had been summer and passion was no more than a chill little wind of regret.

Involuntarily, a slight spasm shook the figure in the four-poster bed. Lying there she knew she had been right in her course. With Henry beside her she had been strong and able to muster her resources and great vitality for the common good. He had loved her well and capably in his fashion, and left enough over in her for those countless audiences who, during the years of her life on the stage, had found inspiration through what she had given. Her life had not been without its vanity, but it was a vanity which at least had formed itself into warmth and light, had given a flame unforgotten by those who had been warmed by it. Beauty of words, nobility of thought and the despair of passion, the bright conflicting pattern of life with all its seeking and fulfilment and tragic frustration, had burned for a brief time in her eyes and voice. She had kindled the hearts of thousands to smiles and tears; spent herself on their behalf; sown where she went the soil of humanity with pain and beauty; conjured a vision which for a short spell had turned the mediocre to the divine. This had been her life, as it had been Henry's. For he had made it possible. He had neither taken from her nor exacted more than she could give to one person. He had given her children, yet left her freely herself — 'the lovely Shane' in those veins the blood of countless adventurers had danced for this end. Had it not been so, she would have destroyed him and defeated herself. She was grateful to Henry; though it had not been to him she spoke when her first Juliet had swept London off its feet these sixty years' ago:

> Thou knowest the mark of night is on my face,
> Else would a maiden blush bepaint my cheek
> For that which thou hast heard me speak tonight;
> Fain would I dwell on form, fain, fain decry
> What I have spoke; but farewell compliment!
> Dost thou love me? I know thou will say aye
> And I will take thy word; yet if thou swearest
> Thou mayst prove false; at lovers' perjuries
> They say Jove laughs. O, gentle Romeo!
> If thou dost love, pronounce it faithfully;
> Or if thou thinkst I am too quickly won
> I'll frown, and be perverse, and say thee nay,
> So thou will woo; but else not for the world.

No. It had not been to Henry that the young Juliet had thus revealed herself. But *through* Henry that Juliet had been possible. And she was grateful to him. The fever of life was over now, and passion spent. But memory of Henry remained as one of the good things of her life — a corner-stone on which her safety had been built.

Chapter Twelve

Chetwyn spent the Saturday morning with Dame Julia in her room. In the afternoon he went into St Taloc with Hugo. Despite the twenty years' difference in age, there was the bond of experience between the two men. Both had been through the war. Both had suffered. But whereas Hugo was battling ahead to a new life of different values, Chetwyn had wilfully stepped back into the past, endeavouring to recapture the old illusions and elegance of a former age.

In the small, deserted room of a cafe overlooking the quay, they started talking.

'I may be an escapist,' Chetwyn said, 'but quite frankly I can see little ahead for this civilisation. It's shattering itself, and I don't care to think about it. During the time left to me I mean to move as much as I can in the world I know. I like pleasant company and a congenial environment, and see no reason why I should tear myself out of it for the sake of modern hysteria and commercialism. I'm young enough, and old enough, to know what I want, and to find it where and when I can.'

'You're lucky to know your own mind,' Hugo said, 'most of us don't.'

'Meaning yourself?'

Hugo's brows were knit. 'I know where I want to go. But the going's difficult. To be quite frank, the idea of settling down to lecturing in Lynchester looms ahead like imprisonment.'

He'd confessed, and was then silent, watching through the window of the cafe the dark shapes of the boats on the water, where a few gulls rose, dipping and circling against the line of sea and cloud.

'Well, then,' said Chetwyn presently, 'get out of it.'

'I have Merlynne to consider.'

'She has courage, she's been through the war. She wouldn't be afraid of change.'

'I'm afraid *for* her,' Hugo said.

'But why?'

'She's not happy. She's burning herself out. She needs roots.'

'Change doesn't necessarily mean no roots,' the other man pointed out. 'At periods in life it becomes necessary. You'd find probably that it would do her a world of good. Though I haven't seen much of Merlynne in recent years, I know her pretty well. She's a Shane. She needs adventure. Something to get her teeth into.'

'That's it. Something to get her teeth into. She should have married a younger man.'

Chetwyn laughed, 'My dear fellow, you talk as though you were ninety.'

'In some ways I am,' Hugo said. 'In some ways I feel I know all there is to know about life, that there's not a single sensation I haven't felt or tasted. It's not true, of course, but that's how I feel at the moment. Dust in the mouth, Dry as dust. All the lecturing in the world isn't going to help. The inner me wants an open door — if you know what I mean — a door to pass through.'

'That applies to all of us — having an open door somewhere,' Chetwyn agreed. 'Mine's in the theatre, when I can become all the things I've not had the courage to be in reality. But it serves. Yours should be in your work, and life with Merlynne.'

'Maybe. But unfortunately we're pulling in opposite directions.'

'Reaction, dear fellow. It'll pass.'

'How do you know? How can anyone say that it's not going to be continual conflict?'

'My dear chap,' Chetwyn said, 'I don't like hearing you talk like this. It's defeatism.'

'No. I must face facts so that I can get my mind in

perspective. Once I've done that — well, maybe in time we'll find a mutual course.'

'You and Merlynne?'

'Exactly.'

'Hm.'

'It won't be easy. But she's my wife. I love her still, although she finds it hard to believe.'

'Unless Merlynne can see and taste and touch a thing, she'll not accept it, Hugo. You know her well enough to realise that, surely? She has all the Shane greed and Shane exuberance, without, I'm afraid, the Shane humour. That's your difficulty. As a small child she was the same — could never be objective. Now Susie-Jane's quite different. Uncomplicated. Life may not be easy for her — who's to say? — but she'll be all right. She'll come through, because her values are her own. Merlynne maybe hasn't found hers. That's what you have to watch. Forgive me for preaching.'

'There's no need,' Hugo gave a faint smile. 'A touch of the old soap-box does no harm. In my case, though, the long and short of it is — I've failed my wife.'

'For Pete's sake, man — ?'

'Oh, yes. I've failed her.'

There was a pause before Chetwyn said sharply, 'Then what about putting things to rights? Children? Have you considered starting a family?'

Hugo winced. 'At one time. Most men do. But what a world to bring them into!'

Chetwyn shrugged. 'The world is as it is. You can't change it. All anyone can do is hope for the best.'

'That's where we differ. I still believe that it's possible for men of integrity to take a lead if they have a will to do it. Society could be entirely altered by a change of heart, and human beings en masse have the power. But the initiative, the will's lacking. We exist as half-men, frustrated by circumstances and small human apetites. We're not big enough. We talk of the open door, you and I. But dare we walk through it, given the chance?'

'My dear fellow, we're men, not gods. There are moments possibly when we may contact the divine. But those are moments only. Our main concern's with the mundane business of living life as it is.'

'Even you, with your many parts?'

'Especially me,' Chetwyn asserted. 'I couldn't exist without my luxuries and accessories, my little pleasures and comforts. They're the drug to my humanity, as my different roles on the stage are. If I had any real sense of "godliness" I shouldn't have to strut before the footlights as an actor. I'd know, and be – walking the world like the proverbial John the Baptist in sackcloth, proclaiming and living my belief. Like it or not, Hugo, we live what we believe. The rest is mere words.'

'That's just it,' answered Hugo, 'I'd get up here and now, if I followed my conscience, and leave everything behind – spend my life spouting my own doctrine from my own little orange box.'

'Such as?'

'Brotherhood. Peace on earth. It may sound bilge to you, but I believe in it. It's possible.'

They were both silent for some minutes until Chetwyn resumed, 'Of course it's possible. But it isn't probable, and therefore, if you'll forgive my saying so, hardly worth your losing sleep over. Maybe you'll think it strange that I, an actor and artist, should be speaking like this, but I damn well don't believe in sacrificing the reality to the shadow. As I said, I'm an escapist, but I know I'm an escapist, and the world I escape to is comfortable and does me good. Don't become too fanatical, Hugo, old man. Don't miss all the sunshine. We need what we can get of it. I know I do.'

This conversation, revealing as it was, did not really clarify matters for Hugo. If he could have taken Chetwyn's easier way of compromise things would have been far simpler for him; but his whole being struggled towards a positive path. There were times even when he considered going to Merlynne and saying, 'Look here, we can't go on as we are. Let's leave all this. Let's go away for a time – anywhere – and live simply. A caravan in the mountains – find ourselves again. Of if you prefer it, I'll go on my own.'

But, somehow, he never quite came to the point. Her femininity, which he had first fallen in love with, now baffled and distracted him. They were searching so completely for different things. He wondered increasingly if there could ever again be real companionship between them. Whenever he tried to talk to her the veiled look would come into her eyes. She would smile lightly, secretively, or turn away. He would be aware of her only as a woman, something beautiful to look on, but evasive of real issues.

He'd have liked to feel her dedicated and friendly, and capable of marching in mind beside him. But when he looked ahead to the future, to his mountain top, it was not Merlynne he saw beside him but a stronger woman, firmer and more courageous – a girl brown and boyish with the morning light on her, and a look about her of Susie-Jane. The fact didn't worry him, for Susie-Jane had in no way trespassed upon his loyalties. But then, that first rapture could be no woman's again. Even with Merlynne it was something remembered now, rather than experienced. Gradually the essence of it was changing day by day, as he himself was, and unhappily he doubted if he could ever reclaim it, or would even want to. This was his sadness – that before he'd truly fulfilled her, he had in heart let go.

Yet as a human being she was precious to him in a way she'd not been before. He felt for her compassion and tenderness and sympathy which might last beyond physical desire. But she didn't want it. The best he could give her seemed unacceptable. Realising this he felt useless and entrapped. For what point was there in their marriage? And where was it taking them? The future appeared blank. As he had said to Chetwyn, he feared for his wife because he doubted very much if she would be able to stand the course of their life together. And he dreaded what the alternative might be.

Chapter Thirteen

That same evening saw the celebration of Richard's engagement to Deborah Cavin. Sir John and his daughter drove over to Trencathra and Nicholas was present at dinner, for which he had produced a bottle of his best port.

Richard, in evening dress, looked handsome, almost gallant. Deborah was radiant. At first the occasion had been planned as an informal family affair, but at Dame Julia's request the guests had been included. Sam Murgatroyd, she knew, would appreciate it, and following Miss Fothergill-Briggs' gesture concerning the room, her heart had warmed even in this direction. And so, with the lamps burning brightly and the candles lighted on the table, the old dining room took on a forgotten elegance. Above the mediaeval fireplace at one end of the room a former Nankerviss and Squire of Trencathra flickered to life for a moment from the dark oak frame, watching as if from across the years the little scene enacted before him. At the other end Dame Julia, with her face ivory white in the light, sat with Nicholas who for that brief interim was content to be pleasant even to Miss Spring herself.

A toast was proposed by Chetwyn, looking ascetic and distinguished with his actor's face lean and pale above the black bow tie. Sir John attempted to be humorous, sprinkling his remarks with a touch of coarseness which struck an absurd note in the atmosphere. Miss Spring was excited and impressed, breaking on occasion into sharp short giggles frowned upon by Miss Fothergill-Briggs who had a sense of propriety concerning the occasion. Merlynne forced a smile from time to time, but her eyes were absent. Hugo, bored, endeavoured not to appear so. Catherine, faintly stimulated, looked lovelier than ever with a delicate glow tinting her cheeks. Ann Chenoweth, who was serving, had something hostile and unhappy in her eyes. She moved automatically with a tight look about her mouth. Life seemed to have drained from her. Beside Olive, who was helping her, she appeared colourless and almost plain.

Olive's eyes were brilliant under the black fringe of her hair. Never had she seen anyone she so much admired as tall Mr Shane who bowed so elegantly, and had such a fascinating way of moving his hands. She liked the way his eyebrows slanted above his dark eyes, the aquiline features and fine head from which the hair, only faintly tinged with grey, grew away at the temples. Yes, that was the sort of man she liked; distinguished, a gentleman. She really couldn't see what Ann found to rave over in Mr Richard. He couldn't hold a candle to Mr Shane. There was something about Richard really very like Tom Lincoln, the gipsy who lived with his family on the common near Cripples Rest. Evening dress didn't look right on him. He'd never get anywhere, never move in the same world as Mr Shane. But then, Olive told herself smugly, her sister had never been the romantic sort.

Susie-Jane, in a gold-coloured dress which had been converted from one of Catherine's, and with a yellow ribbon looping her hair, was in a state of emotional excitement. She was happy for Richard, proud on this auspicious moment to be sitting in the old dining room of Trencathra, exhilarated by Deborah's fey beauty and the significance of her presence there. But beneath the glow of excitement doubt lingered. Deborah looked lovely and happy; eventually she would be Richard's wife and come to Trencathra to live. She would bear his children and be mistress of the house. Well – though the idea wasn't easy to Susie-Jane – she'd always known sometime that her brother would marry; it was inevitable. But, somehow, Deborah didn't *quite* fit into the picture. The house, Susie decided with her deep intuition, hadn't yet accepted her. She knew that the family would laugh at her for her ideas – she'd learned long since to keep her feelings concerning Trencathra to herself. But sitting there with the candlelight leaping on the glass and silver, sending fitful shadows up the panelled walls, it was as though a crowded company of past Nankervisses rallied to her side, touching the inborn core of her pride and love. Deborah, for a few fleeting instants, appeared a trespasser in that quiet throng, and Susie's mind asserted violently: It's wrong. She doesn't belong here.

Then, as quickly, the mood passed into commonsense.

I'm just being unfair and jealous, she admitted to herself. Mean.

After that she tried to be generous; did her best to face the inevitable with composure. But as the sallies and talk continued the conviction grew in her, as it had done in Ann, that she could never live at Trencathra with Deborah. Since leaving the Land Army Susie-Jane had not bothered to look too far ahead. But now, she knew, she'd have to plan some sort of future. But perhaps that was right. After all, you couldn't always stay in the places and with the people you loved.

She stole a glance at Hugo across the table. He appeared solemn and flatly bored. When he caught her look he smiled at her, and something about his smile cut her to the heart. She hated Merlynne, at that moment, for not valueing him. The set, sensitive line of his lips, and keen yet bewildered glance of his eyes betrayed inner anguish. The light caught his hair, touching it to gold round his head. There was something about Hugo, thought Susie-Jane, unlike anyone else. She knew now almost every line of his face by heart. When, as was frequent, his vision intruded upon the happiness of her days, it left an ache in her chest — a hollow of loneliness. Despite her youth, Susie-Jane recognised that Hugo was cutting himself off from the world. She didn't despise him for it. She admired the struggling thing in him which was striving for single mindedness. But she was increasingly aware of his loneliness; knew that if she had been able to go up to him and say 'I don't know where you're going, Hugo, or what you're going to do, but let me come with you. I won't *ask* anything of you', he would have been grateful and touched. That was all.

Hugo was proud. Deny it he might, but the fact remained

that Merlynne had failed him. She, Susie-Jane, knew it, and so did he. Never, never would he admit it; no one liked admitting these things. But there it was — the marriage was a failure, and had passed the point where anything worthwhile could be retrieved. It was obvious that Merlynne was no longer going to try, and Susie suspected the reason. Her heart burned with indignation at Hugo's innocence. When he discovered the truth — how things really were — what would it do to him? The thought was painful. In imagination, watching his face with the light flickering upon the cheek-bones and hollows of the temples, she saw the muscles already flinch, torn by hard taut lines of pain. Then, quickly, the fear subsided. She had a sudden, swift conviction that he should know. It would be better for him.

But I can't tell him, she thought. it wouldn't be fair to Merlynne. And I don't really know anything definite to tell.

No. There was nothing she could do except wait and be his friend, and try to help him. as adequately as she could by deed and word and thought.

The chatter continued over the table; but sitting there Susie-Jane felt herself gradually drawn away from it all to another sphere, with Hugo. She visualised him going through the world, single-hearted on his quest for a new life. She saw herself beside him — not demanding, but administering. The sensation was so acute that she could even picture the scene — a high, stony road, and Hugo, with his chin raised to the light, struggling along it. She saw herself, too, hurrying along behind him, saw this other Susie-Jane draw up beside him and put her hand into his. For a second, even, she could almost feel him touching her palm, and her heart throbbed with the urgency of her compassion and love. Strength radiated from her; and, looking at him, she perceived that he knew. The guests faded, even the room subsided, leaving only Hugo and herself facing and knowing each other across a mist of unreality. In that moment she felt she could be all things to him, and was both infinitely the older and younger of the two.

Then, after some seconds, she was pulled from eternity to the present again. Lights twinkled once more in the room;

she heard Sir John's bluff voice cracking a joke, and above it the thin light sound of Miss Spring's giggle. She observed Richard smiling down upon Deborah, and heard her father talking of cigars. One by one the figures round her fitted into shape. She returned to their plane, and raised the coffee to her lips. But her hands were shaking, and her heart, full and warm, pounded beneath her thin dress. Life was immense, and beautiful and hurtful. Far too hurtful to bear, she thought, unless she could be of use in some way to Hugo.

For many hours that night she lay restless and lonely in her room. From outside sometimes there came the solitary thin note of a lone seabird, and it seemed to her that it had a haunted quality, like the spirit of Hugo searching for truth. From beyond this came the constant rising and falling of the waves upon the rocks. Rhythmically, like the soothing brushing of a mother's hand, they sought to calm her, to draw her to peace. She struggled for composure, closed her eyes, and let the tides of darkness sweep into her brain. But at the point of sleep she was woken, jerked to consciousness by her love for Hugo – the miracle of its being – and by her knowledge now of his need for her. Against its strength, the spirit even of Trencathra was subdued and still. She remembered what he had said to her on the rocks that distant day: 'Trencathra is only a symbol to you. One day your love for it will be given to some person, and I only hope you won't be disappointed.'

Well, she knew now though it had not been clear to her then. Hugo had been right. Against her love, the house meant little. But it understood. She knew that what was real of it, understood. As she lay there, with the tears damp on her lashes, she felt the silences of the old Tower Room envelop her comfortingly. Thus would a mother have felt and behaved, selflessly and with compassion. And she needed compassion. Her love was strong, and true, and warm. But Susie-Jane was only young, and it was inevitable that she would be hurt. Yet her thoughts, even then, were not of herself but of Hugo.

'Please, dear God,' she said in a whisper, 'look after Hugo

and make him happy. Don't let him be too hurt, and let me help him.'

After this she somehow felt a little more at peace. Some of the tension went from her, and at last, as the old clock on the landing was on the point of striking three o'clock, she slept.

Chapter Fourteen

In the days that followed the announcement of Richard's engagement, Ann Chenoweth was very quiet and reserved about the house. A less capable girl than herself might, perhaps, have allowed the work to suffer from her unhappy mood; but her principles in this direction never flagged, although she meant to leave Trencathra after Christmas. She intended the holiday to be over before she informed the family. Christmas, to Ann, was a special and sacred time, and despite her own unhappiness she could not bear to think of causing worry or annoyance to Catherine. As for Richard, clearly he wouldn't really mind. It was obvious to her nowadays that his thoughts were far away from the people at Trencathra. And yet he seemed to have an extra energy for his work. He went about whistling with a light in his eye and a spring in his step that had not previously been there.

One day he arrived back in the evening with a labrador puppy in his arms. He strode into the kitchen and placed it on the floor beside Ann, saying, 'There! Time we had a little young life about the place. Since old Sally died, I've missed my dog. What do you think of it, Ann?'

The soft black creature nuzzled its way to her toes, wagging its body and stubby little tail.

'It'll need a lot of care,' she said, with a dull ache in her heart.

'Come now,' Richard exclaimed. 'Surely you're not going to say you don't want it? I thought you loved animals.'

So I did, she thought, so I did until you turned all love to pain. Then she answered, 'I do. I like them all right. Yes — of course I do.'

She stooped down and picked the young thing up in her arms. It trembled with excitement and joy, licking her on her nose and cheeks and eyes. At that she had to laugh, and turn her head away.

Watching her, Richard was pleased. There was something about Ann that never failed to arouse a sense of sympathy in him. When she wasn't happy he felt it, and was worried. He knew — but did not realise to what extent — that she had been hurt over his engagement. Richard was too modest to suspect that she could be deeply in love with him, but was aware, nevertheless, that her femininity had in some way been affected. He liked no one to be hurt, least of all Ann.

'Well?' he said again. 'Will you like him?'

Ann nodded; but the smile had gone, leaving still a constrained look about her.

'I think you ought to go out more,' he said abruptly after a pause.

'Out?' she said, looking up. 'But why?'

He shrugged his shoulders. 'Well — who do you see here? You're young. And too nice just to be wasted on the Nankerviss family.'

She flushed. 'There's nowhere particular to go to,' she said. 'I'm all right. I go home once a week. Besides, there isn't a greal deal of time, you know.'

'Oh, well, it's up to you,' he said. 'But there's something changed about you.' He felt ill at ease. He hadn't meant to speak of this.

'Changed?'

He nodded. 'Yes. You're not as contented.'

'I never said so.'

'No. You haven't *said* so. But it's obvious. And I don't like it.'

'I'm sorry, Mr Richard,' she spoke stiffly. 'People can't be things to order.'

He looked at her, puzzled, brows knitted over his prominent nose. Pride, a certain youthful aloofness, made her for a moment almost beautiful.

'Of course not. But a young girl like you shouldn't have to

be happy to order. That is, if you're being treated properly. You are, aren't you?'

'Of course,' she said, in the same controlled tones. 'Why shouldn't I be?'

He shrugged again, and turned to go out of the kitchen. But at the door he paused, and told her, 'If anything worries you at all, you know, you've only to speak to me about it. Anything, Ann – understand?'

She nodded, an oddly defensive expression on her face which for a moment irritated and frustrated him.

What was the matter with the girl? he wondered, going into the yard. Why couldn't she smile as she used to? There was no earthly reason for her moods. Outside he remembered he'd left the puppy with her. He turned and went back again. She was kneeling on the floor, with her face against the small black creature, soft shining hair merging close with the dark animal fur.

He stopped, and she looked up. Her eys were suspiciously moist.

'Oh!' he said, at a loss. 'So you do like the little fellow. All right. I'll leave him with you for a bit. But don't let him get too near the fire. And whatever you do keep him out of the hall or we shall have Miss Catherine after us.'

'I will,' she promised him.

'Good girl.' He patted her shoulder, and after a moment, left her. But he was perplexed. She had been trembling when he touched her, and a person with less imagination that he had must have been aware that she was upset.

That same night when both sisters had gone to bed, Olive came to Ann's room to borrow a comb.

'I've dropped mine somewhere,' she said. 'I'm awful with combs.'

'You ought to be more careful. Combs are scarce now.'

'Oh, don't preach so,' the younger girl said. 'You're getting awful old, Ann.'

She stiffened. 'Someone's got to have a sense of responsibility in this place.'

'Well, I don't see why it should be you. You seem so dull. It's my belief you're in love!' Olive added, with a touch of scorn.

'Mind your own business, Olive Chenoweth, and don't be so foolish.'

The younger girl glanced at her sideways from her black eyes. 'Foolish? I'm not so sure. And for a man like Mr Richard! Pooh! I wouldn't waste my time on anyone like him. I think you're soft.'

'Olive! If you say another word I'll box your ears.'

'You try it,' said Olive.

'I will, if you're not careful.'

'Well – there's no need to get rattled,' her sister said. 'It seems silly to me getting upset like you do. It isn't as if it could do any good – him going to marry Miss Deborah and everything.'

'Be quiet!' Ann almost shouted. 'And I'm *not* in love with him. He doesn't matter a bit to me – understand?'

Olive shrugged her shoulders. 'If you say so, that's all that matters. All the same, I think you're an idiot.'

She left the room jauntily in her blue woollen dressing gown, returning after a minute or two with her hair twisted into curling pins round her rosy face. Ann was still sitting on the edge of the bed with a book open on her lap. Glancing at it curiously, Olive saw that it was the Bible, opened at the Song of Solomon. She observed also that Ann had been crying.

'Oh, Ann,' she said, impulsively going over to sit beside her sister. 'I'm sorry. I'm truly sorry if you're unhappy.'

'That's all right,' Ann said. 'Don't fret over me. I don't need your pity.'

Olive sighed, thinking hard of something comforting to say. 'It's always the same,' she remarked, 'people always have to go falling in love with the wrong people. I wonder why it's got to be like that?'

There was no reply, and after a minute she went on, 'Perhaps it's best not to fall in love at all. That's it. I won't. Not if I can help it. It only makes you miserable. The best way is to be like the film stars and have lots of admirers, and shake your shoulder at them and walk away.'

In spite of herself, Ann smiled. 'You are funny,' she said.

'Ah, but I'm sensible. No man will ever get *me* in the dumps. You see. They'll be the ones.'

'You mustn't think like that. Sometimes people are lucky and fall in love with the right person, then everything's perfect. You mustn't not believe in it.'

Olive shook her head. 'Well, I'm not going to be hurt, I'm going to have fun, and enjoy things. I think it's silly being gloomy over any man. I wouldn't be.'

'Perhaps not,' agreed her sister, thinking how oddly went such worldly wisdom with the round childish face surrounded by its mass of curl pins.

'Go to bed now,' she said presently. 'We have to get up early, and it's time.'

'All right.'

'And thank you for coming back,' her sister continued. 'It helped me.'

Olive was flattered. Really, she thought, Ann wasn't a bad old thing. Poor Ann, if only she would brighten herself up a bit, and go out sometimes. But there — she wasn't that sort of girl. It rather appeared now as though she'd end up an old maid. She looked plain, sometimes, with no powder on her nose, and her hair so straight. She needed bucking up, that was it. As she went to her room Olive thought, I'll let her have my glamour books. There's lots of advice in them that would help her if she'd only read them. But would she? There again, Ann was funny. Fancy sitting on her bed there pouring over the Song of Solomon. What a dull thing to do. As if that could do any good. Suddenly Olive got tired of pondering and commenced instead humming a little tune that Bert had taught her.

'Always, I'm crazy — just crazy for you —'

Life was just beginning for her. It was going to be fun, great fun. She laughed as she kicked off her slippers, and jumped into bed.

Chapter Fifteen

December, came, bringing wild skies and high seas which charged in a fury of foam and force round the rocks and into the small harbour. Yet nightly the small fishing boats put out from St Taloc, and in the early evening could be seen drifting one by one from the harbour out into the ocean.

Hugo commenced his lectures in the Fisherman's Hall, which were attended chiefly by older men. He outlined the possibilities of a Federal Union throughout Europe and ultimately the world. But in the face of contemporary European affairs and the line taken in the press, he felt that he was not getting far in the minds of these men, who having been all their lives up against the forces of the elements and of nature for their very subsistence, could not visualise a world existing without battle. It was not that they wanted war. They were peace-loving men with a culture beyond intellectualism, but the essence of living to them was struggle. How could it be otherwise, when their daily bread was earned frequently at so great a cost? That same year two boats had been lost with all hands off Eagle Point. During the summer a Breton boat had met the same fate. How then could one visualise or accept a world of peace, when it seemed that man was ordained by whatever deity existed for tragedy and effort?

In the face of this fatalism, the pressure on Hugo's belief was intensified.

The evenings left him feeling badly tired. He was seldom free of pain. He was beginning to accept it would be a long time, if ever, before he could walk normally. The wound had healed, but nerves could not be replaced, only eased within certain limits. Still, there were many men, poor devils, in worse plight than himself, and he didn't outwardly complain. His 'old stick', as he called it, still operated, and his aspirations went further than physical matters.

Indeed, as the days went by it seemed to him all personal ties were lessening. Merlynne appeared happier at times, but he knew that she was drifting further away from him. Once, in the night, he reached out to her and would have taken her to him like a child. But she hadn't wanted it — just sighed, and turned her head away, and he had let her go with a sense of failure. Since then, he'd left her alone. They lived together almost as strangers. There were poignant moments when he was struck anew by her mobility and charm, when through a glance or a sudden swift gesture she was transfigured for an instant into memory and desire. But this was for a second only which fell away leaving them both lonely, and it was at these times that he turned in his heart to Susie-Jane. for whereas Merlynne had been a 'taker', Susie-Jane, he knew, was supportive in her loyalty and youth. He might never be able to speak of it, but the fact remained that in spirit they were strangely united.

Sometimes when the winds swept round the house beating in a fury of force and rain upon the walls and windows, it seemed to him that her courage was carried along with it. At lowest ebb, he fancied frequently that she was there beside him, could almost visualise her shadowy, boyish form, and hear her in imagination saying, 'I am here, Hugo. I am always with you.'

Susie-Jane, he thought, so young, was yet in essence a mother to men. This was her strength.

One day he was sitting in the hall by the fire when Dame Julia entered. She looked a little restless and perplexed; indeed since Chetwyn's brief visit something in her had been longing to get away. Emotional confusion — and there was plenty of it, she felt, at Trencathra — stimulated for a time, but in the end it was apt to become tiring, and she was feeling now in need of respite, of a little relaxation in her own world.

Seeing Hugo sitting there, she took the chair opposite to him beside the fireplace in which the logs were burning merrily. It was almost dinner time, and the light was fading. Outside the trees lifted wan grey arms against a grey sky. There was very little wind and no sound penetrated the silence save the distant rattle of pots and pans from the kitchen and the crackling of the wood. She placed her stick on the floor beside her, smoothed out the creases of her black silk dress, and after a little silence said, 'Hugo, my dear, I've been thinking about you.'

He looked surprised. 'About me? What? Tell me.'

'I've been thinking you should go away.'

'Away?' he said. 'But why? What's the hurry?'

'Cornwall's not any good to you and Merlynne at the moment,' she said. 'Don't think I'm being dramatic, but it's too intense. Oh, not that I agree in giving in to whims – but there are limits.'

'Just what do you mean, please?'

She shook her head. 'Oh, face facts, Hugo. There's too much for you to tackle here. I'm telling you, dear boy, to take Merlynne away.'

'Why should I? This is her home. She's happy enough at the moment,' he lied.

'No, she's not,' the old lady said, sitting up straight with a jerk, and facing him with very shrewd bright eyes. 'She's in danger, and you know it.'

'Danger?'

'Don't hedge. It's no light matter. That's why I'm telling you. Unless you're very careful you'll lose Merlynne.'

'You're not telling me she's ill?' he said. 'Is there something the matter with her that she's not told me – is that what you mean?'

'No, I don't mean that at all. Really, Hugo, in some ways you're incorrigible. The point is that somebody else is likely to give Merlynne what you've *not* given her – unless you look out.'

For a few seconds he made no answer and showed no reaction of any kind. Then, as the implication fully registered, he went perceptibly paler, with a faint greyness colouring his lips.

'I don't believe it,' he said presently.

'You're very foolish then.'

'Who?' he began. 'Who is it?' Even as he asked the question he already guessed.

She shook her head. 'I'm not telling you. I don't want to become an ordinary vulgar gossip. But I had to speak out. Merlynne's my granddaughter. I'm fond of you both. You both seem to have lost your way. I don't want that to happen, Hugo. Merlynne's a nice little thing, really; look after her.'

Shortly afterwards the dinner bell rang. Both got up, and accompanied by Miss Spring and Sam Murgatroyd, who had entered the hall upon the tail end of the conversation, filed into the diningroom. That evening nothing more was said. But afterwards, when the meal was over, Hugo remained in the room smoking his pipe, while Merlynne helped Ann to clear the table. Dame Julia's words had shocked him. Even now his heart was beating more heavily than usual, and his throat felt dry. He watched his wife as she walked quickly from place to place collecting the cutlery, and pausing at moments to shake the tawny hair from her face. He tried to put himself in the place of any man other than himself, seeing her for the first time.

It was not easy to do this because, inevitably, he was taken back to the past, and with a sense of unreality was once more facing her in the war canteen. Even old tunes slipped into his mind – 'Roll out the Barrel', the 'Pensylvania Polka' – all the nostalgic tin-pan collection which had provided the background to those hectic years. The hundreds of different faces, the easy camaraderie bred of a hopeless gallant spirit, the laughter and chaff floated back to him in its sea of smoke and sound. And through it all he saw Merlynne's pale face with its fair hair and dewy eyes. He was gripped by emotion, a feeling of overwhelming grief, and a sudden impulse to snatch her to safety. He knew this was what he should do. As her husband the moral obligation was his. But she who had once desired him so passionately, now he knew rejected him sexually with equal force. He remembered moments int he past when she'd clung to him and humiliated them both through the intensity of her emotion. Had he then done wrong not to play-act to her? Should he have simulated what he did not feel, in order to keep her satisfied? He still shrank from this course.

He felt wretched and defeated – ashamed of his lack of foresight, and of her deception – if what Dame Julia had hinted was true. The deception of a hole-and-corner business was surely the worst thing of all, and the most damaging to Merlynne. It showed that she couldn't trust him, had not even the courage to face him squarely in the daylight.

Later, as they were getting ready for bed, he said to her suddenly, 'Merlynne?'

'Well?' She spun round, surprised at the note of force in his voice. He was facing the window, standing in his dressing-gown, looking out to sea.

'I want to talk to you.'

Oh, dear, she thought, another dreary scene. I hope he gets it over quickly. I hope there's nothing wrong. Perhaps people have been talking. Perhaps it's about Laurence.

She stifled her nervousness, and with affected nonchalance remarked, 'OK, get on with it, Hugo. What is it?'

He turned round and crossed towards her, placing his hands on her shoulders, staring straight into her face. 'A lot might have been said between us lately,' he said, 'which hasn't been. We've been cowards, both of us.'

'Really, Hugo, I don't – '

'Oh, yes, you do, Merlynne,' he contradicted her. 'You know perfectly what I mean.'

She wriggled slightly under his touch. 'Is there any need to be quite so intense?' she said. 'It's just wearing me out, all this intensity.'

'I know,' he said, releasing her abruptly. 'I don't want to pry into your affairs, and I don't want to exonerate myself. A lot of the trouble between us has been my fault, but it won't be any more.'

'What do you mean?' she asked, half whispering.

'I think we should go away,' he said, 'do what many other couples are having to do – make a new beginning somewhere else. We'll start all over again. And I promise you I'll do *my* part – to make things go.'

He waited expectantly while the minutes ticked away in the silence which was electric, tense.

Then suddenly she faced him with her mouth contorted and her breasts heaving. He had never seen her so before.

There was something Medusa-like about the angry passion of her voice as she answered, 'No. I won't go away — why should I? You think you can come back into my life like this, spoiling everything I've found and done, and then calmly expect me to go where you want, trotting after you like a little dog — I won't do it! I tell you I *won't*. My life's been sickening with you these past months. What life has it been? What do you think it's been like for me, day after day, week after week, while you've scorned me and gone your own self-pitying way? How do you think I've stuck it — the humiliation? And now you want me to have more of it. Well, I won't. I'm staying here, and you shan't drag me away — no one shall. I —'

She broke off, and turned away, fumbling for her handkerchief. Hugo still stood there, quite rigid, as though turned to stone. When she faced him again she saw that he had gone deathly white. His eyes looked strained, glazed almost, and seemed to stare beyond her, into something she could not see. It was as though pain itself had frozen his features into anguish. Before it, she weakened, and was afraid. After a moment she ran up to him, grasping the reveres of his dressing-gown with shaking hands. Tears of emotion and strain flooded her eyes. 'Hugo — I don't — I didn't mean all that. Don't look like that. Hugo — Hugo — I didn't mean it.'

He unclasped her hands with his own and put them from him. 'It's all right,' he said. 'I understand. It's quite all right.'

'But, Hugo —'

He smiled bitterly.

'Please don't try to explain. It's quite unnecessary.'

'It *is* necessary. I've hurt you. Oh, Hugo —'

'You will never hurt me again, Merlynne,' he said.

'What do you mean?'

'Just that,' he said.

'You mean —?'

He shrugged his shoulders lightly and remarked, 'Go to bed. You need rest.'

Quite suddenly she felt dreadfully tired. Emotion had exhausted her. The room appeared unreal, and it seemed that the proud, hurt figure of Hugo still standing at the window like some legendary and disillusioned Galahad must be some figment of a nightmare sent to taunt her. She lifted her hand to her forehead, and sat on the bed weakly. Her eyes felt swollen, and her heart burned with a pain she had not known she could feel. In that moment despair overcame all other issues. She forgot Laurence even, conscious only that somehow this dreadful thing had come upon her and Hugo. She had not wanted to hurt him. Always now, the memory of his hurt would be with her, she would be struggling in it like some wild thing caught in a net. She was struggling now. In a torment of conflict her unhappiness spurred her to further effort. She stood up and went over to him again.

'Forget what I said,' she pleaded. 'Can't you forget it?'

He looked at her, very straight, from his clear cold eyes. Then one word framed itself on his lips. 'No.'

'Oh. I see. You mean, you'll hold it up against me?'

He smiled, shaking his head. 'No,' he said. 'I shan't do that. I don't blame you, Merlynne.'

'Then why?'

'Please,' he begged her, 'Can't you see? It's been a shock. Won't you please go to bed, leave me alone for a bit. There's nothing more to be said, is there? I put a suggestion to you – you rejected it. That's all.'

She left him, moving to the bed slowly and with effort. In her tired state the poignancy of the situation swept over her. This room so short a time ago had been prepared by her for Hugo's return. The peach-coloured hangings, the walnut furniture, the reading lamp at Hugo's side – all this had been thought out for their mutual happiness and comfort. The book shelves in the recess she had painted cream herself, and had arranged there all his favourite editions. With what love she had bought the large Cloisonné bowl in Penzance, and placed in it red roses for his home-coming. How happy she had been going to the hospital that day.

She remembered driving back with him through the soft grey summer dusk. A thousand impressions had been written on her mind then, returning now to disturb and hurt her; the ghostly silhouetted heads of the scabious waving on the wall, the warm drift of sea air blown through the window of the car, the feel of Hugo's hand in hers, the brave, clear outline of his profile which she had so loved. Their unspoken communion, and plans for the future; and beneath it all — she had to admit it — the faint intangible awareness of the change in him. But she had not allowed it to distress her that first night. For in the face of his return such minor doubts were negligible and as nothing.

But now — what had they come to? What had happened to bring them to this? For a second she wondered wildly if it was yet too late, if even now something could not be done to save the dream that had once been theirs. Then, in a sea of weariness, the answer came to her. There was no way out. Things happened as they did. She was no longer fighting for integrity or even for her own ends. Forces came into life on which one was carried away, having no will to combat. She, Merlynne, no longer had the will to steer her own course. She was floating now on the dark tide of her passion to some end which might save or destroy her.

For some time she lay on the bed staring unseeingly at the ceiling. She was aware that Hugo still stood by the window. Once he slumped into the chair, only to get up again after a minute or two. She wondered whether to speak to him, ask him to come to bed. But something about his posture — the rigidity of his square shoulders and set of his chin against the light — forbade her. She sighed, and turned her face away; presently she heard him move across the floor and leave the room, closing the door quietly behind him. She was alone.

Chapter Sixteen

The following day a queer atmosphere of suspense seemed to hang over the household, conveying itself even to the guests. Miss Spring, coming down at nine to breakfast, found only Sam Murgatroyd and Susie-Jane present. Miss Fothergill-Briggs it appeared had a headache, had taken some aspirin and was staying in bed. Nicholas was at the lodge, Dame Julia was breakfasting in her room; Richard was already at work, Hugo, strangely, had gone for an early walk, and Merlynne wanted nothing to eat. Catherine had taken what she wanted and Ann appeared with the teapot looking rather sombre in her navy print dress. It was all rather bewildering. Sam suggested that there was a heaviness in the air. But it was more than that.

Miss Spring whose room adjoined Merlynne's and Hugo's had heard queer things in the night, including poor Mr Lane leaving the room and later the sound of his young wife sobbing. There had been no mistaking that muffled unhappy noise, and Miss Spring had been unable to sleep for quite a long time. It had been impossible not to wonder about things. And yet the matter was their own affair, and nothing to do with her. All the same her sympathies, on the whole, were with Hugo rather than with Merlynne, who in her opinion did not always behave as dutifully and kindly to her husband as she might. There was something subtle and secretive about her these days not entirely to be trusted. The odd, half-veiled glance of her eyes, and the slow half-dreamy curve of her lips endowed her at times with a dangerous changeling quality. She was not, Miss Spring decided, deep down a really nice girl. Nice young women did not look like that, neither did they visit young men like Laurence in their studios. That was one of the things she would have to speak to him about – his friendship with Merlynne.

Laurence was all right, bless the boy! So enwrapped in his art that the danger of gossip, the risk of public opinion, would neither touch him, nor enter his head. He lived in a dream world. All the same, if she was going to launch him upon the world, his reputation must be guarded. Accordingly, she determined to visit him that afternoon.

The previous week Miss Spring had rashly spent all her coupons upon a lilac-coloured two-piece, which she now wore, with a heavily embroidered foreign-looking blouse that had long sleeves gathered in tightly at the wrists. The ensemble was far too young for her, and with the gold drop earrings, made her look not only eccentric but bizarre. Nevertheless, she felt confident in the clothes, and set out with a feeling of exhilaration in her heart that was accentuated by the still, dreamy quality of the afternoon, by the faint tang of wood smoke intermingling with sea drifting to greet her as she stepped outside the door, and the sight of the little boats lying contentedly upon the water. This was the sort of day she liked – this still, quiet, unexciting weather when one could walk along unmolested by wind which left one's nose red and blew drifts of hair about one's eyes. She was glad now that she had been reckless and bought the costume, because she felt sure that Laurence would like it. And before she went into the studio, she meant to spend a penny in the ladies' cloakroom for the sole reason of using the mirror adjusting her hat, and powdering her nose.

A feeling of beneficence flooded her as she mounted the bus. She smiled at the conductor and a labourer sitting opposite to her, beamed upon a little boy who sat on the seat next to her gazing at her with round eyes from a grubby face. After a minute or two she magnanimously handed him a sixpence from her bag. He took it solemnly without smiling, and his mother said to him, 'Say thank you, 'enery.'

Henry rubbed his eye and looked away, burying his face against his mother's coat.

'He's shy,' the woman said, jerking him up. 'Now, 'enery, – say thank you to the lady.'

'Oh, please don't bother him,' Miss Spring said. 'It's not worth that. Let him buy some sweets with it.' She beamed back complacently, a warm little glow about her heart. It was so nice being able to do things for people, she thought. And did not the happy feeling inside of her but prove the truth of Karma – that all was a law of cause and effect, and that what one gave was returned a hundredfold?

The sun was shining when she left the bus, glinting in a pale wintry radiance upon the water. She walked along the harbour, glancing at odd moments towards her reflection outlined in the windows. Once she lifted her chin in a gesture emulating youth. She was again profoundly thankful for the money left to her by the aunts, for this chance she had been given of living before it was too late. Several fishermen turned to look at her as she passed, and she beamed on them revelling in their attention, in the sensation it gave her of fraternity and understanding.

I'm becoming quite accepted here, she thought. Soon I shall be one of them, and they will not think of me as a foreigner at all.

The thought gladdened her. She hurried on, and reached the studio just as the church clock was striking three.

She went lightly up the steps, and with a sense of pleasant anticipation, knocked on the door.

For a moment there was no sound, then after a short pause she heard a man's footsteps approaching. The latch was withdrawn, and Laurence appeared before her, with a lock of hair fallen over his eyes, his loose blue shirt open at his neck, and his face surprised. But how charming he looked. A stab of emotion went through her because she felt she had a right now to intrude on him in his sanctum. She smiled, and gave him her hand.

'I just *had* to come,' she said. 'I've been thinking things over, and I – '

At that moment she became aware that he was not alone; someone had moved in the shadows of the room behind him. Miss Spring involuntarily took a step forward, peering in. Laurence, with slight confusion, stepped aside, recovering himself with admirable self-control, saying quickly, 'Come in, Miss Spring, I was thinking about you. Merlynne's here – she just called in for a minute. But she's not staying.'

Miss Spring felt a tight, unwarrantable little feeling of resentment. So that girl was here again. And Laurence apparently quite enjoying it. She stiffened perceptibly.

'Well I haven't much time – '

'Oh, but of course you have,' he said, coaxing her. 'Now do come in or you'll make me think you don't really want to. And I shouldn't like that. In a minute or two I'll put the kettle on for a cup of tea.'

Weakening, Miss Spring allowed herself to be propelled into the studio. But she was aware that a jealous look had come into Merlynne's face. Her mouth was sulky, though her voice was pleasant enough.

'Hallo, Miss Spring, nice to see you.' Her eyes were angry. Really they were extremely unpleasant eyes, Miss Spring thought, cat-like, although some men, no doubt, would think them attractive. Laurence, bless him, was not likely to be impressed. Anyone could see, she told herself with increasing determination, that it was Merlynne who was pestering him, not the other way round. Well, she had come to talk to him about this very matter, and she would do so. However long the girl stayed, she would stay longer, and if she did not go by six o'clock, she, Miss Spring would inform Laurence that she had to talk to him on urgent and personal business. But over this she needn't have worried; when she had ensconced herself in a chair, Merlynne got up abruptly saying she must go. Laurence made no effort to detain her, but saw her to the door then closed it after a moment upon her retreating figure in its teddy-bear coat.

Miss Spring breathed a sigh of relief, Laurence came towards her.

'Won't you take your coat off?' he said. 'It's quite warm in here. I've had the stove on all day.'

'All right, yes. Perhaps I will,' she said, flattered and faintly thrilled at the chivalry with which he divested her of the garment.

'I wondered if you'd come,' he said presently. 'Do you know – I had a feeling you might. This morning I thought,

"I wouldn't be surprised if Miss Spring came today." Funny, isn't it?'

She glanced at him quickly, with a burning look in her pale eyes.

'Not so very,' she said. 'I'm not surprised. Some minds you know have an odd kind of telepathy between them.'

'Yes,' he said. 'But those cases are few.'

'All the same –' she persisted '– with you and I it's possible, I'm sure.' She blushed at her daring, and resumed quickly, 'How is the painting going?'

'Oh, so-so,' he said. 'Look! What do you think of that?'

He strode across the room, took a picture from the floor and placed it upon the easel for her approval. It was a queer composition of fruit and flowers arranged against a window through which, minutely in the distance, chimneys could be seen belching smoke. There was something macabre and yet stimulating about the rich curious colouring and strange design that sent an odd emotion through Miss Spring. His previous abstruse surrealistic efforts had bewildered and impressed her because he, himself, had painted them. But this was different. It was really stirring. He knew it, too. He was watching her closely all the time, as though to test on the instant the pulse of her reaction.

She didn't have to flatter this time. 'It's good,' she said. 'It's curious. But it's *good*.' He seemed satisfied. 'Do you like it?'

'I don't know,' she said. 'It isn't the kind of thing you like or dislike. It's – it's strange, Laurence. It's silly to say so, no doubt, but it makes me feel a little excited.'

'There!' he said. 'That's what I wanted to do. And I have. I've succeeded. But you wait. This is nothing to what I *will* do.'

He went to a drawer and produced a further effort.

'See this – what do you make of it?'

She saw before her the depiction of a shattered world of corpses and debris, above which towered the grotesque agonised figure of a nailed figure. The cross was painted in a molten dull red against a sky of lurid swirling darkness. The bodies on the ground were suggested rather than drawn, but the whole effect was one of tense, dramatic struggle, of

147

seething life in the face of corruption. Miss Spring felt a shiver course down her spine.

'Dreadful,' she said. 'But *great* – in its way. I didn't know you could do things like that.'

'Neither did I,' he said, 'until recently. It's only lately I've found my own style. I know now where I am. I'm going to paint – do you understand, Miss Spring? I'm going to *paint*. And I'm going to let nothing stand in my way, nothing at all. Everything I've got that matters is going into this. Everything. Get me?'

She stared at him, fascinated at his intensity, a little unnerved by the daemon that had so suddenly taken possession of him.

'Of course,' she said. 'I always knew you would. That's why I wanted to help you.'

'Ah, but you didn't know before,' he said. 'You couldn't. I didn't. But this last week or two I've discovered it. It's made me a very vain man, and also a very ruthless one. There's always been that in me – a certain ruthlessness – but now I know why, and I'm fulfilled. For, of course, every artist has to be ruthless, otherwise his work will be nothing at all.'

'Yes,' she said a little faintly, 'I understand.'

Already the force of his emotion was overwhelming her, rushing her into a torrent of feeling, of queer upsetting sensations and pictures which left her breathless and very unlike herself. She'd come to see him with the express purpose of guidance, of pointing out certain necessary adjustments in his way of living, and with the intention also of presenting him with the surprise cheque which lay in her bag. It was a large cheque – £500. She had pictured his surprise and delight last night when she made it out – visualised his gratitude, and the sentimental little scene which would follow. Yet, here he was, instead, making *her* feel the child, the patronised. It was all topsy-turvy.

She struggled to assert herself. 'Laurence,' she said.

'Yes, Miss Spring?'

'You're very clever,' she pointed out. 'I am so glad you realise it. You're going to be a great artist.'

He smiled. 'Thank you.'

'And, therefore,' she resumed, 'you must be more than ever careful of your – shall we say – reputation.'

His eyebrows lifted in a whimsical Pannish gesture of surprise.

'Reputation?' he echoed, quizzically.

'My dear boy,' she stretched out her hand to him, 'don't think I want to interfere – who am *I* to do that? But, after all, it's natural I should be anxious over your well being. Even at this moment –' and she glanced towards her bag, meaningfully ' – there is something in here which I don't imagine you will sneeze at. At least, I hope not.'

He appeared mystified. 'Do go on, Miss Spring, about my reputation. You were saying?'

'It's Mrs Lane I was alluding to,' she resumed recklessly.

'Ah! I see.'

'I know, of course, there's nothing serious in it. I wouldn't for a moment suspect anything like that because I know you. But other people – they have not the same understanding, and tongues wag. You see, Laurence? You see what I mean?'

He nodded.

'Now,' she resumed 'do forgive me, but don't you think it would be better at least to curtail the visits of this young woman?'

He faced her with no mark of emotion in his face whatsoever, his eyes inscrutable and cold. Yet after a moment or two his lips smiled. 'You think so?'

'I do indeed.'

He shrugged. 'All right. A thing like that is quite unimportant really.'

The casual manner of his speech shook her slightly. Surely there was something just a little inhuman about him? He was more like a fawn, a satyr, than a human being.

Faintly flurried she started to fiddle with her bag, and presently she drew the cheque from it.

'And this,' she said nervously, 'is a little present to tide you over, I hope, your difficult period.'

She handed it to him, flustered and expectant while he took it, frowning slightly. Then his face cleared, and in his smile she had her reward.

'Why, Miss Spring! Miss Spring!'

'Yes. Well? I thought you might find a use for it.'

'Use for it!' he exclaimed. 'My God! Do you realise what this will do for me? It will mean the possibility of a one-man show, and capital for materials and expenses. It will mean that I shall be free of penury for a time and able to go ahead. It's darned good of you. I don't know what to say.'

'I don't want you to say anything at all,' she answered. 'The knowledge that I can be of help to you is the only thing that matters. You see,' she added pathetically, 'I always knew, in an odd way, that we were linked in some fashion, that there was some secret psychic union of our minds. I think I spoke to you of it before. Of course, it doesn't do to talk of these things lightly, but I felt from the very beginning, that in some past life perhaps − and please don't laugh − we met before, and that I might have some important link with your destiny.'

She waited while the fluttering continued in her heart, jerking the lilac-coloured bodice spasmodically with each breath she took.

He stared as she stood there, with her face faintly flushed beneath her absurd hat. Her earrings were bobbing about below her frizz of hair, and her lower lip was trembling ridiculously and unbecomingly. There was no mistake about it, he thought, she looked a silly old frump, in her stupid finery, with the tears of emotion in her short-sighted eyes. To be with her for long would bore him to death. He'd resented her intensely when she appeared on the doorstep to interrupt his afternoon with Merlynne. If it hadn't been against his own interests he might have slammed the door in her face. But then, on the other hand, she'd been kind to him. He did not respect her for it; she was a foolish creature. Still, he owed her something. So, stifling his boredom, he moved towards her, and very deliberately planted a kiss on each cheek.

'Thank you,' he said. 'You're a good woman, Miss Spring.'

'Oh, I − I,' she laughed, blushed, and raised a shaking hand to her temple. 'Dear boy. I'm not good at all. It's a pleasure to me. A pleasure.'

Her being was alight when she left him half an hour later.

But when she had gone, Laurence laughed to himself. He remembered the occasion when Merlynne had called him a 'gigolo' those weeks before, and wondered what she'd say now. Well, no matter. He had the money, and hadn't asked for it. He'd have been a fool to refuse it. No sane man would. Besides, there were a lot of false scruples about such things. Miss Spring had more money than she needed, and his work was more important than any quibbling convention. He'd found his daemon now, and it was a daemon which possessed him, needing to be fed. He'd spoken truly when he'd told Miss Spring that everything, if necessary, should be sacrified to it. There was no time or energy for false sentiment in his life. Other interests, other people, even Merlynne herself, must, if necessary, be subjugated to what was now a single-hearted purpose. Time had not yet proved him to be great. But he felt now the seeds of greatness in him, a savage burning capacity to paint for the sake of painting, which in the end must prove itself. He had been frank about it, even to Merlynne, during the last weeks.

Only the other day, he'd said. 'I love you as much as I shall love any woman, Merlynne, and I need you. You understand? But if at any time it suits me best to do without you – if you interrupt me – I shall walk out of your life. I'm being honest with you. I can be cruel. The force of cruelty's even coming out in my work – it's *me*! – my fulfilment. Well?'

He'd stood looking down on her, and she'd watched for a moment the cold, detached yet desirous look on him, as though he were some pagan creature, calculating his prey. Then, almost against her will, she'd gone to him and the touch once more of his lips pressed hungrily upon her own had swept all doubt away, and she had surrendered to the delight and anguish of her unhappy love, unknowing of what the issue must eventually be, and quite uncaring. Something had died in her – integrity, belief – but his power over her was the force of something stronger than good or ill, than right or wrong. It had in it the pagan elements of the wind and the rain, and the strength of the sea breaking. It was a wild, lost, lonely thing, which swept morality and purpose into oblivion. Like that other Catherine, with Heathcliffe, she had become but an echo of himself. And the same cry might have come from her lips.

'I *am* Laurence. He *is* me.'

At first, she'd fought against it. But that time was past. She no longer wanted to, or tried to. Her life for good or bad, was linked to his as surely as the great rocks to the earth from which they sprang. There was no retreat for her. No turning back.

It was too late for that.

She lay beneath him, satin-smooth, while he took her on a wild delirium of passion that was both sweetness and pain. Pale flesh became one with the darker gleam of his own — her hair a soft halo of light through the shadows. There was no time and no tomorrow, no conscience or regret, nothing but the mounting ecstasy of fulfilment which had been inevitable from their first moment of meeting.

Following the climax a little sigh left her lips. She relaxed, and saw his eyes, brilliant slits of darkness, staring down on her. The soft touch of his hands was about her breasts, and her two white arms reached to his neck. Shudders of delight passed through her.

And so the night passed.

Outside a lone seagull called.

The rest was quietness except for their rhythmic breathing and the gentle murmur of passion appeased.

Chapter Seventeen

As Christmas approached, heralded by a period of rain and gale, Sam Murgatroyd was troubled by a nagging pain in his side and an intangible feeling of depression which had been with him on and off during the past months. The most recent attack was considerably worse than the preceding ones, so one day he went into Penzance to a doctor who had been recommended to him.

The doctor was kindly, inconclusive at first, with the misleading vague optimism so frequently a characteristic of the profession.

'Hm, hm!' he said, after making a thorough examination. 'And how long have you been suffering like this, Mr Murgatroyd?'

'Six months or so,' Sam told him. 'But not so badly, you know. At the first, it was just a touch of indigestion like. I took little notice of it. But this last attack was bad, doctor. I had to see someone.'

He spoke apologetically, as though in defence of his weakness.

'Why, of course. Of course. Hm.'

'Is it much?' asked Sam, after a pause, when the doctor still withheld his verdict. 'Is anything wrong – seriously?'

The doctor professed uncertainty, raised his brows and said presently, 'Well, now, it's not easy to say from a first examination. I think it's a pity that you did not come before, Mr Murgatroyd. That's the worst of you businessmen. You're so anxious to dispel a pain as though it were something to be ashamed of, without doing anything about it.'

'But,' Sam said, with a faint intangible fear at the back of his mind, 'so many people have indigestion, doctor, I thought it would pass.'

'Yes, I know. But these things don't always pass without something being done about it. Pains need attention.'

'You mean – ?' The little man looked perplexed, uncertain, faintly shocked. 'D'you suspect anything then?' he asked abruptly. 'Go on – tell me, I'm man enough to hear.'

The doctor regarded him thoughtfully for a moment or two. He saw before him an innocent puzzled face, with nevertheless a certain character about it – something courageous, which he couldn't lie to.

'Well,' he said, 'since you want to know, the symptoms point to some obstruction.'

Beads of perspiration gathered on Sam's forehead. For a moment the room went dizzy while he fumbled for something to say. 'A growth, you mean?'

'It's possible. Mind you,' the doctor continued more cheerfully now that the worst was over, 'mind you I may be quite wrong; I'm not at all sure of it. It is impossible to say at first. But I think you should have a further examination. I could fix it up at the hospital here – or, if you preferred it, you could see someone in town. That's up to you.'

'I'll see Jefferies,' came the answer in a commonplace, rather lifeless voice. 'He's a good man. Harley Street. I now him well. He attended Tilda – my wife.'

'Oh, I see. Yes, he's *the* man, of course. You couldn't do better.'

The doctor waited, anxious now for the interview to end. It always depressed him having to suggest a possible death warrant to a patient. There was so little one could do or say to alleviate the shock. But after a pause Sam resumed, 'And if it *is* what you think it may be, doctor, would an operation help?'

'Well, now as I have said one cannot predict. Everything depends on what the trouble is, and what the X-rays reveal. There's always the chance, you know, that there's nothing much wrong at all. And my advice to you in the meantime is to look at it in that way – optimistically. For the present I shall make up some tablets for you, which I want you to take every three hours. That should prevent a further serious attack of pain. Meanwhile, shall I contact Jefferies for you?'

Sam shook his head. 'No,' he answered. 'I'll fix up with him myself.'

The result of this interview was a trip to town the following week, where in the luxury of the Harley Street surgery Sam Murgatroyd learned the truth. All the signs pointed to cancer. At first he could not believe it. The pain had been such a trifling thing in the beginning, a mere stab, a pin-prick, and it was over. Was it possible all the time its insidious roots had been spreading, attacking further the regions of his vital organs? That in the space of a few months only, it had gained a hold on him which in the specialist's opinion was inoperable?

'You mean then,' said Sam slowly, at the conclusion of the interview, 'that I'm − that I'm going to die?'

Jefferies attempted nonchalance, seeking by cheeriness of word and gesture to lift his patient from the despondency into which he'd been forced to fling him.

'If it comes to that,' he said, 'we all are. It's only a matter of time for all of us. I may go first, or you may. Nothing's certain. And, also, while there's life, you know, there's a good deal more hope than we sometimes think. All the time research is teaching us more. Any day now a cure may be found. You should bear this in mind; it is most important.'

'Yes, thank you. I will.'

It was raining when Sam left the surgery. An air of oppression hung over the quiet street − over the grim houses and impersonal windows which had witnessed the deaths of so many hopes − heard so many sentences passed − seen men come and go, as he was going, with doom in their hearts. Yet later, in Oxford Street, the world went on still. The cars hooted and women hurried by with their umbrellas in front of them, like shields in his face; the buses stopped at their accustomed places. The commonplace, everyday sights and sounds went on around him: motor-horns, the tramp of feet, a newsboy's whistle and occasional shrill laughter as a girl passed by on the arm of her boyfriend. Life that had a future − movement, initiative, thousands of people with thousands of days ahead. Yet to him it was meaningless, because he was to be cut off from it all.

He stumbled along until he saw a taxi approaching. He got into it, and gave the address of his hotel. Back there, in the comfort of his room, he realised how unimportant that comfort was, now that he was going to die. He did not want to die – why should he? It was all so meaningless; to work hard for a material success, and then, having achieved it, to go out like a candle slowly guttering because of little cells gone wrong inside which insisted upon growing. Perhaps if he'd continued with the work he'd started upon, he would not have come to this. Perhaps there was something wrong in it all – both morally and physically – in this striving for power and achievement which resulted only in death eventually, and a feeling of frustration and waste. Those men, his friends, who had stayed on in the mines, had possibly done a better job than his had been; they had worked with their hands and bodies, sweated their strength away in what was, after all, man's work. They had not stooped to propaganda or pretence. No slogans or slick phrases or sleek business acumen. They had worked side by side as men.

As he sat there by the electric fire, wave after wave of nostalgia swept through him. He remembered Barny Bud, who had been his friend; and Charles Strang, who had lost a leg in a fall. Memories of their choir returned – the singing as they returned from work. The wash-down in the old tub, followed by the fish and chips, and afterwards a game of darts in the 'White Horse'. He remembered farther back than that when, as a young boy, he had tramped home after school; the certain hot sweet smell of summer lanes, with the tall cow parsley dusty in the hedges and the drift of cowslip scent in the air. Sam, to whom life had been such a vital thing, who had thought in some way to impress the world by his presence and make it better, now had a year – six months maybe, or three – left to him. A few short months in which to round off his life in the best way he could. A dying man.

All of a sudden he thought of Susie-Jane, and wished she was with him. He would have liked her there beside him, because there was something about her so essentially courageous and real. He remembered the night of the shooting stars and her remark to him, which he had never forgotten.

'You've probably done more than you think. Probably it's the little things that count, Mr. Murgatroyd, you know – like talking to people, and cheering them up – the little, friendly, funny things.'

Yes, and perhaps it was. Perhaps she was right. He hoped so. He thought back, trying to remember any such incidents in his own life. There had been some. Though he had got on, he had tried not to do it ruthlessly. He had tried to keep at heart the welfare of his workpeople – endeavoured not to lose the common touch, although this had not been too easy, hedged in as his existence had been by the red-tape and conventions of a business life. Still, perhaps a few might have cause to be grateful to him. There was, for instance, poor John Beal who had diddled the firm's books a bit to his advantage and afterwards, conscience-stricken and neurotic, committed suicide. Sam had not given him away; on the contrary he had withheld any such knowledge, and seen that his wife and child did not want. Tilda had never known of this, but it was, he saw now, one of the few things perhaps which might count in his favour when the judgement day arrived – if there was any judgement.

He was not sure what he felt of religion. As a boy he had sung fervently in Sunday School, and later in the choir of the small Methodist Church attended by the family. But now all this seemed to count little in the face of what he'd just learned. Doctrines and dogma – what did they matter compared to the few essential simplicities of living? A man was born, and died; and in the end, it seemed, his claim to immortality lay chiefly in what he had done for others – the friendly smile, the helping hand at a difficult hour, the kindly thought, and the place he had earned in the hearts of those whom he'd known.

For some hours he sat there, silent and alone with his own thoughts, while the twilight deepened outside, and at length darkness came to the room relieved only by the dim glow of the fire. At seven-thirty he roused himself. He rose mechanically, switched on the light, washed, changed and combed his thinning hair. Except for a slight tenseness about the eyes and a faintly yellowish tinge of skin, his face in the mirror looked unchanged. Yet the reflection was that of a doomed man. In a few short months, unless a miracle occurred, he'd no longer have the power of action or thought. A funny idea, that. One accepted death as the common sequence to birth. But it was hard to believe in one's own. Hard to believe that the 'I', the personal ego, could ever 'not be'. But then one had no certainty of that. The mystics said otherwise. They might be right. Yet, whatever the answer, it was mysterious and unknowable; frightening to a man such as himself – practical, of no great intelligence or faith.

Presently, realising that despite everything, he must eat, he left the room and went down to dinner. He was sitting at a table by himself, and was glad of the solitude. On his own he could act normally, keep up the pretence of being like other men, cause no concern. Had there been others with him he would have found normal conversation difficult, felt his courage flag in the effort of his pretence.

Later, he read the paper in the lounge, striving to discipline his mind to everyday matters. But he was unendurably tired. Quite suddenly all energy went from him, and all he wanted was to sleep in forgetfulness of the day and what it had revealed to him. He went to bed early, and mercifully slept. The next morning he packed his bag and caught the Cornish Riviera Express. Back there in Cornwall things might fit into some sort of shape, appear easier. He was tired of the traffic and the bustle and the seething throngs of human beings, which collectively represented something in which he could never share again. The thought of Trencathra meant escape to him. All the way down in the train he was visualising the coast and the lonely shores. In the constant rhythm of sea and the strange wild call of the cormorants and gulls was something which was eternal and beyond the limited comprehension and span of man. He would stay there as long as his condition permitted. He would learn to face the future, or his lack of it, with equanimity if possible, and all the courage of which he was capable. He would not go down trembling or afraid. For after all, as Jefferies had said, all men, at some time, came to it.

Seen in such perspective, a little of the strain went from him, and when, that night, he reached Trencathra, save for a certain gravity and slight reserve which was accepted as natural tiredness, there was nothing about him superficially in any way different from the Sam Murgatroyd who had departed three days before. He divulged nothing of the specialist's verdict, but passed it off as a trifling affair. Later, perhaps, he might have to explain. For the moment he preferred that the household should be in ignorance. He would obviously not be able to remain there long, but until the time for going arrived, it was pleasanter for himself and all concerned that he should be regarded as a normal man.

Chapter Eighteen

Christmas came, and everyone remained at Trencathra except Richard, who spent it at Stark End with Deborah and Sir John.

The house looked pretty that year. Susie-Jane had spent many hours cutting and collecting holly, which she had placed generously about the rooms and corridors. Richard had seen that there was enough wood to burn, and Catherine, on her shopping expeditions, had purchased plenty of chestnuts which were roasted in the hall. There were besides tangerines, nuts, and all god things for the table; and every evening there came the sound of carol singing from outside. The age-old excitement of Christmas seemed to penetrate every nook and corner of the house with its air of well-being and hope. Nicholas was affable and sociable, and Dame Julia, stimulated by the festivity, amused and delighted everyone with her vivacity and charm. On Christmas Day everyone except Catherine and Ann went to the village church in the morning. Hugo drove Dame Julia, with Merlynne, Susie-Jane and Sam, in the large car. Nicholas walked with Miss Spring on one side and Miss Fothergill-Briggs on the other. It was a clear day, faintly frosty, and the bells pealed melodiously across the cliffs. The slight nip in the air brought a glow to the cheeks, and a sparkle to the eye.

Throughout the service Dame Julia sat very erect in her velvet cape. She wore a lace scarf about her head which accentuated her aged individual elegance. Interested looks were thrown in her direction from other pews but she appeared not to notice, sitting with her eyes fixed on the vicar, chin up, her head a little to one side. In the pale light from the window her profile had a waxen, carven look. In youth she must have been lovely; and in age there was something noble about her. Her thoughts that morning were hidden and to herself, but there was an enigmatic look in her eyes which suggested she knew more than the rest of them put together.

The vicar would have been surprised had he been able to see into her mind, for the main impression registered there was that he read very badly, and that the essence of true religion was not to be found in the orthodox service, although the singing was very nice. It was pleasant to be sitting there with the family, despite the aching of her shoulders. She was already looking forward to her lunch, and would enjoy the drive back in the sunshine, with the prospect of fowl or turkey ahead.

The rest of the day was passed quietly enough following the meal. In the afternoon the old lady went to rest, also Catherine who was tired. Ann and Olive went home to Cripples Rest, and Susie-Jane prepared the tea. Hugo retired to the library with a book, leaving Merlynne sitting in the hall. Miss Fothergill-Briggs decided to take Tito for an airing, and shortly before three o'clock could be seen striding along the cliffs in her mannish tweeds with no hat, the little dog trailing at her heels in his fancy coat.

Miss Spring struggled with the choice of either walking into St Taloc and back to see Laurence, or relaxing in her room. Eventually she chose the latter course, because she remembered that Laurence had said something about a party on Christmas Day. Nicholas took himself off to the lodge. This left only Sam at a loose end for something to do. In view of the weather and sunshine he decided to go for a walk. At first he had thought of asking Susie-Jane to go with him; but there she was working, so he set off on his own following the road across the moor in the direction of Cripples Rest and Penzance. He started off at a good steady pace, and after a mile or so was well in form, his muscles and heart working in perfect unison. Indeed, it seemed incongruous that there could be anything seriously wrong with him; and just for a moment he wondered if there was? If, after all, the whole thing was not a professional mistake, a blunder of opinion? The thought cheered him a little — such errors had been known to occur — but a stab of pain some minutes later brought the whole thing into perspective again. He paused to rest, waiting until the spasm had passed. Then he walked on.

A faint haze hung over the winter landscape, leaving a blueish soft bloom on the berries and trees. There was no breath of wind, the gulls circled and dipped lazily above the ploughed red fields with a few crows. Until now he had never been so acutely conscious of the beauty of nature, and it occurred to him that only in the face of death could man adequately appreciate what had been given to him. This was a queer thought, indicating that in some way to die could be a privilege. Was that, then, true? He remembered the old adage 'Whom the Gods love die young', and thought also of his own son who had gone out in his prime, with thousands of others, before life had been properly tasted. He had not seemed afraid on the last leave of his, and yet he must have known that in the job he was doing the odds against his surviving were heavy. But then, the boy had gone out in the full flood of action, he had not been doomed to die slowly, each day a little more, until at last the bed claimed him with the attention of nurses and the sick room. That was what was so horrible. That was the spectre confronting Sam Murgatroyd — the slow torture of knowing.

He walked on, trying to escape the depression, to accept this day as though it were like any other, philosophically and with calm. But this day was different; it was, to begin with, incredibly beautiful, and it was Christmas, the symbol of birth and new beginnings. For nearly two thousand years now this day had brought a message of hope to millions of people. He wondered if, somewhere perhaps, he might find some bit of it for himself. He did not believe in miracles. But he was human enough to long for a sign — some material indication that indeed it was so — that life was not in vain, and that from the dead ashes of material experience there could be resurrection and new beginnings.

Without realising it, he had walked further than he intended, and was on the summit of the hill facing Tor Crom before deciding to turn back. He sat down for a minute or two on one of the great slab rocks to rest, taking in at a glance the view all around him – on his right some miles away the Mount glistening like a jewel in the sea, and to the left the strip of coast opposite Godrevy, stretching eventually to St Taloc itself. Nearer at hand he observed the small things that were happening. A tiny wren fluttered from the brown undergrowth of bramble and bracken at his feet. Presently, from some yards away, a rabbit emerged, stopping for a second to listen, before hopping away towards the hedge. A hawk hovered high above the field below. The sun glistened on its wings for a moment before it dipped quickly and suddenly like a stone towards it prey. Nature – so beautiful and so ruthless. There was something sinister about its relentless pattern, unless one had also the inner faith.

Sam got up at this point of his conjecturing and proceeded down the hill again, only along the different path which led the opposite way back to Trencathra.

Long shadows filtered through the trees to the ground when he at length reached the road. At the corner, where he branched off into the secondary lane, he saw a small grubby child standing by the gate of an impoverished-looking cottage. Something dejected, a little uncertain, about his face and manner caused Sam to pause and say, 'Well, sonny, how are you?'

The child hung his head, and for a moment made no reply. Then, quite suddenly he looked up and smiled. Sam couldn't have said why, but a queer stab of emotion went through him – perhaps because it was Christmas, a period symbolising the innocence of youth. He put his hand into his pocket and drew out a half-crown.

'There,' he said, 'take that, sonny, and buy yourself some sweets.'

As the child's grubby fist closed over the coin, a woman came out of the cottage followed by a man, who was obviously attired in his Sunday best. But the woman looked harassed, tired.

'Come along, my 'andsome!' she said. 'I must get you washed.'

Then she noticed Sam.

'Good afternoon,' she said.

He returned the greeting. 'Nice day,' he said.

'Yes. It's all right for some.'

The child ran inside the cottage with the man, but the woman lingered behind for a moment and resumed confidentially. 'Sad case, that.'

'Sad?' asked Sam. 'The child?'

She nodded. 'Father killed on a tractor a month ago, and now his mother gone, poor thing, in child birth.' She shrugged her shoulders. 'I'm taking him for Christmas — she was a relation of my husband's — but after that he'll have to be got in an institution. I'd keep him, but I can't afford it. Five already.' She broke off, and continued, 'Still, they say these places are all right now. But it's not like a mother's care.'

'No,' he said. 'It can't be.'

'Well — these things happen, and there it is.'

She moved away, and presently Sam also started walking back. For an instant he had been prompted to say to the woman, 'Look here — if you'd like to keep the child, give him a good home, I can pay for it. I'll see that he's all right.' But on second thoughts he'd checked the impulse. The woman had been all right but calculating, — a little too business-like and thin-lipped to warrant the gesture. Besides, the little fellow would probably be just as happy, and better cared for, in one of the orphanages they had for such children nowadays. That is, if he got into one of the best. But would he? One could never tell. Accommodation was limited, and although no child nowadays was neglected by the State, some homes were still preferable to others.

This trend of thought inevitably led him to the scheme discussed earlier with Miss Fothergill-Briggs for founding a Home of his own. He might have done it, too, given a little more time and energy. He knew now that he would have liked to accomplish something of the kind, which would have been justification for his own life.

But — as the woman had said — these things happened, and there it was. Plans could be made only to be smashed inexorably by some freak trick of fate. That was the rum thing about life — its freakishness! The way it had of turning round on you just when you thought you were getting somewhere. He walked on, pondering again over the whole problem; and then, from a cottage nearby, he heard children singing. A moment before all had been still – no sound but the occasional crackling of the undergrowth and the hollow echo of his own footsteps going along the road. Then the soft clear rise and fall of youthful voices.

He paused and stood quite still, while it seemed to him that everything around, – the small wild creatures, the deep earth pulsing with new life to come, the trees, the very air – also waited, listening. And, as he stood there, something happened to him. He saw, in imagination, crowds of little children – happy children – swarming the hillsides and fields. They were laughing, they were running. They had the morning in their eyes – symbolic somehow of a fruitful future ahead. They were picking flowers and playing together. They were crowding round him with soft fresh faces pressed close against him. He could feel their warm eager hands about him; their chatter and laughter filled the air. It was a wonderful thing, this awareness, suddenly, of children. His heart seemd to swell in his breast to something immense, so that the hunger of love embraced all things. Compassion flowed from him; fear fell away and he was conscious of nothing but his desire and capacity to give. His life! How little in the face of this need to serve all life. Death, what was it when eternal life went on, reborn in the hearts and minds of the young? His 'self' dropped away. He became for that interim transfigured. Before he had been afraid, mortal. But for a fleeting interim he had shed his mortality – looked into the darkness, lost himself, and found light.

As the vision faded he slowly became himself once more – Sam Murgatroyd, a lonely sick man, standing in the lane listening to the carol singing of children.

He waited until they'd finished, and then walked down the hill. All was the same as it had been before – the light on the fields, with the gulls and crows flying above them, the berries red in the hedges, and the frosty salt tang of winter and sea in the air.

He was still going to die. The verdict was true, he had to accept it. But he was no longer afraid; neither was his life dead-sea fruit. Some months still remained to him; and in that time, with luck and initiative, he could do much. He could plan his money for the greatest good. He could plan, even at this late date, the home for children which would bear his name. It should be a happy home. Somehow he'd contrive to see the main essentials safe-guarded.

A blackbird rose swiftly from the undergrowth, flying some yards ahead of him to a small ash tree where it started to sing. Its note was akin to the triumph in Sam's heart as he quickened his pace. He'd wished for a miracle, and had been granted a vision which would help him face what lay ahead.

No human being could expect more.

Chapter Nineteen

In the early days of January Ann informed Catherine of her intention to leave Trencathra. Catherine was upset but not unduly surprised. She'd sensed for some time the girl's unhappiness, and had suspicions concerning the cause of it.

It was early morning with a cold damp wind blowing outside. The catkins swung on the lean black branches of the trees; yet the ditches were already starred with the first celandines gleaming like small golden suns in the wet grass. Soon it would be spring, soon the greyness would pass into a world of light and shade and new young life. Already the intangible sense of it was astir in the air; beneath the ground the earth was pulsing with a myriad leaping, pushing things which in a short time would rear their strong young shoots to the sunshine.

Ann being young sensed all this, and was frustrated, wanting to be away where she might have some chance of forgetting Richard, and able to find new interests.

She and Catherine were standing in the kitchen when she announced her decision. Catherine looked up, frowning slightly, and said, 'But why? I thought you were happy with us.'

'So I was,' came the answer. 'Please don't think for a moment I haven't appreciated working for you. I've enjoyed it – mostly. But a time comes for most people when a change is needed. I – I just can't stay here all my life. I'm sorry, Miss Catherine, but that's how it is.'

Catherine shrugged her shoulders helplessly.

'Well, if you've made up your mind I suppose we'll have to accept it. But I'm sorry. And I hope you won't regret it. What do you think of doing?'

'I don't know,' Ann admitted frankly. 'I shall probably stay at home for a bit and then go to some town.'

'A town?' exclaimed Catherine. 'But you've told me so many times how you detested cities. I can't understand you.'

'I don't like big places, but it'll be an experience. It isn't good to stop in one job.'

'And when do you want to leave us?' Catherine asked a trifle coldly.

'I'm not particular,' Ann said uncomfortably. 'I don't mind – so long as it's not too long to wait. But as soon as you can get someone to take my place.'

'And what about Olive? Will she want to go too?'

'I don't know. I hope not. Not yet anyway.'

'Well, all I can say is that I'm sorry. I wouldn't want to keep you here against your will. But we're going to mis you – especially me.'

The suggestion of tears glistened briefly in Ann's eyes. Catherine saw her swallow hard in an effort to control her emotion. So she has got some feelings, she thought, and was on the point of trying to clarify things more satisfactorily when Ann burst out impulsively, 'If I could explain better I would. It isn't easy for me. I'm not leaving for nothing. I just have to go.'

She spoke so urgently and with such sincerity that Catherine was moved, putting her hand affectionately for a moment on the girl's shoulder.

'Don't worry,' she said. 'You know your own affairs best. You must do what you choose. I only hope you won't be disappointed. If you are, remember any time you want to come back we'll be only too pleased to have you.'

Ann thanked her and turned away, striving to keep her expression hidden. Not wishing to embarrass her, Catherine pursued the matter no further at that point but left her to her own thoughts.

The following Saturday Ann and Olive took the bus to Cripples Rest, where Ann informed her parents of her decision to leave Trencathra. Her mother accepted the news with less surprise than might have been expected; but Nathaniel Chenoweth looked worried.

'But what's made you do this, girl?' he asked. 'Have you had a row or something?'

'Oh, no. Nothing like that at all. It's just that – just that I want to go. I'm tired of it.'

'But you always seemed so settled there,' Nathaniel objected. 'Now if it had been Olive I could have understood better. But to want to walk out of a good place for no apparent reason whatever, beats me.'

'It'll do Ann good to have a change,' Olive interrupted. 'She's been at Trencathra long enough, anyhow, and there isn't much to do except work.'

'You keep quiet,' her father said. 'I was speaking to Ann. And what do you think of doing?' he resumed. 'Anything? Or will you be at home for a bit?'

Ann nodded. 'I expect Mum could do with a bit of help. I'm sorry about the money – but it won't be for long. If I take a job in the town it will be better pay, and I'll be able to help you more.'

'Hush,' her mother said. 'You – to go talking about a town. I can't see you there, that I can't. You're a country girl, you always were. You'd be fair miserable in a large unknown place with nothing but streets and traffic round you. Don't tell me, I know.'

There was a slight quiver of Ann's lips, but her voice was firm. 'It's what I want. Experience. I'm not a child, Mum. I do know what I'm talking about.'

But Mrs Chenoweth was not satisfied.

Later, when Olive had gone out to see a friend and the children were in bed, she tackled her daughter. Nathaniel was upstairs washing.

'Look here, Ann,' she said, 'what's the matter? Tell me. As your mother I should know.'

Ann drew her lips together tightly, lifting her chin a fraction higher. 'There's nothing the matter; I'm quite all right. A bit tired, perhaps, that's all.'

'It's more than tiredness,' her mother said. 'You aren't all right. I've seen that look come into your face times before –

since you were so high – and it's certainly not happiness. Now then, what's fretting you? There's something. Come on. Out with it.'

Ann shook her head slowly. 'I – one day perhaps. I'll tell you one day. But not now. Not yet. Let's leave it, shall we? Please?'

Lizzie sighed. 'You were always a wilful proud one when your mind was set,' she remarked grudgingly. 'But I should've thought you could've trusted me with whatever it is. A man, is it?'

When her daughter didn't reply Lizzie continued, 'Ah, I thought so. And I can make a good guess at who. That Mr Richard, I reckon. Don't think I've not noticed the look on your face every time his name's been mentioned these last months. I've hoped I was wrong, because I didn't want you hurt. But he's done it, hasn't he? And I thought he was a gentleman. A *real* one. I wouldn't have expected it of him – to let you think – '

'He didn't,' Ann interrupted hotly. 'It's nothing to do with him, he's said nothing; and done nothing. And he is a gentleman. That's just it. Don't you see?' Pride, defiance, and the anguish of love flamed in her clear eyes. 'We don't mix, his class and mine. Not as equals. I've always known that. But somehow – ' She broke off helplessly.

'I know – somehow your feelings got mixed up with commonsense and brought you to this state. But there are other men in the world, love – respectable comfortably-off men like John Feathers, country-born and bred, who'd give their eyes to have a girl like you as a wife. Another thing, don't you get thinking the Chenoweth's count as nobodies. Poor we may be, but in the past we were high up in the district. You just remember that, and think of that slab in the Church bearing your ancestor's name. You father's not one for bragging about family – there's no sense in it, as things are. But facts remain. Servant you may be now, but – '

'Oh, Mum, don't go on. Just leave it, will you? I've told you, I'm going away. Whilst Richard was free I could stand it. But not any more, now he's for marrying that Deborah Cavin. It's all settled. And she's rotten, you know. Rotten to the core. Loose and wild. She'll destroy him.'

'That's no way to talk,' Lizzie said sharply. 'She could change when they're married. Let's hope so. And it's not for you to sit in judgement. You should know better.'

'Why?' Ann demanded bluntly. 'I'm only speaking the truth.'

Lizzie sighed heavily. 'Yes. Well — there's nothing you can do about it. So mebbe it's all for the best you're leaving.'

'I know it is.'

'All the same, I never thought to see a girl of mine running away.'

A strange half smile tilted Ann's lips, though her eyes were misted. 'If I could sprout wings I'd fly,' she said, with a catch in her voice.

Lizzie had a sudden impulse to take her daughter in her arms and make an effort to comfort her. But the girl's aloof manner, which was, she'd guessed, merely the enforced icy armour to disguise pain, forbade her.

And so the unhappy interim ended.

A little later Olive returned and the two girls had supper — cheese and pickles, and mugs of cocoa. Shortly afterwards they said goodbye to their parents, and commenced the four mile walk back to Trencathra. They took the high moorland road across country, and were soon going at a quick pace between the stony hills on one side, and on the other the small rough fields bordered by grey stone walls and alternating hedges of bramble and thorn. It was moonlight; the landscape stretched pale and mysterious before them, patterned with long dark shadows flickering in the faint wind, reaching and leaping as though creatures of the night itself. It was not difficult to believe in spriggans and ghosts. Ann remembered a tale that she had been told in childhood by her grandmother about a lovesick girl who'd sold her soul to the 'little people' for forgetfulness. After that she'd never grown old, but had wandered about the world from place to place, a pale beautiful shape unable to laugh or smile or to love humankind. It was said that all who looked on her had been afraid, and rushed away. Then there was the story of the dark Elvin King who had stolen a mortal maid for a night, and when the morning came a hundred years had passed, leaving her as an old, old creature on a wild hillside, with her family gone and none to care for her. These were only legends but Ann had half believed in them, and as she walked along the impression that she and Olive were not alone, but surrounded by fey wild things, stirred her imagination until she was conscious of every slight sound and movement around her. When a bird rose from the undergrowth, she started slightly. The dancing pattern of light and shade kept her ever on the alert and uneasy.

So at first, as two riders appeared over the ridge of Starcroft Hill, she imagined her eyes had deceived her. But when they dismounted near a windblown tree and tethered their horses, she knew the dark forms were real; for a second or two the man and girl were silhouetted starkly against the greenish sky. Ann tensed. She stood quite still against a granite slab, one hand gripping Olive's.

'What's the matter?' she asked. 'Whatever — ?' her gaze followed Ann's, and a note of conspiratorial understanding left her throat. 'Ooh! now I see. It's them, isn't it? The Cavin girl and Stokes. What do you think — ?' She gave a little giggle as the two forms drew close, and the man bent forward, drawing the girl's slim figure so they merged and became one — a passionate picture of abandon and desire holding an emotional hunger as lost and wild as the sweep of lonely moor under the rising wind. A sudden drift of mist obscured what followed. When it had cleared the interim was over. The girl had turned and was swinging herself into the saddle. The impression even from that distance was that she had rushed away in anger — that there had been some difference between the couple, ending in a quarrel. When, without looking back, the girl cantered off breaking into a speedy gallop, the man did not attempt to follow her, but stood watching her for a moment, after which at a leisurely pace he took his own mount, and was presently moving off in the opposite direction.

Deborah cut along the moor quite near the two girls; and from the shadows, unobserved, they caught for a second a fleeting impression of her strained pale face, from which her eyes looked wildly bright. She rode as though all the forces of the night were after her, her hair broken free in the wind, streaming silver-pale in the moonlight. Her figure had a demoniacal energy about it which seemed to symbolise the forces of nature itself. Her posture, her defiance, her speed, belonged more to some nymph of the elements than to a creature of flesh and blood. From coldness and tension Ann shivered.

'What's it all about?' asked Olive. 'I mean – '
'You saw,' Ann said, forcing herself to move.
'It was that Stokes man, wasn't it?'
'Who else?' said Ann.
'Well – it's a queer thing; and her going to marry Mr Richard.'

Ann didn't reply, but quickened her pace. She swung along easily, being an athletic, slender girl. Olive tripped along beside her, running a few steps now and again to keep up with her. Once she enquired, 'What do you think it's all about? Why were they out together like that?'

'Ah!' Ann expressed contempt. 'Use your brain, Olive.'
'Well, I think Mr Richard's soft to be taken in like that,' Olive said. Then as an afterthought she added, 'Will you say anything, Ann?'
'Me? What good would that do? Besides, it's not my business.'
'No. But you like him. I should've thought – '
'You know nothing whatever about it,' Ann said tersely. 'And you keep your mouth shut, Olive, please. If it's got to be, it's got to be. But maybe – '

Her voice, with her thoughts, trailed off vaguely into nothing. Olive glanced at her sister curiously. But there was little in her expression to indicate what she was thinking. Her mouth was set, and her eyes had a faraway look in them, lost and cold, different indeed from the brilliant, wild glance of Deborah Cavin as she rode by. Ah, but she was beautiful, Olive thought. Wicked she might be – but you couldn't somehow help getting excited by her. She could imagine any man falling in love with Deborah. A pity it was, though, that she had to come and spoil poor Ann's life. Yes, poor Ann.

Olive sang a little as they went down the hill, a strange tune for such an eerie night, a tune they used to sing at school:

> As I was going to Strawberry Fair,
> I met a maid with golden hair,
> Singing, singing, buttercups and daisies –

This made her feel better, more ordinary. It had really been a spooky walk, with Ann so solemn, the shadows dark, and those two in the moonlight. She would be glad now when she was back at Trencathra and in bed.

Quite soon they reached the main road, and crossed it again where it met the lane leading to the house. The wind had strengthened, and was blowing in cold gusts when at last they got there. The back door had been left open for them with the lamp burning in the passage. But it was later than Ann had thought. Looking at the clock she saw that it was past ten.

'We're late,' she said to her sister. 'Hurry up, Olive, I'll go and tell Miss Catherine we're in.'

She hurried into the hall, and Olive, still singing a little, went up the stairs. She wished she had some chocolates and a nice book to read. It would be nice to read a proper love tale – one with lots of adventures in it, that ended properly. Something about Ann discomfited her slightly. She never said much, but you had a feeling all the time that a lot of things were going on inside her. Olive wondered what she was going to do about the meeting between Deborah and Barry Stokes. Nothing, she had said. But you never could tell. Somehow she felt the whole thing was not ended yet, and that more eventually would come of it. Well, they would see. She, Olive Chenoweth, was not going to worry about it any more. None of them was worth it. It was silly to fret over other people's affairs. With which piece of sound philosophy she undressed and got into bed.

Chapter Twenty

When Deborah Cavin had passed the spot where Ann and Olive were standing she cut abruptly to the right, in the direction of the path leading across the moor to Port Kerryn Cove on the opposite coast. She rode recklessly because she was unhappy and because wild action of some kind was the only outlet for her feelings. Not only her pride but her heart was outraged. Barry Stokes had just said goodbye to her. Against her wishes he had said it, his cruel, loved face merciless and hard in the moonlight. And she had sneered at him; she had said, 'Of course it's for the best. I always knew you weren't much good, anyway, Barry. And I'm going to marry Richard.'

'I wish you well of him.'

'I'm sure you do. So you should. He's at least decent, with a sense of responsibility.'

'Look here, Deborah, there's no need to go off the deep end. You knew very well this would have to end sometime. You've had your fun, and I've been damned grateful. But I was open with you, I told you I didn't intend a divorce.'

'Oh, yes! Thanks. You've been marvellously honest and straight-forward. A hell of a fine fellow.' She had flung up her head and laughed.

God! he had thought. What spirit she had. If circumstances had been different and he'd been free, a younger man ...

'Don't fret over me!' she had said, jumping to her horse. 'I can assure you *I* shan't. Bye-bye, Barry – good hunting.'

And she'd plunged into a gallop, almost before he'd realised she was away. He had not known that the pain in her throat was choking her; that though her eyes were dry, anger and bitterness had frozen the tears so that they had crystallized there, blinding her.

For some time she continued in a straight line, lashing her horse at intervals to greater speed. Something was unleashed in her now which she could not control. As a child this same emotion had displayed itself in an abandon of temper for which the only efficient treatment had been to allow it to run its course, to die down through sheer exhaustion. But she was adult now — a young woman of excessive vitality, and excessive feelings. Though she had defied Stokes with the whip of her contempt, her heart clamoured for him. If he had come speeding after her and ridden with her by force into oblivion, she would have welcomed it. She hated him, but she loved him. Not as she loved Richard, with affection, but with the whole force of her wild and reckless heritage. As she rode along she imagined, darkly, that he was with her. His smiling, lascivious face was in every corner of her mind and heart, in the swirling clouds also, which billowed above the dark swaying furze and rushes, and in the stars which seemed tossed now in the wind.

'On, Sheba,' she shouted, kicking her mount with fury. 'Get on with you — on — on —'

Her wild shouting turned to laughter. Before the cove was reached, her hat blew off and was whirled away. She didn't stop, but rode straight ahead in her course. At one point the moon was temporarily extinguished behind a cloud, thrusting the whole landscape into blackness. When it appeared again the edge of the cliff rose dark against the water which was lit to an angry splendour in the eerie light. Its fierce challenge startled her. With her pulses hammering, her lips and cheeks stinging from exertion and the cold air, she visualised one monstrous leap into the silver glittering sea.

Through her fevered imagination she pictured herself defying death and hell itself in one extravagant gesture which would take from her this excessive burden of living, and on Barry place the sting of remorse. Yes, he should suffer! Why not? No one cared about her suffering. No-one ever had cared — not even as a child when she had rolled on the floor, gnashing her teeth because of the dark violent thing inside of her. They had pitied her, and later when it was over petted her. But she had despised them always – even her father who had given in to her over everything. That was it. He had been weak, despite the bluff bulk and success, unable to control either his will or herself. No-one had been able to control her, ever, not when she was like this. It was a terrible strength she had – a mad, hungry kind of joy and devastation that went beyond all reason or restraint. Her mother had had it also. She remembered her mother only dimly, but she, Deborah, was probably the only person in the world who could properly understand her. They were alike. They had always been alike, but in a way her father had never suspected, because his blood was different, and because it took a Trevane to understand the bad, mad blood of another Trevane.

Yes – mad! She had always known somewhere that there was a streak of madness in her. From very young she had suspected that she was different; later, when she had grown older, she had tried to forget it. But couldn't quite. A day came, or a night like this, when the dark thing rose in all its force and beauty, shattering sanity and the puny restraints of ordinary behaviour. Why should she bother to be ordinary, anyway? Why should she try? Why not embrace the devil that was in her, and in so doing appease the lingering anguished memory of Barry's kisses on her lips – his hands at her breast.

Fools, she thought of society in general. Fools not to have known it was like that with us! But soon they will know.

She laughed to herself again, as the thought took possession of her, but her laughter was disintegrated, thin, rather childish laughter, which rose shrilly as she headed her horse to the cliff.

'On, Sheba. On, Sheba!'

Her teeth and eyes were straining in her face, her hair now a flying silver cloak about her shoulders. Before her the water stretched, iridescent and glittering, its breakers white with spume in the light. She flung back her head, and for a moment as she rode was silhouetted there, straight as a larch, lovely as the goddess Diana, before a cry left her lips, a scream that penetrated the night shrilly, disturbing the gulls whirling in a squawking cloud around her. As horse and rider leaped into the darkness, the thin high screaming of the birds persisted, until at last quietness came again leaving only the mournful sighing of the wind round the cliffs, and from the shore the rise and fall of the waves breaking on the rocks.

Chapter Twenty-One

Letter from Julia to Chetwyn Shane

Trencathra
St Taloc
Cornwall
February

My dear Nephew,

    Since writing to you last many things have been happening here, and I must say I am getting a little tired of Cornwall. It is all so intense and restless. In the first place there has been a tragedy here. That lovely girl, Deborah Cavin, whom Richard was engaged to, was killed riding one night – her horse went over the cliff near Port Kerryn. It was all very terrible. There was an inquest, and a verdict of accidental death brought in. But other things were involved; it appears there was another man – Olive Chenoweth, one of the maids here, saw them together that same night, and like most young things she started talking. Ann, her sister, was quiet about the matter, but this did not prevent her having to give evidence at the inquest. It was all most upsetting. However, though, I believe the question of suicide was hinted at, she was given the benefit of the doubt. Poor Richard has taken it very badly. He is working hard, but seldom speaks. It is a tragic business, and Sir John is almost demented, but if what rumour says is true, the marriage would never have been a success. Her mother and grandfather were both unbalanced, and the taint, I believe, goes back further, though the Trevanes have always denied it.

And so you see, a gloom has fallen on the household. But that is not all. There is something wrong with my little Yorkshireman. He went up to Harley Street about Christmastime, and is under a Penzance man whilst he is down here. He is looking much thinner, and suffers pain, I know, sometimes. Yet he has a marvellous spirit, and refuses to discuss his malady. All his thoughts seem concentrated on the founding of an orphanage home for children. He has all manner of men and women to see him about it – chiefly from Town; and though I by no means agree on many points with Miss Fothergill-Briggs, she is turning up trumps in this matter and giving him all the practical help she can.

My opinion of the woman is changing. Her ideas are less masterful and eccentric, and she is no longer trying to inflict them upon Sam. Do you know, Chetwyn, I do really believe that the root of her aggressiveness and eccentricity is nothing more than a deep loneliness. Have you ever stopped to consider the millions of lonely people there must be in the world? It is sad when you think of it – it makes me long to create some kind of bureau dealing with the problems of loneliness and the furthering of human relationships. But of course the business is more subtle than that. To introduce a number of people to each other does not mean that mutual sympathy will arise there. Sympathy can only be instinctive and spontaneous, or it defeats its end.

I wish I had something really cheerful to tell you. Susie-Jane is the one bright spot. She is doing her best for Hugo these days, and believe me he needs it. For if any marriage is heading for the rocks it's his and Merlynne's. I've talked to them both on several occasions, but I don't really think I got very far, and have come to the conclusion that it is better now to let it follow its own course. I don't agree with taking marriage lightly – a lot of these new-fangled divorces are quite unnecessary. But if two people have tried hard and simply can't get on, then I think it's better to end it. What will happen in this case I can't say. But it certainly won't go on as it is. Both would be nervous wrecks.

Nicholas, I am glad to say – and this really *is* cheering – has had a complimentary letter from his publishers concerning his last book. It is more alive apparently than any of recent years, and they are expecting it to have good reviews, and consequently high sales. I'm glad for him, and from a monetary point of view it is a good thing. Catherine has shouldered a good deal here. The others all help, of course, but the brunt of it falls on her, nevertheless, and if the guest house business could be dropped, I should feel happier for her. Still, although I complain, although Nicholas has likened Trencathra to a lunatic asylum during the past six months, the fact remains, Chetwyn, that living with so many completely different people has, even at my age, enlarged and enriched somehow my capacity for experience. I have learned, for instance, to have quite a friendly feeling for Miss Fothergill-Briggs. Miss Spring who in the beginning irritated and amused me to a somewhat cynical contempt, now rouses in me a queer kind of sympathy. I can't explain it. It is just that, seeing day by day her pathetic little efforts to impress people – her sentimental devotion to the long haired young man in St Taloc – I have become more aware gradually of the tentative, half-frightened child in her which lurks deep down beneath her stupid exterior. What is her strange religion and delving into past lives, after all, but a seeking for self-justification and a yearning for company? Aren't we all searchers at heart? As Shakespeare said:

> These cloud-capp'd towers, the gorgeous palaces,
> The solemn temples, the great globe itself,
> Yea, all which it inherits, shall dissolve,
> And, like this unsubstantial pageant faded,
> Leave not a rack behind. We are such stuff
> As dreams are made on, and our little life
> Is rounded with a sleep.

Poor Miss Spring, with her dreams and visions. He knew it all, Will Shakespeare. As I write to you, Chetwyn, I would give a great deal – the rest of my old days – to have one evening more watching my father play Prospero or Lear. Are you contemplating a Shakespeare season in the future? These modern plays are stimulating, and may have their literary merit, but the test of acting is one's capacity to play Shakespeare well.

By now, I suspect, you will be getting tired of all this,

and wishing me away. And so, for the moment, au revoir. I shall not, I think, be here much longer. Any day now you may see me in my accustomed box, with Marianne. I am looking forward to that. My heart and mind and brain, dear boy, are sick for the sight of the footlights, and the glimpse of a Shane walking across the stage.

Till then − your affectionate aunt,

Julia Gort

Chapter Twenty-Two

February passed into March, and the crops showed green in the fields. The dark hedges frothed at intervals with the first frail white cherry blossom, and the snowy splendour of blackthorn. Lambs played in the fields, and the purplish pink of sea-thrift showed on the headlands. Keeping to her decision, Ann left Trencathra at the beginning of the month. Richard had shown no sign of wanting her to remain; on the contrary he appeared moody and abstracted, anxious only to get on with his work and to forget, it appeared, human beings. If she could have helped him she would have stayed. But any gestures of friendliness on her part had, since Deborah's death, appeared unacceptable to him. And so it was with a heavy heart and a sense of finality that she went one Saturday when the wind was cold and clear and pale spring sun spilled its radiance over the fields and ditches and waking hedges. Never had the blackbird sung so poignantly, and never had the heart of Ann felt such sadness as the old gate swung behind her, closing for good, it seemed, on her brief, unhappy love. Richard, for some reason of his own, had not offered to take her but had arranged to run over with her cases the following day. She didn't mind. The constraint between them did not make his company easier to bear, and she was afraid of saying something which would make him despise or dislike her.

She wondered, as she'd wondered so much of late, whether he blamed her for having spoken at the inquest. But he must have been aware that she'd been subpoenaed, that she would never, otherwise, have divulged Deborah's meeting with

Stokes. What else could she have done on oath but speak the truth? If Olive had kept silent, of course, the necessity would not have arisen. But it was not in the girl's character to do that. Besides, surely, eventually, the truth must be best. Richard might dislike her now – but later perhaps, though she herself might never know it, he would think more kindly of her, and see the whole matter in better perspective.

Catherine didn't know what to think of her going. She knew now that Ann was in love with Richard. It was all painfully obvious to her. And while socially the possibility of a permanent relationship between the two might have presented problems, there was a great deal to be admired in Ann and she did fit into the atmosphere of Trencathra. The house would not be the same without her. Even Miss Fothergill-Briggs was visibly depressed by her going.

'It was a pity she couldn't get on with Lotte Eberhert,' she said to Merlynne one day, 'but I must say, I'll miss her.'

'Well, it can't be helped,' Merlynne said absently. 'People come and go. No one can be static.'

'Aye,' said Sam. 'That's right. You never spoke a truer word. We have to go where life takes us. No one can stand still, it's not possible.'

Looking at him, Miss Fothergill-Briggs thought with pity that he was standing still rather less than other people. Indeed, the change in him from day to day was alarming. Each week he appeared to lose more weight, and his skin to become yellower and more dry. The plump rotundity of his cheeks had sagged into a haggard pouchiness. His eyes were heavy, and yellowish also.

'How are you feeling these days?' she asked one morning, after typing a few letters for him concerning the future orphanage on her own small portable machine.

He looked up, a faint quizzical smile on his lips. 'Not so bad,' he said, and sighed. 'Not so bad – considering.'

'Are you still under the doctor?'

He nodded.

'He is helping you, I hope?'

'As much as anyone can,' Sam replied.

'Would it not be advisable, Mr Murgatroyd, to see the specialist again?' Miss Fothergill-Briggs enquired as casually as she could, with a pretence of adjusting the ribbon.

'Why? What makes you say that?' He looked up sharply.

'Oh, nothing. I – nothing really,' she said. 'But – you are losing weight. Possibly you need a strong tonic, or a course of treatment.'

Sam was silent, looking out through the window across the fields to the headland above which a few white clouds floated like silver boats sailing into the face of the sun.

She waited with a helpless sense of anxiety. There was, she knew, some reason for that pause of his which was more serious, more tragic than she had anticipated. At last he spoke.

'No treatment can help me,' he said.

'Mr Murgatroyd! Why not?'

'Just that,' he said. 'I'm beyond it.'

'Beyond it – what do you mean?'

He smiled again wistfully. 'I'm a dying man, Miss Fothergill-Briggs,' he stated simply.

'Dying?' She gasped the word, letting her hand instinctively go to her heart.

'Aye.'

'Oh, Mr Murgatroyd, are you sure?'

'Quite. I've known for some time,' he said. 'Ever since my visit to Jefferies in December.'

'And you never said anything?'

'Why should I. I don't want to talk about it. I don't want to be pitied; it doesn't help. I'm telling you now because I know you can keep it to yourself, and because it explains my hurry to get this job finished.'

She was shaking slightly, with emotion and distress.

'But – and you've been so brave about it,' she said. 'Keeping it all to yourself, and planning things as you have. Oh, Mr Murgatroyd, I'm sorry. *Sorry.*'

'So am I,' he said. 'It's no use pretending. Life's sweet. I don't want to go – but in a rum way I've got kind of resigned to it. Thinking of my son, I guess, and getting myself into proportion. After all, I've lived almost my three-score and ten. That's not so bad, you know. It's not like being cut off before you've ever had time to see or know anything. Although I must admit, I'd have liked to see another summer with its blossom and everything. Aye! I'd have liked to see another summer.'

'Perhaps you may do that.'

'Oh, no,' he said quite definitely. 'I shan't even be here much longer. Another month will see me away.'

'Do you mean you're leaving?'

He nodded. 'It's all fixed up. A hospital in Penzance. That's why I have to be so quick about all this home business – my kind of complaint doesn't lag. Once it's started it goes ahead at some pace.'

'Oh!' She fumbled with her handkerchief, agitated, distressed.

'Don't upset yourself,' he said in a kindly way. 'I'm not any more. We all have to go sometime. And taken from the long view it isn't our little personalities that count, not in the end, Miss Briggs. It's the little good we may have done – the little difference we may have made in the pattern around us towards bettering human society. Aye, that's it! Values. Queer thing, isn't it, how we clutter ourselves up with conventions and codes and all manner of pretences, yet it's only when a man like me realises he's going to die that he sets the value of himself into perspective.'

'Perspective?' she echoed.

He nodded. 'Bless you, the things I thought counted in life for forty years aren't really that important at all. It's been pleasant to get on – it's been pleasant, too, to be able to be generous, and give a present or two when the mood was on me. I've not been mean, Miss Briggs. But all the time I had a hankering for something else. All the time I've been conscious of my lack – education, and all that sort of thing. Tilda used to rub it in, too, and it made me look up to culture almost as though it was God.'

After a pause he continued, 'There – that's the truth. And now I see what an old fool I've been.'

'Oh, no.'

'Oh, yes, Miss Briggs. A real old fool, to think those things were really important. What's culture matter unless it teaches you to live right? What's talk unless it gets you somewhere?

And what's the use of all the cleverness in the world unless it somehow touches the hearts of people?'

'No,' said Miss Fothergill-Briggs, in a whisper.

'That's what dying is teaching me,' Sam said, 'to know myself, and where I stand. I'm glad I've been given grace enough to put things in order before I go. I'm glad, too, to have been able to talk to you like this. You seemed a funny woman to me at first, with your strict vegetarianism and all that. But now I see you were working to something real. It was your heart and love for animals that let you appear ridiculous to other folk. And you didn't mind. Funny, isn't it, how wrong we get about each other? It's generally so much easier to scoff than understand. It's a short cut. A kind of laziness.'

'I don't think you've done much scoffing,' Miss Fothergill-Briggs said gently.

'Well, I've tried not to,' Sam said. 'Maybe that's not one of my worse faults. But I have plenty.'

'We all have.'

For the space of some minutes neither spoke. Then in a low voice Miss Fothergill-Briggs resumed, 'I appreciate it – your talking to me like this. I shan't break your confidence. And I must say, although it sounds rather odd, that it's helped me too, quite a lot.' She stopped, flushed nervously, her eyes bright beneath her Alexandra fringe.

Sam, seeing how moved she was, replied, 'Nay. But that's your kindness, Miss Briggs. I've done nothing but talk about myself. You must forgive me.'

'No. You've done much more than that. You've shown me something – something that most of us spend our lives looking for.'

Sam could not speak, but he patted her hand, remembering his Christmas walk and the vision of the children. A sense of compassion swept over him, keeping him silent.

A few minutes later she left him. But at the door he took her hand, and wrung it hard. It was strange – the sensation of life in that dry palm. Dying he might be. But the spirit lived and was strong.

April came, with warm quiet days heavy with the nostalgic scent of lilac and may. The gorse was lit to flame on the moors, and great clumps of it burned like fire along the cliffs, brilliant against the sea and blue sky.

In St Taloc, Laurence was painting hard, getting work in hand for an exhibition which Miss Spring wished him to hold in Cornwall, but for which he had other ideas. She had made over to him another generous gift; and it really appeared now as though some kind of recognition must come to him. In the Winter Show of the local society he had sold two pictures, and had, as well, good reviews from the press. Miss Spring should have been happy. He was justifying himself, and doing credit to her interest in him. Yet she felt all the time — especially recently — as though his work in some powerful yet intangible manner was drawing him away from her. She had no material evidence of this, he was polite and complimentary to her as he had ever been — perhaps, on the whole, more so. But even her faith and admiration was disturbed on occasion by a certain look in his eyes — callousness, was it? Contempt? — which belied the flattery of his speech. The suggestion was only fleeting; and afterwards she told herself that she was being silly, she had been mistaken and suspicious, her nerves were awry. Still, the feeling did not make for peace of mind. It was not that she was possessive with him, she argued with herself, she didn't want him always to be thinking of her and admiring her — or even to have half the affection for her that she had for him. Still, she had given him a great deal — not only money, but of herself. It was hurtful to imagine he could ever be casual about her, or consciously use her.

Then again, though he had said that Merlynne's visits were unessential to him, Miss Spring had an uncomfortable conviction that the girl still went there. Laurence could not be entirely to blame of course — Merlynne was quite capable of intruding where she was not wanted — *if* she was not! But of that Miss Spring was not sure. She recollected the early days of Trencathra when he'd hardly kept his eyes off her, and certain incidents since, which had been significant to anyone shrewd enough to see.

The climax came one evening when she took it into her head to make an impromptu call. She had been in the previous day, Wednesday, and had told him she would not be in St Taloc again until Saturday. But on the spur of the moment she'd caught the five o'clock bus in order to do a little shopping — she needed some blue sewing silk — and with the intention of dropping in on Laurence for a little chat perhaps, and a late cup of tea.

The twilight was deepening as she made her way up the narrow cobbled street, lurking in the doorways, and under archways and in the maze of corners and alleys, in deep blue shadow shapes from which a cat emerged from time to time, or the dark form of a fisherman strolling comfortably in the direction of the ships.

It was nearly six when she got there. She had intended to be earlier. As it was she would only have a quarter of an hour or so, for she must catch the six-thirty bus back in order to be in time for dinner. So, in her hurry, and without thinking, she did not knock at the door as she generally did, but opened it softly and quickly, and called, 'Hullo — is anyone there?'

There was a confused stirring in the semi-gloom, and with shaken nerves and a sick sudden feeling of shock, Miss Spring saw Merlynne disengage herself from Laurence's arms, spring to her feet quickly, shake her skirt down to cover an unseemly expanse of pale thigh, and adjust the collar of her blouse which had been far too revealing for modesty.

Then Merlynne gasped, 'You again, Miss Spring! We seem to have a habit of meeting here.'

Miss Spring could find no words for the occasion; and after a moment, Laurence, smoothing his hair from his brow, came towards her and in a voice bordering between anxiety and contrition said, 'Come in, dear lady, don't stand there. I'm sorry, you know. I didn't expect you.'

'Evidently not,' she said coldly, hating herself for what would naturally be taken as jealousy by that wanton, wicked girl standing so contemptuous and self-contained in the shadows. Had she no sense of propriety or shame? Miss Spring felt herself shaking with anger as Laurence took her by the arm, guiding her forcibly to a chair.

'There!' he said. 'Sit down, you're tired. I'll explain it all later.'

'It seems to me,' Miss Spring continued in the same smothered voice, 'that there's no explaining to do.'

'Oh, come now,' Laurence said, 'you mustn't be upset at a little natural fun.'

'Fun?' she echoed. 'You seem to have a queer idea of it, although no doubt,' with a bitter accusing look at Merlynne, 'Mrs Lane evidently encouraged you.'

Merlynne flushed angrily and retorted, 'Really, Laurence! If you intend me to stand here and be insulted by that women — '

'Now, now, you two! *Please.*'

'I hardly think I was insulting you,' Miss Spring resumed with an icy thrust. 'Surely it isn't the normal thing for a young married woman to take her fun in another man's arms?'

'Is it, in any case, any business of yours, Miss Spring?'

'Yes,' she said, 'under the circumstances I think it is.'

'What circumstances, may I ask?'

Miss Spring started to speak when Laurence interrupted her.

'Look here! I'm sorry, but whatever the rights and the wrongs of the business, I simply won't have you two women squabbling in my studio.'

'Squabbling!' exclaimed Merlynne. 'I like that.'

'Well, aren't you?' he said. 'It's not exactly pretty, anyhow, and if you can't both stop it, I'm off.'

'You needn't,' Merlynne said. 'I'm going.'

She turned and picked up her beret from the chair, pulling it savagely on her head at a rakish angle, over one eye. Then she put on her coat, and drawing on her gloves faced Miss Spring with the angry colour still in her face.

'For a long time,' she said, 'I know you've resented my visits to Laurence. I think it's a pity you've felt so personally about it. It doesn't help matters. I'm not going to discuss my affairs with you or explain them. But in future I hope we can arrange together to come here on different days. It might perhaps be pleasanter and less embarrassing.'

She swung round and marched to the door with her head held high, her tawny hair swinging above her shoulders. At the door she paused, and said to Laurence, 'Goodbye. See you again.'

As the latch closed he breathed a sigh of relief. 'Really, Miss Spring,' he said in conciliatory tones, 'you take everything far too seriously. You shouldn't. It isn't good for you.'

Feeling the threat of hysteria constricting her throat, Miss Spring agreed, 'No, it isn't. You might have thought of that, mightn't you?' Her voice rose shrilly. Under the lace blouse her heart pumped painfully, the shred of handkerchief became a tight ball in one hand, 'It wouldn't have been so bad,' she continued, 'if you hadn't promised me not to have her here.'

'I don't think I promised any such thing,' Laurence corrected her. 'How could I? I can't be rude to anyone who comes to see me – including Merlynne.'

'There was no need to make love,' Miss Spring objected, 'especially to a married woman.'

He smiled, with his eyes cold as glass in his face, and said equably, 'You use altogether the wrong expression. Love doesn't enter my scheme of things. Why should a few harmless kisses worry you?'

'I've told you. Your reputation. And I did think, when we talked things out before, you meant to keep your word. You said emotional matters were completely unimportant to you.'

'So they are,' he remarked lightly. 'That's exactly my point.'

'Well, then!' she said a little stiffly. 'I don't think they should be – not that kind of thing – playing about sexually. Such an awful word. I may be old-fashioned and a little dull, Laurence, but I believe there are some aspects of life that shouldn't be mocked. Besides, there's Mr Lane. Don't you see that it isn't as if the girl was free – she has a husband and responsibilities to him.'

'Has she?' he remarked significantly. 'Maybe.'

She stared at him, shocked. 'You speak so callously. Sometimes I think you try to hurt people.'

'No,' he said, 'not consciously. But people, in the main, don't matter to me much. Their feelings and little emotions are, on the whole, rather ridiculous.'

'Thank you.'

'I said "on the whole",' he resumed, with his slow charming smile upon her. 'You're quite different!'

In spite of herself, she couldn't help feeling faintly relieved.

'That's all very well,' she said. 'You're trying to flatter me now.'

'Oh, no, I'm not,' he lied. 'You're my friend. My benefactress. How could I feel otherwise?'

'You know, Laurence,' Miss Spring said, weakening suddenly, 'I think very often you can do what you like with me.'

'Can I?' he said teasingly, with a boyish look on his face.

'You just twist me round your little finger,' she answered, with a slight sigh, 'although I know half the time you're laughing at me.'

'Not at you,' he said. '*With* you sometimes. That's different.'

'Yes,' she agreed. 'I suppose it is.'

He strode across the room and picked up a canvas which was standing with its face to the wall.

'This is my latest,' he said, showing it to her. 'What do you think of it?'

Miss Spring saw before her a strange composition; abstract and yet queerly personal, painted in his characteristic dark, exotic colours, which although abstruse in meaning, suggested to her a whirling elemental force from which shapes and forms were emerging.

'Well?' he said.

'There's something – frightening about it,' she answered, after a brief pause.

'Good. That's what I wanted.'

'Is it? Why?'

'The whole idea's conception,' he said.

'Oh!'

He gave her a sidelong glance. 'I wonder if you get me?'

'Well – not quite clearly perhaps,' she admitted. 'But I felt – I feel – something. I think I know what you mean.'

He laughed. 'And you still like me?'

'Why not?'

'That's me' he said, 'in that painting. That's myself. Far

more clearly than the man you see before you, Miss Spring. My truth! To me that's life — beauty, horror, sin, virtue, all of it bursting forth in a tremulous gust of energy — completely amoral, without principle or puny restraints. The dark god-head. I'm not, I'm afraid, a very nice man.'

Miss Spring stared at him, fascinated. 'Oh, but —'

'Don't try to excuse me,' he said. 'I'm stating a fact. I'm being perfectly honest at this moment. No one shall ever preach at me, Miss Spring. No one shall order my actions or tell me what to do. Anyone who is my friend must put up with me as I am.'

'But — but of course,' she said, a little lamely.

'I feel,' he said, putting the canvas down, 'as though all forces, both good and bad, work through me to some creative end. Perhaps it's stupid of me talking to you like this, but as far as I can, I want to be truthful with you.'

'Oh, yes, of course,' she said faintly.

'A psychologist once advanced the theory to me,' he resumed, 'that *all* art — of any medium — only arose through frustration. In the majority of cases this may be true. But it isn't so with me, Miss Spring. With *me* the work, the creation, is the appetite — and the personal affairs of living merely subsidiary. That's why you should never fear Merlynne or any woman. Because, as I have already said, in my case sex is a secondary and unimportant thing.'

'Why have you told me all this?' she asked presently.

'I have just been explaining. Strange as it may seem I have a relic of a conscience somewhere. You've been good to me. I may disappoint you in every way as a man, but I won't disappoint you as a painter.'

There was a pause, after which Miss Spring said, 'I quite understand. I realise that — that any genius — real genius — is bound to be difficult, in some way. I wouldn't expect you to be ordinary, Laurence. Just — just a little circumspect, that's all. Just careful, where your work is concerned. To be talk about in a degrading sense, at the very beginning of your career, might be bad for it. Although, of course, with your talent, I realise you will eventually overcome all that.'

Her voice trailed away while a hint of impatience hit Laurence's eyes and twitched his mouth. With finality, he said, 'Yes. But you needn't worry. Merlynne shall not interfere.'

With this Miss Spring had to be content. The interview ended, satisfactorily on his side, with an additional cheque to meet further exhibition expenses, and on hers with a self-induced sense of satisfaction which was, however, assumed.

On the way back to Trencathra she told herself repeatedly that everything was all right, that her confidence in him was justified. But a gnawing at the back of her mind held a jealous intangible fear which persisted, even in the face of her belief.

Later, however, she pushed it into the background, telling herself that all artists were difficult, and had to be humoured. And Laurence, after all, had been honest with her. Yes, he was a dear boy, despite his shortcomings. He had been truthful, which was something. She knew where she was with him. But *did* she? This was the question she refused to answer or even acknowledge; because it involved, also, her own feelings which were becoming far too complicated to be comfortable.

Chapter Twenty-Three

April came, and high above the cliffs and harbour apple blossom frothed against the sky. Quieter, longer evenings came, and the sun was warm, splashing the sea to a still radiance on which the boats drowsed comfortably now, no longer tossed by storm or rain. In the small town the shops already had a holiday air, and visitors appeared week by week in the streets and in the small harbour. The old fishermen had a dreamier, more contented look in their eyes; for the season of hardships and storm was over. In a short time the pleasure boats would be about their business – tourists would bring money to St Taloc, and there would be opportunity for a little leisure and enjoyment.

On a day of pale sun, with the primroses yellow in the hedges of the narrow lanes, Sam Murgatroyd left Trencathra for good.

As Richard was working in the fields Hugo drove him in the car to a hospital near Penzance where, unless a miracle occurred, he had decided to spend his last few months. Susie-Jane went with them, her heart heavy with pain and sympathy for the little man, yet conscious, nevertheless, of a tremendous admiration for his fortitude.

They spoke as casually as possible of ordinary things, but time after time the conversation returned to the one topic now in which Sam seemed to have any real interest – the orphanage. He expressed a wish that Susie-Jane should concern herself in some slight way with the welfare of the children involved; and on the way told her that he had directed his lawyers to add a codicil to his will in which she was to be an honorary director of the organisation for her lifetime.

Susie-Jane was surprised and a little shocked.

'But Mr Murgatroyd,' she said, 'I can't! I mean, it wouldn't be right. I haven't had any experience. There are heaps of people far more capable than me.'

'There are altogether half a dozen directors,' Sam told her, 'and provision for an elected annual committee as well. I don't expect you to give up much of your time, my dear, you're under no obligation. But I like to think of you as there in some way. Aye, from the very beginning – do you remember that talk we had at the gate? – I had a soft spot for you. I believed in you. If I'd had a lass of my own I'd have wanted her to be like you. And I'll like to think now that you were going to carry on a little with what I've set my heart on. You're young. You're kind-hearted. You like children. You've got a conscience. Don't disappoint me.'

Susie-Jane was touched. 'Oh, very well,' she said. 'I'll do what I can. But you're overrating me.'

There was a pause as he lay back in the car, eyes closed for a second or two, then remarked, 'No, I'm not. I know what I'm doing all right. And it's no tie, you understand? If you want it to be only nominal – it *is* only nominal. But if you choose to interest yourself in it, and if circumstances permit – well, you'll be doing something grand.'

The matter was left there. There seemed little more to say. Several times Susie-Jane was prompted to make the conventional remark of encouragement, of hope for his recovery in the future. But a glance at his face made a travesty of the suggestion. For never had she seen one more emaciated or yellow-looking. The flesh sagged now into hollows and haggard folds. The eyes were dark-rimmed, filled with pain and courage. But the lips still had a touch of whimsey at the corners. In the face of suffering he could still smile. And Susie-Jane felt, therefore, that to attempt to delude him with false hope would be, in a sense, to make mock of his integrity. So she was silent.

They reached the hospital a little before four o'clock, and were given tea in the Matron's sittingroom. She was a kindly, efficient woman; the room was cheerful, with a fire flickering in the grate and the cream distempered walls gay with framed prints of Cezanne and Van Gogh. But Susie-Jane, as the minutes ticked by, was filled with a sadness she could not control. There was at all times something depressing to her about hospitals, with their unmistakably anaesthetic smell and bare clean corridors, the business-like nurses and ominous doors which gave her a sense of being caged and cut off from reality. How much worse it was when someone one was fond of was about to enter for good. She strove to be bright, however, though her eyes on occasion were misty. If Sam noticed this he did not say, but smiled encouragement at her.

She's young, he was thinking, and this hurts her. She shouldn't fret. The time's done for that. Aye, on the whole I'll be glad when the things over now. It's a strain — this last part.

Later, when they had driven away, having given a promise to call again at the end of the week, Hugo said to Susie-Jane, 'You musn't be too sad about old Murgatroyd, Susie. He's got something few of us have.'

'I know,' she said in a quiet voice.

'Look here,' he said, 'what about taking the coast road past the Mount, and back through Marazion? It's a nice evening. Would you like the run?'

She looked up at him and smiled gratefully. 'Yes, Hugo,' she said. 'I would.'

'Right.'

He accelerated, and soon they had left the town behind and were driving along the front. There he slackened his speed, and drove easily through the dying light, which left long faintly flickering shadows on the water. The Mount, half-silhouetted in its tones of soft blues, greys and green, rose like some mediaeval fairy-tale castle from the water. Everything was very still, holding a painted quality in which life for a moment became remote and dream-like, far removed from the disturbing conflicts and activities of human beings.

On the summit of the hill he stopped the car and sat for a few moments saying nothing. She, too, did not speak for fear of disturbing the rich current of unspoken communion between them.

Then he said, still not looking at her, 'It's nice being with you. You fit in. I never seem to have to explain anything.'

'Perhaps the biggest things don't need explaining,' she replied.

'You're a composed person,' he said, turning to look at her, 'and yet it isn't that you don't feel things. You do – in a way most people never realise.'

'Perhaps I don't terribly bother about myself very much,' she answered. 'You once told me I expected a great deal from life. Well, in a way I do. Yet I've never believed things would turn out exactly right for me, Hugo. And so I've sort of got used to not wanting things.'

He smiled faintly. 'You're young to be learning the impersonal path of self-renunciation, Susie-Jane.'

'Perhaps it's been forced on me,' she said.

'What do you mean?'

'Well . . .' She faced him with very candid eyes, and then smiled. 'Oh, what does it matter?' she queried, deciding to prevaricate. 'After all, Hugo, your affairs and mine, they're not the whole world, are they? Especially when you think of people like poor Sam Murgatroyd. And it's not true that I don't expect a good deal, you know. I do. But I can enjoy myself in my own alone-ish kind of way. You see, even when I'm alone, Hugo, I'm not really lonely – '

'No?'

'I might be sad,' she admitted, 'I might be terribly unhappy, but there'd be something with me all the time – a kind of other me that helps me through bad bits. It's always been like that – ever since I was a child. A sort of unseen companion that I've been able to fall back upon in any gloomy time. Do you understand a bit? Or does it all sound dreadfully silly?'

'No,' he answered. 'Not silly, Susie-Jane. But it does show an innocence of spirit. Yes, you're very innocent. You must be, to be able to take comfort from yourself. Most of us are afraid to.'

'Why?'

'Well – there you are!' he said. 'That's the difference. That's where your power lies. You're unspoiled. You haven't been tainted like many of us.'

'Oh, but I – oh, no, Hugo. I don't know what you mean by power,' she said.

'You make people feel a hundred per cent better,' he said. 'There aren't many about like that.'

She flushed. 'Do I? It's nice of you to think so, Hugo, but you mustn't think I'm too good. I'm not, you know, I'm very ordinary, really.'

'Of course you are,' he said. 'Thank God! You're so ordinary, Susie-Jane, that being with you is to feel the wind and air keener, and smell the earth with richer senses. You make things live! You're strong, and natural, and good. And yet, you're a funny kid, too.'

She laughed. 'Am I?'

'How we talk about ourselves, don't we?'

'Does it matter?'

He knit his brows. 'No. Sometimes it's necessary. And this is one of those times. If we didn't babble on we'd be gloomy perhaps.'

'You mean about Sam?'

'Yes. We do our best to feel strong, Susie-Jane, we philosophize and try to read reason into things, but the fact remains that seeing a fine character like that having to suffer so, *does* something to you. Something we can't escape from, because we're human.'

Susie-Jane slipped her hand into his, naturally, without embarrassment. 'You always tell me not to be so sensitive, Hugo, but you're the one, really. However much you pretend, you get hurt dreadfully. More than me, I think.'

'Because,' he said, 'when it comes down to real issues I'm less certain than you. You live your belief. I don't.'

She didn't answer. In the dying light a few gulls drifted through the grey air in the direction of the Mount. From the distance somewhere the rumble of a cart sounded in the silence. Presently the shape of it emerged, silhouetted darkly against the hill. Hugo gave Susie-Jane's hand a tight little squeeze and dropped it.

'Thanks,' he said, simply and irrelevantly. And when she did not speak, 'Well?'

'Oh!' She pulled herself together, 'I was just thinking.'

'Of what?'

'I was thinking,' she said, in her clear young voice, 'how a moment, really, can be like a lifetime, Hugo, how everything can be crammed into it so perfectly that time dies.'

'Like the legendary monk,' he said, 'who in listening to a bird's song let years slip away, and did not know it. Out of Time.'

'Yes,' she said. 'Something like that.'

He felt for her suddenly an immense tenderness which was deeper and stronger than any emotion she'd yet roused in him. He'd have liked to slip his arm round her, and draw her to his breast. He nearly did so. But a quick instinctive consciousness of her womanhood prevented him. Had she been the child he'd so often imagined in the past, he'd have kissed her. But she was not. Though innocent, she was, he knew, mature. He must not trifle with her; for her sake, and for his, they must not run the risk of new issues. And so he said abruptly, 'Well, we must be getting on.'

He started the car with a jerk, his face set. And feeling his constraint, she wondered a little sadly what had gone wrong. A moment or two before the understanding between them had been complete. She'd been content just to have him there with her. She'd not asked anything, had not even required him to speak. Now, somehow, a shadow had fallen for which, in some unknowable way, she felt she must be guilty.

Realising her perplexity, sorry to have hurt her, he said a little later, 'Don't worry about me, Susie-Jane. Forgive my moods. It's been good, being with you.'

'Me, too,' she said. 'I've enjoyed it – this last part.'

'You know,' he told her, 'it helps being with someone who understands. I wish I could do the same for you.'

She looked at him, starry-eyed. 'But you do, Hugo. That's just it – you do.'

He shook his head. 'You're far too unselfish. So different from –' He broke off, and in the darkness she sensed that his eyes had clouded.

'From Merlynne, I suppose you were going to say?'

'I didn't mean to *say* it.'

'But you *thought* it, Hugo.'

'Yes, I suppose so.'

'I'm sorry. You still worry about her, don't you?'

'I can't help it,' he said. 'She's my wife.'

'Yes, of course.' Susie-Jane spoke in a flat, subdued little voice.

Then he said, half apologetically, half in self-recrimination, 'We have to remember that, always. You see, when two people have lived together as we have — whatever happens, however wrongly things go — there's the tie just the same. It can't just be not there.'

'I know that. Of course not. You needn't explain, Hugo.'

'There!' he exclaimed. 'What a blunderer I am — always talking about myself. Good Lord, I'm sorry.'

'You needn't be,' she said, thankful he couldn't see her face. 'But let's not talk about it any more. There really isn't any need.'

He was silent, and presently the car swung into the lane leading to Trencathra. It was darker now, and the trees had deepened into black shapes against the sky. In the distance the turrets of the house loomed, with odd lights twinkling here and there from the windows. The sight brought a feeling of relief and comfort to Susie-Jane.

Her brief depression lifted a little as she got out of the car. She smiled at Hugo, determined he should not sense her mood. She was home. In a minute or two she would be safely within her room. It would not matter then what she felt, or looked like. She could cry, if she chose, and no one would be any the wiser. And tomorrow everything would be different. A new day would be beginning. She would be herself again, and strong. If it was fine she would get up early, before breakfast, and go down to the headland in the early dew. She would find the ledge where the gull's nest was, and see if the young birds were hatched yet. The mother bird knew her, and was not afraid. There was something friendly and comforting in thinking of the mother gull. Merlynne considered them cruel-looking creatures, but nothing was cruel if you showed you were not frightened and had no wish to harm. Susie-Jane believed this implicitly. It was also, she knew, Hugo's belief.

But he argued more with his mind, whereas to her it was simpler to accept from the wisdom of the heart. In this lay the great difference between them. Her way was clear and straight, but Hugo's always would be harder and stormier to travel. Nevertheless, she loved him. She would always love him, even if he went away and never saw her again. And after all — it was the loving that mattered, more than being loved. If you loved properly you could not hurt anyone by it. That was why her love wasn't wrong, either to Merlynne or Hugo himself, because she asked nothing from it, and was content only to give. Yes, she only wanted to help him. She would never cause him pain or worry. She would be his friend always. This thought, as ever, was her comfort. That, whatever happened, she could still be Hugo's friend.

Chapter Twenty-Four

One night towards the end of the month, Miss Fothergill-Briggs could not sleep. The previous day she had been to see Sam Murgatroyd in hospital, and the visit had depressed her profoundly. Beneath her mannish, somewhat agressive exterior, Miss Briggs had an uncomfortably soft heart, which starved as it had been in youth, was the more ready now to expand itself in any likely channel. There had been very few such opportunities in her life, and friendship until now had not come easily to her. She had been born the eighth and most unattractive daughter of a poor and obscure country parson in Norfolk. Her childhood had been lived in an atmosphere of confined, stuffy poverty, of narrow religious views and rigorous discipline, which together with her lack of charm had bred in her at an early age a sense of inferiority and repression, later resulting in her domineering manner and passion for animals. Of her sisters, two had died unmarried, two had married missionaries, another a country doctor, and a sixth taken up nursing. Ann, the most beautiful and rebellious, had run away to London when she was eighteen, and had been swallowed up in the back row of a third rate theatrical chorus, thus cutting herself for ever from the annals of her respectable family.

Miss Briggs had only been ten when the disgraceful affair took place. But she could still recall, even after forty years, the terrible anger of her father's voice at breakfast time, when he had informed his trembling family of his daughter's wickedness, and that henceforward she was to be unmentioned and unremembered by any of them.

'And may God,' he had added, 'be her judge.'

In the years that followed Miss Briggs had frequently wondered with a guilty sense of curiosity if God had done anything about Ann. The bomb-shell had come twenty years later, in the shape of a lawyer's letter which had informed Miss Fothergill-Briggs that on the death of her sister, Miss Ann Laverick, the actress, who had died in New York, she was beneficiary to the sum of £20,000.

The Reverend Henry Briggs, retired on his meagre pension, was by then well on the way to a crusty senility. That his daughter – the daughter he had cut off and forbidden his doors – should have done well for herself, enraged and embittered him.

Miss Briggs had never forgotten the twisted look on his face as, gripping his stick in his hand, he'd sought to rise from his wheelchair.

'You send it back,' he'd said. 'None of mine shall touch that sinful money. Send it back, do you hear?'

All her life Miss Briggs had been afraid of her father. During her youth she'd served and cared for him through fear rather than affection. Since her mother's death, when she was sixteen, she'd known no tenderness, and very little joy. She'd grown old before her time as on her young shoulders had fallen the onerous task of running the household economically, of striving to keep up appearances, wearing mended clothes and endeavouring to keep her irascible father content. She'd had no parties, no boy-friends, none of those pleasures which, even in Victorian times, fell to most middle-class girls. Being plain to look at – as her father had constantly reminded her – it was highly unlikely she'd find a suitable husband. The only male friendship she'd experienced had been with a medical student who came for a holiday to the district when she was twenty. But the Reverend Briggs had successfully ended it, and she'd settled down with a sense of apathy to 'doing her duty' and looking after her father for the rest of her life.

The windfall from her sister, however, had completely changed everything. Listening to the snarling old man in the chair as he poured his contempt and hatred into her ear, she had suddenly seen him clearly for what he was – seen the household objectively for the first time — the dreary joyless routine, the smothering atmosphere of the rooms, the eternal struggle against constant grumbling over expense and money. How she had hated it all — the lovelessness, the ugliness! The warped possessiveness which under a guise of piousness had spoiled and eaten into her best years.

And so, as he had waited, with his old hand still gripping his stick, for her acquiescence, her instant obedience to his wishes, a decision had formulated in her mind which transformed her from a drudge to a woman of decision and action.

'I shall do no such thing,' she'd said clearly.

'What — what did you say?' he'd spluttered, unable to believe his own ears.

'I said I shall do no such thing. We need the money. It would be ridiculous not to take it.'

Never had she experienced anything equal to the rage which possessed the old man when he realised the import of her defiance. He had staggered to his feet, with the blood purple in his face, unable to speak for the anger which was choking him. Her own heart, too, was pounding with a heavy rebellious emotion which, however, left her mind quite clear and cool.

'Sit down, Father,' she'd managed to say, 'you'll be ill.'

She had sought to help him, but he had pushed her violently away and a second later, with his eyes staring and mouth half-open, had sagged back into the chair.

Almost at once she'd known that something was wrong with him. He'd not spoken, but had sat with a curious glazed expression in his eyes, looking straight before him, his mouth drawn a little to one side, the fingers of his left hand twitching at the air. Behind him the large macabre china dogs on the sideboard leered at her with the same glazed evil quality. She had shuddered, and raised her hands to her eyes, suddenly sickened by the scene.

The doctor had later diagnosed a stroke, which he said might easily have been brought on by some excessive emotion or temper. Miss Briggs had confided in him concerning the scene over the money, and he'd been kindly, reassuring, patting her shoulder and saying, 'Well, well! I shouldn't say this I suppose – but for your sake, Miss Briggs, it may be for the best. You'll be able to have a little freedom now. And high time, too. Don't you go blaming yourself. You've sacrificed yourself far too long. It was bound to come sooner or later. Besides, you know, his life hasn't been much pleasure to him.'

That was true, and it had certainly meant nothing but trouble to others of recent years. Indeed, she'd thought, watching him that evening as he lay breathing stentoriously in the mahogany fourposter bed, despite his calling had he ever really helped any human soul in any warm personal way? She doubted it. And, because of it, had felt a stab of pity for him. It must be dreadful to have to die like that without the knowledge of friendship or affection in one's life.

At that moment he'd opened one eye and looked at her, a hard malicious, tormenting look which had a suggestion of triumph in it, as though to say, 'Look! You've killed me. Your defiance has killed me. You'll never forget that – how you killed your father.'

She'd winced, and felt again a stab of the old fear. He had died that same night. But she had not, as he'd anticipated, let his death prey on her mind. Indeed, she'd admitted to herself quite frankly that she was glad he was gone, leaving her free to make a new life for herself. She certainly wasn't going to brood over the past whims and lusts of a crazy old man.

But it had not been quite so simple as she'd imagined. Though her mind had rejected her father's influence, the unconscious effect was still there, making her uneasy in company, inducing her to affect a certain outward bravado as armour against her thwarted youth.

For a time she'd travelled abroad, returning to Britain eventually to interest herself in social welfare work and various other organisations and societies. Because of her innate shyness of human contact she became devoted to animals, an interest which eventually was to absorb her life.

Sam Murgatroyd, however, had touched a chord of softness in her that was quite new. She not only admired and respected him as a friend, but lavished on him, despite his seniority, something of the maternal thought and care which, under the circumstances, she might have given to a husband and children.

On that certain sleepless night at Trencathra, she was ill-at-ease and unhappy because she knew now that Sam had very little longer to live, and that there was nothing she could do for him.

It was a warm night. Several times she rose and went to the windows for more air. The moon was bright, and below, in the garden, the daffodils glinted pale in the grass between the long dark shadows of the trees. It was odd, she thought, however unattractive and unwanted a woman might be there could be, deep down, as in her case, a compassion and awareness of beauty ready to blossom forth, however shyly, only given the incentive and opportunity.

And yet, she decided, going back to bed, it was silly for an old spinster like herself to get such ideas. The time for romance was past, even if she'd had more charm.

Even friendship – that rare friendship of hers for Sam Murgatroyd – was already passing, because he would soon be gone. She was grieved for him, but she suffered also for herself. The days would not be the same. They would be incredibly grey without the chance of a little chat with him, the friendly confidences which had grown to mean so much to her in the past months. Lately, naturally, they had been seriously curtailed. But even so there had been up to now the prospect of her visits to him, the knowledge that he looked forward to seeing her, and that she was of some use. But that afternoon he had been almost too exhausted to speak to her. She'd not stayed long, realising with pain that the point had been reached now when her company took from him more than it gave.

Still, she must really try and rest. Fretting would only make matters worse. Presently she took three aspirins in some water, and after a time she did manage to get a little restless sleep.

She awoke in the early hours of morning, disturbed by Tito who was whining softly from his basket. She switched on the light and leaned out of bed, with her hand out.

'What's the matter, Tito?' she said. 'Sh! Go to sleep.'

But the little dog would not be soothed. He sat there with his ears pricked as though on the alert, listening. Then, quickly, he gave a short excited bark.

'Sh!' she said again, looking at her watch. 'Be quiet. There's no one there. It's only half-past five.'

She spoke more sharply, but Tito refused to obey. Now thoroughly disturbed, Miss Briggs also found herself listening. After a few moments she, too, thought she heard a sound below.

Who can it be? she thought. It's too early for Olive, and Mr Nankerviss hasn't his light on. I wonder ...

It might be Catherine, of course, making an early cup of tea – there could be numberless commonsense explanations. But for all that, she was suspicious. Perhaps someone had broken in. Perhaps, even now, some tramp or other was tip-toeing away with some of the silver.

Miss Briggs was a naive soul. Instantly the suggestion had formed, she half-believed in it. She jumped out of bed again quickly and pattered over to the window, peering cautiously through the curtains.

The first pale streak of dawn was lighting the sky, throwing into vague relief the soft dark half-light. All was very still, the flowers standing like small ghosts in the grass, the trees, bunched together in dark shadow shapes and the glitter of dew over the lawn and hedges. The only sound now was the note of a young thrush twittering, and from beyond, the surge and fall of the sea. But, as she listened, something else came to her ears. The click of a latch and quick soft sound of footsteps.

Miss Briggs felt her heart jump. It *was* someone then – someone on some secret mission perhaps – up to no good. She wondered in her excitement whether to rouse the household or attempt herself to catch the intruder. She was still pondering when the figure of a woman emerged from the gloom and made its way hurriedly along the path leading to the side gate. There was something vaguely familiar about the swing of the coat and the character of the walk, and as she turned in the direction of the road, Miss Briggs knew with certainty that it was Merlynne. Mrs Lane of all people, and she was carrying something, too, something that looked like a case in her right hand.

Bewildered, a little shocked, Miss Briggs left the window and moved to her bed, where she sat for a few moments trying to find an explanation for what had occurred. Why was that girl going out at such an early hour, and carrying a bag, too? Why was she stealing away so quietly, as though fearing to be seen? It was common knowledge, of course, that she no longer slept with her husband, poor man. For some time he'd been in the yellow room on account of his nerves and insomnia. Could it be that she was running away from him altogether? No. Surely not. And yet, like Miss Spring, Miss Fothergill-Briggs had never entirely trusted Merlynne, although being less personally concerned she was more generous.

There was something, despite her disapproval, that she'd always like about the girl. Dangerous? Yes. Without conscience? Possibly. But it had never appeared as though she got much fun out of her marriage. Hugo Lane might be a very fine young fellow and a hero, but no one could deny that he might be difficult – even frustrating to live with. It was not that she, Miss Fothergill-Briggs, approved of broken marriages. Still, the fact remained that Merlynne was a woman, and human. And Hugo did appear on occasion to have forgotten the fact. The knowledge of this, and of her own broad-minded attitude to the affair, faintly stimulated Miss Briggs. The mystery of Merlynne's departure intrigued her now, and she was on pins to know the truth of it, and what the outcome would be. She resolved that until questions were asked she would say nothing of the matter to anyone. It might be that there was a perfectly ordinary and rational explanation. But she rather doubted it.

Nothing was said at breakfast time, for which only Susie-Jane and Catherine were present. Miss Spring had neuralgia, and was still in bed. Richard was already at work, and Dame Julia as usual was upstairs. No reference was made either to Hugo's absence or Merlynne's. But Miss Briggs sensed a certain tension, an air of strain which was significant.

Only Olive was her usual jaunty self, although in her bright black eyes there was a lively air of curiosity.

Something's up, she told herself, clearing away the dishes. A row or something. *I* know. Bet she's bolted. Miss Catherine can't fool me, with talk of headaches and bad colds. Miss Merlynne's gone. Her room's empty. And I don't blame her neither.

But it was not until the next day that the full facts leaked out. Somehow the truth got about for such affairs can never remain secret for long. By that time most of the household had come to the conclusion that Merlynne had left Hugo, which was true. For a whole day and night he had nursed the knowledge to himself, hurt and dazed by the letter which he had found waiting for him in his dressing room. For a long time, though comprehending, he had been unable to believe the evidence which confronted him. It was true they'd not got on well lately. He was well aware of her unhappiness and of her friendship with Laurence, but had thought it would pass. He'd trusted her, more fool him, believed she had more sense than to break all marriage ties for a sordid affair with a third-rate arty philanderer. Well, he'd been wrong.

Now, confronted with the fact, he was amazed at his own cold rage. It wasn't physical jealousy he felt. He was too proud, too little concerned with the body for that, but a sense of outrage at her deception which was humiliating to both of them. Despite their recent quarrels and coldness he had still clung in his heart to the vision of Merlynne as she had been when he'd first met her. Desire had faded, but a lingering quality of romance had remained in him. Through this last act she had plundered even that innermost shrine, and through spoiling herself had spoiled something in him also.

As argument after argument circled through his brain a little of his first anger died, and was replaced gradually by sorrow. She could never, he felt, be happy with Laurence. There was something sadistic about him, and pagan, which would make tenderness from him impossible. For a time they might satisfy each other physically, but after that, what? What would become of her when the dark tide of passion had exhausted itself and she found herself without friends at the mercy of an intolerable egotist?

There was no answer. No feeling left in him but contempt, and a sickening sense of pity.

Time after time, as though fascinated by an icy disbelief, he took the letter from his pocket to fortify his condemnation. He knew it almost by heart now.

Dear Hugo,
   When you receive this letter, I shall have gone with Laurence. I'm sorry to have to do it in this way, but I can't stick family rows, and in any case you'll all think badly of me anyway; so what does it matter?
   We're going to London. Laurence is sick of St Taloc and wants to get out before he's possessed body and soul by a certain person. I only decided tonight to go with him, but I know it's the best thing for all of us. Nothing has been any good with us for a long time and I'm pretty certain it never would have been. I'm sorry if it hurts you, Hugo, but I don't really think it will, much. In any case, I'm in love with Laurence. We're very alike really, two people without much conscience. And I must *live*. You will never know how chilled I've been, how depressed to death by your mysticism and aloofness. Perhaps that's my shortcoming, my limitation. Maybe. I know you're a far better person than me. You really ought to have married someone like Susie-Jane. Divorce me or not; it doesn't matter. I shall never live with you again.
   Merlynne

And that was that! Cold. Brutal. Final.

For a moment the memory of her pale flower-like face floated into his mind, fanning a desire in him for revenge – to hit out somehow in the effort to erase the shock. Then as quickly it died, leaving him just overwhelmingly tired.

What right, after all, he thought, had he to demand faithfulness after neglecting her physically for so long? How could he expect her to be true to something she'd never understood?

He sat down presently in a chair by the bed, head in hands, feeling nothing but defeat and futility. He was still there when Susie-Jane entered the room an hour later, carrying a cup of coffee and sandwiches for him. He was in darkness, for twilight had already fallen; and the sight of his lonely bent form moved her to quick compassion. She stood there for a moment or two before speaking, then moving forward said in a soft voice, 'Hugo – dear Hugo – I'm so sorry.'

He did not immediately look up. But when he did she was still waiting, silhouetted against the dim light. He felt rather than noticed her distress, sensing the deep sympathy which held her for a moment at a loss, uncertain what to do.

He smiled at her faintly, and said, 'Don't worry about me, Susie-Jane. It's all right.'

'Oh, but Hugo – I –' she spoke, and paused impulsively, then continued with some of the gallant self-consciousness of a child who feels too much. 'Look, I've brought you some coffee and something to eat.'

'Thank you.'

'And –'

'Well?'

'Grandmother sent a message. She said – but it wasn't really important.'

'You'd better tell me.'

'She said, "Tell Hugo if he's a man, and loves Merlynne, he'd better take a horsewhip and catch the next train to Town. But if he *doesn't* he'd better have something to eat, and show a little sense". That's what she said,' Susie-Jane concluded half-apologetically. 'But you know what grandmother is – everything's generally either black or white to her. I don't suppose she understands quite. No, I'm sure she doesn't.'

She touched his shoulder gently. 'Dear Hugo.'

He did not move, but beneath her fingers she felt the iron control of his nerves quiver. She drew her hand away, struggling with the desire to put her arms round him, easing tension and unhappiness to peace.

He looked up at her, and the soft lines of her figure, the quiver of her voice, the expectant troubled glance of her shadowed eyes, jerked him from bitterness to a momentary tenderness.

'Susie,' he said, reaching for her hand, 'you really mustn't worry about me. What your grandmother said is probably right. But I'm not that kind of man, my dear. There must be no prisons.'

'Prisons?'

'One doesn't,' he said, 'attempt to cage a bird once it's flown. Affection must be free, Susie-Jane. No locked doors. To run after her, to imprison one's wife ... Oh, no!' He shuddered, and at the same time dropped her hand. She stood there, slightly chilled, until he resumed. 'This is *my* battle, I've got to face it out alone. It will pass.'

'I hope so, Hugo,' she said.

'I am sure,' he spoke through dry lips.

'Yes,' she agreed. 'For all our sakes. For yours, and for mine, too.'

Disturbed, he patted her hand. 'Go, my dear,' he told her. 'Leave me now.'

And with that she had to be content.

Chapter Twenty-Five

It was inevitable that Merlynne's elopement should put a certain strain upon the household, and two days' later the tension was deepened by Miss Spring having a hysterical fit which resulted in a half-hearted attempt to drown herself in the cove below the cliff. She was discovered and brought back by two fishermen who had found her, they said, half lying in the water, fully clothed, her handbag with her identity card in it on the wet sand above. At first they thought she must have been paddling and had fainted from the cold, or else been taken suddenly sick. But her words had belied this suggestion. Between chattering teeth she had been murmuring incoherently about 'betrayal' and 'common seducer'.

They could have thought, the elder man had remarked with a twinkle, that the bedraggled lady had really been assaulted, but it was obvious that she was labouring under some illusion or other which had caused her undue distress. Anyhow, they had done what they could for her, and there she was — a pathetic sight on the couch with her face yellow and drawn, her artificially golden hair lying in unbecoming sodden streaks about her forehead and face.

'And after all I did for him,' she was saying, between the sips of brandy which Catherine was forcing upon her. 'After all the money he's had — and encouragement. Oh no, I can't bear it! I really can't!' she gasped, and started to moan again. Whereat Dame Julia said irascibly, 'Fiddlesticks! Slap her someone. The woman's hysterical,'

'No, I'm not. It's not true. I wish I were dead – I really do.'

'The more fool you, then,' the old lady stated harshly. 'I'd be ashamed to get into such a state over any man, that I would. Pull yourself together, my good woman, or you'll end in the lunatic asylum.'

'No. Oh, *no* – don't *speak* like that. I can't bear it – I *can't,* I tell you. It's all too much for me – '

Dame Julia, deciding to act at this juncture, gave her a smart tap on the cheek. This, miraculously, stopped the flow of speech, and temporarily at least seemed to bring Miss Spring to her senses. She gulped, sat up, and asked for her bag.

'Here you are,' said Catherine, handing it to her.

From it Miss Spring took a handkerchief, and proceeded to dry her eyes.

'I must look so awful,' she remarked with the first glimmer of apology.

Catherine laid her hand on her forehead.

'You mustn't worry about that,' she said soothingly. 'In a little while you'll be all right, when you've had something to eat and a good sleep.'

The tears flooded Miss Spring's eyes again. 'You're very kind, you're really *very* kind to take pity on a – on a poor woman who's been betrayed like this.'

'Oh, rubbish!' interjected Dame Julia. 'Who's betrayed you? Do try and stick to the truth.'

'He promised me he would have nothing to do with her,' Miss Spring resumed once more. 'He promised.'

'Who promised – who?' asked the old lady. 'What are you talking about?'

'Laurence! And Merlynne – that girl! I've been helping – I've given him quite a lot of money recently to help him with his art.'

'More fool you then!'

'On the stipulation,' Miss Spring continued, 'that he would not see so much of her. But he did, you see, he broke his word.'

'Of course he did, if he wanted her,' Dame Julia stated mercilessly. 'If he could have his cake and eat it too, that man wasn't going to the miss the opportunity. What did you expect?'

Miss Spring sniffed, and Dame Julia continued, 'Now, I don't want to be unkind, but at your age you should have learned a few things. I'm sorry you've been so upset, but you really must pull yourself together. What good has it done you, lying in the water like that? I tell you, my dear, all the men in the world wouldn't get me down to that extent.'

'No. But – '

'But what?'

'Oh,' said Miss Spring more coherently, 'you're different. Everyone admires you. But people laugh at me, really. I've always known it; only Laurence seemed different.'

'But people do like you, Miss Spring,' Catherine said, 'and we all have our amusing moments. Does that matter? Isn't it rather nice to have people laugh with us sometimes?'

Miss Spring looked at her gratefully.

'With us, yes. But – '

'Well,' Catherine resumed, 'I'm sure no-one laughs at you unkindly, Miss Spring. We're all fond of you, really.'

'I wish I could believe that.'

Catherine pressed her hand. 'You really must,' she insisted. 'It's true.'

Later Miss Spring was put to bed with a hot water bottle, and warm milk to drink and an aspirin. It was not long before her exhausted nerves induced her to sleep, though her dreams were confused and discordant, coloured by a nightmarish melancholy which even in unconsciousness caused fitful moaning and incoherent murmuring to come from her open lips.

Downstairs, meanwhile, a family conference headed by Nicholas was in process, attended by everyone except Hugo.

Nicholas for once showed command and dignity, and a certain precision quite at variance with his usual vagueness.

'From the very beginning,' he said, 'when we first started this guest house idea, I've known it was wrong. And, as it turns out, I was right. You see what the effect of its been – my daughter's marriage wrecked, a lot of unhappiness in the house, and now the fresh scandal of this hysterical woman throwing herself into the sea. If we hadn't taken in a lot of cranks it might have been different.'

'There's no use in going on like this. Catherine's worn out – Susie-Jane's getting nowhere muddling about at housework all the time – Hugo's life is wrecked at the moment, and I tell you frankly, these affairs one on top of the other are wearing me down. I think on the whole we'd better take a stand now, and see that these two women leave as soon as possible. It isn't as if we couldn't manage now, with the help we've had from your grandmother, and my new book with prospects ahead. Richard, too, is getting a grip on the land. Yes, we'd better end the guest idea. This affair of Merlynne's,' he paused for a moment, then resumed, 'well, it's done something to me. I'm not surprised, but I can't help seeing that if it hadn't been for this new-fangled idea, she'd never have known that rotten blighter, and things wouldn't have come to such a pass.'

His voice trailed off moodily, his chin sunk a little to his chest. He was thinking, as a little one, she was always the most vivid and wilful. Difficult, she always was. But she had charm. She was a loving little thing, naughtier than the others, but easier to forgive. I don't know – it's an aching business this love affair! What good will it do her! How will it end? If Hugo was more human he'd run off and bring her back. But he won't. He's a queer fellow. That's why, in my heart, I don't blame her so much.

He was jerked back from his ruminations by hearing his mother-in-law saying, 'There's something in what you say, Nick, but you're not altogether right about Merlynne.'

He jerked himself up, 'Eh?'

She shook her old head shrewdly. 'No, my dear. They'd have met in any case. If they hadn't, it would have been someone else. Well, what did you expect? It isn't just what it appears, a freak trick of circumstance. You know that as well as I do. No, it's deeper. It's the war, Nicholas.' She sighed. 'Men don't go through all that unchanged – not sensitive men nor women neither. And in that sense we have betrayed these youngsters, by allowing such things to arise. They come back changed. Their spirits have suffered, their values have altered. Some come through stronger; others weaker. Merlynne, I'm afraid, found her foundations gone. We mustn't judge too harshly.'

'Judge?' said Nicholas, 'I don't judge at all. But she's my daughter — I'm fond of her. How do you expect me to feel? It's not only a matter of convention. I can't see any future for her with that man. And at heart she's not a bad little thing. But here we are — doing nothing.'

'What can we do?' asked Richard grimly. 'For two pins I'd go and find the fellow myself, have it out with him and bring her back. Perhaps I should?'

Catherine shook her head. 'No, Richard. We've discussed this before. The damage is done. Besides — Merlynne's not a child, and you know her temper; she wouldn't stand for it. In any case, it's Hugo's affair. He's her husband.'

'A fine job he's made of it!' Richard exclaimed bitterly.

Dame Julia clicked her teeth impatiently. 'Yes, I agree. I like Hugo but really! In some ways I can't help being a little irritated with him. He was so cool to her. And now you see — there he is eating his heart out.'

A silence fell upon the gathering; a silence filled with a deep unhappy questioning which in that old room assumed a living quality as though the house itself were breathing and participant in family troubles. And as she sat there, with the rest, it seemed to Susie-Jane that its very soul urged her to action, to some show of vindication of what had occurred.

Much has happened in these rooms, it seemed to suggest. Commonplace everyday things, comedy, a little tragedy. That's the way of life. It can't all be fun; and here, perhaps, living has been more vital than in most places. But at least things have *happened*. People have felt, and loved, and hated, been born and died here, suffered, and been happy. And it hasn't been in vain. A pattern, a rich and varied tapestry, has been woven into the very air and atmosphere — a pattern of experience which will never entirely die while these four walls remain. And who is to say that the last months have been a failure? A mistake? What of these lives, so divergent, which have been brought together? It's easy to scoff and condemn and miss the best. But what of the real truth? What of Sam Murgatroyd and the help he's found here? The idea which is to mature for the benefit of countless children? What of

Miss Fothergill-Briggs and her friendship for him? Though she will suffer through his death, the memory will remain with her to enrich all her life. Is this of no account?

And Miss Spring herself — when she has recovered a little she'll remember the kindness in Catherine's voice, the look in her eyes. This will give her confidence. She'll learn to live again on a basis of reality which she has never before experienced. Friendship. The common bond of understanding which must arise eventually from the intermingling of many lives. Isn't this important? Isn't it the thing so needed in the world? Merlynne has gone. But who is to say whether she is right or wrong? She has always been tempestuous, like the sea. As a small child her thoughts were tempestuous. I, the house, knew it. There was something wild and fey in her which wanted always the unobtainable. And maybe in his dark pagan way, her lover will give her what she wants. Who dare judge?

Life is not a static thing. It is constant and flowing like a river — I have its life-blood in my ether. Memories are writ here, which can never fade. The memory of Julian, as a young boy, running from the garden through the front door and up the stairs; the sight of him later, in his uniform, whistling and smiling gallantly before going back after his last leave. Of Catherine and her young lover, saying goodnight by the old tree. And further back — memories, thousands of them, crowding back from the past, so that the air trembles with a rich and thrilling unrest. In vain? No. Never say that any life here has been in vain. For something, always, of human experience is salvaged into eternal ends somewhere. Nothing can be completely valueless or lost.

'Well, Susie-Jane?' Richard said as though from a distance. 'What's bothering you? You look lost.'

She pulled herself into the present with a supreme effort of will, and remarked, 'I was thinking.'

'Yes. Obviously.'

'Yes — but I was thinking it wasn't exactly right to believe it had all been a mistake,' she resumed. 'The guest house, I mean.'

Nicholas looked at her sharply.

'No? Well, I can't agree with you, Susie,' he remarked. 'I'm afraid it's proved to be so.'

'But it hasn't!' she said, with lightened eyes. 'Don't you see, Daddy — it's *not*. We've learned lots of things from each other. Although there have been heaps of annoyances it's meant something to every one of us. To old Sam especially. If it hadn't been for coming to Trencathra he'd never have known Miss Fothergill-Briggs, or thought of the orphanage. Miss Spring — she's miserable now, but in the end she'll have benefitted. And we know her better. We know that she's only a timid little thing with an inferiority complex because she's never particularly been liked very much — and Miss Briggs, too, she's different somehow, she's human. Even you admit that. And your books — they're better books, like I said they would be. Oh, don't you see, it's not been a mistake? We're *all* richer — even Gran admitted it not long ago. And Merlynne — it would have happened, I expect, anyway.'

She broke off, her cheeks flushed, with lips parted like a child's. Dame Julia found it hard to resist an impulse to go over quickly and kiss her. The dear child, she thought. So eager, and so loving. With a flame-like quality about her that did somehow bring new belief into the room.

Even Nicholas had softened, and was smiling.

'And what has it done for you, Susie-Jane?' he enquired. 'What have you got of value from our cultured cranks?'

She paused. 'A lot of things.'

For how could she say: 'I've found Hugo's friendship — that's meant more than all the rest to me.'

'Ah, well!' Dame Julia strove to turn the conversation onto commonplace issues. 'Maybe there's something in what the child says. If it's taught you to sell your books better, Nicholas, that's certainly something.'

'I think Susie-Jane's right,' Catherine said quietly. 'It's given us all more than that. I know it's brought me out of myself a good deal, and though I get a bit tired, the hard work hasn't hurt me — not really. And somehow,' she resumed, with feeling in her voice, 'I wouldn't want to ask Miss Briggs and Miss Spring to go until they want to. It may be better to take no more guests for the moment. But in a queer kind of way I've got quite fond of the old things.'

Don't think me sentimental, but I do feel they depend on us in a way now; and I suppose it's a little gratifying.'

Richard flung her a warm look.

'If that's how Cathie wants things,' he said, 'let it be like that. After all, she's done more in a practical way than the rest of us put together. I think sometimes we overlook the fact. But it's true. We others have had our complications and difficulties – I know I've been a boor myself, following Deborah's death – but Cathie's just gone on in her quiet way, seeing that we were all fed and cared for and made comfortable. It's up to us I think to do what she wants now.'

'Very well,' Nicholas gave in quite quickly. 'If you feel like that – that settles the matter.'

Later, when the gathering had broken up, Dame Julia had an interview with Hugo in the library. Her manner was brisk, but her eyes were troubled in her old face. She was looking very elegant in a black tafetta frock, with a flimsy white lace scarf over her head. Hugo, she thought, looked strained and ill. She noticed that a nerve was twitching in his cheek, below the right eye, and that his mouth had a set, almost twisted look.

'My dear boy,' she said. 'I don't like to see you brooding. I *am* sorry. But you know – I did warn you.'

He nodded. 'Oh, yes. I've been a fool.'

She faced him quizzically, with something of a bird's bright shrewdness in her eyes.

'And you're not going to fetch her back?' she queried sharply, after a second's pause.

'Why should I?'

'Why not?' she questioned, more irascibly than she had intended. 'In my young days a man didn't lie down calmly while some young gigolo ran off with his wife. I can't understand you.'

'If Merlynne hadn't wanted to go, she wouldn't have,' he said coldly. 'I certainly don't intend to play the outraged husband, however badly I may feel about it. In any case, I've partly asked for it. You must know, since everyone else does, that we'd not lived together for quite a time. I'd hoped matters would be all right in the end.

But apparently it was too late. And I suppose that's that.'

She was puzzled by his formality – the almost callous quality of his voice. Yet he was not really cold-blooded; he was acting, then, a nonchalance he did not feel. The hurt, she thought, must have gone deep indeed to have produced so bitter a mood.

She shrugged her old shoulders, and adopting his light tone said, 'Well, I suppose you know your affairs best. But be sure you are not cutting off your nose to spite your face. Such things can happen when one is too proud.'

She left him then, and slowly, trembling a little, for she was tired, went upstairs to her room. The agreeable smell of Marianne's coffee came to her nostrils as she reached the landing, and she was suddenly overwhelmingly glad that the day, with its excitements and conferences and arguments, was over.

I'm getting too old for this sort of thing, she mused, opening the door of her room. Elopements, suicides, hysterics, and drownings! Whatever's the world coming to? I must really get away. I'm sure Henry would have wanted me to. He never could stand neurotics of any kind. That's what I liked about him. That's what this age lacks – balance.

A fire was burning cosily in the grate, and Marianne had already drawn up her chair, with the footstool nearby and at its side the small table with her cup and saucer and sugar basin on it.

She sat down gratefully while the French woman arranged the cushions at her back.

'You are tired?' she queried in her clipped speech. 'Ah, poor madam! It *is* a house – this!'

'Yes, it's a house indeed,' Dame Julia replied. 'Do you realise, Marianne, that in my father's day none of these extraordinary happenings would have taken place? No. There would have been *real* things to do instead. Merlynne would have been playing Titania and Rosalind, and that young Casanova of hers would have had his nose to the grindstone. Yes, people had more discernment then – more sense. They had better things to do than waste time gaping at cranky smudges on paper. Masterpieces? Hm! It's all a tremendous hoax, Marianne. So much is hoax nowadays.' Her voice trailed off in tiredness while Marianne agreed soothingly.

'Of course it is, Madam.'

'You know —' Dame Julia began again — 'it's wrecking the young people. What can you expect of a generation that has no values? All this new-fangled psychology — what use is it if a spade's no longer a spade?'

'None,' agreed Marianne.

'Hm! Well! I feel like a cup of coffee,' her mistress ended abruptly. 'And one of those little biscuits — you know, Marianne, with the icing on them.'

When coffee was over, and Marianne had carried away the tray, she decided to go to bed early and write, from there, to Chetwyn.

She undressed, with Marianne's help, and was soon arrayed in her nightdress and frilly bed-jacket with a becoming lace cap on her grey curls, a bottle at her feet, and in front of her the painted pink bed table, on which was placed her writing pad and pen. The cushions were piled up behind her and the bedside lamp placed at a convenient angle, so that she could see clearly what she was about.

Letter writing came easily to her, especially when it was to Chetwyn, who in some ways was nearer to her in sympathy than the more immediate members of her family.

My dear boy,
    Next week I shall definitely return to town for a time, because to be quite frank I am utterly tired of scenes, and far too much is happening here. In the first place Merlynne has run off with that blatant young opportunist, and Miss Spring has tried to drown herself. Hugo, who is fretting, is behaving most unnaturally, too, and on the face of it I think I should get out before the next climax arises. I don't wish to discuss Merlynne's affair too much on paper, but when I see you I shall be able to explain more. Then, dear boy, I shall look forward to a little peace and culture, and spring along the Embankment.
    I am looking forward, too, to taking a gentle walk with Marianne down civilized streets, of buying violets for myself from my old flower seller at Cheyne corner. Or will you

buy them for me, Chetwyn? That would be nicer. I am starved, you see – wicked old woman that I am – for a little masculine attention. Nicholas is no good at that sort of thing. But then, bless him, he is not a Shane! For the young, Cornwall is pleasant in the spring. It is strange, and wild, and a little fey. But for the old – ah, London is a nostalgia and a dream! One day you must take me driving through the Gardens. Does old Geoffrey Drewhurst still take his constitutional there, I wonder? I should like to have a chat with him again.

Now there is an artist who is an artist! None of your dots and dashes and repulsive ideas – but something one can recognise. And elegant in himself, too. Always impeccable with his gardenia and tall hat. I must say, Chetwyn, I do like people to look pleasant. Somehow it makes a difference to life. This idea that to be clever one must be dirty – fiddle-dee-dee! How stupid that is.

Well, well, there is no need either to spin out the news or my own thoughts. In so short a time now I shall be seeing you. I shall arrive by the Riviera Express either Tuesday or Wednesday. Do not attempt to meet me as I know it would interfere with your performance. I will let you know the exact day later, and then we must soon meet.

With best wishes,
Your affectionate Aunt,
Julia Gort

'Ah!' she sighed with contentment, as duly signed and addressed in its envelope, the letter lay ready for Marianne to stamp and post in the morning. Then she lay back, with eyes closed, imagining herself back again in the cosy bedroom of her London flat. It would be pleasant to return. She had not realised, until then, just how nice it would really be to hear the comforting drone of traffic from beyond her window, to be able to wake up each morning with the anticipatory pleasure of wondering just who would call that day to see her. For there was always someone of her own world with whom one could gossip agreeably over the things and people with whom one was familiar. Yes, there was a pleasant little thrill in that. It gave spice to life. Where was the harm, after all, in a little friendly gossip so long as it hurt nobody? It was the aperitif to existence – that filip without which, things, to the old, might become unendurably dull. And she had no intention of becoming dull. Not she. Where was the sense?

Thus ruminating, and half-dozing, she chuckled as amusing little scenes from the past returned to tickle her senses and memory.

Shortly afterwards Marianne entered, to take the table away and see that her mistress was made comfortable for the night. Already the old lady was asleep. Managing not to rouse her, the Frenchwoman gently took the pillows away, and when she was comfortably at rest, drew the eiderdown round her shoulders and turned the lamp down.

Still smiling, Dame Julia slept on.

Chapter Twenty-Six

The following week she returned to London. The next afternoon Chetwyn called and had tea with her in the sittingroom of her flat. It was an attractive room, significant of its owner's personality, furnished in light walnut of the Queen Ann period, with maroon-coloured hangings and upholstery, relieved by touches of green. The cream walls were bare save for two paintings, a water colour by David Cox, and a Landseer. Above the mantelpiece were two miniatures – one of her father, and the other of Henry, her husband, when he was a child. On the sideboard stood his photograph, looking very resplendent in his Guardsman's uniform.

The firelight flickered comfortably on the tea table and tray, on the George III silver, the Dresden china figurines poised elegantly on the mantelpiece, and on all the small knick-knacks and treasures which she had stored and cared for during the years. There was an ivory-handled paper knife with which some wild and adventurous ancestor was supposed to have stabbed a lover of his wife, a diary with a silver clasp which had been her grandfather's, and, among other things, a wax doll with yellow curls that had been her own when she was a child. The childish streak in her liked to have the doll there. Indeed, throughout her career, it had been her mascot and accompanied her during her various tours – even to Rome and Prague. And so, as she sat there pouring tea, with her nephew opposite looking so handsome and distinguished, a warm little glow of comfort and security surrounded her.

She was glad she was back. She was grateful to Chetwyn

for having come round so soon; and happy to be surrounded by her own things. It was good to travel a bit – she did not regret her visit to Trencathra. But at her age it was better still to return. She was not a morbid person, and the thought of death did not worry her – indeed she seldom thought about it. But the fact remained that she was an old woman. A day must come, not so very far ahead, when she would take the long journey into the unknown. She would feel safer, as it were, to embark from her own sphere. It would be pleasanter to take her departure with her old friends around her, rather than from unfamiliar scenes. Not that she was afraid – dying, like birth, must be right since it was in the natural course of events. And she believed in a God. But say what one would, it was an adventure – something known little about, for which certain homely fortification would help to face. Chetwyn, for instance – no-one perhaps gave her so much reassurance as that nephew of hers. Her grandchildren meant a great deal to her; she loved them. But they didn't really understand her with the bond of unity existing between Chetwyn and herself.

She thought he was looking very handsome that afternoon, and age would only emphasize the air of breeding and elegance which despite their vagabond origin seemed to be the heritage of the Shanes.

He, in his turn, could not keep his eyes off his remarkable kinswoman. Her eyes sparkled in the firelight, her skin was flushed and warm at seeing him, and her voice eager, giving a momentary illusion of youth.

'You said you had more news for me,' she said, leaning back in her chair following tea. 'Now, tell me, Chetwyn – what is it? No secrets!'

'Well,' he said, 'you'll be surprised, I think. It's quite a bombshell. I saw Merlynne only yesterday.'

Dame Julia leaned forward quickly. 'You *saw* her!'

He nodded.

'Where?'

'At the Blue Frog in Soho!'

'Well! Was she alone?'

'No. The artist fellow was with her.'

'Ah! What did she say? Was she ashamed?' The question

held a hint of petulance. 'Did she give any account of herself? How was she dressed? Did she look happy?'

He smiled. 'My dear aunt! You bewilder me. If I remember rightly though she was looking quite striking in red.'

'Hm! Must be new – Merlynne never wears red.'

'She certainly didn't look unhappy,' he told her.

'Did you find out where they were living?' she asked presently, more quietly, following a short pause.

'I asked,' Chetwyn replied, 'but both were non-committal. They were in temporary lodgings, I believe, in Bloomsbury. But I gathered from him that a one-man show of his was to be opened in a small gallery near Leicester Square early in May.'

'What is the name of the gallery?'

'The Greville, I think.'

'I shall go,' the old lady said with a sudden somewhat aggressive decisiveness. 'I shall certainly go and confront that young man. Did he say what date?'

'Yes, the fifth.'

'Good. I'm glad I know. And what did Merlynne say – anything? Did she give you any message for any of us?'

He shook his head. 'No. Not exactly. Just a remark or two. Something like, "I expect the family's in an uproar. But it can't be helped. Anyhow – I'm happier than I've ever been if that's anything. Tell Gran if you get the chance, will you? Somehow I think she'd understand."'

Against her will, the old lady's eyes sparkled with a hint of triumph. 'Hm! She said that, did she? The jade! Well, never mind. Maybe I do – better than the rest. Between you and me, Chetwyn, Hugo was no good to her. The longer I stayed there, the more clearly I saw it. Not that I condone what she did, there should have been a better way than that, and a better man to do it with – still, the girl has spirit, and I hope things don't work out too badly for her.'

'I don't see why they should,' Chetwyn remarked. 'As you know, I didn't care for Laurence – but he has something that women like, and Merlynne's very feminine. It may be that the rest – the disadvantages – won't matter in comparison.'

'Not at the moment, perhaps,' Dame Julia said. 'But

permanently, Chetwyn – what about that? It's never easy, you know, for a woman to defy convention. There may be occasions, perhaps, when a great love makes it worth the candle. But somehow I don't believe there's anything of that in their affair.'

'Certainly not on his side,' Chetwyn agreed. 'The man's a complete egotist. But Merlynne – I'm not so sure.'

'Then Heaven help her!' Dame Julia said fervently.

'Perhaps Heaven may.' The remark was light, inconsequential. 'You never know. In any case, it all remains to be seen. There's nothing that anyone can do about it now.'

'No, I suppose not. Too late to alter the course of events.'

Long after Chetwyn had left her, however, his aunt was disturbed, albeit a little intrigued, by the news of Merlynne. Chetwyn's meeting with her had alarmingly brought her into immediate perspective again, and Dame Julia found herself on tenterhooks to see her.

Here I am, she chided herself, only just back from Cornwall, determined to have a rest from emotional scenes, and almost the first thing I do is to get drawn into a situation immediately. For, of course, I shall go to his opening, and of course I'm quite excited at the thought of it, for which I should be thoroughly ashamed.

Nevertheless she was not – in the very slightest. To the contrary, the prospect stimulated her immensely.

'You see,' she confided to Marianne, 'I'm not so tired and old as I thought I was. That's what London does for one. And I must say, whatever she's done it will be pleasant to see the dear child.'

The day arrived, warm and springlike, with clear sunshine spilling its radiance over the London streets, on the shop windows and upon the baskets of flowers heaped gaily with violets, rose and lilac, at street corners and along the thoroughfares.

The opening of the show was at three-thirty. Dame Julia lunched early, and at three o'clock Chetwyn called for her with his car. She wore her black velvet cloak, trimmed with fur and lined with purple silk, and a small frivolous hat arrangement of flowers and lace, with a veil thrown back from her face. She took her ivory cane with her, and carried also her small silver chain hand-bag. A bunch of violets was pinned near her throat. Never had she looked more regal. She was quite excited, with a pink flush on her cheeks and her eyes piercingly bright.

'You mustn't get too concerned about it all,' Chetwyn said, as they drove along. 'I don't know that I should have let you in for all this excitement.'

'Tut, tut, my dear! It's doing me good. Best tonic in the world,' she smiled at him with a hint of archness. 'Why? Do I look so decrepit?'

'On the contrary,' he affirmed. 'You're bewitching. That's just it – you look positively dangerous.'

'Now, now, Chetwyn! You're flattering.'

But she was pleased. She could not keep the gleam out of her eyes, or pleasure from her voice, and there was, he saw, a self-conscious twitch of gratification at the corners of her mouth.

A small crowd of people were already assembled there when they arrived, including Lincoln Green, the critic from the *Clarion*. There was the usual smattering of obviously 'arty' youngsters with bows, earrings, and long hair, but few faces that she knew. But then, there wouldn't be! she told herself. Most of her generation and standing were either dead or had the sense to keep away from an exhibition of that kind.

Presently she saw Laurence himself emerge from a little group of the far end of the hall. He came towards her, smiling.

Brazen! she said to herself, trembling on Chetwyn's arm. Quite brazen! To confront me openly, after running away with my own grand-daughter. Where is she, I wonder?

She waited while the young man approached. He looked the same as ever, she thought with hostility; just as odd, in his arty clothes, a little tidier perhaps, but Pan-ish with his mouth and eyebrows curled in the same expectant mocking way.

Nevertheless, she allowed him to take her hand, although she withdrew it quickly, saying tersely, 'Where's my grand-daughter, young man?'

'Oh!' he said. 'It's Merlynne you want, Dame Julia. How disappointing.'

'What did you think it was?' she queried. 'Your pictures?'

Chetwyn laid a slight restraining pressure on her arm, and a little more quietly she added, 'Don't play with me, or you'll be sorry, Mr Dale. Merlynne, I presume, is with you?'

He shook his head. 'No. As a matter of fact, she isn't.'

'Not? Where is she then?'

Without answering her question he muttered, 'Excuse me for a moment,' and moved away to have a few words with a couple nearby. When he returned he merely continued as though there'd been no interruption, 'About Merlynne – I can assure you she's perfectly well, but prefers to stay away from crowds. Satisfied, madam?'

'No,' answered Dame Julia tartly.

'Then I'm afraid – '

'Look here,' Chetwyn interrupted. 'It's understandable my aunt should be concerned. Why don't we meet for a short civilized interlude later at Polini's for drinks?'

The young man's face took on a certain grimness. 'I doubt if I can make it. Hang it all, this is my opening!'

'And I'll have you remember, young man,' Dame Julia interposed with rising temper, 'Merlynne's my granddaughter, and if all the rest are too namby-pamby to say what they think – I'm not!'

'Hush, Aunt!' said Chetwyn, taking her arm again. 'Come along! We mustn't make ourselves conspicuous.'

A gleam of irony lit her eyes. 'Conspicuous? My dear Chetwyn, I'm *always* conspicuous. Indeed this young man will be well advertised. Green has already seen me.'

Looking round Chetwyn saw that it was so. The famous art critic had his eye on her, and after a moment came towards her. That clinched matters. Slightly mollified, she said to Laurence, 'Well? Are you meeting us?'

'All right,' he agreed. 'Six. Inside. But I shan't be able to stay long.'

'You won't be required to,' she answered.

Laurence left her, and a second later Lincoln Green was shaking her hand.

'Well, Dame Julia,' he said. 'What a surprise! They say this outrageous young man is quite promising. But I didn't expect to see you here.'

'No,' she said, 'and I shouldn't be – but for a fluke.'

'A fluke?'

She tapped him on the hand playfully. 'Now – no questions. I don't want you to think I like the stuff – I don't! So don't be spreading any pretty tales in your gossip columns, Mr Green.'

He looked interested and vaguely bewildered, then said, 'One has to have a taste for modern stuff. But of its kind it's not bad.'

She was surprised. Green had the reputation for being a hard critic, with a bitter edge to his tongue. Her eyebrows went up. She queried, 'Do you mean you like it?'

'It has something no painter has had since Gauguin perhaps,' he admitted. 'This one, for instance.'

Against her wishes, she was compelled by him to cross the floor, where he stood by her, Chetwyn on the other side, confronting 'Resurrection'.

Dame Julia did not like the painting. But something in her was stimulated. She was both taken aback and startled by the energy and lurid force depicted in the strange passionate colouring and composition. For a moment, it seemed to her, indeed, that the soul of some primeval satyr, some immense pagan entity, had materialised in that vortex of emotion and was summoning her to recognition of its being. She was a little shocked at herself, feeling that to be moved at all on the subject was an insult to her intelligence.

'Well?' queried Green. 'It speaks, doesn't it?'

She shrugged her shoulders, feigning nonchalance; but admitted grudgingly, 'It has a certain power. But what *is* that power? Nothing good. I don't like it. What's the point of spreading evil about?'

'Perhaps we're on the verge of a dark age,' the journalist remarked incomprehensibly. 'Looking at life from a completely amoral point of view, you know – there are two sides to it, a dark and a light side, which are correspondingly mirrored in a man's nature as evil and good – one the counterpart of the other.'

Dame Julia tapped her stick impatiently on the floor. 'I don't like abstruse arguments,' she said. 'This thing has doom in it. No ultimate beauty or meaning. Power ill-used. If we, as human beings, want the light, we shall have it. If the dark – well, I suppose we shall get that too. But why should we?'

Green smiled with faint irony. 'We are perhaps a generation without fairy tales,' he said. 'The war has done it. Something has died.'

'Oh, the war!' she spoke impatiently. 'It's easy to blame the war. Everyone does. But if individuals lived properly there wouldn't be war; and there wouldn't be this sort of thing.'

'Well,' the young man said more equably, 'that may be so, Dame Julia. But whatever the moral issue, Dale has conveyed a great idea in this painting. It may not be pleasant, it may not be true. But he's *conveyed* it. And that, to an artist, is success.'

'Hm! have it your own way,' she conceded grudgingly. 'You will, anyway. You always do. But don't ask *me* to approve.'

'I don't,' he said. 'Your disapproval, Dame Julia, is of more use to me in any case.'

'And remember, young man, there's a law of libel.'

He smiled at her brightly, and left her some moments later.

Now what, she thought, is he going to make out of what I've said?

But the thought did not trouble her unduly. She liked Green. If it meant any kudos to him he might use her name, so long as it was not said that she had sponsored Laurence.

She did not stay long at the exhibition but left following the short opening speech which was given by Julian Dallas, the poet, a contemporary of Chetwyn whom, she thought, should have known better than to support the young man. However, despite her irritation, the visit had not been entirely wasted; she had learned something, and at Polini's later she would find out more concerning her grand-daughter.

The afternoon was spent agreeably in Chetwyn's company. He escorted her from shop to shop where, among other things, she purchased a new smart evening coatee and handbag. It was gratifying, after her isolation in Cornwall, to be indulging herself with fripperies again; a pleasure emphasised by Chetwyn's company — the evidence of his affection, and the knowledge that together they did indeed make a handsome pair. She was warmed and heartened by the attention she received in the shops, by the pleased smiling faces of the assistants, their hurry to find for her a comfortable chair and to supply something suitable to her taste. She, in her turn, smiled and joked with them, flattered a little, and was pleased once more to find her charm working.

When, later, they were sitting in Polini's at a table in a quiet alcove waiting for Laurence, Chetwyn said to her, 'It's always an education being out with you, Aunt Julia. The longer you live, the subtler you become. Your methods are devastating.'

'My dear boy! You make me sound positively immoral.'

'Aren't you?' he teased.

She smiled. 'Chetwyn, I believe in making life as pleasant as possible, and believe me there are few people who don't respond to friendliness. That's where, as a race, I condemn the English. They are so chilly — so gauche.'

'And you, of course, are *not* English?'

'Me?' she shrugged her shoulders. 'I'm a mongrel, Chetwyn — so are you; our disreputable ancestors, after all, though English born had a touch of the Basque in them, a dash of French and Irish, and goodness knows what else. That's why we have a sense of humour. That's what keeps us healthy.'

'Agreed,' he said. 'And I suppose, also, it's that touch of Irish which makes you so blatantly rude to Laurence?'

'No. My good sense,' she responded sharply, 'and now here he is.'

Looking up, Chetwyn saw Laurence threading his way between the tables towards them. He sat down next to Dame Julia and said, looking at his watch, 'I haven't long. I had to leave Ericson in charge, and quite a number of people are in.'

'Have you sold any?' Chetwyn enquired.

'Two.'

'Oh! Not bad in the time.'

'Very good,' Laurence said easily. 'And if I get good reviews, that will help enormously.'

'Never mind about reviews,' Dame Julia said a little testily. 'Tell me about Merlynne. I'm not going to moralise because, quite frankly, I believe you're beyond any moral sense whatever, and I don't intend to waste my breath. But the fact remains you've behaved abominably and I want to know where my grand-daughter is.'

'Well,' Laurence regarded her with something between admiration and hostility, 'at the moment we're in a fourth-rate hotel in Bloomsbury. How long it will be for I don't know. We're getting out as soon as we can find a small flat or better digs.'

'I see. And why, may I ask, wasn't she with you this afternoon?'

'As I said, she isn't keen on crowds. And there was no point in flaunting our relationship.'

Dame Julia leaned forward, a dangerous gleam in her eyes, 'In point of fact, young man,' she told him, 'you mean to keep Merlynne in the background for your own pleasure while you gad about at exhibitions and parties, enjoying yourself. After seducing her and luring her away from her husband, you are not even prepared to face the music openly.' There was contempt in her voice.

Laurence's face tightened. 'Nothing of the sort. Merlynne determined of her own free will to join me. I didn't even know she was coming until the last moment when she appeared. It was true we'd been lovers for some time. Eventually, I knew it would happen. But that moment was hardly the most opportune for me with the exhibition so near and circumstances as they were.'

'You're insolent.'

'Agreed. Where would I be if I wasn't? I've no illusions about myself. Nothing you can say will surprise me. If I'd been rich I could have afforded to have a conscience and be a perfectly nice moral man. But I happened to be poor, with a burning obsessional talent. Hence I am as I am.'

'Poverty played no part in your elopement with Merlynne,' she told him.

'No. Mutual need,' he said.

'An if Hugo never divorces her, what then?' she queried, with the first faint gleam of anxiety. 'Are you going to allow Merlynne all her life to be discussed and whispered about – to be the subject of gossip and secret vulgar taunts? Don't you think she is worth more than that?'

He faced her frankly, yet with so cold a look that she was repelled.

'Merlynne made her own choice. As for gossip – once I'm established, it won't hurt us. In any case, an artist is expected to lead his own life. In the autumn we're most probably going abroad.'

'I see!' There was a sneer in her voice. 'You're going to run away. Well, maybe you are wise to. You may think it's possible, now, young man, to ride rough-shod with impunity over other people's feelings. But I can tell you this: no art, no achievement, lasts if it's built on heartlessness, at the cost of other human beings.'

He smiled. 'That's a debatable point, Dame Julia. Take for instance Gauguin – '

'I did not come here to discuss Gauguin,' she told him. 'I came for Merlynne's sake. Also – ' and she looked at him fixedly, pausing for a brief second before continuing ' – it may interest you to know that Miss Spring tried to drown herself recently.'

She had delivered her bomb-shell. She sat back, a little gratified to have penetrated even his cold egotism. She could see he was shocked. Just for an instant he paled, before the swift colour flamed into his face.

'What did you say?' he asked in level tones. 'Did you say *drown* herself?'

She nodded. 'You heard.'

'Why?'

'Neurotic, obviously,' the old lady said. 'And far more interested in you than she should have been, or than you're worth. Still, after what she did for you, I should have thought even you would have had more decency than to have behaved as you did.'

He did not at once reply, and she sat watching him closely, wondering if at last she had touched some shred of feeling in him. But he was hard to read; obscure and tantalising, with his longish enigmatic eyes and tilted mouth. There was something attractive about the mouth, sensuous and beautifully curved, but cruel, too. Still, some women, as she well knew, liked that sort of thing, the foolish creatures.

At last he said, 'I'm sorry about Miss Spring. But you said "tried". Well,' he made a gesture with his hands, 'that's not the same thing, is it? She was probably just being sensational.'

'Probably,' Dame Julia agreed shortly. 'But a woman should not be driven to these sensational moods.'

He drank a martini quickly, put the glass down and said, 'Dame Julia, I'm sorry, but I think this interview should end. Ten minutes of my time have been given to listening to your recriminations. I have "seduced" your grand-daughter – well, have it your own way, if you like. I am responsible for Miss Spring flinging herself into the water – very well, if you wish to think so. But I tell you quite frankly, it just doesn't interest me at all. No, not at all. Merlynne and I can get along if left to ourselves. As for Miss Spring – well – I'm quite sick of her, you understand? Kind? Yes, she's been kind to me. But she's been kinder still to herself. Have no illusions, it's given her no end of a kick.'

'Oh! You're impossible.'

He stood up, smiling. 'Quite,' he agreed.

Seeing that he was determined to go, the old lady said sharply, 'Give me your address. I must see Merlynne.'

'There's no point in it,' he said. 'We're moving tomorrow, and I'm not even sure where to. But she has your address. She can write.'

A bright colour suffused Dame Julia's face. 'Young man,' she said, trembling, 'if I want to see Merlynne, wild bulls won't deter me. I'm warning you.'

Chetwyn put his hand on her arm, restraining her. 'Now, now,' he said. 'Don't get excited, Aunt. It's quite true – if she wants to, she can contact you. She told me she would, you know. And I believe she meant it. In any case, there are other ways if necessary.'

'Yes, of course. There are other ways.'

She allowed herself to be settled back into her chair. But

her hands were still trembling. Thought he could defy her, did he? The good-for-nothing! Ah, but he was a scoundrel. An impudent rogue. If she was a younger woman she would teach him a lesson. Indeed her hand itched at that moment to strike him. It would not have been the first time she'd fought a man. No. There had been that fellow in Paris! Against her will a sly, reminiscent little smile curved her lips, in contrast to the anger in her eyes. He had been her devoted slave ever afterwards, following her wherever she went. But then, circumstances had been different; and herself a young woman. Still, one couldn't help wondering ... Her fingers relaxed on the cane.

'Well,' she said, more quietly, 'you'd better be off before I make a scene.'

He bowed ironically. 'Thank you.'

'Tch!' She made a gesture of impatience. 'But understand that when I want to see Merlynne, I shall do so. And I take nothing back. I dislike you, and consider you've behaved abominably. That's all.'

'Thank you for being frank,' he said. 'We at least know where we are with each other, although I was under no illusions. Well, goodbye Shane. Goodbye, Dame Julia. I'll remember you to Merlynne and tell her what you've said.'

He left them, assuming a pose of nonchalance, a sangfroid, which despite his jaunty air did not, however, completely convince.

'I've touched him,' Dame Julia said to Chetwyn, with faint triumph. 'He's incorrigible; quite amoral. But I got under his skin, Chetwyn, I did him good. But that poor child! What's to become of her when the romance wears thin? No, the more I think of it, the more hopeless it seems. It won't last. Not with a man like that.'

Seeing that she was becoming depressed again, Chetwyn refilled her wine glass. 'Cheer up,' he said. 'Things aren't that bad.'

She took a sip, and there was a silence between them. Watching her, Chetwyn knew that something was going through her mind. Her eyes had an abstracted, far-away look in them, and her chin was sunk forward in a manner which belied her age – a posture revealed seldom in public.

Presently she sighed, and looking up, remarked, 'Chetwyn, I've been thinking.'

'Yes,' he queried encouragingly.

'We must try and keep in touch with Merlynne. Even if the running abroad comes off. And I've been thinking also that if, at any time, she should break away — which I think she will — we must do something for her. You can, Chetwyn.'

'Me?'

She nodded. 'I'm an old woman. I have a lot of silly ideas no doubt. But I do know life, dear boy. And I know Merlynne. That girl's wasted, Chetwyn. It's because she's been wasted that she's got in this mess.'

'No doubt,' he agreed. 'She's never properly found her feet yet. She's a Shane — greedy for life! It was always apparent.'

'Exactly. She should have been with you, Chetwyn. On the stage that girl would have been good. I can see her as my father would have seen her — Ophelia, Rosalind, even Juliet. She has a lovely voice, the Shane temperament. Lacking in humour, perhaps, but all the rest.'

'Yes, I can see it.'

'Hm! Well? What about it?'

She glanced at him intently, a little smile about her lips, and a sudden warmth spread through his veins.

He reached across the table, placing his hand momentarily over her own.

'Of course,' he agreed. 'If she needs me, I'll be there — I promise you. I'll take her, and I'll train her. I'll do what I can.'

Moisture filmed her eyes. 'Thank you, I knew you would. You're good. The best friend I ever had. That's made me feel better. You see after all she's my daughter's child. And whatever she's done that fact remains. My own blood. And yours, too.'

He nodded.

'Maybe,' she went on, 'I'm an incorrigible sentimentalist. But I can't change at my time of life. I should be criticised, no doubt, by the prudes. But what did they ever do in the world, Chetwyn, except make it a little harder and more difficult for those in trouble, eh?'

'Nothing,' he agreed.

'No. Well, let's be grateful anyway that we've been given a little more human kindness, you and I. We may be fools in our way, but I think on the whole we're quite happy fools. What do you say?'

He smiled, and she took a nut from the silver dish. 'Do you know,' she went on, 'I feel better after all that. I do really. The afternoon has not been such a failure after all. No, on the whole, I've quite enjoyed it.'

'Good,' he said. And he was thinking, she may have a sharp tongue on occasion, but her bark's worse than her bite. Underneath her heart's soft.

'Come,' she said presently. 'We must be going, Chetwyn. You should be getting to the theatre. And Marianne will be waiting for me.'

It was nice, after all the excitement, to visualise once more her own fireside, with her slippers put to warm. She had, as well, quite a lot to tell Marianne who would be gratified, no doubt, to hear all about the young man and how she had told him off. Yes, for all his high and mightiness, she had humbled him a little. That was good. Nevertheless she smiled remembering his impudence. A rascal, undeniably, but he had been honest. She didn't approve. His morals were offensive. All the same, he had something! What was it – charm? No, hardly that. An indefinable quality which had nothing to do with good or bad, right or wrong; something, she knew, which would appeal to many women. The knowledge brightened her spirits, because in one sense it did exonerate Merlynne the more. It was natural for the girl to want something in her life rather than vague dreams and high falutin' arguments. Who, with any red blood in her, wouldn't? She did not *approve*. Merlynne had been foolish as well as wrong. But there! This applied to many former Shanes, adventurers and playboys that they were. Greedy for life – yes, that was true. And a hunger of deep love quickened Dame Julia's heart for this sheep that had strayed. There was, after all, something highly coloured and romantic about their affair which appealed to the dramatic in her. And on the whole Hugo deserved what he had got.

Having come to this conclusion, her mind was more at ease,

because the fact simplified the moral issue. Before she went to sleep that night she had successfully managed to convince herself that Merlynne had been the victim of circumstance rather than her own actions, and that all in the end must turn out for the best.

Chapter Twenty-Seven

That same evening Laurence told Merlynne of his meeting with Dame Julia. He spoke casually, almost flippantly, yet she knew he was disturbed. His eyes were still angered at the recollection of their conversation; she knew the signs now – the cold stare and narrowing of the lids, the brief, callous curl of his lips. Seen thus, Laurence's was not a pleasant face. But it had a power to move her more than anything in the world. If he left her, if their life together broke up, whatever happened to separate them she knew that although she might hate him violently, she could never forget him. Indeed, it was doubtful if her hate, even, could endure for long. There had been times already since leaving Trencathra, when his selfishness had stimulated her to a violent anger. But always, in the end, it had died. With his arms around her, his sudden swift alternation from one mood to another – from contempt to charm, from coldness to warmth – her defences were down, and she was mere clay in his hands. His dominance, while it frightened her on occasion, pleased and lulled her to forgetfulness in the grip of their mutual passion. There were, too, those rare times when he was more human, more of a boy and lover. Then she was tempted to forget his other side and the ruthless will which, when necessary, subjugated everything to its own ends.

But there was little of the boy about him now. This was the Laurence she feared and yet who fascinated her so that the primitive streak in her responded and was possessed utterly. He was not strictly speaking handsome. Yet there was something lawless and proud about him which had the quality of some pagan god, almost frightening in its contempt. As she faced him, the dingy sittingroom with its cheap furniture and faded wallpaper of trellis and roses receded into nothing. She forgot to notice the tawdry lace curtains, the hideous pot vase containing the aspidistra, the mingled smell of dirt and turpentine. All these details became of a sudden insignificance, obscure and quite meaningless against his vitality.

'And so I told her,' he was saying, 'that we were moving tomorrow. That's final. If there's one thing I won't have, Merlynne, it's your relations interfering. Even so remarkable a character as your grandmother.'

'Of course not,' she agreed. 'Although I think you have probably misunderstood her. Grandmother is not narrow-minded.'

'Oh, no,' he said. 'We understood each other perfectly.'

'And in any case − ' she continued ' − I can't ignore her. If we meet, which we're almost certain to, you can hardly expect me not to welcome her.'

'What you do with yourself is no concern of mine,' he said lightly, cruelly. 'All I'm saying is that *I* won't be bothered with family arguments. I'm warning you, Merlynne. I refuse to be drawn into your affairs.'

Her lips curled. 'How nice of you, Laurence. You're so kind always, aren't you? Such a help!'

'There's no need to be sarcastic.'

'Well,' she lit a cigarette with fingers which trembled, 'sometimes, you know, you really are the limit.'

'I've never denied it. But you were aware of it. Don't nag.'

'Oh!' She turned away with a hurt impatient toss of her head. Her eyes were bright, and the colour flamed in her cheeks, but his gaze was arrested suddenly by the lines of her back, the curve of waist and hips and gallant swing of the shoulders.

His mood changed. He laughed. In a second he was across the room, his arms round her, straining her to him. And she in her turn felt resistance go from her, so that she slackened and let her head fall against his shoulder, chin raised.

He turned her round, smiling, hungry lips travelling the cool skin of her cheek and neck, while a hand closed seductively against the curves of breast and buttocks.

'You know, Merlynne,' he said, when he had released her, 'you're a terribly arrogant person. I want to beat you. Why fight me so?'

'I, Laurence?'

'But of course you do. Pretending and arguing. Words, words, words! Such a waste of time.'

'Well, I have to say what I think. Anyway, you'd never want a "yes" woman. And you must realise that the whole thing hasn't been easy for me.'

His lips tightened.

'There you go again. Criticising. As though I were responsible.'

'No, Laurence. I didn't mean that. You're so suspicious.'

'Something else wrong,' he sighed. 'Very well, I'm going out.'

He reached for his coat, and went towards the door, but she was there before him with her arms outspread, flushed and bright-eyed, a pale fringe of hair fallen over one temple, looking very young in her agitation. He took her by the arm and would have pushed by. But her arms were suddenly round his neck. He became aware of her scent and warmth and subtle sweet femininity, noted the tremor of her scarlet lips flower-like in her white face, and desire to punish her was gone. He drew her to him, his eyes bright and triumphant above her, his breath warm on her cheek.

'Don't leave me, Laurence,' she whispered. 'Never leave me.'

She could feel his hands caressing her, felt herself submerged and lost in the delight of his proximity. The present, the knowledge of what she'd done, all doubts faded. This was the one reality, this wild thing sweeping all other considerations aside, and which, through its own sensual fire, brought new life to her, and a delight which was beyond all other delight, all joys she had ever tasted, all rapture she had ever imagined. In such moments she knew herself to have been right. For in comparison the world was a small and tawdry thing, and the moment longer and deeper than eternity. To have rejected it would have been to dam the strongest currents of her own being. In succumbing she became, in truth, no mere flesh and blood but of the elements of which all life was comprised. Civilisation fell away, and she was wind and sea and rain, sunshine and the thrust of life from the earth, her breasts as mountains, her body a fountain for his pleasure. And he, in his mastery, knew, and was triumphant.

So that when at last they saw each other with their eyes again, they knew that while this lasted they were bound together more strongly than by any man-made laws, for good or ill. Man and woman – possessor and possessed.

He might hurt and taunt her, and she in her turn rebel and hate. But always, in the end, she would come to him again and follow him where he chose to go. He was not 'good'. Never had a man been less tender to her, less kind. But she loved him. And late that night, long after he slept peacefully, his head on her breast, she lay awake, afraid to disturb him, her heart warm and at peace. It was always so. After the turbulence came this strange new quiet which transformed her from restless girl to woman. All wisdom was hers then, and she felt temporarily as a mother does – protective and wise in her knowledge of man. She had no illusions. According to social standards she'd strayed. Her future, she realised, would be difficult. She was not even certain of the outcome. But she accepted it, and at such times had no fear. The morning would bring its anxieties and problems, its adjustments and uncertainties, its miasma of doubt. But for the present she was fulfilled. This, it was, which made the rest worth while.

Chapter Twenty-Eight

On the last day of the month when the may frothed white in the hedges, and the aching call of the cuckoo sounded across the fields and hills, Sam Murgatroyd died. After a heavy dose of morphia he passed away quietly in his sleep, without regaining consciousness. Lying static and silent on the hospital bed, the strain miraculously passed from his features, leaving round the lips the semblance of a smile, an innocent benevolence which seemed to suggest: 'Don't fret. No pain can touch me any more. Death isn't difficult, it's kind. The rounding off of a pattern.'

Following the turmoil of life, the last secret was his and had stamped him with a strange dignity. There was no fear there. Only renunciation and peace.

He was buried in Penzance, on a day when the larks sang and a haze of sunshine lay over the town and sea beyond. Susie-Jane, with Hugo and Miss Fothergill-Briggs, attended the funeral. Susie, pale and strained-looking in a loose grey coat and hat, Miss Briggs openly crying into her handkerchief. More than had been expected were present. During his time in Cornwall something of his kindly nature had penetrated the hearts of the people, and among the gathering were several fishermen and country people with whom he'd struck up acquaintanceship during his rambles in the vicinity.

'There was nothing brilliant about him,' Miss Briggs said later, driving back. 'He wasn't particularly clever. But he was a good man. He never hurt anyone. The world would be a better place if there were more of his type in it.'

Yes, thought Hugo, that's true. We thought him a funny

old boy at the beginning. His jokes, at first, used to irritate me. But he was direct. He saw straight. And that's something we more sophisticated blokes seldom do.

He realised though that the time was quickly approaching when a decision about his own future must be made. He couldn't stay for ever at Trencathra with his wife gone, and Susie-Jane beside him offering her faith and love which at the moment seemed too much for him. There were times when he caught her off her guard, watching him, when he was both elated and humbled by what he saw in her eyes. Mildly irritated too. He knew the time wasn't ripe for any decision. Concern for Merlynne still troubled him, and he was still tired, his spirit still wanting solitude and regeneration. Beyond his natural need of woman — of *any* woman, even Susie-Jane — was this searching of his inner self. He was too weary to tackle the conflicts of personal relationships. Other things lay waiting before him — necessities dealing with humanity rather than with himself. Reading the papers, watching the trend of world affairs, he saw, despite lip-service to peace, the Crucifixion being enacted all over again. There was praying in churches, obeisance to a creed, while wars were still hatched and men revenged themselves on each other. A great deal was talked of goodness, but the so-called 'good' forgot that the basis of Christianity was forgiveness.

In the days following Sam Murgatroyd's funeral, Susie-Jane sensed more than Hugo realised of his conflicting moods. With feminine intuition she knew he cared for her, recognising at the same time the wound both to his pride and heart caused by Merlynne's desertion. His mental conflict was clear to her, and hurt. Friends they would always be, and lovers perhaps in spirit. But being young and vibrantly alive, she longed for physical fulfilment and reality. She wasn't even certain whether or not he intended to divorce Merlynne. She did her best to feel loyal to her sister, but it was obvious to her that Merlynne no longer cared a rap for Hugo, and for them to be tied in any way now was a travesty and mockery.

Somehow though, Susie-Jane could never bring herself to speak to him of these things. In the earlier days, before their mutual feelings had taken such root, it had been easier to approach him. But with the sensitive awareness of their new relationship a certain restraint had developed, so that neither cared to mention the subject.

In order to keep herself from brooding too much, and because there was a good deal to do following Merlynne's departure, Susie-Jane busied herself more actively than she'd ever done in household matters.

Catherine so far had not managed to get an efficient girl in Ann's place, with the consequence, now, that except for Robin, the simple-minded boy, everything fell upon the two sisters, with the help of Olive.

Strangely enough, she seemed more contented with Ann away. There was a chance now for her to shine, and earn praise other than mere reflected glory. She was strong, and energetic, and it pleased her to get up early in the mornings, singing or whistling a dance tune as she rattled the dustpan and brush, or cheerfully laid the breakfast things. She was noisier than Ann and seldom brooded. She banged about a good deal, but when there was extra work to do always managed to smile, provided encouragement and praise were given her. Without this she would have lost interest and flagged.

One morning, when Richard came in for his early cup of tea, he said to her, 'How's Ann these days, Olive?'

She flashed him a brilliant sideways glance from her dark eyes. 'Oh!' she said perkily. 'She's okay, Mr Richard. She's fine now. You wouldn't know her.'

'No?' he queried, half absently.

Amost too casually Olive remarked, 'She's had her hair waved. And she's got a new blue frock. But then that's natural, having a fellow always bucks a girl up!'

She continued to roll the pastry on the board, humming a little tune nonchalantly under her breath. A dark curl of hair escaped from her cap and lay black as ebony against the rick glow of her cheek.

Richard's brows met for a second above the bridge of his prominent nose. He was not sure whether she was serious or not. 'What did you say?' he queried. 'A fellow? Ann?'

She nodded. 'Charlie Traill – he's wanted her for a long time. There's another, too, Bill Tredegle from Shortways farm. But Ann – she doesn't care for him. She likes Charlie best. He's nicer to look at. But Bill's got better prospects, my father says.'

'Indeed.'

'Yes. It makes you think, doesn't it? After all a girl could so easily make a mistake. Ann doesn't think much about position and all that. But *I* say you have to look to the future. After all, love doesn't last, does it, not for ever? And then where are you?'

'Quite right,' said Richard, faintly amused. 'But I shouldn't be too cynical, if I were you, Olive. You may miss a lot of fun.'

'Oh, no, I shan't.' She tossed her head. 'I know what I'm doing Mr Richard. I'm not a fool.'

'Certainly you're not,' he agreed. 'I can see that.'

There was a pause while he helped himself to a hunk of bread and cheese. After a moment he said almost lightly. 'So Ann's in love, is she?'

'Mm,' Olive made a gesture of prevarication, 'I wouldn't say that exactly. She hasn't said so. But she doesn't tell much. She's not like me. I let folk know things. But Ann's kind of quiet about herself. She thinks a lot.'

At first Richard was mildly surprised at the suggestion of Ann having a lover. She had seemed to him too remote, too quiet. But after all, he mused, as he left the kitchen for the fields again, it was only natural she should. She had character, and was attractive in a subtle feminine way. There had been always something fresh looking yet elusive about her, holding the fitful glint of sunlight on ripening corn – a quality that would mature and deepen with the years. There'd never been anything bold or tantalising in her nature – no wild charm such as Deborah had possessed, wilfully calculated to entrance and torture; but one day, if she married, some man would find fulfilment and a rich peace in her as wife and mother of his children. She'd be loyal and decent, single-hearted in her love, and unquestioning in her trust. With her there might be no wild rapture, no journey to the stars – on the other hand who could tell? Quiet waters sometimes held a hidden mystic beauty. One thing was sure, union with Ann would have roots too deep to be disturbed by temporary difficulties of temperament or circumstances.

He walked on, past the orchard in which a few late apple trees were still in bloom, through the gate at the bottom of the slope and upwards to Starvecrow, one of the five acre fields which had been ploughed up in the early autumn and now showed a good yield of young potatoes. Beyond it a field of barley was gently astir in the wind, and to the right several acres of greens ready for cutting and marketing in Penzance. He thought of Ann as he swung along, and could not help wondering about her affair with Charlie Traill.

He knew the boy; a nice young fellow, pleasant to look at in a country way. He would probably make a good husband, and he and Ann came from the same world socially. But somehow Richard couldn't see her married to him. A country girl she might be, but there was something proud about her, and too intelligent surely for kindly Charlie. Richard felt in his bones, and couldn't have said why, that if Ann *did* take Traill for her husband it would only be because he was a good fellow, and because she wanted a home and children. For many marriages this was a sufficient basis but Richard didn't feel it would satisfy Ann. In her quiet way she had a strong capacity for affection; it was difficult to imagine her mating unless love also were there. Perhaps it was, though. Perhaps after all she had, in her isolation, grown really fond of the young fellow. The suggestion made him unduly ruminative. He wanted her to be happy; he wouldn't like her to make a mistake. Another thought occurred to him which came as quite a shock – he didn't really wish to see her married to anyone at all.

This was the first time, consciously, since Deborah's death, except for Merlynne's elopement and certain family matters, that he'd allowed his interest to be engaged by the affairs of anyone else. For a time, indeed, following the tragedy, he'd shut himself away from everyone – hating, even, the daily necessity of conversation and of those domestic issues which demanded some of his time. His only relief had been in his contact with the earth and his own physical labours.

All through that grim winter, through the long hard days when he'd worked in the open on windy frost-bitten fields, or when the grey winds blew over the wet cold earth, Deborah's image, like a ghost, had risen to haunt him; sometimes when the stunted trees were bent groaningly against the gales, he'd pictured her shadow speeding across the leaden sky, imagined, as the gulls wheeled and cried, that it was her voice he heard, in her last scream before going over the cliff. He'd tortured herself then for not having managed things better, for neglecting to take a stronger line in protecting her from Stokes. Though his mind was well aware that the deciding factor had not been in his hands – that it lay in something deeper, which even she could not control, her heritage and blood – the possibility that he'd failed her would not leave him alone. All those lonely months he'd been obsessed with arguments of – *if* things had been different – *if* this had not occurred – *if* he had married her earlier – need that final issue ever have arisen?

Then, when the spring came and the first warmth penetrated the young earth, something in him had gradually relaxed a little. He'd felt himself responding almost against his will to the resurrection going on around him, and in time the horror and anguish had given place slowly to an ache which had become now a confused memory of beauty and desire. There were moments still when a chance word, a scent or tune brought back the past with a sudden vivid pain, jerking him away from the present to a startled longing. But as the days passed these intervals were less frequent. He knew now that he would live again one day as a man, and that passionately as he had loved Deborah, desire had not entirely died with her but slept on somewhere in his being, and would one day wake again; not with the wild longing of his first love, but in strength and wisdom, with direction and purpose. For his was not a character intended by nature to live celibate or alone. Unlike his sister, Catherine, his feet were too firmly on the earth and he knew that whereas she might manage to live by memory alone, he, ultimately, could not. He was not sure that anyone should, and quite frequently was worried when he contemplated his sister's future.

Catherine, for her part, was content in her own 'aloneness', and the unique position she held at Trencathra. Only once had her security been threatened, at the time of Deborah's advent into the family circle. Catherine, unlike Merlynne, was not a physically passionate woman, and what there had been of it in her own character had been given completely to her husband. She recognised that for her no one else could count in the same way, and preferred to keep her memories ever fresh and faithful rather than take a secondary love. If people pitied and were sorry for her, they were mistaken in doing so. For Catherine, despite her apparent flower-like fragility had a flower's resistance also in meeting the whirlwinds and problems of nature. All she asked for now was the chance to make and retain her own environment — which was at Trencathra — to be able to please people, and look nice, and to feel that she was being useful in some way to others.

During the days following Miss Spring's nervous outburst this capacity of hers had been well tested and proven. For never had anyone so clung to her, been so dependent upon her for encouragement, and never had Catherine felt so warm a stab of sympathy for any living soul.

Following the episode Miss Spring had wandered about the house curiously dumb and defeated-looking. Her briskness, her simulated girlishness, had cracked, as it were, in the night; she had emerged in her true guise, as a middle-aged, disillusioned little woman who had been hopelessly fooled. For the first time since the affair had begun, she had seen matters as they really were, known the extent of her own gullibility. She was not only ashamed — something in her was beaten. For her, the bright prospect of rosy romanticism was completely gone. She tried to lose herself once again in the retreat of her mysticism, but for a time even this was Dead Sea fruit. The only comfort she obtained was from Catherine, who took her completely under her wing, went on walks with her when she had time, talked to her at nights, and began subtly to make her feel as though life, after all, was not quite in vain, and that there might still be a place for her in the world.

Then one day a letter came for her in handwriting which she knew. It was waiting for her on her plate at breakfast time, the unmistakably scrawling writing staring up at her like a message from some other world which she had been doing her best to forget. She opened it with fingers that trembled, tearing a corner of the paper in her agitation.

Dear Miss Spring,

    I'm aware that I owe you — if not an apology, for I never believe in one person apologising to another — at least an explanation after your help and encouragement in the past.

    I'm not going to say much; I know you'll condemn me. I realise that you'll be imagining your trust betrayed, and that I've been completely ungrateful. But this isn't so. I sold a dozen pictures from my show in The Greville which should prove to you that any belief you had in my work was justified. I'm enclosing for you several cuttings of reviews, which I hope you'll appreciate. I didn't ask you to come to my opening, because quite frankly personal issues would have been very complicating and irritating, and I know you wouldn't have wanted that any more than me.

    I'm not going to attempt to make excuses for any of my actions — as I've said before, I lead my life the way I want and feel beholden to no one, including you. But I hope you'll realise in the end that my work has been worth your interest. One day, when any annoyance you feel now has passed, you'll possibly be gratified to have had a share in its beginnings. I intend somehow to put my stamp upon contemporary art.

    I'll let you know, from time to time, how matters go with me. I'm giving no address. There's no point in it, and I'm by no means settled at any permanent place. Later we hope to go to Italy, when things are possible there.

    Once more, with thanks.

    Sincerely,

    Laurence Dale

She was breathing rather quickly when, the letter read, she put it down beside her on the table. From the other end she saw Catherine's glance upon her, a hint of anxiety in her eyes.

Miss Spring gave her an agitated, quick little smile, reaching once more with trembling fingers for the note which she replaced in its envelope and deposited carefully in her bag.

Later, when the meal was over, she followed Catherine out of the room and caught her up in the hall.

'It's from him,' she said breathlessly. 'It's from Laurence. He's written after all. You see, he – he didn't quite forget.'

Catherine laid her hand gently on Miss Spring's arm, 'No,' she said, 'of course not. What did I tell you? No one short of a brute could. I'm glad, Miss Spring. What did he say? Did he mention Merlynne?'

Miss Spring's face clouded slightly. She shook her head. 'No, not at all. He – I don't suppose he wanted to upset me.'

'I see. Did he by any chance repay you anything?'

Miss Spring shook her head again, with more vigour. 'Oh, no. I don't expect him to. I didn't – you see, that money wasn't a loan. I gave it to him. That's why it seemed so unfair.'

As the memory of the past week or two returned to her, tears momentarily filled her eyes.

'Well,' Catherine said, 'you're very charitable, Miss Spring. I'm glad, anyway, he had the decency to write.'

'Yes. It does make a difference.'

And, indeed, the difference showed. Her expression was brighter, her skin had more colour, and already a certain sprightliness had come back to her walk. Catherine wondered what he'd said to her, and if, in fact, the letter had been impelled by conscience or opportunism concerning the future. Miss Spring herself didn't delve too far into the motive; that he'd written at all, even at this late date, was balm to her pride. She no longer tried to deceive herself, she recognised she'd been foolish and that he'd played without scruple upon her feelings; but this one gesture of his had elevated her from a status of complete contempt to some show of recognition, and she clung to it as a drowning man might cling to a straw.

In the early days following, something of her dejection lifted, and in early June she could once more be seen taking walks by herself along the cliffs, her cape flapping in the same old way, her chin poked upwards in her characteristic manner.

Nicholas caught sight of her frequently as she passed the

lodge carrying the paper bag from which she fed the gulls with crumbs and bits left from the table. He had thought her odd and affected before; her high voice, nervous manner, and queer ideas had irritated him profoundly. But since the day when she'd thrown herself into the water he'd seen her in a new light. Whatever her motive, whether the desire actually to drown herself was genuine or not, the poor little thing had obviously suffered keen emotional distress. He hadn't wanted her to remain; at the time he'd thought it far better for the family to be peacefully on its own again. But her continued presence now only served to remind him how easy it was to underestimate an individual's capacity for suffering, and how the least likely people might contain the seeds of tragedy beneath exteriors that were ludicrous in the extreme.

Susie-Jane had been right. He was learning something about human beings which was subtly affecting his work and giving a new filip to his creative urge. Apart from its success his writing nowadays came more easily to him and was altogether more fun. Odd to think that a queer little creature like Miss Spring could in any way have helped. But there it was – which just went to show, one never stopped learning, even an established writer of sixty-four summers.

Chapter Twenty-Nine

Letter from Julia Gort to Catherine Vernon
My dear Catherine,

　　Though I told you in my last letter that I was hoping somehow to contact Merlynne I have not yet done so, and I think now, unless I force matters myself, it is extremely doubtful if I will. I told you, I believe, of my little dénouement with Laurence? He is really an outrageous young man! However, that is neither here nor there. I really *did* expect Merlynne to get into touch with me sooner, but doubtless 'the opportunist' influenced her. Until last Saturday I heard nothing. Then a letter arrived in which she informed me that under the circumstances perhaps it would be better to arrange no meeting for the present. Here is a quotation, in her own words:

> Please don't think I don't *want* to see you, Gran dear — it would make me so happy I should probably cry. But at the moment I just couldn't bear to hear news of the family. I know, you see, that I have cut myself off — of course I have. And I think I'm a coward. I think now I just want to go on in my own way, without having my conscience jarred, which it would be bound to be. Things have been too complex for such a long time that at the moment I want only to keep to a direct course. I have chosen mine, and I hope you will be able to forgive me, some time.
>
> 　　I know you don't care for Laurence, any of you. But I only seem to live properly through him; my time with

Hugo — even the best time — was nothing compared to this. I am sorry about Hugo. But you know, he's never really needed me, and he'll be able now to do what he wants — divorce me, and marry Susie-Jane if he wants, she's always looked up to him — or go on in his queer way trying to set the world right. Hugo, in every way, is so much better than me, we could never have got on. But Laurence and I are alike. We both have a dark wild side — perhaps we are pagan and lost. But we fulfil each other.

So you see, Gran, I don't want you to worry about me — and please tell the others — because whatever happens, I shall have lived, and I shall get through. Give my love to Daddy. Later I will write to him. We are thinking of going abroad soon, and I will keep in touch with you.

I'm not giving you my address, because we both think that it's better not.

Try and understand.

Yours lovingly,

Merlynne.

Well, before doing anything further I thought I should let you know. And in view of everything, having thought things over in cooler blood, I have come to the conclusion that if that's the way the child feels, it *is* perhaps better at the present to leave things as they are. It may be, of course, that we shall meet by chance at some function or other — but I rather think that they will not be for long in the country. Perhaps, all things considered, this is for the best. I should like to know if Hugo has any plans in view. Whether or not he has any intention of divorcing her. I know most men feel badly about divorcing a woman. But in this case it would obviously be best, both for Merlynne's sake and his own. She could, then, marry the young man, which would simplify things from her point of view.

To me, it is a grievous thing having to discuss divorce in this cold-blooded manner. I have never believed in this casual jumping in and out of marriage, and I wished something better for Merlynne. But from the beginning, her marriage to Hugo, I'm convinced, was ill-starred. And this is one of those things for which we may rightly blame the war. If they'd had a better chance of knowing each other, probably it would never have come off. However, there is no point in bewailing the past, the future is what we have to look to, and according to the trend of modern affairs, this is none too rosy. Still, I for one, refuse to be depressed unduly, either by the income tax, rationing, or the insidious State control which is doing its best to get us into the mass-machine. Well, let it do its best or worse! One day it will overeat and burst itself. But whatever happens, and for the time I have left, I shall remain *myself* – Julia Shane – the individual. I shall fight tooth and nail for the personal freedom which is one's birthright, and I shall fight, my dear Catherine, in a manner which most women unfortunately are forgetting, or have never known – with a woman's best weapon, her charm.

Ah yes! Charm is a subtler, a more powerful thing, than most people realise. With it many a heart can be softened and issues altered. God did not make women to wear breeches and storm man's domain, but to lure him with her skirts to pleasanter territory. This is what women are forgetting nowadays. This is where life is going wrong. The strength of a nation lies, primarily, in the strength of the home life. When that goes, either civilisation breaks up, or over-reaches itself.

Well, I did not mean to philisophize, but when the pen gets into my old hand I just forget myself.

Take care of yourselves, and God bless you all. Whatever the old pessimists like to say, we shall come through.

With love, your affectionate Grandmother,
Julia Gort

Chapter Thirty

When Sam Murgatroyd's affairs were settled, and all death duties and legacies paid, the sum of £400,000 was left with the bank in trust for the Murgatroyd Home. It came as a surprise to Susie-Jane and Catherine that both had been remembered in his will to the extent of £2,000 each, free of tax. 'In gratitude,' the Will read, 'for the friendship and consideration always shown me during my happy stay at Trencathra.'

Details were then expressed concerning his wishes for the orphanage, in the hope that a suitable site or sites would be found in country districts where the children would benefit from fresh air and freedom. He expressed a hope that so far as possible the home or homes would be run without the necessity for outside financial help or charity, and that all the house staff should range under the age of fifty and have proved themselves to be conscientious and keen youth-welfare workers, of humanitarian principles. The question of salaries he left to the Committee, but stipulated they should not come below a certain range.

Both Susie-Jane and Miss Fothergill-Briggs were nominated as life guardians, among whom also were several public names – men and women of high principles whom Sam had for long held in esteem.

The bank was left as sole Trustee, which, in conjunction with his lawyers, was to see that his directions were carried out. He ended on a note of hope, 'My wish is that the orphanage will be named the Murgatroyd Home, or Homes, and that all who carry on this work for me will remember that I wish to found it for the sole sake of children who otherwise might not have known the comfort and happiness which this bequest may provide. I wish them to be brought up free of dogma, yet in the spirit of true Christianity with a respect and affection for each other, so that when they come to adult age they will go out into the world as men and women having a happy background, with courage and brotherhood in their hearts, on which, I believe, the new world of peace may be built.'

Many other details concerning the administration and organisation were defined and suggested, certain plans for the training of the children when they had reached school leaving age, and a special fund set apart for this. There was little he had not considered.

Though she had known about Sam's wishes before his death, Susie-Jane was touched and humbled at his mark of esteem. It was something, she knew, which would affect her for the rest of her life, and in her innocence she was convinced with a sudden upwelling of emotional faith of the truth of immortality, and that dying was no more than passing from one state of life to another. She had no clear mental vision of the exact form of her belief – it went deeper than that. It was, to her, a sense of rightness and harmony, and the ultimate survival of good over evil. As the days grew longer, passing into young June, she had the illusion sometimes that the spirit of Sam walked with her when she went for her evening stroll along the beach. Belief in his unseen presence comforted and helped her, because Hugo these days seemed remote and withdrawn. She never doubted his love, but was frustrated at being unable to show all she felt for him.

At times, walking in solitude where the gulls basked on the wet sand, she saw her brother as she last remembered him, in his uniform, clear-eyed and young, trying hard to smile as he said goodbye to their old dog and pulled her hair before he kissed her. She was not being morbid; it made her happy to believe these people she'd been fond of were together, neither lost nor gone but still caring, and remembered. It made dying seem less lonely, and it occurred to her frequently that though Sam had left them, he'd gone to good company, and that nothing of him which really mattered had been taken from them. With this conviction a curious peace came to Susie-Jane.

If Hugo goes away, she thought, I must try not to mind too much. If he goes it will be because he has to. I don't believe it will be for ever – I don't believe what I feel for him could ever be destroyed, because it's beautiful, and it belongs to the good things, and it will live on somehow. It's stonger than life and death – it's like Julian, and Sam. They're not dead, not really; and my love for Hugo will never die. Neither will his for me. I know that. I know it more strongly than anything. And perhaps in the end, he won't go at all?

Always her conjecturing ended on that note of hope, opening the gates of Heaven for her, leaving her warm and expectant with something inside of her singing – so joyous a thing that her heart trembled in mere anticipation, and it seemed the world rejoiced with her. Never, at such moments, was there so happy and vivid a creature as Susie-Jane. Life indeed was miraculous then; the young flowers, the scabious swaying in the grass, the soft west wind, the early mornings when the dew shone bright on the thrift and thyme, and the gulls dipped low over the headlands – all the miracle of awakening life symbolised the depth of her love. And if at times the song was saddened, if following the morning's glory, warning of maturity's pain touched her, the song nevertheless was still there. And she knew it would always be so. If in the years ahead suffering came to her, that singing thing would still go on, hoping, loving, giving, believing. There was that in her which would never be entirely defeated by circumstance. Life was too rich and full; too precious ever to lose its value.

One Saturday afternoon towards the middle of the month, when she was arranging flowers in the lounge, Hugo opened the door and seeing that no one was with her, entered the room. He had, she saw at once, some purpose in his mind. He walked deliberately, his limp hardly noticeable. He came over to where she stood with a flower in her hand, watching him, and said gravely, 'I have something to say to you, Susie-Jane.'

She smiled, 'Yes, Hugo?' She paused, trembling a little. 'Sit down then.'

He shook his head, 'No. I – this isn't going to be very easy for me.'

A half-frightened query leapt into her eyes, and instinctively her hand stole up to her breast where her heart missed two beats and then, with startled urgency, started hammering. She forced a smile to her lips. 'Why?' she asked.

He did not at once answer her question but, evading it, said with a hint of wonder in his voice, 'How pretty you look in that blue dress.'

'Oh, but I – but it's old!' she said quickly. 'I had it ages ago. I worked the little daisies on it myself.'

'Did you?' He smiled at her, and seeing the expression of his face, so warm and candid at last, no longer withdrawn or strained, anxiety and shyness left her. She went forward and let him take her hands returning his smile.

'Oh, Hugo, I –'

He kissed her gently on the lips. 'Darling Susie-Jane!' he said.

'Dear, *dear* Hugo!'

After a moment he released her and walked over to the window where he stood for a minute or two contemplating the garden and distant view of the headland and cliffs. She waited until he turned and came back to her. But he didn't attempt to touch or kiss her again. He took his pipe from his pocket and lit it, half sitting on the arm of an easy chair. She said nothing more, though longing for his nearness, for the feel of his arms enclosing her. That brief contact had fanned into consciousness all the pent-up emotion of the last months. Now more than ever she knew their love was right; with physical contact had come an overmastering sense of belonging – of coming home. It was as if for a long period she had been searching restlessly and at last come to her own haven. And she knew that for her it was for all time.

At length he spoke.

'For a long time,' he said, 'we've cared for each other. It's true, isn't it?'

She smiled, 'Oh, yes!' she half-whispered. 'Of course it is.'

'I wouldn't admit it openly,' he went on. 'You know that too. But as things were I think I was right.'

'Yes.'

'And now it's different of course.'

Her heart waited for some sign, for some indication of what he had to tell her; but his eyes had torn themselves away from her, and he was staring past her into something she did not see. Presently she saw him lift his hand to his left temple as though some nerve beat there in pain. Then he turned to her again and said, 'Susie-Jane, I love you. But I'm going away.'

The seconds ticked like a clock in her brain. Everything in the room was suddenly accentuated in detail, in the silence which gripped them; yet it seemed to her that colour had gone swiftly from the roses, that the air had quickly chilled, and that though the sea outside was the same sea, and the sun still shining, a shadow had darkened everything, temporarily obscuring all meaning from the day. Yet she must be brave! Because, all the time, she had half expected this — it was not as though she hadn't been prepared.

'Are you?' she said, forcing herself to answer. 'Very well, if you think that's best.'

'I've got to go, Susie, otherwise all this — you and I — would be no good. First of all I have to find myself.' He paused. 'But how unconvincing it sounds — just talking to you, like this.'

He turned and sat down again, leaving Susie-Jane still standing nearby. She saw how difficult it was for him; without fully comprehending his enigma, because she herself was so direct. She could only wait for him to explain, to make his decision, and then muster courage so that when, as he said, he had 'found himself', he could return to her if he chose. If not — She swallowed hard, and forced the vision of emptiness from her.

'I know what you mean, Hugo,' she forced herself to say. 'Tell me. Go on.'

He shrugged his shoulders, 'What more is there?'

Then his expression changed, and he faced and spoke to her for the first time perhaps as individual to individual. She was no longer child or girl to him; her sex became briefly unimportant through this new knowledge of equality. Looking into her fearless eyes he saw, with wonder, that she did indeed open the gates of freedom to him. His bonds were gone. It was as if for the first time in his life he was really able to follow his own course. And she had done this for him – this young girl, who had the courage to say 'Go' when her whole being yearned for him to stay. He was aware that he had hurt her, that beneath her pride she was suffering; but he knew, also, that to have pretended and stayed through pity would ultimately have hurt her more.

'Susie-Jane,' he said gently, 'do you believe in me?'

'I always have,' she answered. 'There's no need to ask.'

'No. I know. Well then! Some day, when I've thought it all out, when I've done what I have to do, I shall come back. I'm sure I shall come back,' he said, looking at her. 'And then our lives may be clearer. I wish for you,' he resumed thoughtfully, 'that you could have loved a more normal man.'

'Oh, no. Never,' she asserted passionately.

'Because,' he went on, 'you were so obviously made for normal things, Susie-Jane. You have a right to them. And it may be that they will never be mine to give you.'

'Never mind,' she said stubbornly. 'I don't care, Hugo. I love you.'

'Even if things work out for us,' he said, 'I shall never be young again, as you are. There is a whole hunk of experience between us.'

'Does that matter?'

'No. But it makes a difference. It's the reason for my going. If I'd never fought through the war, never married Merlynne, never lost my faith and found it – well, something of it – again through such desolation –' His voice faltered. 'Well, my dear, there'd be no need for this involved conversation, or for me to hurt you. It grieves me to cause you pain. You know it, don't you? Rather than that I'd give up everything I have, sacrifice it all – except this one thing. That I can't do.'

She bowed her head. 'Yes, I understand.'

'It may not be for long,' he continued. 'It may be longer, I don't even promise to return, and you, too, must feel free. But somehow I think I shall – no, that's not true. I'm sure of it.'

'Yes,' she whispered. 'And I shall be waiting.'

There was a silence between them until she asked presently, more steadily, 'Where will you go, Hugo?'

'For a time I shall just journey,' he said. 'I shall go back to Wales. There's a little cottage I stayed at, in the mountains. Then, if my leg's good enough, I shall walk.'

'I see.'

'I have to be alone,' he resumed. 'Not only because of my own problems, and Merlynne's, but to get life into perspective. Maybe I've worried too much, or even too little. It may turn out that the mystic's path isn't mine. I don't know. But anyway I must see. And then, afterwards, I want to know Tom, Dick and Harry. I want to be free to mix with all types of men and live as they live, to contact what's possible of the very worst and best of life. Superficial knowledge is no good. I want to be able to walk into the lowest dive, and shout my belief, and *win*! If I can do this I'm proving myself, and proving to them, in their own language, that it's possible for all things to be born anew given faith and mercy. But I must be able to speak their language first. Mercy to each other – that's my lesson.'

'It was Christ's, too,' Susie-Jane said.

He nodded. 'That's what I mean. I want time to learn and understand it. Oh, it's not that I imagine myself in any way worthy of preaching Christianity but I can see this clearly – that through it the world could be swept clean of war and hypocrisy and corruption and greed. This has been said before, it's preached in the churches every Sunday. But the real Christ is not confined to dogma, Susie-Jane. He's at the street corner, and in the pubs. He's with the sinners and those who, in our arrogance, we think we have the right to judge and destroy. What right have we to judge anyone but ourselves? When we haven't even learned the first lesson of kindliness.'

He continued, 'And that's what I want to do. I want to help somehow in tearing down the blindness of individuals, so that they can see each other clearly as human beings with weaknesses and virtues like themselves, to release the spring of compassion, to help restore decency and gentleness and kindliness of spirit.'

'I think most people are kind at heart,' she said. 'It's only when they're together they go wrong.'

'Then,' he said, 'when I've done what I can, worked the urge out of my system, I shall perhaps be able to rest. Perhaps one day, in the autumn, or in the spring when the lambs are about and the young things growing, I shall come back and find you. And you won't look any different – I'm sure of that,' he said quietly. 'You will still have that grave look in your eyes, with your mouth half smiling, and that funny little breathless way of talking – oh, Susie-Jane!'

He jumped up suddenly and went over to her, catching her in his arms, his face buried against her hair.

And she thought a little faintly, I must remember this. This moment must be eternity to me – so that when he's gone, I can escape and be with him again in memory. A warm little wind drifted in from the sea, stirring the curtains, carrying with it the faint scent of brine and bluebells. She stirred and sighed, raised her face to him and let her hand reach up, touching momentarily his cheek and hair.

Then he turned and left her.

She was still standing there, minutes later, when Catherine entered, some sewing in her hand.

'Why, Susie-Jane!' she said.

Something in the young girl's face when she broke from her reverie, arrested and silenced her. Never had she seen so passionate an avowal of grief and triumph, pain and joy.

'I'm sorry,' Catherine said, sensing a little of the truth, for she had met Hugo going down the passage. 'Did I startle you?'

Susie-Jane shook her head. 'No, I was just thinking.'

She turned, and replaced the roses on the table. But her eyes were still far away, as though, having looked on some vision, she had returned to the world unseeing of the things that went on around her.

Chapter Thirty-One

How quiet was the old house. How strangely the cuckoo's call sounded through the open windows from the fields beyond. A haunting cry – forerunner of spring's passing. And yet it was only morning, and the risen sun had not yet driven away the first mist which lay over the garden and fields. Light, like a golden net, quivered through the trees and above the grass, in which the dandelions shone as small round suns, their petals open to the dew. Everything was indeterminate and hushed, caught in a spell of beauty which, to Susie-Jane, who stood at the door, was timeless and poignant, aching with the sadness and the hope of her own heart. Above her, through the haze of sky, there was the whirring of wings as two wild geese flew to the west. For a moment their shapes quivered against the light; then, as though drifting to eternity, they passed and were lost to view.

In such a way had Hugo gone from her a short while ago. She had watched him walk up the path to the waiting car, seen his form grow dimmer and more far away until, at the gate, everything about him was vague and indistinct, everything except the urge in her to follow him, to snatch the shadow back to reality, and by her touch compel him into her life again. But she hadn't stirred. She'd let him go as they'd arranged, without fuss. And when he had turned at the gate she'd been unable to see him through the mist, and the sun, and the tears in her own eyes.

Seconds later she had heard the car start up, and the whirr of its engine as it moved away, along the lane and down the hill to the station from Trencathra. She'd stood there, unable to move, listening until the sound of it had quite faded, leaving her alone in the doorway of the old house. All was as it had been — the white rose tree round the porch, the lawn with its familiar sundial, the yew tree at the corner, and beyond the hazey glitter of sea. The scent of bluebells crept with its nostalgic unhappy sweetness through the long grass, heavy with childish memories which like forgotten ghosts crowded round, impelling her to the past. But this could never be, now. No more could she return to that world of escape. Childhood had gone. It was to the future she must look. She must have the courage to face it; for some day he would return as he had said. She was sure of it. And if he did not? Ah, but he would. Like a challenge the certainty swept through her. He would come back. Her faith couldn't lie. Whatever happened, she knew that she would see Hugo again.

And presently, as a shaft of sunlight pierced the top branches of the old yew, she turned and went into the house.

The summer passed, and autumn came, with the potatoes to be lifted and sorted, and the crops to be harvested. From early morning till late at night, Richard was at work in the fields; labour was short, and whenever they had a spare moment Susie-Jane and Olive gave him a hand. But this was not sufficient for all that had to be done. He had help occasionally from German prisoners from a distant camp. The Agricultural Committee did its best to see that the farmers were provided with labour, but Trencathra was not a priority case, with the consequence that Richard was left very largely to face his own difficulties. Robin was very little use. The two regular men worked well, but could not be expected to achieve the impossible. Nicholas, in a sporting mood one day, offered a hand. But he was soon tired, and found himself unable to cope in any useful sense with the outdoor work. The result was a reliance on any casual labour which could be obtained, and this was all too infrequent.

One Saturday afternoon, as Richard on the tractor was lifting the potatoes in the field below Starvecrow, with only two school children to pick up and bag them, he saw on the brow of the hill the figure of a girl in a blue frock. At first he didn't recognise her, then, as she drew nearer, swinging down the slope, he saw that it was Ann. It was some months since he'd spoken with her, and her appearance came as a pleasant surprise. He waited, wiping his brow for it was hot, and waved to her as she approached. She was looking her best, with her hair burnished to deep chestnut from the sun, her skin warm and glowing. At one glance he noted everything about her – the athletic easy way she moved, the glint of gold freckles on her slender, rounded arms, the proud arch of her neck when she raised her head. Yes, she was proud, but very human for all that, he thought, remembering with a touch of humour her spurts of temper in the past, the toss of her head, and the manner in which, when challenged, her eyes could flash. She was smiling now, facing him candidly though a little shyly, with a tentative query in her glance.

'Well, Ann,' he said, jumping down. 'This is nice.' He went forward and gripped her hand. 'How are you?'

'I'm all right,' she said. 'And you?'

He grinned. 'A grease spot. I was thinking about a drink. I've some cider by the hedge. What about it, Ann? And you can tell me all about yourself.'

'All right. Actually I'm here to help you with the potatoes – if you want. We heard you were hard up for labour, and my father suggested I came along.'

'That was kind,' he said, walking back with her over the brown earth. 'Haven't you enough to do at your own place?'

'Oh, yes, but it can wait.'

'Well,' he said, looking at her, 'I'm not sure that I should let you, but I'd be a fool not to.'

He called between his two hands to the children in the distance. They came running to him, pigtails flapping, their faces grimed with soil and blackberry juice.

'Here you are,' he said giving them each half-a-crown. 'It's after five, your mothers will have tea ready for you. Are you hungry?'

They nodded. 'Ooh, yes!' one of them said. He patted her on the head. 'Run along then. Come on Monday if you can. You've done well today.'

'All right, Mr 'kerviss,' they agreed, giggling at each other and running away. 'Goodbye.'

He returned to Ann, and uncorked the bottle of cider which was lying in the shade of the hedge. There was also half a loaf and a hunk of cheese which he insisted upon dividing.

'But I don't want any,' she protested. 'I'm not hungry. I've had my tea.'

'Nonsense,' he said. 'Come on, let's have a picnic.'

She laughed, showing a glint of white teeth, unable any longer to restrain her happiness at being with him.

'Oh, very well,' she agreed. 'But it does seem soft, when I'm not a bit hungry.'

'You will be when you relax. What about a drink first? It'll have to be out of the bottle I'm afraid. I hope they didn't leave any vinegar in!'

Like a child, almost, she entered into the spirit of the occasion, and took a drink from the bottle. Then thrust it at him.

'I'm enjoying this,' he said presently. 'Why didn't you come before?'

She shrugged. 'We're a busy family.'

'You could have called in some time,' he accused her. 'Why didn't you?'

Her eyes became grave. 'I didn't like to. Not after the way things happened.'

'I see. No.'

He sat silently for a minute or two, while the golden afternoon darkened for a second. Or was it his imagination that a shadow fleetingly obscured the brightness of the sun? He fancied briefly that the brilliance died and that the air stirred with the first breath of evening chill. Yet when he turned to look at Ann she was still sitting in a pool of sunlight, hair and frock unruffled by any wind, the blackberries luscious and dark on their prickly stems behind her. A few late buttercups shone in the long grass at her feet.

Presently she gave a sudden exclamation of suppressed tenderness, as a small shrew mouse made its way along the earth under the hedge towards her.

'Look,' she said, in a soft voice, touching his arm. 'The pretty thing.'

It didn't appear to fear her, but crept towards her open

palm, and after a tentative pause, crept into it, the small trembling body soft against her flesh. Then there was a quiver of fur, and the tiny creature slipped away again, darting through the grasses into safety.

'The *little* thing,' Ann said. 'I don't know how people can kill them.'

'You've got a soft heart.'

She shook her head. 'Not me. Not always, Mr Richard.'

'Richard, please,' he corrected her.

'I can be very hard when I want to be,' she almost boasted, ignoring his interruption. 'You've no idea how hard I can be when it's necessary.'

'Oh, yes, I have,' he asserted. 'You were pretty hard when you went away and left us.'

She knit her brows in honest distress. 'Ah, but I didn't mean to be. Not then,' she said. 'It was for – it was because –'

'Well?'

'It seemed the right thing to do,' she finished, 'and that's all. I can't explain properly now. But it seemed the right thing for me to go.'

'Well, there's no understanding a woman,' he said. 'But perhaps it was to be near that young man Traill, was it, Ann?'

He hadn't meant to mention Charlie Traill, but the words were out before he realised his intention.

She flushed and looked away. 'Charlie? Who told you that?'

'So it's true, is it?' he said. 'Never mind. A little bird.'

She gave her quick characteristic toss of the head. 'I suppose it's Olive,' she said. 'Olive could never keep her mouth shut. The silly meddlesome.'

He didn't look at her. 'Well, if you're happy – happiness is important, and meant to be talked about. What harm does it do?'

'Ah, but it's not,' she said quickly. 'Not with me, I mean,' she added with confusion. 'I *like* Charlie, but not the way you think. Oh, no. It never could be that.'

She spoke with such finality that he asked curiously, 'Are you sure?'

'Quite,' she said.

'Hm! Well – in that case,' he remarked lightly, yet with an odd sense of relief, 'what about a cheese sandwich?'

She smiled, relieved that the embarrassing interim was over.

'I don't mind. But only a small one. No – not so much. Here, let me cut it.'

He handed her the knife and watched her slice the bread.

'Thanks, Mr Richard – thanks, *Richard*!' she said, passing it back to him.

'That's better.'

They ate and talked, while the sun lowered slightly in the west. Then suddenly jumping to his feet, and stretching himself, he said, 'We must get to work. We've waited long enough.'

She agreed and herself rose, packing the cider bottle and remains of the bread into the basket. A flock of gulls rose shrilly as they made their way across the brown earth to the tractor. He had been well ahead of the two children and many rows of potatoes lay waiting to be picked up. She left him and crossed the patch of ground, taking a sack with her to commence the bagging.

She worked rhythmically and almost tirelessly. Many women brought up under easier circumstances would have wilted by the end of the first hour. Not so Ann, who already had a hard day's work behind her. The feel of the air and earth was always good for her, and the knowledge that she was working for Richard stimulated her, even when her muscles were beginning to ache.

At rare intervals he stopped for a cigarette and a short chat with her, but these moments were few, for daylight would soon be on the wane, and the light too low for her to see.

At last, at half-past eight, he told her she'd better go. 'You've quite a way to walk,' he said. 'In fact, if you can wait another hour or so I'll drive you over.'

But she refused. 'No,' she said. 'I promised I'd call at Mrs Jenkins on the way back for some magazines for Mother, and that means going the field way, and across the moor.'

'Well, Ann,' he said, 'you've been a help. And it's been nice having you with me.' He smiled warmly from his dark face, and she noticed, with a pang of emotion, how white and strong his teeth were, how his eyes appraised her from beneath his level brows. His green shirt was open at the neck revealing skin tanned to a deep mahogany from the sun. The black hair was damp on his brow. This was how she liked to see him. In any setting he appealed to her as no one else ever could. But in his working clothes, his figure outlined sturdily against the sky, he represented reality to her, something which was stronger and had more meaning than his background of culture which, though it had its place, was something she couldn't entirely appreciate. It belonged somehow, she thought, more to the old world than to the new, and would divide rather than bring them together.

Not that she had much confidence in any lasting relationship between them. At the moment it was enough for her that Richard appeared to have recovered from Deborah's death, and that he seemed to bear her no grudge for her revelations at the inquest. Walking back across the moor her mind went this way and that. Perhaps she had been too sensitive and imagined more than was really true. For Ann that period was now tinged with horror and would hardly bear looking back upon. His engagement to Deborah had been hard enough to bear, but Richard's coldness and disregard of her – his seeming contempt following the inquest – had been far worse. Indeed she had never dreamed then that a day would ever come when she'd be able to walk over to him, as she had done that afternoon, and be met with friendliness. Only a chance remark of her sister's had impelled her to do this.

'He was asking for you,' Olive had said, on her last visit home. 'He asked how you were, and what you were doing, and I reckon it would please him an awful lot if you went over, Ann. And they're short of help, too.'

She had not replied. But her mother had supplemented, 'Yes, why don't you? It would do you good to get away from here for a bit. Goodness knows, my dear, we don't get much change.'

No, Ann had thought, that was true, although lately she'd been going out with Charlie Traill again occasionally. But those jaunts into Penzance had not excited her very much. She liked Charlie, he was a good sort, but still he was not Richard. Nobody, for her, would ever be the same as Richard.

And so she'd taken her courage into her hands, and on her first free evening made her way to Trencathra.

Now, on her way home, she was surprised how easy it had all been, how naturally glad he had been to see her, and how perfectly they had worked together, with no shadow of misunderstanding on their evening.

There's no difference in us, really, she thought. We like the same things, and we've got the same sort of strength. All this business of being a Nankerviss – what does it matter? If I'm looked on differently to his sisters by most people it's only because I work and haven't learned quite so much from books. But there's another kind of knowledge that I could teach them. It isn't that I don't admire them, and I respect Miss Catherine. But I respect my mother more for having brought up nine children on three pounds a week. There's something in that to be proud of. It takes grit and lots of common sense and elbow-grease. And nobody's thanked her for it, except the family, and we've not cared enough. But if I had my way it's people like my mother who'd be looked on as grand ladies, and presented to the Queen. But nobody takes any notice. It's just taken for granted that they should wear themselves out being good and doing their duty, and stinting and saving to bring their children up for the sake of the country. And then after all that, folks of our kind aren't considered good enough to mix with the gentry. I may not be clever, but I can see clearly. And I know it's not right. It hasn't any sense to it. Besides – and for the first time ever she considered her own heritage seriously – the Chenoweths were something in the past.

Richard, making his way past the sheds, was quite unaware of the revolutionary thoughts which he'd stirred in Ann's heart. To him it was unimportant to what stratum of society she belonged. He had never consciously thought of her as a servant; indeed he'd always respected her as a girl of character, his equal in commonsense and all the essential qualities of personality.

He was tired that night, but his spirits were lighter than they had been for some time. He was whistling when he entered the house later, and Catherine said to him, 'You sound happy, Richard. Things going well?'

'Fine,' he said. 'I had a visitor, too. Good help she was!'

'Oh?'

'Ann,' he said.

'Ann?'

He nodded. 'It was a surprise. She walked all the way from Cripples Rest and back again. Wouldn't wait for me to drive her, and worked like a navvy.'

'She always put her heart into things. It was a pity she left. I've often wished she was back with us.'

'Well,' he lit a cigarette, 'there's no knowing.'

Now what did he mean by that? Catherine glanced at him curiously, but he was not looking at her. It appeared rather as though he didn't wish to discuss the matter further. The next moment he said, 'Where's Susie?'

'She's gone to bed,' Catherine told him. 'She was tired. Unusual for her. By the way, she's had a letter from Hugo.'

Richard started. 'Oh? What did he say?'

'Oh, nothing much. He's in some settlement or other in South Wales, helping with the unemployed. She showed me the letter – he seems better, more contented. Perhaps it's really for the best things turned out as they did.'

'Maybe,' he agreed thoughtfully.

'There's something fine about him,' she said, 'but complicated – difficult to understand. In his way, he's before his time. And Merlynne's behind. She belongs to the past.'

'I should have said that she was typical of post-war disillusionment.'

'No, it isn't quite that. Not merely. She's primitive. They'd never have got on, even without Laurence. I'm sure of it.'

'Well, you may be right. I hope so. It means nothing we could have done would have changed things. I just hope Susie will be OK and doesn't get hurt.'

'You needn't worry about her,' Catherine said with certainty. 'She's very young but mature, too. She sees clearly.'

'Has she ever said much – about Hugo?'

'No. Susie doesn't talk. She seems to be just waiting. Whatever happens she'll accept it. It's made her happy knowing he's finding his feet. And in the end, somehow, I've got a feeling they'll be together − she and Hugo, whether he divorces Merlynne or not. You know Gran said once, and I believe it's right, there *is* a kind of pattern in life, if you look for it.'

'She's a born optimist. Sometimes it gets on my nerves a bit. But no one can say you haven't done your bit. All these things happening − the guest house and everything − that period when everything seemed to go wrong, and yet you battled on uncomplainingly.'

'What else could I have done? Sat down and cried, and let life swamp us? I had to have an aim. It helped me. And in one way I'm luckier than most people. I've known what it is to have the perfect thing.' Her voice softened in retrospection. 'It's true, too, isn't it? We've got a lot to be grateful for. It isn't many people who get a windfall like we did, just when we needed it most.'

'I know,' he said. 'And it was damned good of you to put what you did into the place, Cathie. It'll help a lot next year when we have more fertilizers to buy, and the whole heap of other expenses to tackle. The year after we should begin to see daylight. That's my aim.'

'Good.'

And she was thinking, he's really recovered now. Some day perhaps he'll realise that to have married Deborah would've been disastrous. Poor Deborah.

She visualised Sir John and his lonely existence at Stark End. Since his daughter's death he'd shunned Trencathra. But soon, Catherine decided, she must really ask him over. She didn't like to think of him living alone in that great place, nursing his bitterness to himself, although recently he'd launched out into company again and had put up for, and been elected to, the City Council. Nevertheless his life, at the core, must be a lost one. Despite his forced worldly exterior, his face now had a settled hardness which revealed a man without much hope or reason for living. Acquaintances he had in plenty, but she suspected few friends; and meeting him by chance one day in St Taloc, she'd been touched at his genuine pleasure in seeing her.

Richard and Sir John had little in common, otherwise she

might have arranged something before. It was only natural that her brother so far had discouraged social overtures on her part. Any reminder of Deborah must have been painful. But with shrewd insight she suspected, now, that he would not be so affected by a meeting. And she proved to be correct in her judgement. When the matter was broached to Richard some days later, he agreed without restraint.

'Of course,' he said. 'Ask him over. We should have done so earlier.'

Catherine accordingly wrote to Sir John and a date was arranged for three weeks' ahead. But before the day arrived something else had happened which was to change once again the pattern of Trencathra.

Chapter Thirty-Two

On a day in late September, when the air was rich and heavy with the damp smell of decaying leaves and blackberries intermingled with brine, Charlie Traill walked over from Cripples Rest to see Richard. He was in the stables attending to one of his horses, Nelly the mare, who had a sore place on her flank. He was rubbing in some ointment when Charlie appeared at the door, looking fit and handsome in his boyish way, with his fair curly hair ruffled from the wind, his corduroys and boots caked with mud. At first Richard thought the young man had come to help him with the extra work. They exchanged greetings affably, and presently went out into the mellow afternoon sunlight. The fields, golden and brown, stretched before their eyes in a patchwork of tone against the green and yellow of the moor beyond. Once again Richard felt a thrill of satisfaction when he contemplated this practical outcome of his labours. From once stony ground, acres of cultivated soil now lay rich in yield before him. True, it was mostly potatoes and green stuff, with a small acreage of barley and corn, some of which had already been taken in; but next year he would have peas and beans as well. Already some of the fields were ready for ploughing. And a sudden sense of freedom and security swept through him with the consciousness of what, ultimately, he and the land together might achieve.

'How are things at your place?' he asked the other man, who worked for a farmer in the vicinity of Cripples Rest.

'So, so,' Charlie said. 'We had the wireworm bad.'

'Oh, tough luck. How are you for labour?'

'Short,' the young fellow answered.

'I see,' Richard said. 'When I saw you here I hoped you'd come to help me out a bit.'

'No,' Charlie answered. 'Not that, surr.'

He looked down, appearing slightly confused and at a loss for words. Richard had a strong feeling that there was something urgent he wished to say for which he had hardly sufficient courage. Perhaps the boy wanted a job? Perhaps Ann had after all consented to marry him, and was hoping that he, Richard, would be able possibly to offer something better in employment. The suggestion came as a shock to him. Since Ann's assertion that there was nothing between Charlie and herself he'd never doubted it. But then – all women changed their minds sometimes. There was no reason why she should differ from the rest of her sex in this respect. A momentary feeling of alarm possessed him. Without analysing his reactions he knew that he was against Ann marrying Charlie Traill.

'Well, Charlie?' he forced himself to say in a cheery voice. 'What have you come to see me about? Any way I can help?'

Charlie Traill lifted his face and regarded him squarely, with a sudden look of determination on his rugged countenance.

'Yes, Mr 'kerviss,' he said. 'There be. It's about Ann I've come to see you.'

'Ann? You mean Ann Chenoweth?' Richard asked, prevaricating.

'Yes.'

'Oh? Well, you'd better explain,' he said. 'Though I don't see Ann very much, as you know. She left here in the spring.'

'Ah, but she's been coming back again lately,' the young man asserted.

Richard laughed. 'Just to help me,' he said. 'That's all. And I've been very glad of her assistance, I can tell you.'

'Maybe you have. Anyone would. But what *I* have to say, Mr 'kerviss, is this – if you aren't fond of her, you haven't a right to encourage her. That's fair. And that's what I came to say, surr. And I'm not going to apologise, neither. I was walking out with Ann until she started seeing you again.'

Despite a feeling of relief, Richard was both startled and amused to be so accosted and accused of something of which he was so entirely innocent. This human reaction obliterated any sense he otherwise might have had of insolence from a subordinate.

'But, my dear man, Ann has been coming over simply from kindness of heart, nothing more. Now, don't be a stupid fellow. If she's fond of you, I can assure you there's been nothing between her and myself.'

Charlie looked first distressed, then a trifle sulky.

'Maybe,' he said. 'But her feelings are her own. She won't even go with me to Penzance Fair on Saturday. Before it was different. She'd go out with me sometimes. Now she won't.'

'Well,' said Richard, 'you can't expect me to do anything about that.'

'No. But there are things it's best to be straight about,' the young man persisted. 'If you love Ann, say so. And if you don't, then it'd be best to give me a chance.'

Richard, though slightly annoyed, nevertheless saw in the other man's simple assertion a certain logic. To Charlie, uncomplicated by the complexities and frustrations which beset less simple natures, life was either one thing or another — black or white — and love a thing to be admitted or not. There was no half-tones, no middle courses, or doubtful issues. A thing was plain or it was not. And though Charlie's affection might not possess the subtle ecstasies, the joys and anguish, experienced by more sensitive individuals, it was honest and strong and direct and demanded to know where it stood.

Richard put his hand on the young fellow's shoulder.

'I can't tell you that,' he said kindly. 'That's a matter for myself and Ann. But, you know, don't they say that all's fair in love and war?'

'Ah, but —' The young man's eyes looked miserable.

'If Ann was fond of you, she wouldn't let me come in the way.'

'Yes, but if she knew you weren't fond of her — if you showed her plain — she'd give up thinking about you. That's what I mean.'

So Ann had been thinking of him; thinking of him so much that even this young man had discovered it. Yet she would not talk, he was sure of that. She was too proud consciously to divulge her feelings. He remembered how she had sat in the sunlight in the field that first day, the serene quiet little smile round her lips, her composure and the glint of gold on her arms and hair, the confident easy way she had worked for him, and the sight of her later, swinging up the hill as though she owned the world, free and proud, despite her humble background, as the corn swaying or the gulls soaring over the sea. He saw suddenly, with clarity, why he had never been able to think of Ann as a subordinate. It was because she was not. She had a strength of character beyond class or status or social distinctions. She was the kind of woman who would be a pioneer in a new land, sticking grim things, bearing children, making a home for her husband and family, unafraid of adventure or loneliness, accepting without reserve whatever difficulties might be given her to tackle.

And this was the woman young Charlie Traill was asking him to discourage.

'I can't, Charlie,' Richard said, almost gently. 'I can't act what isn't true.'

'Do you mean that you care about her then?' Charlie asked miserably.

'Let's leave it,' said Richard. 'Let the future show.'

But it was some time before he could persuade Ann's persistent swain to leave matters at so inconclusive a point.

'Well, Mr 'kerviss,' he said, before leaving, 'you must excuse me, surr, for having said what I have. But you must also understand that I love Ann, and to have her played with would just make me see red.'

'I'm quite sure no one's going to play with Ann,' Richard asserted rather shortly.

After Charlie had gone Richard was reflective, and quiet with Catherine when he came in that night.

'Tired?' she queried, noting his mood.

'Oh, no more than usual. But I shall turn in soon.'

On the way to bed, however, he was seized with a fit of reslessness, and decided to have another look round, telling himself in justification that he was not sure whether or not the tool shed had been shut. But in truth it was more than that. He went downstairs, out into the night air which was warm, faintly exciting, holding still the hovering tang of woodsmoke. It was one of the nights which are never quite dark, with a harvest moon hanging like a huge orange in the sky above the peaked line of elemental-looking hills, Torcrom way. Opposite, beyond the dark line of cliffs, the sea glittered in a broken surface of black and silver, splashed here and there with a rosy glow from the moon's light. The house stood dark and solid in the background, its towers reared like some ancient fortress above the sparsely scattered trees. An owl called from the old yew, and its low piercing note awoke an answering loneliness in Richard's being.

Something was alive in him, clamouring for expression, which had been sleeping for many months. His love of Trencathra, and his satisfaction in the plans for the future, demanded suddenly a deeper alliance of companionship, someone with whom he could share his pleasures and difficulties and personal ambitions for the place, in the most intimate possible relationship of a man and woman. The beauty of the night stirred in him a longing which he knew could be appeased in no other way. It was not enough only to have the family round him, good as they were, and much as he cared for them. With the possible materialisation of his plans came also this natural overmastering desire to perpetuate himself with bone of his bone, flesh of his flesh deep into the heart of the place. To have sons, something of himself that would go on, after him, and a wife who was with him in spirit and in the flesh, someone who would unify rather than sunder him from the things and those he cared about. This was what, now, he needed above all things. And he knew, too, with a rush of conviction, that Ann could give and be this to him.

Ann. Desire hardened in him. He saw her for what she was – loyal and true, courageous and shrewd, with a certain Celtic intuition which could make her on occasion provocative and tantalising – shy, yet despite her independence, utterly feminine. He pictured her as she had been when she left him the previous night – the glow of her face and sweet full curve of her smile above the gently rounded chin. The swing of hips as she went gradually further from him, disappearing at length beyond the ridge of Starvecrow. He had been, then, strangely reluctant to see her go, but had refused to face the import. What a fool, when of all the women in the world there could be for him, surely, no one better fitted to be his wife. With this certainty determination fired his mind, flooding his veins with renewed vigour and warmth. The minor issues of social barriers, the fact that Ann had worked as servant in the house, counted for nothing. If she cared for him, which facing the matter squarely he believed she did, and would marry him – though criticism might arise in some quarters – Catherine and Susie-Jane would understand and welcome her. Of that he was sure.

And after all, who was he? And who in the past had they been, those early Nankervisses who had toiled with their hands, and sailed their boats to the China seas? Strong, hardy men, bred to the Cornish soil and salt. Men not afraid to work or sweat or adventure. Men with the open air in their lungs, and purpose of life in their blood. Trencathra was their heritage. Without them, those later squires and ladies could never had been. And he, Richard, was the throwback to his ancestors, that answering cry to a race of men who, in a world gone sick, refused to sicken; for their roots were in the soil and sea. Something of their spirit lived on still in the blood and bone of all like himself, who in the face of international and economic disorder could turn still to the hoe and the plough – to the integral and fundamental purpose of growing food, without which men and women could not endure. This was what mattered. This was the challenge which came to him from the past, and which was also his challenge to the future. With Ann beside him he could face that challenge. All who wished could have their cities and big finance, their luxury and comfort and soulless ease, their nervous distractions and faded pleasures, their clamour and race for power. The world was tired, out of focus, its values shaken. But for some – for himself, thank God! – it was possible yet to stand on a hill in the great silence and know that life was good. There was earth and air and water still, and much to do for those with the will to do it.

And there was Ann. The thought of her was revitalising

and sweet. Not sweet with the bitter wildness of his first love; but with the steady sweetness of a clear stream which would strengthen and feed his life in the course he had planned for it. As he turned and went back to the house, it was almost as though she were with him and he walked already in the company of those who were to follow.

Chapter Thirty-Three

Letter from Catherine Vernon to Julia Gort

20th November

Dear Grandmother,

     We were all so pleased to hear from you, and Richard and Ann of course were delighted with your good wishes. I was not really surprised at the quick marriage, although Nicholas was privately taken aback, I think. For a literary man he is rather 'old hat', and intrinsically a bit of a snob, though he'd never admit it. However, he behaved well, and now makes the most of any chance that comes along of referring to the Chenoweth family's former standing in the vicinity centuries ago. Aren't human beings funny?

    It will be a relief to me to have somebody capable like Ann about the place. Actually I'm delighted.

    I should like to write you an amusing gossipy picturesque letter about the wedding, because I know you'd like to imagine it all. But I'm afraid I'm not very good with my pen – and of course the ceremony was a very quiet one. They were married at the small chapel at Cripples Rest. Richard would have no show, and Ann wanted it there; Nicholas would have preferred it to be away somewhere, but I don't blame them for sticking out. Ann wore a blue costume and a small blue hat, and looked very nice.

    Olive was the bright spot in petunia-coloured velveteen; where she got it from, I can't imagine. She sang very loudly and had a lively eye for Ann's discarded suitor. Her lipstick matched her costume, and there's no doubt about her being the dashing one of the family. Nathaniel Chenoweth had waxed his moustache in the style of the Victorians, and had unearthed a pair of very tight trousers from somewhere which gave him the appearance of having stepped out of a wedding group of sixty years ago. However, nothing can destroy a certain look of dignity about him, and I must confess that when I saw them together, that stalwart hard-working man with his wife leaning on his arm, it occurred to me, Grandma, that it was really a kind of insolence for any of us to have had social qualms over the affair. Mrs Chenoweth has a great pride about her. If I was an artist she has the kind of face I would chose to paint, kind and tired, but so patient, a kind of settled peace in the face of grim circumstance. You know what I mean, don't you?

Richard looked really happy, for the first time for many months. And so handsome. Dear Richard. He hasn't let civilization spoil him, has he? Not even the war. He's kept always very close to the real things, and has had the sense to get back to the essentials. I think − no, I'm sure − that in marrying Ann he's done the right thing.

They've gone away for a week to Torquay − Richard could not spare longer, and Ann wanted a town − she's never been out of Cornwall in all her life. Odd, isn't it? They return on Saturday, and the home-coming is causing great excitement to Miss Spring and Miss Briggs. You knew, didn't you, that they were both here more or less permanently? When Richard and Ann decided to get married we had a further discussion about it, and Ann agreed with us about keeping them on. At first Nicholas made the suggestion that the young people might perhaps prefer to take over the lodge, but Ann was quite hurt. I believe − bless her − she's genuinely concerned about helping me, and I'm sure we shall work together well on the new footing. Anyhow, I shall do my best.

Well, I think that's all about the wedding.

You say that Merlynne and Laurence are still in London. I'm sorry you've not seen her, and I wish she'd write. I wish too with all my heart that Hugo would divorce her. In the end I think he probably will. But at the moment − according to Susie-Jane who's heard from him once or twice − he's very concerned with his settlement and unemployment work in South Wales.

I'm sure Susie would like to be with him, and if he was free I think it would work, because I know she loves him. Although so young and childlike, Grandma, there are strange depths in her, and although she loves Trencathra so much, she needs other things. Well – naturally. When I suggested the other day a change might be good for her, she said, 'Not yet, Catherine. I'll wait a little and see.' That, of course, means Hugo. Well, no one can say what will happen, but I hope everything turns out happily for her.

Thank you for your invitation to me to come up and stay some time. How I would love to – just to be civilised and luxurious for a week, and to see the kind of clothes they have in the shops now. But I don't know when it will be. Perhaps in the early spring. With Ann here I ought to be able to arrange a break then.

Now I must go. Take care of yourself – and give my love to Uncle Chetwyn.

    Yours affectionately,

    Catherine.

Chapter Thirty-Four

On a day in late November, Richard brought his wife back to Trencathra.

They walked hand in hand along the lane towards the gate where, the previous year, Susie-Jane had first discussed life with Sam Murgatroyd. The pale wintry sunlight struck slantwise across the landscape, catching the dark glint of Richard's hair and the firm line of Ann's young cheek half-turned towards him. She was smiling and a deep happiness lit her eyes.

'They won't be expecting us just to walk up like this,' she said. 'But I'm glad. It's nicer!'

He pressed her hand; and thus, they drew nearer to the old house.

It watched. It waited. Its windows like friendly eyes welcoming them. Within was a stir of activity; for all, including Miss Spring and Miss Fothergill-Briggs, were agog with a pleasant, anxious excitement to receive the young couple.

Beyond saying, 'Some time in the afternoon', Richard had mentioned no time of arrival in his letter to Catherine, and on the impulse of the moment they'd decided to walk from the station, leaving the bags with old Abel Trewinnion, the postman, to drive over later.

'Still,' Richard said, 'I hope there's a good cup of tea waiting. Or if we're lucky – champagne!'

'I'm sure Catherine will see to that,' Ann said.

And she was right. A meal was already prepared, and the log fire burning in the hall. There was a clatter of china, and chatter of conversation, but the soul of the house was quiet; satisfied in the knowledge that its life would now go on, that another thread was being woven that would bring young feet and laughter to its corridors — a furthering of that vast pattern which included so many lives and personalities, so varied and rich a scheme. All were part of it, from those far-off ghosts of the past to these of the present and future: Nicholas, Susie-Jane, Catherine, Julian, Hugo, and Merlynne; Richard and his Ann.

All of them, breathed the house, are part of me. Not one of them that has been unimportant. And if a thread has wavered sometimes and stretched far afield, it is well; for it means that something of me has penetrated deep into the world. But the heart of the pattern is here, and will remain while my structure holds and my walls stand strong to the gales and sea.

A gust of wind, blown tangy and clean from the shore, swept across the headland, up the lane, disturbing the grass and trees in the garden, catching Ann's hat so that she took it from her head and smiled, with her chin up.

'It's been nice away,' she said. 'But I'm glad to be back.'

'Yes,' Richard agreed, taking her hand. 'So am I, darling. It's home.'

'Our home,' Ann echoed. An echo of contentment seemed to fill the air with promise for the future.

Epilogue

On a late September afternoon in 1949, Susie-Jane stood at a side door of Trencathra staring across the moors towards the high lane above. She had an instinct that something wonderful was about to happen – the day was so hauntingly quiet and golden, filled with the nostalgic scent of tumbled leaves and drifting distant tang of bonfire smoke.

A year had passed since Richard's marriage to Ann – the guests had now all left, and Merlynne was living with Laurence in Paris. Nicholas's last book had been sufficiently successful to give ballast to Trencathra's agricultural progress, and Susie-Jane had proved to be useful in the gardens and on the land. But she knew that without Hugo she could not continue there indefinitely. Life had become for her mostly a matter of waiting. He had written to her regularly; loving letters, but evasive of the future – until that morning, when a note had arrived telling her to expect him some day soon.

> I know I've found my proper niche here. It's taken some time to find, but I feel *needed* – a change from the moody failure I'd become at Trencathra. There's a lot of hard work to do, both on the humane and administrative sides. But I'll tell you more about things when I see you. The visit will be brief – just long enough to say 'hello' to the family and find out what you intend to do with your life. Could you bear to leave Trencathra and join me here? Think about it, but remember, love, we have to be absolutely honest with each other – no doubts or regrets. And, of course, there'd be the final situation

with Merlynne to sort out. I had a brief note from her recently. She seems completely satisfied and OK with Laurence, thank God.

    Enough for now. Take care of your precious self.

    Yours eternally,

        Hugo.

Susie-Jane, still with the warm glow about her, took the slip of paper from her pocket and re-read it as she'd done many times before.

Possible. Was it *possible*? he'd asked, as though being with Hugo wasn't the only thing she'd ever wanted, or would in life.

Through the quiet air a bird chirruped from a bush nearby, and against her cheek for a second she felt the frail brush of a late butterfly.

The next moment, looking up, she caught the glint of a blue shirt rounding a bend in the moorland path.

And as the figure swung nearer, limping only slightly, a beam of slanting sunlight caught his face – Hugo's face. He was smiling. Even from that distance she recognised it, and realised without a shadow of doubt the wonderful thing had actually happened – he'd come for her at last. It was no dream. Bitterness and despair had left him. For the rest of their lives they could be together.

He waved, and with a little cry of joy she ran to meet him.

You have been reading a novel published by Piatkus Books. We hope you have enjoyed it and that you would like to read more of our titles. Please ask for them in your local library or bookshop.

If you would like to be put on our mailing list to receive details of new publications, please send a large stamped addressed envelope (UK only) to:

Piatkus Books, 5 Windmill Street
London W1P 1HF

PIATKUS

The sign of a good book